THE JOURNEY HOME

A NOVEL

LEGACY'S ROAD
BOOK FOUR

M. DANIEL SMITH

 BAY LEDGES PRESS

ISBN: 979-8-9873731-0-1 (paperback)
ISBN: 979-8-9873731-1-8 (ebook)

Published by Bayledges Press, Inc., Phippsburg, Maine

Bay Ledges Press, 2022

I'd like to thank my grandmother, Bertha Beryl Boone, for having introduced me to the proverb: all is grist for the mill. It has been my favorite saying ever since, reflected throughout the diverse landscapes, people, and events populating the pages of my novels, poetry, and advice (when asked) to family and friends. Reading, important to me as life itself since an early age, has provided a wealth of opportunities to explore other writers' minds. To plumb the depths of the worlds they create. To experience their character's emotions, opinions, and a diversity of concepts regarding life and death. Helping to expand my mind, providing a multitude of alternate viewpoints. Again—all grist for my mill. I have come to trust what my own characters reveal to me. Allowing them to paint themselves fully into the canvas of my stories. All of them, lingering in my thoughts, long after the writing has concluded.

I would also like to extend a special thanks to Maggie McLaughlin. A fellow traveler in the world of words, lending her talents to helping me bring my character's stories to a larger stage.

CHAPTER ONE

UPPER SANDUSKY

SPRING, 1782

C aptive's Town was in mourning. The remaining inhabitants moved about as if ghosts, drifting along paths, emptied of people. They gathered in a temporary church, forming a few handfuls of elderly parishioners, along with a scattering of pregnant women, toddlers, and elderly men deemed too infirm to have made the journey back to their long-abandoned homes in Gnadenhutten. Remnants of a once thriving community, they sat in stunned silence, their heads bowed as they tried to come to terms with God's plan for them and their loved ones.

Lukas stood in front of his diminished flock, hands at his sides, voice trembling as he stared at the congregation, guilt weighing him down. Eliza caught his eye, offering a thin smile, encouraging him to find the words to lead his people back to the grace of God. Noah sat at her side, with a lost expression on his youthful face, his dark eyes lowered, having witnessed the worst of what men could do to their fellow man.

Aaron stood apart from the rest, his face set in a neutral look as he stood in the doorway, clad in gray-brown leather clothing bearing bloodstains from several animals slain, then abandoned. He held a sheaf of arrows and his longbow in hand, having guided his wife and her brother on a sober trek back to their temporary home. Moving through rough terrain, avoiding the narrow roadway threaded between Captive's Town and the destroyed village of Gnadenhutten.

The massacre of Anna and the others had been a horrible tale, told to Lukas in halting sobs by his daughter, witness to the slaughter. Prevented from joining the others in their martyrdom by Aaron's protective embrace. Holding onto her with his hand over her mouth, muffling her desperate pleas to go to God until the colonial militiamen vacated the village, with every building set afire.

When he released her, Eliza had run to the largest structure where the militiamen had taken the parishioners, two at a time. Aaron, following close behind, grabbed her hand as they entered the building, discovering a mound of bodies tossed into the cellar, killed by blows from wooden mallets, their scalps removed. With valuable bounties earned in return for proof of each native slain. Paid them by the Pennsylvania Colonial government. Ninety-six people, men, women, and children, including several still at suck. Slain while reciting prayers for their slayers and themselves. Not one resisting, accepting their fate as an extension of God's will.

Eliza had collapsed, wailing in misery as Aaron carried her away from the horrific scene as flames climbed the walls. He took her to the edge of a wood line where Noah waited, locked in place by a sharp command not to move. Her sobs, muffled against Aaron's chest, ended with limp-limbed exhaustion, her mind lost to depthless grief.

They traveled home by night, taking an angle away from their former home. Aaron navigated by the stars, careful to avoid contact with the column of soldiers who'd left several of their younger comrades behind. Men who'd lost their souls, minds torn asunder by what they'd done, or been witness to. Wandering in aimless circles before collapsing, heads in their hands, sobbing with vacant stares. Left morally and emotionally bankrupt, unable to return to their former lives. Their lives ended at their own hands.

Eliza recovered her senses by the second day, with anger replacing sorrow. Aimed squarely at Aaron, cursing him for having saved her. Denied the opportunity to have ascended to God. Noah had watched the exchange with a stone-faced stare, unable to rationalize his sister's feelings, or the harsh words flung toward a man he considered part of his own family.

Eliza worked through her feelings during a week of furtive movements, helped by Noah's constant attention to her needs until they finally reached Captive's Town, having come to the end of what had turned into a horrendous journey. Aaron watched as his wife broke the news to her father, with Lukas moaning in anguish as he learned the bitter truth. That the dream of a peaceful existence between native converts and colonists was over. Left without answers in hand on how he might turn back the hands of time, returning to what had once been a bright and promising future.

His belief in God shattered, Lukas fell to his knees in front of his people. Unable to find the words to bring them hope. His heart and soul, in pieces, the ground left coated with his tears. Eliza, her hand on her father's head, faced the others and gathered herself, struggling to clear her throat from a lump of emotional pain. When she finally spoke, her voice, soft in tone, was firm with conviction.

"We're left burdened by this challenge of our collective faith. One we shall face *together*, as brothers and sisters. As a family. One we are *still* part of. Each of you left to find, then reclaim, your belief in God's plan for us. Helping bind us together, again. Every one of us gathered here, helping to create a *new* beginning. Honoring those who went willingly, *without* fear, walking the path God put them on. Including my mother—Anna."

Eliza stopped, her eyes gleaming, tears streaming down her cheeks. "She rose from a place of concealment. Free to walk away, choosing to stay. Her only concern was the safety of my brother and myself. Telling my husband—my hand-fasted husband—that the end of her journey was before her. That the sound of our people singing psalms, waiting for death at the hands of those about to deliver them into God's hands, had *strengthened* her faith. Going of her *own* free will to die *with* them. Committed to the teachings of my father. *Trusting* in him. In his words. His actions. In his beliefs."

Eliza paused, squeezing her father's hand, feeling a slight pressure of a response. "Knowing, without a doubt, she would *see* him again. See *all* of us again when we walk to God in the light of our unshakable faith."

Lukas pulled himself up. He raised his head, looking at those gathered before him, his eyes holding more pain than he could imagine himself capable of bearing. When he spoke, his voice hoarse from waves of grief, the words flowed as if from a source outside himself.

"I abandoned my faith. Once before. But God did *not* abandon me. My hubris, in thinking I alone was the arbiter of our brethren's futures, is a cross I shall bear for the rest of my days." Lukas hesitated, a wash of energy rising within his thin frame. "God has led us to this day. Has led us all *to* and through the darkness, delivering us into the light. Once again. The light of his everlasting love. Ours, not to question why, but to accept. To find the answer in prayer. In dedication to our cause. To rise and go forth, continuing to spread his love before us, helping to enlighten those unable to find their way to his glory. People looking to us, the shepherds, to help guide them safely home."

Aaron didn't move, his jaw set, watching as the small congregation came together, embracing Lukas and Eliza, surrounding them with their arms. He slipped away, heading toward the road leading back to Gnadenhutten. A thin voice from behind pulled him around, Noah standing with hands on his hips, a dark scowl on his face.

"You'll not take me with you. I know. But you *could* have said goodbye."

Aaron shrugged, then nodded. "You're right. You deserve as much and more." He waved the boy forward, placing one hand on his shoulder. "I'm going to find my redemption. Placing myself in the path of those who've committed a great and unforgivable sin. To discover, when I find them, what God bids *me* do."

Noah shook his head, his eyes moist with tears of frustration. "You'll *kill* them. Until they're all dead. Or until they kill *you*. In forgoing the new Bible, following words from the old one. An eye for an eye. Tooth for a tooth." He stared at the arrows. "Using *those* to justify your actions."

Aaron nodded, then let go, moving away. "We *all* die, Noah. Just a matter of where, when—and for what cause."

"And what of my *sister*?" Noah's face twisted into a mix of anger and despair. "Is she to wait until you return? And then what—forgive you your sins?"

Aaron stopped without turning around. "Eliza's on her own path. Same as me. Same as you."

"Then take me *with* you!"

"No. You're needed here."

Noah ran over, burying his head in Aaron's side, clinging to him. Aaron pulled him away, holding onto his thin shoulders, looking him in his dark-brown eyes. "You know how to provide food for others. To find wild game. To kill—then take care of it. I'll be back, with blood on my hands or not. And you'll be here, tending out on the others. On your father and sister." Aaron paused, listening to the sound of singing from within the church. "Promise me."

Noah nodded, his nose running. "Alright. I'll *stay*. But *you* come back to us. *Promise* me that."

Aaron hugged Noah, then let him go. He took a moment to look around the empty, temporary town, wondering if he'd ever see it again. If he'd see Eliza or her brother again. Then he turned away, leaving without looking back. Without speaking.

Noah watched as Aaron slipped away into the woods. He lifted one hand and waved goodbye, tears streaming down his dust-colored cheeks.

The light from a stub candle flickered, sitting on top of a small wooden desk, drops of wax dripping down its sides, congealing in the cool, nighttime air. A leather-bound muster book, discovered in an office drawer in the large town where the militia force had formed up, sat cradled in Aaron's hands with the cover open. A list of one hundred and forty-six names printed by a clear hand. Followed by a handful of signatures in perfect loops and whirls, along with dozens of others in careless scrawls or crude marks.

Aaron nodded, then closed the book, satisfied he had what he needed. The identities of all the men involved in the massacre. Not all of them were guilty of the same crime, with a handful having died by suicide, unable to bear the weight of their associated guilt. The neatly formed signatures of those holding a higher station in life would be the first to face judgment. Leaders of the raid. Responsible for their actions and those of their men.

A single officer spared, with the moral courage to stand back, along with eighteen soldiers, refusing to join in. Left sickened from the soup prepared by A'neewa, providing an opportunity for him to enter the barn and carry Eliza away. Tossed over his shoulder while she beat him with her fists, demanding he put her down so she could join the others.

Aaron lowered his eyes, staring at the floor of the small office. He recalled the moment during their journey back to Captive's Town when his bride had returned to her senses, her strength spent from a lack of sleep, and the mental and physical trauma suffered over the previous two days.

"You should have *left* me there. It was *my* choice. Not *yours*."

Noah, curled in his sister's arms, looked up, confused by her wanting to have stayed behind. Aaron shook his head. "You swore the same vow as me. In front of the others. My feelings as your husband are as worthy of consideration as yours. And I *need* you. Your *brother* needs you. Today. Tomorrow. Throughout the rest of his life. Would you have him left abandoned and alone, having lost both mother and sister?"

"He would still have *you!*" Eliza tried to rise, her legs weak, failing her. She took Aaron's hands, letting him help her to her feet. "And our father, too."

Aaron shook his head. "I could *never* have left you. Would have rushed in, taking as many of them with me before joining you and the others, seeing where the next path leads. Whether to heaven with you, or to hell, for what I've been party to. With no guarantee of my ever being able to find you again."

"God would have lifted—"

"God wasn't *there*, wife. Only the *Devil*. The one beating in the hearts of men, rearing his ugly head, spreading death and destruction to all corners of the *earth!*" Aaron released Eliza's hand and moved away, facing the darkness, the moon hidden behind clouds.

She came over, standing beside him. "You did what you did—out of love for *me*. For my brother. For my father." She reached out, slipping her hand into his. "Out of *love*, Aaron. God's gift to us *all*. *His* love for you. Waiting for you to fully accept him into your heart."

"Not much room left in there for that." Aaron lowered his voice to a whisper. "Not with what I've seen. Done. Been witness to—and didn't put a stop to."

Eliza squeezed his hand. "He *will* forgive you if you'll forgive *yourself*. With your sins washed away, leaving you free to walk an alternative path. One of salvation, *not* revenge."

Aaron shook his head, letting go and turning around, facing her, the light from their small fire casting a red gleam in his eyes. "I'm only wanting to get you and your brother *clear* of this. Wanting the two of you safely back to your father. That's *all*. That you can let him and everyone else know what's happened." He paused. "What comes after that is beyond the horizon for now."

Their conversation dwindled to an exhausted slump of weary bodies. Two more days seeing them back to Captive's Town, where Lukas met them with questioning eyes and quivering lips. Left unstrung by the horrible news, his knees folding, with Aaron grabbing his shoulders before his head could hit the ground. Eliza cradled him in her arms, holding him while he wept. The rest of the community slowly gathered together with bowed heads and heavy spirits, waiting for guidance from their leader.

Now, after seven days of cautious travel away through wilderness woods, Aaron had slipped into the settlement fort to the east, where the bloody journey had begun. With over one-hundred death notices held in his hand. One for each man involved in the massacre. Prepared to hunt them down, executing them one by one. Made to pay with their lives for their terrible sin.

He tucked the roster book into his pack, then slipped away, longbow in hand, a quiver of two dozen arrows slung over his shoulder. His eyes focused straight ahead as he whispered the names of the first men on the list. The scent of them hanging in the air, his finely honed instincts pointing him along the path.

CHAPTER TWO
MID-ATLANTIC
SPRING, 1782

S inclair wrapped her arms about her chest, clinging to a heavy cloak as a cold sea breeze tugged its edges. She shifted her stance, maintaining her balance as the large ship she'd boarded in Philadelphia, bound toward Glasgow, struggled to make its way into the teeth of a stiff, easterly headwind.

She stiffened her shoulders, keeping her emotions in check as she searched the horizon, knowing she'd wait until stepping on clan land to release them. The death of Eldritch by her husband's hand had broken her spirit, leaving her numbed by the man's betrayal. Doubting her instincts, unable to absolve herself for having misjudged the serpent. One she'd allowed into their lives. Into their home. Into her heart.

"Excuse me, Lady Sinclair-Haversham, for once again intruding on your privacy." A deep, soft-toned voice, familiar in Sinclair's ear, pulled her head around. The ambassador at large for the upstart Colonial Government, Arthur Lee, removed his hat and bowed. He straightened up, a welcoming smile on his face, eyes gleaming beneath a wash of bright sunlight, finding its way through a break in a scattered layer of thin gray clouds.

"Ambassador Lee." Sinclair gave him a stiff nod. "We seem destined to cross paths—whenever I'm aboard ship. One of several dozen leaving the port in Philadelphia every day." She paused. "I cannot imagine the odds of it happening—*twice*."

Arthur shrugged. "I will admit to having noted your name on the ship's manifest before selecting my date of departure. The choice made then to alter my plans, with the sole intention of engaging in a lively discourse on matters of mutual interest. Should you prove open to such?" He bowed once more, then resettled his hat, clamping it in place with a firm tug against the breeze. "I've waited until catching you out on deck to make my reacquaint. The weather easing a bit, leaving me hoping you'd make your appearance."

Arthur paused, taking a moment to sweep the horizon, searching for a sign of sails, the British navy haunting the sea lanes, eager to inspect the passenger lists of any ships encountered. "The captain's disappointed by your decision to take your meals below. We, my fellow voyagers, and I—feeling the same."

"*We?*" Sinclair's response was a degree above freezing, well below the current temperature of the air. Arthur suppressed a grin, enjoying the caustic tone displayed by the famous and still beautiful Lady Sinclair, known for her philanthropic ways. "I am traveling alone. Although there are several other men of—*note*, in regular attendance at the captain's table. Influential men who, though known to me, shall remain nameless. Unless, of course, they choose to reveal themselves to you."

Sinclair turned away, staring across the bow, measuring its rise and fall against the curved line of the horizon, pleased her stomach was in fine fettle. No complaints registered as yet from the constant movement of the deck beneath her feet. "I have little interest in such things. My life is now one of *simpler* means."

"Understood, my lady. I humbly apologize for the intrusion, bidding you a good day, and taking my leave." Another bow followed, Arthur a few steps away when Sinclair called out.

"I *would* have an interest in learning more of what you can *safely* reveal regarding recent events. Over a pot of tea, perhaps? In my cabin. After the next bell."

Arthur hesitated a moment, her invitation catching him off guard.

He quickly recovered, spinning around. "Of course, Lady Sinclair Haversham—"

Sinclair raised one arm, the cloak slipping free, whipping at her side. "Sinclair will suffice." She lowered her arm, gathering up its fluttering edge. "Arthur." Then she moved away, a tug by a spiraling gust causing a lock of her dark hair to pull loose, falling across the exposed skin of her cheek.

Sinclair pinched another helping of tea leaves into a pewter diffuser. She closed it with a press of thumb and forefinger, then dipped it into a thin-walled China cup. The aroma filtered through the cabin air, adding to the light fragrance of perfume she'd applied to her neck shortly before the tall aristocrat had arrived.

"Do you require sugar, Arthur?"

"Without it, preferable. Allowing for the full enjoyment of the leaves, left unadorned except for the flavor of oil of bergamot, scenting the air."

Sinclair prepared another diffuser, then filled their cups with water from a steaming kettle, delivered along with a platter of pastries by a uniformed steward, shortly before Arthur's arrival. Along with a note from the captain, inviting her to join his table that evening, if so inclined. The steward left with her reply enclosed in a note, sealed with a dollop of candle wax.

Arthur tasted the tea, sighing with pleasure, watching as Sinclair did the same. "I'd not expected to be invited to your cabin." He narrowed his eyes, head angled slightly to one side, full lips pursed. "I'm sensing you have *pointed* questions for me, having to do with the current state of affairs between Colonies and Crown."

"I am *fully* aware of developments regarding ongoing discussions and associated *rumors*. Information from a variety of sources arrives in Philadelphia regularly. Forwarded to—" Sinclair stopped. She studied Arthur's features, gauging his reaction as she continued. "To a farm. And a warehouse store. Tucked away in the hinterlands, well outside the environs of the port city."

Arthur nodded. "I'd heard whispers of such. A surprise change in location and vocation *indeed*. Often remarked upon by those in high society, wondering why someone of your reputation would choose to abide in the wilderness. Personages of *note*. One, in particular, making a crossing with you and your late husband, many years ago."

Sinclair held the cup to her chin, inhaling the mixed scents, her eyes locked on Arthur's, neither one looking away. "Another time. A far different world, now." She reached down, sliding a plate with fruit-stuffed scones across the table. "Will you join me?"

Arthur nodded, then reached out, touching the back of her hand. "I would like nothing better, Sinclair."

The small shipboard cabin lay at an angle, the ship heeled slightly to starboard as the hull slipped through the Atlantic Ocean with a steady hiss. For a moment, Sinclair was uncertain of her whereabouts, having awakened from a deep sleep. Untroubled during the night by worries or doubts, or a mother's concern for loved ones, left behind. Or of those still ahead, lying the better part of two weeks away.

The smell of pipe smoke brought her fully awake, the scent of blended leaves familiar to her nose. She took in a deep breath, holding it, losing herself in memories of happier days. Before she'd lost her husband to his destiny. Then having lost him again, going off in search of their wayward son. Losing him the last time, slipping away into the night, leaving death in his wake. A rumor filtering down from the western hills a month later of an enormous explosion there, with several bodies left torn and tattered, strewn about a small glade.

He's dead, Sinclair told herself, for the thousandth time. Never to return. Along with Aaron, lost to the tide of war. A faint hope, still, regarding her son. Her daughter was insistent he was out there, some-where. Still alive. That she'd seen him in a vision, standing with a bow in one hand, a book in the other. His sister, brimming with confidence that they would see him again.

Sinclair opened her eyes, gazing at Arthur's profile. He stood in front of a small window, cracked open, letting in a draught of cool air.

He sensed her eyes on him and turned his head, a warm smile on his lips as he held out the pipe.

"Did the smell disturb your rest?"

"No. Quite the opposite. It is—reassuring. My late husband and his father were fond of the same leaf, in a similar blend." Sinclair sat up, the sheet slipping to her waist, leaving her upper body exposed. She held her head high as Arthur returned an appraising stare.

"You are a *vision*, truly, my lady."

"I am a mother, thrice over. And *grandmother* to boot. Your sight failing you. No doubt from your constant perusal of documents, by candlelight."

"And a severe case of *advanced* age, which you have provided the *cure* for." Arthur emptied the bowl of his pipe through the porthole window, resealing it. He came over and sat on the edge of the bed, shared with Sinclair during the night. Neither of them had wished to join the captain for dinner. Forgoing food for the pleasure of holding one another, giving, and receiving what each one needed, and both could offer. "But I am *clear-eyed* and will repeat my statement. A *vision*, truly. One beyond compare."

"A *gifted* liar. But *sweet*." Sinclair reached up and cupped Arthur's chin, beardless, with a thin covering of light-colored hair. "You need to go, my friend."

Arthur pursed his lips, considering the situation for a moment, then nodded. "Of course. Parting as if two ships having met at sea, sharing a moment of connection, before moving on."

"But not without leaving an *impression*. A *wonderful* impression. One I shall not soon forget."

"Nor I." Arthur sighed, then stood up and crossed to the door. He turned around, taking in the sight of the dark-haired goddess who'd haunted his memories since their first meeting. "Farewell, Sinclair. When next we meet, it will be as strangers, protecting your sterling reputation."

"Appreciated, kind sir." Sinclair settled back as the door closed behind Arthur, a smile spreading across her face. The hours of intimate embrace had helped untie a knot of tension within her body, relieving her from years of emotional turmoil. Ready now to move on with her life. To focus her energies on both sides of the Atlantic. Determined to find a path leading her family into a promising future. One that would allow equal progress for all.

As the passengers of the ship disembarked, a solemn-eyed man in gray clothing moved along with the crowd. He kept his attention focused on a tall, well-dressed man, holding an unlit pipe in his left hand. Watched as the mark kneeled to check a buckle on one shoe, then straightened up, the pipe still there. Left behind for the furtive figure to scoop it up, tucking it away in a large pocket. A scrolled message, secured in the bowl, sealed with wax. One he'd deliver to another gentleman, waiting at a nearby inn, with a fat purse due to him upon completion of the assigned task.

He crossed the docks at a casual pace, surrounded by crowds of people coming and going. Then he slipped away, disappearing into the shadows between a line of tall warehouses.

Pierre unrolled the thin paper, the enticing scent of tobacco leaf stirring the hairs in his nose. He studied the symbols, able to decipher the message, with a frown curling the edges of his lips. Too familiar, he thought to himself; the tone of the message signifying a potential breach of gentlemanly conduct regarding the woman mentioned within.

He paused as an image formed in his mind's eye, shoved aside as he focused on how best to arrange an impromptu meeting with Lady Sinclair. A reunion of sorts, intended to provide her with his assurance he'd had nothing to do with what transpired at the highland manor. The men he'd paid to escort him there and back, hired out from under him by someone else. Disappearing from the ranks of nameless men under unknown circumstances.

The cabal had met to discuss pursuing the matter further, Pierre convincing the members to narrow their efforts, altering events in the colonies. To lay the foundation for what would come next. Instigation of a period of financial instability, pitting each colony against a nascent federal government hovering on the edge of insolvency. Owing enormous debts to foreign governments. Left pleading for funds. Going from capital to capital, tri-cornered hat in hand, begging coins enough to stay relevant.

Pierre knew countless opportunities would arise, providing the secretive group he was a member of to place their hands deep into the pockets of those seeking to gain power. Men, the cabal would eagerly support, until having them removed from their seats in government at a later date.

Countless chests of gold were surrounding the edges of a multi-tiered gameboard, played by handfuls of men cycling through, one generation at a time over the past dozen centuries and more. Encouraging political unrest, to the advantage of the few against the many. Common people made pawns, guided by carefully worded speeches. Influenced by words printed in ink, along with rumors circulating from hovel to home. From humble manors to expansive estates. From privy all the way to gilded thrones. With obedience enforced, here. Insurrection supported, there. Leading to the slaughter of the best and brightest of young men of each new generation. Fighting for national pride and personal honor, while helping to fatten the purses of men, with no love for them in return.

Pierre frowned, unsettled by the role fate had forced upon him. Torn at the moment by his admiration and warm feelings for Sinclair and her daughter. Either of them, a woman he'd gladly see at his side. Each a vision of loveliness, with cutting wit and nimble minds.

He sighed, using the flame from a candle to destroy the message, his lips widening into a smile as he considered the thought of having both women sharing his bed. Stirred by the image, he left his private room at a local inn with a jaunty bounce in his step, heading to a nearby house where such services were readily available. For a price.

CHAPTER THREE

HIGHLAND MANOR

LATE SPRING, 1782

A ngus bent to the repair of a heavy leather harness. His thick fingers worked a large needle through the resistant layer of leather, using a pair of pliers to push, then pull it through. The work settled him, each stitch carefully placed, adding strength to the whole.

He pulled out a thin, well-honed blade, carried with him at all times, using it to sever the waxed string. Then he smiled, remembering how easy it had been to slice the throat of the gut-shot man at the warehouse in Glasgow. Along with the other two, their bodies fed to the pigs at the remote croft farm.

The brutality of their deaths hadn't bothered him then. They didn't bother him now. The memory of his black stallion lying with a gaping wound in its throat in a nearby stall did. Still. It had been his first mount, gifted him by the former laird of clan Scott.

Another now stood in its place. A stout, large-chested sorrel mare, easy to climb aboard with good lungs and a solid frame. Able to run at pace or climb steep hillsides with ease. A stalwart and cherished companion. Angus determined no harm would ever come to her. Not while he was alive.

He leaned into his task, placing another series of stitches in the thick leather, then pulled back as a red-framed vision stole his senses. A woman on horseback, with long black hair. A smile on her face as she approached the Squeeze. Just down from the narrow, rock-face cliffs of the Pinch, leading up to the highland reaches. He slid out from under the harness, heading to the manor to let Lady Marion know her mother, Lady Sinclair, would soon be home.

Declan smiled as he watched Marion hug her mother. Lorna in Sinclair's arms, a confused look on her wee face, eyes searching for and finding Angus, reaching for him. The short man went over and plucked her out from between the two women, both engaged in a loving embrace. Angus glanced at his laird, then started over to hand him his daughter. Declan sniffed, then waved him away. "She's all yours, in need of a change of garments." With a smile and nod of his head, he headed outside to gather up Sinclair's belongings, delivered in a cart pulled along behind her by a hired team.

Marion separated herself from her mother, taking her hands and stepping back. "What news of Meghan? And little Patrick?"

"They're fine. Allwyn too, though the work can be difficult, having to do most of it alone." Sinclair buried a frown beneath a thin smile. "Your sister doing what she can to help."

Marion released her mother's hands, her arms dropping to her side. "And—my brother?"

Sinclair lowered her eyes, hands clasped together. "Still no word. Not even rumors." She looked up, tears in her eyes. "Both he and your father, missing from my life. With no word—with nothing from them to hold in my hands."

"There's no one who's heard *anything?*" Marion stepped to the window, watching as Declan carried a chest up the front steps, followed by three young men hired by Angus. All with strong backs, dedicated to working in the pastures and protecting the manor. "I thought he, my father—thought he'd been working to get Aaron safely back."

"He was. At first. But things changed after his last attempt to convince your brother to come away with him. Your father with a shadow hanging over him. Growing distant. Staying away for weeks at a time. Leading to a—" Sinclair shook her head. "He killed a man. One close to us—to Meghan, Allwyn, and I. As close as kin. Killing him for having turned against us. Paid in silver for providing information to *another* man. Someone close to our entire family, back in Scotland. Then over in the colonies, during the war."

Marion found a chair, her knees trembling. "Who?"

"Charles."

"Charlie?" Marion touched the fingers of her hand to her lips, eyes wide. "But he was as close as an *uncle* to us. Lost at sea. Drowned, according to Father."

"He's been supporting the Colonials. I'm uncertain how. Your father keeping that information to himself. It was Charles who revealed where Aaron was, allowing your father to go to him. Twice. With the journals belonging to your brother brought back with him, the last time. Which I brought here with me, so you could come to understand what Aaron has been witness to. Been part of. Might *still* be a part of, for all we know. Your sister and I."

Declan came into the room, pausing for a moment, eyeing his wife and mother-in-law, then going over to kneel beside Marion, taking her hand in his. Sinclair came over and placed her hand on Declan's shoulder.

"I'm sorry for not bringing you brighter news, daughter. Our family suffering its way through *another* war, with damage done to our loved ones. Again. Without our being able to help them in their time of need."

Marion opened her mouth to respond, hesitating when Declan squeezed her hand, a look in his eyes letting her know to hold back the story of their involvement to supply arms to the colonies. To keep it a secret between them, at least for a while. He stood up, smiling at Sinclair.

"I've had your things put in the master bedroom. Marion and I will move into—"

Sinclair cut him off, shaking her head. "I'll want some of them taken to the croft house, where I'll be spending *most* of my time. After

I've had a day or so to recover from the journey, getting to know my granddaughter. You're to stay where you are, as laird and lady of clan Scott."

Angus entered the room as if on cue, handing Lorna to her grandmother, having to pry her tiny fingers from his forearm as she clung to his arm. Her mouth puckered into a tearful wail as he nodded, then walked away. Sinclair eased Lorna around, cradling her in her lap, leaning down to inhale the scent of her head, and giving her a cooing greeting with adoring eyes.

"The lad, or rather, the man. Angus. He's a hard one to place. His —*demeanor* unusual." Sinclair stood beside Declan in the salon window, studying the short, stocky man as he moved around the grounds, posting men with muskets at positions with a clear view of the surrounding area. "*He* seems a serious sort." She turned her head, giving Declan a quiet stare. "Is he sound of mind?"

"More so than any man *I've* had the pleasure to meet, including Shaun. May God bless and keep him near to our hearts and thoughts." Declan shook his head. "I understand you questioning his role, with our Lorna looking on him as if an uncle. Closer to him than myself, I swear, in how she reaches for him whenever he's in sight."

"I hardly imagine *that* being true." Sinclair crossed her arms, leaning back against the frame of the window. "I've watched you doing the same with my daughter. Following her with your eyes whenever she's in the room. And I've noted the change in *her*. From a stubborn child—the *willful* young woman I left behind. Turned into a partner to a man she trusts. Willing to share the responsibility of tending to clan business." She paused, staring at the floor. "While I was away, seeking news of my wayward son." Then she sighed. "Turning out to have been a fool's errand."

Declan shrugged. "Nae. Only a mother, seeking an answer to the why behind it, from what your daughter shared with me. Keeping yourself busy, providing opportunities for women and their families in the colony of Pennsylvania. Helping them regain their feet. Same as you were doing on *this* side of the sea, between."

Sinclair leaned her head against the thick glass of the window. The surface was cool against her forehead; the view filtered by a wash of tears in her eyes. She felt separated from the life she'd once shared here with her husband. With Eira, Shaun, and her three bairns in rush-and-tumble games of chase throughout the flower gardens.

Memories now turned to dust, along with the bones of those buried in the hills above. With countless others in the colonies, loved just as much by their dear mothers, lost to the futility of another war, fought in wilderness woods.

Declan's hand found her shoulder, pulling her around, holding her as she laid her head on his shoulder, without speaking. Waiting until she finally pulled away, wiping her eyes with the edge of a thin shawl.

"Only an old lady, letting her feelings get the best of her. You must think me weak—or feeble-minded."

He shook his head, his voice reassuring. "I see ya' as the mother to the woman I love more than life itself. With your *same* strength of will, from what Shaun shared with me, his voice near to breaking whenever he mentioned your name." Declan reached out and gently squeezed Sinclair's upper arm, then turned, looking toward the kitchen, hearing Marion call out that the scones were ready. He offered his elbow, escorting Sinclair from the salon.

Marion served the fresh pastries with mugs of strong tea. Declan nodded his thanks, taking a second kettle and plateful out to share among the men, leaving the two women and his sleeping daughter to themselves. Once he'd gone, Marion busied herself cleaning the dishes used for baking, unable to look at her mother, unsettled by what she'd read in Aaron's journals during the previous night.

Sinclair watched patiently, until Marion finally turned around, hands on her hips, giving her mother a hard look. "Are you *not* to speak to me about it?"

"Meaning the writing. In Aaron's journals." Sinclair shrugged. "The images, painted with words or drawn on the pages, in direct opposition to the memories of the brother you grew up with."

Marion nodded, tears forming in her light-gray eyes, unable to reply. Sinclair reached out, bidding her distraught daughter to come and sit with her. The two of them shared a small bench, Sinclair's arm around Marion's shoulder, pulling her in, her fingers reaching up, brushing through her long dark hair.

"He left to save a friend from harm. Failing in the attempt. Drawn in, as so many young men are, by a need to seek revenge. To prove himself capable of meeting fear with courage." Sinclair leaned away, finding her daughter's eyes. "To enter the cauldron, daring the flames, exposed to the raw intensity coming from men doing what they *have* to in order to survive. Left stained by the—*insanity* of it. In the taking of another's life."

"Meghan did the same, without losing *her* way."

Sinclair smiled, shaking her head. "Led to it by Aaron, in defense of our family. *His* decision to dole out death that day. *His* burden to bear. The seed planted, left to lie fallow, until sprouting anew in the spilled blood of a boy named Rory. Growing into a root, twisting its way *deep* into his soul." She nodded, looking at the journals sitting on the countertop.

"What came next—the pain inflicted on tormented men by a woman who was herself a damaged child—*another* twist in his path. Leaving your brother caught between and betwixt. Drawn to the rush of strategic maneuvering, pitting himself against those who were hunting him. Caught up in his need to have someone to hold on to, even if it meant burying his innocence during moments of *extreme* violence."

A moment of pause filled the space between them, each trying to imagine the scenes described in the books, many of them stained with water, sweat, and blood. Unable to do so, both clinging to the image of their son, or brother, his blue eyes shining with an inner light as if it were emanating from the center of his gentle soul and remarkable mind. Gone off and become a ghost, hovering somewhere out there in the wilds of Pennsylvania. A loss far worse than learning of his death, with his body recovered and brought home. Buried in the croft glen, high above.

"What does *Meghan* have to say? She was *closest* to him. Closer than *any* of us." Marion leaned forward, grasping her mother's hands, the tone in her voice stirring Lorna in her cradle, causing her to wake.

"She is—convinced he'll return. Someday. Return and be the same as before. As if the past few years have been nothing more than a dream." Sinclair glanced at the leather-bound volumes. "Or rather, a nightmare. One I fear he'll never be able to awaken from."

CHAPTER FOUR
OHIO BASIN
SUMMER, 1782

Smoke drifted in a desultory haze, stirring Aaron's instincts. He scented the air, knowing the fire was emanating from a pit in the ground. Not from coals in a hearth, channeled through a chimney, with no sign of habitation discovered anywhere throughout the length of the small valley he was moving through. More likely, he told himself, a campfire warming food for a band of men, come seeking the pelts of beavers. The local area was rife with stretches of slow-moving water. Prime territory to find valuable animals by the hundreds.

He slipped forward, probing the shadows for the scent of unwashed clothing, mounds of offal from flayed animals, or leavings from the bowels of men. Found them scattered about, with a footpath threaded between thickets of alder and birch, pointing to where their camp would be. Enough of a trail, Aaron whispered, his beard breaking around the line of his teeth as he smiled, to lead me to them.

His hunt had pulled him to all corners of a depthless wilderness area. From large settlements, well on their way to becoming small towns, to scattered handfuls of small farmsteads interspersed with encampments of military men. No corner of ledge or fall of rocks left unvisited, searching for those whose names were in the book. Having unknowingly signed their lives away.

Several of them made to pay the bill he'd presented them, left pinned to the ground by arrows with unique fletching. Distinctive, revealing a pattern unlike any of those from native tribesmen still using such a primitive weapon.

The first man he'd tracked down had been the commander of the militia group. A man of distinction, responsible for the massacre of Eliza's community. Too late to exact revenge, his death coming at the hands of native and English forces who routed his band of Pennsylvanian militiamen shortly after they'd departed from Gnadenhutten. Taken captive, then burnt at the stake by the natives with the English looking on.

The survivors of his force made a disorganized retreat east, including the officer who'd been second in command. Struck in his lower back, with a lead ball shattering his spine. His legs numbed, no longer working. Abandoned during the retreat by panic-stricken men, unwilling to take the time to carry him out of the thick woods. Two men with grievous wounds lying alongside him, reaching out to the men moving past. None willing to help. Not even to put them out of their misery.

Aaron had approached the wounded officer with a war club in hand. A knife in the other. The middle-aged man stared up with a frightened expression on his powder-stained face, hands scrabbling to find purchase on the leaf-littered ground, trying to find a place to hide.

"Time. To atone for your sins." Aaron kneeled alongside him. "Given the *same* opportunity to sing a psalm to God. Or beg for forgiveness. For mercy. Though you'll receive *none* from me."

"You're *not* English. You're *not* my enemy. We're on the *same* side." The man's eyes widened in desperation, his voice trembling as he stared up at the face of the man staring down at him.

"I am the *wolf*. And you are—the lamb." Aaron looked away, studying the other men's faces, their features gray, unaware of the outside world, clinging to their lives, feeling them slipping away between their clenched fingers.

The officer tried to sit up, his numbed legs no longer a concern as he saw the distant look in the eyes of the man to be his judge, jury, and executioner. "I'm *innocent*. Have not done you *any* harm in fighting against the *damnable* English and their Indian allies."

"Killing of innocent men, women, and children. For their hair. For *coins*. The Governor of Pennsylvania colony paying you blood money, in return for proof of murder."

"No. *Not* true. They were *guilty. All* of them. Guilty of aiding the raiders. *Their* people, coming into our lands, slaughtering innocents. The *same* villainy you accuse *me* of. Our men, women, and children. Some of them with babes in their arms. *Their* hair—taken. English coins paid to *them* in return." The officer reached up, his fingers spread wide. "It was revenge, *yes!* For actions taken against *us*. For deaths dealt us *first!*"

Aaron nodded. "A pre-judgment on your part used to tie innocent victims to the crime. Spurred by the gleam in your eyes of the bounty you'd receive." He leaned in. "Laid upon the heads of people praying for your *souls*, along with their own. Led, two by two, to their *deaths*. Still praying. And singing psalms." He lifted the war club, the polished knot of hardwood poised, reflecting a gray, uncaring sky. "So—sing to *me*. Raise your voice, you *god*-fearing man, as I deliver you into his *arms*."

"*Wait!* Please, *wait*. I'll give you anything. *All* I have. My lands. My wealth. If you'll only set aside your desire for vengeance. I'll do *anything*. Give you *anything* you ask."

"Names. Of yourself. And them." Aaron motioned with the end of the weapon he held. "Leaving you to receive far better treatment than deserved."

The officer glanced over, wetting his lips with his tongue. "I'm Captain Mills. Those two are Andrews and Scott. Their first names, unknown to me."

The club descended in a blur of motion, cracking the skull of the officer, the sound of it loud in the hushed woods. A tremor of arms followed, his fingers outstretched, eyes bulging from the force of the blow. A swift circle of a knife blade removed a blood-splattered ring of long hair, held up to the sky, then flung away, deep into the woods.

Aaron stared at where it landed, beyond feeling any compassion.

Beyond forgiveness. His voice was firm, in control as he parted his lips. "One." He killed the other men, leaving them their hair, an expression formed of cold stone on his face as he slid the war club back into place at his side, then slipped away without leaving tracks for others to follow. Three names in the book, looked for when he stopped for the night. With thin lines drawn through them, the book closed and slipped back into his pocket.

Now, several days and miles of cautious travel away, he bent his course to avoid contact with the trappers. Leaving them to their destinies. To be determined by God, or the natives claiming the lands on which they were trespassing.

Noah finished his meal, a thick soup of venison, with vegetables gathered from the extensive gardens planted in the community's fields outside the English fort. There was more than enough to go around, with the number of mouths in the community reduced to a few dozen. He sighed, feeling guilty for being so full, applying the sin of gluttony to himself.

His sister kept insisting that he eat more, his body outgrowing the limits of his clothing. New ones provided from garments no longer needed by the men who'd worn them. More guilt self-assigned. Everywhere he looked, and everything he touched, a reminder of the ghosts of those left behind. A funeral pyre formed from the burning walls and roof of the building. A scene of horror, one he'd never forget. The image seared into his mind's eye.

Eliza came over and offered another ladle of soup. Noah stared at her arms, knowing they were much too thin, even for someone of her kind. He blushed, ashamed by the comparison to his own people, watching as she held out the ladle. Aware his sister was not eating enough. Her hair thinning. Face framed by sharp-edged cheekbones. Her eyes shadowed by what had happened, despite her forced smiles.

"Eat up, my brother. Your efforts are the provider of food for us all. You need your strength, that you may continue doing God's work."

Noah frowned, lowering his bowl, refusing the offer. "It is *hunting*, sister. Without prayers offered—or needed. I follow their tracks. My arm holds the bow. My fingers pull, then release the string." He gave Eliza a measured look. "Killing is *easy*—when you've done it often enough."

"It is not *killing*, brother. It is a provision of God's gifts to those in need. Only *that*, as our father explained to you before." Eliza angled her head to one side, her thin neck looking as if it might snap. "We must give thanks to the bounty God sends us. Whether crops in the field or animals gathered from the woods."

Noah muttered under his breath, resting his empty bowl on the table. He stood up, heading toward the door. His sister reached out, stopping him. "What is it, Noah?"

He squared his shoulders, facing her, the two of them now equal in height. "I said I'd rather be hunting down those who stole our way of life from us. Like *Aaron* is doing." Noah tried to hold Eliza's gaze, failing, looking away, his thick hands clenched at his side.

His sister looked back, unfazed by his outburst. "Aaron—is on a *dark* path. One leading him deep into the shadows. But he *will* regain his way and then return to us. Contrite. Head bowed. Ready to cleanse himself in our love for him. In *God's* love for him. For us all."

Noah hesitated, wanting to scream in frustration, telling her it was not true. That no God, as taught to him and the others, would allow such a horrible thing to have happened. He held his tongue, reaching out, finding her hand, and squeezing it. "It is often difficult to remember the lessons you've taught me. But I promise to try *harder*."

Eliza smiled, overwhelmed by her love for her brother. She leaned forward, kissing his cheek, the scent of wood-smoke and wild on his skin and clothes causing her heart to leap in her chest, reminding her of Aaron. She quickly shoved the feeling aside, watching as Noah slipped outside and strode away, knowing God had his soul firmly in hand.

Lukas came along the path, noting Noah's direction and demeanor as he headed away from the fields, into the edge of the woods. He turned and stared at his daughter, standing in the doorway of her cabin, giving her a warm smile. He knew she was still not fully herself again. The months since the tragedy had done little to lift her spirit, weighed down with guilt for having survived the killings.

He walked over and took her hand, respecting Eliza's unwavering faith, having only grown stronger since returning with Aaron and Noah. Though he remained concerned about her lack of appetite and occasional tears. Unable, as yet, to help her shed her sorrow in a sobbing release, helping to cleanse her soul. Aware, from his own painful experiences of having lost two wives, how important it was to allow grief to have its say, that joy could find its way back into one's heart.

Lukas turned his head, his eyes searching for any sign of his adopted son, unable to find him in the shadows lining the edge of the forest. With a long breath, followed by a deep sigh, he nodded, leaving it in God's capable hands, confident Noah would soon regain his steadfast faith.

CHAPTER FIVE
CROSSROAD STORE
SUMMER, 1782

Meghan cocked her head, giving Allwyn a hard look. She held it for several moments, waiting until he crossed his arms on his work-thickened chest, then sighed, knowing he would not give in. This time.

Patrick, sitting in the packed dirt of the yard, hands holding onto a stick and a rock, looked up, a smile on his broad-cheeked face. "Da." He swiveled his head, looking at his mother. "Ma." Meghan broke her firm stance, giving in to the wash of love felt for her son. She bent down and picked him up. Her son, heavier now, two months slipping by since his grandmother's return to Scotland. "That's right, wee one. Ma *and* Da."

A chicken came on the run, herded back into the coop by their rangy hound. Patrick grinned, then pointed at the large dog with a dirt-stained finger, the tip clean. Used to probe his gums, with several teeth working their way through. "*Da!*"

Meghan smiled, nodding her head, her unbound hair gleaming in the sunlight, a headband used to keep the curls from her bright-blue eyes. "That's right, Patty. Your *Da*. Heading into the coop where he *knows* he belongs." She gave Allwyn a nod, then started into the house to begin the evening meal. Her husband's voice caught her before she reached the steps.

"I'll be hiring *two* more men. Sons of those families we've been trading with these past few years. Trustworthy lads." He saw his willful wife stop as she reached the door, her hand on the latch. "Then I'm joining the group of men looking to head west to secure furs from trappers. For sale here. With a sizable profit, gained." He watched as Meghan ignored him, continuing inside, the door slamming shut behind her.

The hound came up and nosed his hand, then sat down, scratching its side with a gangly hind leg. Allwyn gave him a rub between his long, dangling ears, trying to convince himself he was making the right decision in heading into the Ohio Basin to secure a valuable haul of pelts. Moving west into the edges of the Ohio Basin, putting himself near where he sensed Aaron would be, if still alive.

Men, with dark clothing and hard eyes, still wandering the city of Philadelphia and outlying towns with the same goal, based on rumors related to him during his bi-weekly trips to the city. Friends at the docks and warehouses asked sideways questions over tankards of ale. The subject was always the same, concerning the whereabouts of a colonial warrior, formerly known as the Wolf.

Allwyn sighed, watching as the hound stood up and stared at the house, then back up at him, a questioning look in its brown eyes, eager to call it a day. He gave him a slow nod, then closed the door of the coop, sighing as he headed inside to mollify his beautiful and feisty wife.

Later that night, Meghan rolled onto her side and stared at Allwyn's shadowed profile, the moon a sliver of silver in a cloudless sky. "Are you awake, husband?" A soft murmur was her answer, encouragement enough for her to slide over and put her head on his chest. She listened to the steady beat of his loving heart. To the slip of air in and out of his tireless lungs. To the feel of his fingers stroking her thick hair.

"I know the *why*. Understanding the *want* to do it. But I'd be telling a weak tale if saying I'm in favor of ya going off with the others." She lifted her face, her pointed chin resting on his ribs, aware it was hurting him, though he showed no sign of it. "I won't hold you back. You know that, right?" She touched the side of his face, feeling him nod. "Besides — I already *know* what's going to happen."

Allwyn slid back and sat up. Meghan got to her knees, facing him, the light catching her eyes, with no sign of concern. "A *vision?* Of me there *and* safely home again?"

"No. Not of *you*. But of Aaron. One where he finds, then brings you back to me. Alive, standing with your head down. Come home to both of us. To Patrick and me. Hale, and as strong as ever. Just as stubborn as when ya' left. And still *madly* in love with me."

Allwyn reached out, pulling his wife close, his lips on hers, his heart swollen with his need for her. "*Always*, lassie. Forever. Ever, and a day."

֍ ֍ ֍

Allwyn finished strapping satchels of goods in place on the back of a sturdy pack horse. They held dozens of fine steel blades and the tools needed to hone them to a razor's edge, added in with dozens of other necessities required for pulling a living from dark waters threaded throughout the Ohio Basin. Small fortunes in hand, pinned to bales of beaver pelts.

Meghan came over and touched her husband on his upper arm. She'd packed enough preserved food to see him through the next month and more, with additional supplies purchased along the way from small towns and outlying settlements as the group of eager adventurers passed further west. Any wild game they encountered would help extend their store of dried beef, along with several thick packets of dried plants, carefully pressed and stowed away, used to reduce fevers, supplement their meals, or cure sour stomachs, upset from foul water.

Allwyn glanced at his wife, noting her carefree manner. "Still no sign of an ill wind heading my way — lying over tomorrow's horizon?"

"None, as *shown* me." Meghan reached out and tugged at Allwyn's thick shirt, adjusting its line. Her fingers clenched the thick fabric, pulling the hairs on his chest, causing him pain, though he didn't wince as he took her face between his hands and kissed her.

The other men laughed, accusing him of being weak-kneed. A babe, tied to his wife's apron strings. Allwyn smiled, giving Meghan another lengthy kiss, as tender as any they'd ever shared. Then he reached down and picked up Patty, who was using the back of the hound to support himself, his blanket tossed across its broad back, mimicking his Da's saddled mount.

"Take loving care of your dear sweet Ma for me, son. I'll be back before ya' miss me."

Paddy grinned, three small pearls of newly budded teeth showing in his ripened gums. Then he squirmed as his father handed him to his mother, wanting to be set back down, his eyes following the men as they moved away. Meghan held him against her hip, ignoring his squall of protest, as she watched her husband until he disappeared, without once looking back.

Meghan dropped to her knees and corralled a wayward chicken between the folds of her skirt chased there by the hound, the woven material in clan Scott colors, creating an impenetrable wall. She wrung the squawking bird's neck, tired of chasing it back into the coop at the end of every day.

The hound looked at her with bewildered eyes, staring from the feathered body dangling from her fingers to the coop, where the rest of the laying hens were moving about. Meghan gave the hound a firm stare, shaking her head. "I've no *use* for a *willful* chicken. Besides, there are plenty of *other* animals needing *your* attention."

She stood up and moved toward the house, where an elderly woman from the growing community was tending to Patrick. As she neared the corner of the barn, a shadow slipped across her vision. Gray-edged, not solid black, prompting a moment of dizziness that spun her thoughts. She stumbled, the hound coming close, leaning against her leg, looking up.

"I'm fine. Just stood up too fast." She continued toward the house as her heart skipped several beats, worry framing the lines of her slim face. Not a true vision, she reassured herself. Not like her others. Then she saw a man leaning against the side of the store. A piece of straw in the corner of his lips, with a wide-brimmed hat, pulled down, shading his eyes.

The hound stiffened, catching the unusual scent, the hair on its neck and back rising as it swung his head, emitting a low growl. Meghan glanced at the house as she reached to control the hound. Then hesitated, the large animal stiffening under her fingers, preparing to leap.

The stranger straightened up, hand in one pocket. "I have a weapon. Prepared to use it, should the beastie attempt to bite." The man stayed locked in place, a thin smile on his face, the angled sun painting his cheeks with a red glow.

Meghan kneeled, pulling the large dog's head around, looking him in the eyes. "To the house. To Patrick. *Guard*." The dog whined, looking back over at the unknown man, then lowered his head, slinking away with its tail down. Once it reached the house, it curled up on the top step, staring back across the yard, ready to come to her aid, if needed.

"I'm *no* threat to you, miss. To your family, or dog. Just here to ask a few questions. Having to do with your husband. Gone missing these past few weeks, from his normal deliveries to the docks." The man pushed himself away from the wall of the store, moving in a nonchalant motion, crossing the yard, stopping several feet away, eyeing the dead chicken in Meghan's hand.

"Skillfully done. The killing of the bird."

Meghan shrugged, wondering if she could reach for the knife beneath her skirt before the man could stop her. Her instincts whispered in her ear, telling her to ride out the storm, wondering if the violence surrounding her brother and father both had now come home to roost.

"I can offer you a meal and drink."

The man smiled, the straw in his mouth wobbling as he spoke. "I'm not here for any of that, though the offer's appreciated. Would have expected nothing less from a woman known for her

—generosity toward those in need. Mostly women and their children."

"The chicken." Meghan held up her hand. "Easier to pluck, while warm."

Another grin, as thin-lipped, followed the first. The straw let fall to the ground, another step taken, bringing him an arm's length away. The hound lying on the steps stiffened, half-rising to its feet, held back by an upraised palm from Meghan.

The man shrugged. "By *all* means. Go ahead with your task. I'll talk while you work. My questions will be easy enough to answer with a simple yes. Or no."

Meghan moved toward the refuse pile behind the barn, a ripe mix of manure and hay, added to with waste from the garden and house, creating a dark, peaty compost. "Ask away then, getting on with what you came here to find out. I've got a dinner to prepare."

"Your man, going off with the others. *Where*, exactly?"

"West, to the edge of Pennsylvania colony. Then inland, to the Ohio Basin." Meghan sniffed as she tugged feathers from the limp body of the large hen, then blew a feather away from her lips. "To trade goods for hides. Along with hundreds of other men doing the same, returning with pelts. Beaver, fox, mink, and bear."

"A common enough venture. Told with a—*rehearsed* tone. Though your family is hardly *common*. Headed by a woman of high social status, and financial means, with an *impeccable* reputation."

Meghan sat the half-plucked chicken on the ground, a stray feather stuck in her curls as if placed there by an invisible hand. She eyed the man, her expression fixed. "You're looking for information concerning the whereabouts of my brother. Which means you haven't found him, or his body. Leaving you, or more likely those who've hired you, shaking in—" She stared at his footwear. "Their boots."

"A smart woman, as told me you'd be." He shook his head, glancing around the yard, measuring the shadows on the edge of the woods with a practiced gaze. He glanced over his shoulder, noting the hound had left the steps, coming over and sitting by the corner of the large barn. "A bit too *full* of yourself, but understandable, with you being red-haired, and of highlander stock."

Meghan nodded, her demeanor relaxed, the fingers of her right hand on the hilt of her knife. She recovered the chicken, holding it in her left. "If I knew my brother to be alive, and where I could find him, he'd be on a boat back to Scotland where he belongs. Clear of this nonsense between King and Colonies. Unsupported by *most* colonists, unlike men of your sort. Hired and paid to keep things well stirred, muddying the water."

"It's words like *those* that encourage a close inspection of *what* you know. And *how* you came into possession *of* it."

"From journals. Lost in a fire in Bristol, long ago. My *father*—lost in another fire, over here, if the rumors are true. Performing an act of futility, from the stories told of it. A *poor* ending to a *foolish* quest. My father, with a reputation for fighting for the rights of the common man, including natives. Ending up, pulling my poor brother along in his wake. Leading him to come here, suffering the same fate. With us, his loved ones, never to know what's happened to him. A fate *my* son will avoid." Meghan straightened up. "Politics, and war. Both are a double-edged evil, destroying those most innocent. All of it, an *abomination* in the eyes of God."

The man held up one hand. "Enough." The moment stretched, Meghan's fingers on the handle of the knife, trying to stay calm. To find stillness in the moment of impending violence, as her father had taught all his children to do. Along with the art of defending oneself with a musket, pistol, bow, or knife.

"You're under *suspicion*. Under *watch* for as long as you remain here. Your only protection to date is strict orders from a man who has—" The stranger paused. "*Had* friends in high and powerful places. His orders obeyed—for now." Then he leaned in, hands at his side, his throat exposed. "You're good. *Exceptionally* good. Relaxed, measured by the pulse seen in your thin-skinned neck. Trained, no doubt by your father, before he went too far in his efforts against men like me."

"My father didn't go *far* enough! Leaving men like you *alive*. *Puppets*, dancing to the strings pulled by others. No better—"

His hand cupped her chin before she could register the move. His other clamped to her wrist, trapping it. "I *like* you. Raw. Unskilled. But capable of the *same* violence you oppose in others." He released her, watching as she fell back, her head twisted to one side, yelling at the hound to stand down, already halfway to her.

The man offered his hand, helping her to her feet. Meghan swallowed, needing a moment to regain her balance, her skin gone pale, hands and legs trembling in fear as she watched the man bend over. He collected the dead bird, handing it to her, then slipped away, disappearing into a wall of shadows growing beneath the limbs of a line of trees.

Meghan wrapped her arms around herself, a concerned look on her face as dusk came on in a stealthy approach, moving like a thin curtain drawn across a dark and forbidding sky. Wishing her husband home, again. Wishing her brother there, as well.

CHAPTER SIX

WEST PENNSYLVANIA HOMESTEAD

LATE SUMMER, 1782

Amiddle-aged farmer, having finished plowing a section of a recently cleared field, moved toward the door of a small cabin. He winced as a cramp tightened the calf of one leg, causing him to stop and bend down, working it away with dirt-stained fingers.

The flesh held a stiff knot of scar tissue, caused by a spent ball from an English musket during an ambush near Sandusky a few months earlier. The round had penetrated the skin, nicking the bone, burying itself deep into the muscle. He'd used his knife blade to pry it out, with the wound becoming infected. Forced to reopen it several times a day to drain until healed. Able to save the leg, though it left him with a permanent limp.

He sighed, head bowed, feeling the ever-present weight of shame burdening his soul. One of a handful of lower-ranked officers, he'd led a group of soldiers during a massacre of converted natives. A direct participant in the atrocities committed that day. Rewarded, along with the others involved, with a bag of coins for his share of the scalps taken.

Enough to purchase a mule and materials needed to put down stakes, claiming a piece of the outer edge of wilderness for himself. A

place to start over again, building a future where the memories of the
horror inflicted on innocent men, women, and children could fade. If
given time to do so, rumors in circulation throughout local settlements
of a dozen men slain. All having been involved in the massacre in
Gnadenhutten. Found with arrows in their bodies and their hair
removed.

With a low grunt of pain, he straightened up and pushed on,
needing to find shade. The mid-morning sun was already a beacon of
heat, pointing its finger squarely at him. Then he stopped, seeing a man
sitting on the steps of his cabin. A stranger to him, with shaded eyes
beneath a low-brimmed hat. Dressed in buckskin clothing. A bow in
his hands, an arrow strung.

They stared at each other, the other man finally speaking,
breaking the moment of pause, his words as clear as the blue-bird sky
above.

"Sergeant Nicholas Matthews. Late of the Pennsylvania militia
group. Responsible for the murder of close to one hundred people in
the town of Gnadenhutten. Along with your brother. Killed, by me."

The would-be farmer lowered his eyes, nodding. "I'm him."

Aaron sighed loudly, his voice low. "I'm here to balance the scales
of justice."

"You're here to *murder* me. Same as you did to the *others*." Nicholas
straightened up, his body tilted to one side because of his injury. "I'd
hoped the wound I took after that—" He swallowed as a sour wave of
fear rose in his throat. "That you might consider it a fair price paid—in
my having sinned against God."

Aaron noted the man's stiff posture. "I'm here on behalf of *man's*
justice. Not God's." He nodded toward the man's leg. "You gained that
in the ambush where the English and their allies captured your leader,
torturing then burning him alive. A down payment, made on your
account." He paused, giving the man a long, considered look. "The
balance, now due."

Nicholas raised an arm, wiping sweat from his forehead with the
back of one hand. "Could use a drink before leaving this place. The
work, all but done." He turned, sweeping his eyes along the clearing,
seeing the neat rows of turned soil. The mule tied off to a branch on

the edge of shadowed woods. Still in its harness, though released from the heavy plow.

"Will you attend to the animal, after me?" He hesitated, his breath coming short, chest aching as he faced his death. "Shame to leave her to the wolves. Deserves better than that. A better fate than mine."

"I'll see to it. Afterward." Aaron stood up and moved at an angle, allowing the doomed man access to his front door. "Get your drink."

Nicholas moved ahead, dragging his leg, affecting a pronounced limp, hoping to throw off his killer's aim. Once he gained the first step, he lunged forward, hand reaching for the latch, a loaded pistol left inside. A shove from behind pushed him flat against the rough-sawn wood of the door. He tried to spin around, unable to do so, trapped in place by an arrow through his chest. Another joined the first, both lungs punctured, the iron heads pinning him there.

He felt the vibration of the floorboards beneath his fear-stiffened legs. The press of cold metal against his throat, followed by a flow of warmth down his chest, the world going dark as a wavering bray from the mule filtered through the sun-heated air.

Aaron cleaned his blade, slipping it home in the sheath at his side. He frowned, wondering if he should retrieve the two arrows, deciding to leave them as a calling card to the rest of the men in the militia group. With dozens of names in the roster book in his pack, waiting for him to cross them through.

Men still living and working throughout high places and low in the western border settlements and small towns of Pennsylvania. Nervous men, sharing lurid stories in taverns and other gathering spots. Telling of a phantom native, stalking those with the blood of innocents staining their hands. Taking from them what they owed, with each death creating a growing sense of uneasiness among those still to face the reaper.

The mule called out, braying once again. Aaron picked up a bucket, half-full of water, and walked toward it, admiring the straight furrows as he stepped along them. He removed the animal's heavy harness, then watered it. While it was drinking its fill, he stroked its neck and long ears, filling them with gentle words of encouragement. Once it had slaked its thirst, he lifted its head, pulled out his knife, then slit its throat.

The small tavern was rife with nervous talk. Smoke hung in the air, forming wreaths around the heads of men with pipes in their hands, using them in angry gestures, denying responsibility for actions taken at Gnadenhutten. They were members of the disbanded militia group, with tales of dark deeds done whispered behind their backs as they attempted to move on with their lives.

"*Hunted*. One at a time. Two dozen or more of us already slain. Arrows in their chests, throats slit. Happening *here*, close to our homes. With no one raising a call to band together, seeking the murderous *bastard* behind it." A large man with a broad chest drained a tankard of ale, slamming it on the table he was sitting at, surrounded by half-a-dozen others, glum-faced, nodding their heads in agreement.

"To do what? Kill a *ghost?*" A thin-set man leaned back, his chair tilted against the wall, feet flat on the alcohol-stained floor. "One that's never seen twice in the same area. Striking from every direction. At all times of day—or night." He smirked, shaking his head, his eyes bright with the mixed effects of alcohol and fear.

The large man stood up and walked over, towering over him, hand on the hilt of a knife at his waist. He hesitated, hearing the click of a pistol hammer, the barrel pointed at his stomach, the other man's thumb on the hammer, ready to pull it to full cock, finger on the trigger. The barrel-chested man slowly raised his hands and backed away, while the crowd, barkeep, and a handful of nervous servers returned to their positions, having ducked out of the line of fire.

An unfamiliar voice broke through the tension, coming from a stranger in dark clothes, sitting at a small table tucked away in one corner of the large room. "You talk of sending an army to catch a ghost while waiting for the next one among you to fall." A slim-built man stretched his arms above his head, working them back and forth, settling an ache in his neck. Then he rose to his feet in a sinuous movement, as if formed of coiled steel, stepping between the two men.

"It's a *fool's* game. Either way." He smiled at both men, then sniffed. "*Fear*, in the air. Noticeable, when coming from those waiting on a shaft to the heart." He glanced at the big-framed man, noting his swarthy skin and sweat-beaded face. "Or from a blade placed to the throat, opening it with a simple slip of a hand."

He raised his own, mimicking the motion, a wide smile on thin lips, poised beneath a pair of light-colored eyes. Then he flipped a heavy gold coin in the air, catching it. "Barkeep." His voice, sharp-edged, cut through the thick silence, bringing the aproned man forward. He tossed the coin in his direction, caught with a deft grab, the man staring at it. "A round for all. And *food*. As much of it as the coin is worth, in exchange."

He rounded on the two men. "Same offer made to *you*. Put your coins, along with those of the others, in a purse. Getting on with what needs doing. Hiring a man capable of locating the one you're all in fear of."

The larger man opened his mouth, prepared to deny the charge of cowardice. The stranger raised his hand. A knife slipped from the arm of his coat, held in his fingers, the point aimed at the other man's eyes.

"*Fear*, what I said. Not *cowardice*." He paused, sliding the blade back in place. "Good men, unsettled by a lack of answers, with other *good* men sent to their deaths for a *righteous* act. One done under legal conditions. Soldiers doing their sworn duty under orders of those leading them."

The crowd settled back, the barmaids in circulation again, handing out helpings of ale. The barkeep brought over a tray with a bottle and three glasses poured half-full of whiskey. He nodded his thanks at the stranger, the gold coin heavy in his apron pocket, a gap-toothed smile on his face.

The stranger, choosing to remain nameless, raised a glass, waiting for the other two nominal leaders to join him. "To an agreement between us, with coins put in my hand. Enough to start the hunt. I'll have earned the rest when I provide the location of this ghost of yours. Paid in full on my demand." He gave each man a hard look, receiving nods in response. Then he bottomed his glass, watching with half-closed eyes as the others joined him.

Noah poked with a long hardwood stick, agitating a chicken staked in the center of a small clearing. Several loud squawks of protest followed in response, the sound carrying through the early morning air.

He smiled, knowing several coyotes who'd developed a taste for domesticated fowl would soon arrive, flowing out of a shadowed opening in the dark woods. He'd add their pelts to those from foxes, beavers, and a young bear. One he'd arrowed during a midnight raid on a pigsty. Its blood-stained trail followed, ending in a huddled pile of meat and fur.

Noah's growing proficiency with a bow had drawn the attention of the English soldiers at the fort. Summoning him to a meeting, with the second in command questioning his need for such a deadly weapon. Assured its use was strictly for gathering food to keep the handfuls of converted natives and their spiritual leader's family fed. With the hides and pelts collected, used to trade for manufactured goods.

Two fat deer delivered soon after had helped to supplement the commander's diet of salted beef with fresh venison. Having gained his trust, the English leader gave Noah permission to come and go as he wanted. The soldiers at the gate greeted him with lazy waves of their hands and coarse comments regarding his lithesome sister, walking hand in hand, coming with him to the fort to secure medicinal supplies in return for fresh produce and tanned furs.

The two of them were leaving now, with another trade concluded. A leather pouch clutched against Eliza's waist, her face red. Noah squeezed her hand. "Only a test, sister, of your ability to turn the other cheek. Changing their taunts into the singing of birds in the trees. Their leering faces, the smiles of children at play. Children with *full* stomachs, helping to ease their restless mood."

Eliza returned the pressure of his fingers on hers. "More like the croaking of *ravens* on a kill. Or the braying of *asses*, hauling a plow."

Noah nodded. He was holding his bow in his free hand, brought with him wherever he went, along with a quiver of arrows hanging at his side. "All of us are part of God's plan. Are we not?"

Eliza nodded, her head raised, ignoring the whistles and tart retorts as she moved along. Proud of her younger brother, now more than equal in height to her, with firm arms and legs. At work in the woods or fields, putting in long hours to keep the community's larder filled, and gathering wood for their hearths.

One of only a few men left among them capable of doing so. Her father withered, though still firm in his faith. As was her own, growing stronger each day with God's voice ever in her ears. Telling her to help guide the others. To help guide Noah. And Aaron, when he would decide to give up his need to seek vengeance and make his return to her. Ready to pick up where they'd once been for two glorious days and nights. Starting their marriage anew, helping her build a community made up of people found wandering in the wilderness. Then brought to God's all-encompassing embrace.

As Noah walked beside Eliza, he could read his sister's mind, her thoughts shared with him several times a week, reassuring him she knew God's plans. What he wanted her to do. The messages had increased in number over the past few months. Their constant repetition had left the young man determined to find his own path to, then through the tangled woods surrounding his life. Waiting patiently for his mentor to come back. Ready to help Aaron in his quest to bring the scales of man's justice back into balance again.

CHAPTER SEVEN
GLASGOW
LATE SUMMER, 1782

T he inn reeked of the scent of cheap perfume and sweat. People stood in fan-waving circles, the women trying to keep their faces dry. White powder, caked in the lines of their faces, cracked along the edges of their mouths and eyes as they smiled. Men, equally affected by the unusually warm weather, beamed at one another, beads of moisture dripping down their bearded cheeks, dampening their necks.

Sinclair parted the throng, like a ship moving through dense clouds of fog, passing across the lobby floor, aiming for a stairway leading up to her room. One she'd secured on the top floor, as far from the other patrons as possible, hoping to avoid mindless sessions of inane conversation.

A stale wave of odor from over-heated bodies was nauseating, painfully noticeable after weeks spent in the highlands where the sky was heather-scented, crisp, and achingly clear. Sinclair hid a sudden urge to gag as she smiled her way past a final shoal of people, clustered together, busily fanning the air, increasing the effect of sour smells from people too long from a proper scrubbing in ice-cold spring water.

A voice floated above the murmuring of the crowd of people waiting on transports to depart from the port city of Glasgow. The ships heading there becalmed. Captains and crews left frustrated as they waited for the wind to change, encouraging movement toward the western horizon. With hundreds of passengers exasperated by the week of humid, cloudless weather. Made worse by a thick, clinging blanket of oppressive heat.

"My lady." Small fingers found her forearm, attached to a young boy with an envelope in his free hand, her name on the front. Sinclair produced a thin coin. Taken from her fingertips with a practiced snatch of fingers, the message slipped between. She placed it into her purse, deciding to wait to open it once she was in her room.

Once there, Sinclair shed her outer clothing, left wearing a cotton shift, with a small glass of port in hand. She opened the note, releasing the hint of a masculine scent. Familiar, though she couldn't place it. She closed her eyes and held the parchment to her nose, drinking in a mix of amber with sandalwood notes. Then, with a sigh of loneliness, she unfolded the paper.

The message was from Pierre. Written with a perfect hand, each letter flowing into the next. The words painted an image in her mind of him standing on a ship's deck during their crossing from London to Philadelphia. A voyage that seemed to have been a lifetime ago. Then she gathered herself, reading through the message again.

When finished, she slipped the note back into the envelope and tucked it away. A small frown tightened her cheeks, pulling down the ends of her lips. Her skin, still flawless, left unadorned by the use of powders or creams currently in vogue on both sides of the English Channel.

A soft rap of knuckles on her door pulled her head to one side. She moved away from the window, left closed against the odorous heat of the street, and went to the door where she leaned her head against the thick wood.

"Yes?"

"A friend, Lady Sinclair. Wishing to have a moment of your time. At your convenience."

Sinclair sagged, hearing Pierre's wood-muffled voice. A pang of loneliness tugged at her heart, her throat constricting at the thought of seeing him again. Told by Declan of the Frenchman's earnest efforts on their behalf to help arm the colonists. Told again to her by Marion, in a private conversation, her daughter with doubts as to the Frenchman's loyalty. Those same feelings echoed by Angus when she'd cornered him. The unusual man coaxed into revealing his thoughts and visions. One, in particular, involved the man standing on the other side of the door, still closed.

Pierre hesitated when the door swung open, revealing the woman who'd captivated him from the first moment he'd seen her, on a crowded London dock, husband on her arm. She looked the same to him now, her beauty untouched by the hands of time.

"Please, Pierre. Do come inside."

Sinclair stepped back, noting the scent lingering in the air, matching that of the envelope. Her heart was beating as if at the end of a game of chase with Lorna, the young lass a match in looks and temperament to her red-haired Aunt Meghan, with her chubby legs churning away as she forced herself through tussocks of coarse grass, uphill or down.

The two of them stood a few feet apart, the door closed, then locked by Sinclair. Their eyes joined in a silent appraisal, with Sinclair opening her arms, welcoming Pierre into a warm embrace. It lasted until she couldn't stand the heat, forced to step back, wiping a stray curl of hair from her cheek, her face damp with tears and sweat.

"I must look a mess. This weather an onerous burden for women to bear up under."

"You are, as always, a vision of loveliness, Lady—" Pierre stopped when Sinclair raised her hand.

"No titles between us, Pierre. Too many days and memories shared for such as that."

"My apologies, Sinclair." He stepped closer, inches away from her face, his breath freshened with a sprig of mint before knocking. "You are, as ever, *radiant*. A unique rose, indeed."

"The words of a French gentleman. Gilded with gold. Your eyes, however, tell me a *different* story. The same one shown me in a mirror each day. That of a woman, mother to three, and now a grand-mother. The lines on my face are a fair measure of the life I've lived. Openly. Unapologetically. Resigned to the fate we *all* face. The passage of time, marking us as we grow old—*if* we're fortunate enough to *do* so."

Pierre shrugged. "Then I suffer from the *same* malady. My vision dimmed. For I see only the young woman who crossed the Atlantic, singing her way into my heart. *Still* here. With no apologies offered for speaking so plainly, remembering your penchant for doing the same."

Sinclair nodded, then turned away and crossed to the window. She stared through the thick glass panes toward the horizon, where a line of clouds had formed, harboring a welcome change in the weather. "I am revealed, adorned in a simple shift." She spun around, facing him, arms crossed on her chest, head held high. "With no secrets between us. Only the truth, revealed."

Pierre waited, his hands clasped in front of him, uncertain as to the next move. He took a step forward, with Sinclair doing the same. The air sparkled with motes of dust, a shaft of sunlight penetrating the glass, painting the floor gold as each took another step, entering the circle of light, their lips meeting, arms circling each other's body. Pressed together, they ignored the heat. Ignored the muted noises of fellow patrons, the sound of doors opening, then closing with vibrating thuds.

Nothing penetrated the need each had for what the other could offer. Openly. Honestly. The moment of their reconnection ended with a slow movement sideways into a small bedroom, with Pierre closing the door behind them with the toe of one boot.

Light played on the floor of a large, private berth aboard a three-masted ship, destined for the port city of Philadelphia. Pierre had secured passage for Sinclair and himself, each assigned a cabin. Hers, the one they were currently sharing, both of them unconcerned by any issue of impropriety. Pierre had raised concern for her reputation before agreeing to join her there, with Sinclair dismissing it out of hand.

"I am no longer Lady Sinclair Haversham-Knutt. Only Sinclair, resident of a small plot of land on the outskirts of Philadelphia. A woman of the land, with the scars to prove it." She held up her hands, showing them to Pierre, receiving a kiss on both palms, each finger given the same treatment.

"They are the hands of a goddess, carved in marble. Created for the world to admire throughout time."

Sinclair grinned, then gently slapped him on his cheek. "Gilded tongue *liar*. You've already had what you've wanted from me, ever since our first meeting. There is no longer any need to keep up the pretense."

Pierre reclaimed her hand, his eyes narrowed, holding a hurt expression. "Do you think so little of me to believe I do not *mean* what I say?" He pulled back. "That I would—" He stopped, looking away, the window open, waves in undulating rolls of blue and white, stretching to the curved horizon.

Sinclair reached out and gently turned his face back around. "I do not *deny* your sincerity. It is only a bit of self-protection, knowing the way of the world. Steeling myself for when you return to your senses. When you must return to the world, one you are part of. Myself, back to the one *I've* chosen. One that's become part of me."

"As a colonist?" Pierre shrugged, his mood softening. "And what of England? Your home for more than half your life. Or dare I suggest— Scotland?" He glanced toward the rear of the cabin. "Is there no tug for a return to your highland manor?"

"*Always.*" Sinclair sighed. "At first it was only a move west to close the distance between a mother and her wayward son. Then it turned into a new opportunity, in a new land. One bursting with ripe potential. Filled to the brim, spilling over with boundless energy. With more people arriving each week, thrusting themselves out into a vast wilderness, willing to brave the elements. And native tribes, pushing back against the endless tide of colonists eager to form a new country. Eager to embrace the idea of self-governance."

"Which is why I've been supportive *of* it." Pierre leaned forward. "Encouraging the colonies' movement away from England. A land I admire—despite our frequent dustups."

Their conversation ended with a long, heartfelt hug, leading to another exchange of physical pleasure. Sinclair released herself to the moment, knowing how far between they might be. Determined to grasp the opportunity in front of her. To be a part of something greater than herself, if only for the time left before the ship arrived in port.

Later, with sunlight streaming through the glass panes of the cabin window, closed tight against the early morning air, Pierre stared at Sinclair, asleep in her bed. He could see the thin lines on her face and strands of gray in her hair. Her lips were not as full, though they framed a perfect smile. And though her body was not as sinuous in movement as it once was, it was still firm in tone.

He sighed, aware he was living in a fool's dream. That he'd never be able to share the truth with her, that the group he'd pledged himself to were hunting her son. Same as they'd done with her husband. Unwilling to give up the chase until proof of his grisly death finally reached them. That they would continue to search for Aaron, known to them as the Wolf. Finding, then finishing him. A debt still owed, with his life the only payment deemed acceptable.

With another deep sigh, he went over and leaned down, kissing Sinclair's forehead. She stirred, then opened her light-colored eyes, gazing up at him. He kissed her lips. Loving her. Wanting her. Again. And again. Until he would have to let her go.

CHAPTER EIGHT
EASTERN OHIO BASIN
EARLY FALL, 1782

A small party of seven men moved in single file, leading horses laden down with compressed bales of hides, strapped in place. They'd sold or traded away all the goods brought with them, their remaining rations all but gone. Their legs and those of their mounts were trail weary, eager to reach a place where they could sleep under a roof, instead of another cold Autumn sky.

Allwyn raised his hand, halting the column. He listened for a noise out of place. The fall of a dislodged stone. The splash of a foot, slipping in a pool of water. His instincts stirred by an uneasy spoon, bringing him to one knee where he swept his eyes from side to side, his hand held out, motioning toward the ground.

The other men complied, finding spots to the side of the narrow trail, their weapons brought to readiness. Tomahawks and knives loosened in their belts, preparing for a rush of bodies intent on relieving them of their hard-earned goods, and hair. The moment of attentive silence passed, with no disturbance noted in the local environment.

Allwyn rose to his feet, moving ahead alone, prying back the undergrowth with a slow movement of his hand, finger on the trigger of his pistol. He found signs of other men having passed along the trail, coming in from one side, the tracks left behind a day or so ago.

Reassured the way ahead was clear, he slipped back and motioned to the men. They reformed the column and started forward again. Each man eying the sides of the trail as they slowly advanced toward a rise of cliffs framing the near horizon.

It was late in the afternoon when they discovered what had disturbed Allwyn's instincts. The body of a middle-aged man slumped forward over a small fire pit. His scalp missing, flies buzzing in a haze of iridescent green around the gory circle of exposed bone. A thin trail of smoke rose from between his crossed legs. Nude from the waist down, his lower body charred, with fire used to convince him to reveal information. Any hesitation, or suspected lies, met with the addition of another pine knot, blazing into life, causing their victim unbearable pain.

The line of tradesmen crouched alongside the opening, staring at the remains of two other men, the tops of their skulls showing. Bodies in huddled mounds, the ground stained with pools of clotted blood and twisted coils of intestines. One of the younger men stared at the gory scene, then turned away, spilling his meager lunch on the earth. He wiped his lips with the back of his hand as he walked away, checking the straps of the packs tied to his horse. The oldest man of their group, a veteran of two wars, came over and leaned his head against Allwyn's, his voice a low-toned murmur.

"Are we to be in a fight?"

Allwyn shook his head. "Not sure. It makes no sense. Nothing of value here for them, outside bounties for the hair lifted." He raised his canteen, removed the stopper, and swallowed. Then he moved to the front of his packhorse, cupping the water in his hand, wetting its muzzle. The other man followed his example, with the rest of their group doing the same.

Allwyn had assumed control once they'd reached the wilderness. His instincts of where to go and whom to trust proved out each step of the way. Now, faced with a lack of knowing what to do next, he shrugged, then started forward again, leaning on his former laird's sage advice. The older man with a wry grin on his aged face, telling him that when in doubt, *move*. Let your instincts guide you. Trusting yourself, and those closest to you, to be ready to bring the Devil himself to the fore, if'n caught in a fight you can't avoid.

Aaron watched from a small recess in a rockfall as two natives and over a dozen white men passed below. They were leading five horses, three loaded down with pelts, the others carrying packs of essentials needed for any expedition into wilderness areas. The men were quiet, no one making conversation, all of them with hard-edged stares, weapons at the ready. The natives were in the lead, backed by a thin man who moved with the motions of someone used to the hunting of men.

Aaron relaxed, knowing they were of no threat to him. His movements guarded, leaving no sign behind. Making a cold camp each night, tucked in between the roots of a tree, or a hollow between rocks. Staying away from trails. Traveling more like an animal than a man, trusting the instincts that had guided him since youth. Formed from following stags in the mountains, or feral boars in the lowlands. And more recently men, living in lands stretched between the eastern ridgelines and the mountains of the Ohio Basin.

He settled in, waiting for the column to work its way clear. When the sun moved a finger's width in the sky, he straightened up, then froze, seeing another column of men break free of the undergrowth. Hunkering back down, he narrowed his eyes, studying them as they came on.

One of the men's faces roused his curiosity. The man leading the group below suddenly recognized. Older now, but with the same self-assured stride last seen in the highlands of Scotland. His highlander friend Allwyn, in a constant hover around the manor home, sifting the air for the scent of either of his two sisters. Meghan, the one to have captured his heart, according to his father's telling of it.

Aaron wondered why he was there, leading a group of men returning from the perilous environs of the Ohio Basin. He knew they were heading into trouble, the group ahead of them looking to ambush parties like this. A fight he knew they would not survive.

He lowered his head, frowning, able to sense his sister staring into the western sky, waiting for her husband to return home. The image of her as a widow brought him to his feet. A determined look on his face.

Allwyn came to a sudden stop, spying a figure standing in the shadows alongside the trail. A tall man, clad in doeskin, with a longbow in hand. He dropped to the ground, the reins of the packhorse in one hand, fingers touching the pistol in his belt loop, easing it out, knowing the others were doing the same.

The figure stepped forward, arms out to the side, his face resolving into recognition as the light hit it. Allwyn caught his breath, unable to comprehend that his friend was standing there. Having hoped to hear news of his wife's brother from the men they'd traded with. Something to bring back to her. Any thought of meeting up with him beyond his wildest expectations.

He rose to his feet, waving at the others to stay behind. Aaron, his voice low, gave Allwyn a warm smile. "You've grown. Thickened out some, though I doubt it's from my *sister's* culinary efforts." He touched his brother by marriage on his shoulder, equal measures of joy and concern covering his face, realizing the danger his friend was in.

The group moving through ahead of them would have held up at the next river crossing, where the trail passed between two steep-faced heights, funneling travelers into a deadly chokepoint. Unavoidable when leading horses, especially those weighed down with valuable goods.

Allwyn clasped his friend's upper arm. "*You're* much the same, though a wee bit *older*." He shook his head, having difficulty matching his memories of his wife's brother with the stories read in blood-stained journals, shared with him by Meghan, pried from her mother's hands, claiming the right to read them. He paused, his voice tight with emotion. "Are ya' *still* as wise?"

Aaron noted the shade of caution in Allwyn's voice, understanding the cause of it. He shrugged. "Enough wisdom gained to know you're heading into a tight corner. With the odds stacked to the sky against you."

Allwyn nodded. "We saw their work." He nodded at the trail they'd been following. "Back there. Three men in a small glade. Tortured. One of them—burned."

Aaron considered, looking up, measuring the light left to them. "Looking for *me*, no doubt. Money offered to men everywhere for my head." He gave his friend a wry smile. "I should let *you* have it. Would leave you wealthy enough to buy a nice estate."

Allwyn nodded. "Wouldn't help me out of the *mess* we're in." He watched as Aaron nodded his agreement. "Do we leave the horses—try to work our way around?"

"There's only one crossing. Just ahead. Can your group make the swim downstream, in water over their heads?"

Allwyn shook his head. "Nae. Only myself, able to swim." He smiled. "Taught by *you*. Insisting I learn. Up at the pool at Gran Ma's Mill."

Aaron looked back, seeing the faces of the others staring at him, whispers floating through the air as they shared their thoughts. "It would be a big ask, convincing them to leave the pelts behind."

"True." Allwyn turned his head to the side, spitting, watching as it landed on a column of ants, working their way up the side of an anthill. "Can we win through?"

"Not without losses, and more luck than you've the right to expect." Aaron hesitated for a moment, then grinned. "It's a narrow spot where they'll be waiting for ya. With high walls—*pinched* together. Like the ones back home."

"Meaning we'll need to gather up a herd of red 'shaggies' to drive to and *through* 'em."

"Aye. A hundred head or so would see it done." Aaron glanced back at the other men and their string of horses. "A half-dozen or more beasties—not enough. More of a gift to them than a threat."

"Then we're *fooked*."

Aaron shook his head again. "I have the means to get you clear. With minimal risk to the husband of my dear sister." He reached out and clapped Allwyn on his shoulder. "I'll need the rest of the day to put it in place. You're to wait here until you hear shooting. If it sounds like it's moving away, make for the pass. Make the crossing in the dark. If not, abandon your horses and take your chances in the rapids downstream." Aaron turned to go, stopping when Allwyn's voice pulled him back around.

"You're an uncle. *Twice* over. Our wee one, Meghan's, and mine, a boy named Patrick. After you and your grandfather, both. Marion, with a girl named Lorna. The image of your grandmother, with the same red hair." Allwyn gave his friend a firm handshake, aware he might never see him again. "Thought you should know, before—"

Aaron lowered his eyes and stared at the ground for a moment, then nodded, moving away without saying goodbye. Allwyn watched as he faded from view, then returned to his friends, filling them in on the exchange of information.

The unnamed man raised his head, testing the wind moving through the narrow pass from east to west, preventing the native scouts from hearing the approach of the group of men spotted two days ago. He sniffed, then wrinkled his nose as he scented the assorted odors of the men he'd hired. Their rancid, unwashed bodies slathered with an assortment of oils used to deter insects from making a feast of them.

One man, a tall, thick-set colonial veteran, met at the tavern three weeks earlier, stepped up and belched as he scratched his stomach, his shirt open, insect bites covering a wide expanse of white skin. The unnamed man turned away in disgust, feeling more of an affinity for the man they were in search of than those of his hastily assembled party.

"When are they to arrive? The bastard bugs—a *pestilence* from God."

The unnamed man ignored him as he got to his feet to go check on the scouts, late reporting back, the sun already tucked behind tall rock walls, sheltering them in their shadows. He moved away, enjoying the cleaner air, stopping as one of the two native scouts slipped out from behind a rock, his face wrapped in a frown.

When he spoke, it was in French, knowing the man paying for the hunt understood it. "My brother is late. I was to meet him here. Something is wrong." The native lifted his head, nose angled into the sky, sniffing the air. "I smell death."

The unnamed man stepped forward, probing the edges of the pass, hoping to see the other native scout heading back. "Go. And look for him." The native gave him a hard look. One that would have frozen him in place if he could still feel fear. Events early in his life had beaten most of his emotions from him, including love, trust, and hope.

The dark-eyed native shrugged, then slid away, moving around the nearest curve where he hesitated for a moment, coughing, his body hunched forward, then falling out of sight. The unnamed man stood rooted in place, aware his quarry had shown up, with the chessboard spun around.

He knew both scouts were dead. Knew there would be arrows with unique fletching lodged in their bodies. Knew he would be lucky to escape the night ahead with his life. Then he smiled, looking forward to the challenge. Each one faced to date, in a life filled with violence, having ended with success. A soft whisper of a childhood song sighed from between his lips as he moved back toward the others.

$$\text{❦ ❦ ❦}$$

Aaron completed his climb, finding a perch above the narrowest portion of the pass. He could smell the smoke from a series of small fires lit the group stationed below, waiting for men leading packhorses to come their way. They were moving around, plucking meat from spits, trading stories, unaware they were under observation.

He scoured the shadows, trying to locate the one he'd seen conversing with the second scout. A furtive figure, moving with a nonchalant stride, appearing confident in his ability to deal with sudden violence. Unable to spot him, Aaron slid back, working his way along the steep ridge. He aimed for a spot near the far end of the pass, knowing he would soon become the rabbit, leading the wolves into a deadly trap.

Allwyn edged ahead, alone, leaving the other men behind on watch, ready to move out as planned. He swiveled his eyes, trying to see into every shadow, knowing the group manning the ambush would have posted scouts on the trail. Ready to report back on any movement. Then he froze, seeing a shape on the side of the path ahead that slowly took on the form of a man. One sitting down, leaning back against a rock, arms hanging at his side, a musket lying alongside him. Asleep, Allwyn thought, or dead.

As he closed the distance, it became obvious the man, a middle-aged native, was the latter. With an arrow centered in his chest, placed there by an archer known for his deadly accuracy. Allwyn bowed his head, aware his friend was going to risk his life, trying to save him and his party. A debt owed to his brother by marriage, one he'd repay if given the opportunity.

He slipped back down the trail and gave the others the news, then led them into the narrowing pass. Brought to a halt when they reached the body of a second man, slain by an arrow, waiting there for the sound of gunfire.

The first arrow took the largest man of the group, dead center, leaving him staring at the bloody broadhead jutting from his chest. He reached to pull it out, unable to move it before his eyes rolled back in his head, dead before his body hit the ground. The sight of him lying there startled the others. They stared for a moment, then ducked for cover, aware they were under attack.

The unnamed man squatted down, lowering his profile, sensing eyes in the shadows, seeking him out. A smile played on his thin lips, aware of the press of death's wings, hovering above the confined space. He heard the hiss of a second arrow slipping through the dusk, turning to night by the steep, overhanging ledges. It slid through the throat of a young man who'd raised his head, looking to spot the source of their assailant. Left dying in a gurgle of blood, pouring from his mouth for his effort.

Several shots thudded out from the edge of the confined space, smoke wreathing the end of the pass, clouding the men's view of the water just beyond, where the shallow crossing began. A third arrow whispered in, catching one in the shoulder, the point penetrating halfway through, causing the wounded man to leap up, stumbling back, screaming in pain. Another shaft joined the first, placed in his heart, ending his torment. The remaining men tucked their heads, unwilling to dare the risk of searching for a target.

The unnamed man moved ahead, using his knife to cut the throat of the first one he reached, cowering in fear. He tossed him aside, then slid over to the next, pressing the bloody blade to his throat as the ex-militiaman tried to swing his musket around. The man stared up with fear-shocked eyes.

"Get up and *rush* him. He's somewhere in the rocks ahead. Fire at *anything* that moves, unless you want to wait here, dying one by one." He pulled his pistol, aiming it at the closest man, provoking him into a hunched rush toward a pile of rocks. The terrified man made it across the opening, leaving the unnamed man motioning at the rest, encouraging them to follow.

They all rose as one and advanced, moving in short bursts. Firing, then taking cover as they reloaded, reminded they were killers in their own right. The fight soon devolved into a running battle with several men dropping with injuries, while the others drove the hidden assailant away.

As the sound of fighting moved to the north, paralleling the river, the unnamed man stayed to one side of the others, aiming at a narrow cleft in a wall of rocks ahead. He wanted to get in position before the swarm of men worked their way forward, his eyes focused, attention fixated on locating and then capturing his quarry.

Aaron let the first few men slide past, his eyes on those trailing behind. He knew one of them would break away, moving at an angle, staying clear of the killing zone. A man he'd enjoy taking alive, if possible, knowing he was a member of a cold-blooded group of nameless men. Murderers in gray clothing. Responsible for the deaths of his grandfather, great-uncle, and aunt, along with any others standing in their way. Given orders by men like Charlie, who he'd eventually find and question, if able to survive this engagement.

Once the last few stragglers scurried by, Aaron rose from his hiding spot and circled the open end of the pass, slipping along the steep, wooded slopes, seeking his prey.

Allwyn led the other men into the pinched lips of the narrow pass, listening as the sound of musket fire moved away. He waved at his trade partners, encouraging them to pick up the pace, knowing Aaron had allowed them to escape with their goods and lives intact.

Several bodies lay in twists of legs and arms, strewn across a small opening edged with piles of rocks. The horses shied away at the scent of blood, their hooves striking the hard-packed ground. The men pulled their heads down, soothing them with hushed tones before they could whinny. Everyone was on edge, hoping the way ahead would prove clear.

They cleared the pass; the column coming to a halt at the crossing. Allwyn moved ahead, verifying it was unguarded, then waved the party on, staying behind until they were safely on the opposite bank. He hesitated, torn between joining them and going to help his highlander friend. The faces of his companions stared back as he gave them a slow wave of his hand, then turned away, heading toward the muted thuds of the guns.

Aaron searched for his target, looking for a furtive gray shadow moving through the gloom with cat-like caution. He used the shouts of angry men to guide him to where the chase had come to an inconclusive end. A half-circle of men, their weapons aimed at a column of thick smoke emanating from a fire, started in the fall of rocks. They were calling out to each other, many with wounds in arms or legs, desperate to locate, then kill the skilled archer who'd decimated their group.

Aaron focused his eyes, prying apart the dark curtains of clustered leaves and tumbled rocks, finally finding the one he sought. A thin shape with angular lines, using a series of subtle movements to close on the outside edge of the group of dispirited men. A man with knowledge. One he'd take, then break, using the information to continue the fight against those behind the political and social chaos in the world.

His heart swelled with anticipation of what was to come. A hunger within stirred memories of the light in Chatte's eyes, watching as she carved the truth from men, resisting with every fiber of their will, though they all failed in the end. Spilling their secrets, desperate to stop their torment. As would this man, once he had him in hand.

The questioning calls between the bewildered men died down as smoke from the fire drew them deeper into the woods. Aaron moved to one side, focused on the task at hand, a feral smile on his face.

Allwyn kneeled beside a small mound of boulders, craning his head, trying to pick out the forms of men who were slowly edging forward. Their voices were a murmur of nervous questions, none of them eager to rush ahead, exposing their bodies to the reflexes of the deadly bowman.

He rose to his feet and stepped around a large boulder, startled by a hand lashing out, the barrel of a pistol slamming into the side of his head. A spasm of pain caused him to stumble back, his hands outspread as he fell to the ground, the image of a man's face peering down as his vision faded to black.

The nameless man stared at the unconscious body of his victim, his instincts whispering in his ear, telling him something was wrong. He twisted to one side, raising the pistol, trying to level it, his wrist trapped in a vice-like grip, a knife to his throat. He considered going for his own, the tip of the blade against his skin pressing in, causing his hand to loosen. The pistol fell, landing on the body of the man lying at his feet.

"Your hands. Behind you." Aaron's voice was raspy, tinged with fatigue. His eyes, shadowed by the weak light from a quarter moon, reflected a determined look as he slipped a rawhide thong over his enemy's wrists. With a sharp jerk, he pulled it tight, tying it off, followed up by a swift kick to the back of the man's knees, dropping him to the ground.

Aaron reached down, feeling for Allwyn's pulse, a steady throb beneath the press of his finger, his friend still breathing in a soft sigh, mirroring his own. He reached around, searching through the gray-clad man's clothing, removing two knives. Two more pulled from the top of each of his boots. Another one, found beneath the knot of hair on the back of his head, fastened to his collar.

"Hands." He waited while the man rolled onto one side, his wrists held back as far as possible. Aaron removed the leather strap from one wrist, retying the killer's hands in front, then motioned to the silent man to take Allwyn by the feet. Aaron grabbed his friend by the shoulders, the two of them moving back toward the crossing.

Once they reached the edge of the river, Aaron nodded, following the unnamed man into the flow of the water, forcing him to walk backward until they reached the other side. One of the other men in Allwyn's group stepped out of the woods, musket in hand. He pointed it at Aaron. Dusk now turned to dark, leaving the man uncertain who to aim at.

"*I'm* the archer." Aaron turned to one side, showing him the bow strung over his shoulder, his quiver half-empty, hanging from his side. He pointed with his chin at the man holding Allwyn's feet. "*He's* the one leading the others. Or what's *left* of them."

The man nodded. "I'll run back to the others. Bring back a horse for him." He nodded at Allwyn, who was stirring, his hands clenching then releasing, head turning from side to side. "Will he —*survive?*"

Aaron shrugged, not enough light to check his friend's eyes for a sign of a concussion. "Better odds, if putting distance between us and them." The man handed Aaron the musket, then spun away.

"Are we to talk?" The man in gray squatted down, using the base of a small tree to lean against. "I've made no move to run or call out, doing what's been needed to help you and your friend get clear."

Aaron nodded, then reversed the long gun, hitting the other man in his forehead with the end of the hardwood stock, ending the one-sided conversation without comment.

Fire, the touch of it upon his skin, brought the unnamed man back into the light. His body reacted, pulling back, a gasp of pain slipping from between his lips. Cut off as soon as reason returned into his eyes, with his battle-hardened will preventing an agonized scream from making its way out of his throat.

Aaron leaned back. "*Now* we can talk. For as long as it takes to get the story told. *All* of it. From as far back as you want to go. All the way to your first suck at your mother's teat." He wore a quiet expression on his face. "Your call to make. The *only* control I'm going to give you — over what's coming next."

The two of them were sitting beside a ring of flames, sheltered within the opening of a cave. Aaron, who'd just returned from a scout across the river, had watched as a handful of survivors moved away from the crossing, heading deeper into the gorge. Leaderless, wounded in body and spirits by a ghost, murmuring between themselves as they disappeared into the night.

Allwyn stirred, his condition slow to improve. Left with a large welt on the side of his head, centered by a deep gash, with rough stitches used to close his scalp. He reached up, his fingers touching the wound, coming away wet with blood, his head throbbing. A look of concern spread across his face as he looked for the other men. His vision clouded. Then the world disappeared, taking him with it.

The scent of seared meat filtered through the air, Allwyn's stomach rumbling with hunger as consciousness and an appetite returned. He opened his eyes, hearing a tight-lipped moan, then slowly turned his head to one side. He squinted, trying to focus, his vision filmy, watching as a spiral of smoke rose in the air, coming from the surface of a man's cheek. The odor of burnt meat grew stronger, stirring a wave of nausea, causing him to look away.

Aaron ignored his friend's reaction, along with the shocked gasps of the others, as he focused on his work. The night with hours enough to see it done by dawn. His knowledge of where and how to apply the blade gained at the side of the slim woman he'd loved and lain with for over two years. Left in a puddle at the bottom of a well with a slit throat. Opened by the blade in his hand.

He shook his head, letting go of the image of Chatte's face, concentrating on drawing another heated line across the surface of the captive's sweaty skin. There had been no questions asked of him, with any information shared, whether lies or half-truths, of little concern. Aaron knew the story he wanted to hear would come with blubbering, blood, and snot. Dripping from nostrils open to the air. With pained utterances from a mouth left without lips. Until, finally, a full confession would emerge. Death begged for, then granted. With another life taken, stacked against loved ones lost at the hands of men like this.

CHAPTER NINE
CROSSROAD STORE
FALL, 1782

T he sound of horses in the yard brought Meghan from the house, Patrick holding her finger as the hound loped ahead, it's tail wagging. It was late afternoon, the light in fade. Barely enough left to reveal the expression of hope on her face., shifting to a look of shock as she saw a familiar shape leading a mare. Another, as familiar to her eye, slumped forward in the saddle, holding onto the animal's neck, followed by a heavily burdened packhorse.

Meghan released her son and rushed over, reaching up for Allwyn's hand, squeezing it, her other hand touching the side of her brother's face. There were tears in her eyes as she shook her head in disbelief, looking from one to the other.

"We'll need to get him inside. The ride here — a *difficult* one, causing a return of a severe headache. Your husband, in good health other- wise." Aaron helped Allwyn down, supporting him along with Meghan as they moved toward the house. Patrick reached up, taking the dangling reins of the mare, tugging on them, trying to pull the tired mount over to the closed door of the barn.

Meghan took note, calling to him to leave off. The young boy took a firm stance and shook his head, then relented, seeing the glare in his mother's eyes. He dropped the reins and stomped his way across the yard, leaving the hound sitting between the two animals, watching as everyone moved away.

Once Allwyn was in bed, with a poultice wrapped around his head after his wife inspected his injury, Meghan entered the kitchen, a frown on her face. "*Your* work, I take it—the stitches?"

Aaron nodded. He'd just come inside from tending to the horses, both animals in their stalls and bedded down. He held a bowl in his hand, working his way through a generous helping of stew. "Placed under *difficult* circumstances." He paused. "Not my *finest* work." He spooned out a piece of meat, eyeing it with a smile, putting it in his mouth, and chewing with pleasure.

"I'll have the story told. *All* of it." Meghan stood beside her brother, her tone wavering between the pull of a multitude of emotions. She settled on love, leaning down, placing her head on his chest, her wide shoulders trembling as she released long-held, deep-seated feelings of relief.

Aaron stood up. He took his sister in his arms, holding her while she cried. Wanting to join her. Unable to release himself to the mixed joy and pain of seeing her again. Knowing in his heart that tomorrow morning would find him miles away. That his presence there would be a dark cloud, with the potential of bringing death and destruction in its wake.

Enough of a risk, he told himself, coming here now, letting her know he was still alive. That he would be gone, out there, somewhere, returning when time and the tides of life allowed. If they ever would, his path twisted by events from the past, and those yet before him. Aware the war he was fighting might never be over.

Meghan released him, stepping back, wiping her eyes with a forced smile on her lips. "Welcome, brother. Welcome home." She took his hand, bidding him to follow her into a room with a fireplace. A heavy pot of water suspended over banked coals, steam rising in the cool air. Once they settled in on opposite ends of a small couch, she asked her brother questions saved up for several years, getting answers she knew lacked the full version of the truth. Aaron with hesitant pauses, ones she filled in with the words and images of his journals. Read, then sent back to Scotland with their mother.

Then it was her turn to relate their family's history, from the moment her brother had departed Glasgow on transport to the colonies. Sharing bitter-sweet memories between bookends of reflective silence. The hour grew late, nudging them to their beds. Hers, upstairs with her husband and child. Aaron, heading out to the stable with the horses.

The next morning found Meghan standing outside the storeroom door, the trade goods stacked inside, with no sign of her brother. She headed back toward the house, stopping at the bottom of the steps, staring into the western hills. The hound sat beside her, its head pressed against the side of her leg, looking up as Meghan released a heavy sigh that fogged the frigid air. Then she climbed the steps and went inside, pulling the heavy front door shut with a muffled thud.

Noah raised his head, knife in hand. He'd just begun slicing through the hide covering the abdomen of a fat doe. The animal arrowed as it browsed along the edge of the community garden, feeding on winter squash. It had run off into the woods, finding a quiet place to lie down and die. Tracked to its bed by the young hunter, allowing it time to pass in dignity. Without fear, which could sour the meat.

A shiver slipped through him, Noah sensing the eyes of something or someone on him. He reached up, wiping a bead of sweat from his forehead, cutting his eyes to one side, prying through the mottled hues of leaves hanging from the branches of a grove of hardwood trees. Then he gasped, spying a figure in gray, dark-stained clothing, materializing as if in a vision.

Aaron spread his arms, stepping forward, meeting the young man's embrace, bloody hands, and all. Noah finally stepped back, affecting a more adult demeanor, giving his brother by marriage a considered look.

"You're back. Alive." He gave Aaron's face a close inspection, starting with his eyes. "And not yet finished. I can tell."

Aaron shrugged, a wince crossing his face as he angled his right arm, letting his bow slip from his shoulder. He slid one end alongside his ankle, bending the weapon around his knee and releasing the string. "I realized there will never be an end to it. Enough of a message sent. The others, left in torment throughout the rest of their lives."

He rotated his arm, loosening the scar tissue, trying to ease the constant ache from his old wound. "Found a good friend. A sister and a young nephew, both. And news of a niece."

"You've been *east*. To the coast. Near the *ocean*." Noah could only imagine it, the words foreign to his limited experience. "Are you home —to stay?"

"I'm here—but not entirely home. Not sure it even exists anymore. Not for me."

A voice called out, bringing both of them around. Eliza stepped out from behind a thicket, a thin drag rope dangling in one hand. She tossed it to Noah. "I saw the tracks in the garden. Followed them here, to help you with your work." She came up and gave Aaron a long, silent stare, then smiled.

"Welcome home, husband. If you're finally ready to return to your family *here*." She swung her hand, pointing at the sun, half-risen in the eastern sky, peeking through the overhanging limbs. "Letting go of what's back there." Aaron hesitated a moment, then nodded, his arms open to his wife as she stepped forward. Eliza kissed him, her hands holding onto the sides of his weathered face, looking directly into his light-colored eyes.

Noah returned to dressing out the doe, the others coming over, helping him to finish. Then two men dragged the doe behind them, following Eliza back to the small collection of cabins. Along the way, they passed in front of the fort, its walls manned by a handful of bored soldiers, the interior quiet. No military action seen since an armed incursion earlier in the year, ending with the rout of a large Pennsylvania militia. The English and native allies had pulled back, willing to wait on the next foray, satisfied with protecting the interests of the local tribes, for now.

The peaceful community of people living in Captive's Town, given the freedom to fend for themselves, content to tend their crops. With more than enough food grown to provide for their needs. The rest traded with the English for flour and other needed supplies.

The members of the small group welcomed Aaron home with broad smiles and open arms. Lukas, hearing the commotion, came out of a newly erected small church, standing with his mouth agape, before giving Aaron a warm smile. He came over and embraced him with trembling arms, welcoming him home, his voice thin, with a slight wheeze.

"Such a *wonderful* surprise! Your absence was *intolerable*, with your talents sorely needed. *Here*. But forgo all that. You have returned to us, in both body and soul." The spiritual leader, his hair gone over to white, eyes rheumy with age, stood in a hunched posture.

He peered up at Aaron, his glasses slightly askew, causing him to squint as he stared at his hand-fasted son, wreathed in a halo of dim light streaming through an opening in the trees. A shiver ran through his lean frame, despite the thick coat he had on. "Are you returned in *spirit* as well, my son?"

Eliza went over and wrapped her arm around her father, both of them looking at Aaron, waiting for his reply.

"I am here. Now." Aaron directed his answer to Lukas, his eyes on Eliza, seeing her nod. She wore her hair up, coiled atop her head, her body rail thin, like her father's. "Where a man belongs. Helping keep his loved one's safe from harm."

Lukas grinned, letting out a raspy laugh that turned into a coughing fit, his face going pale as Eliza patted him on his back. She encouraged him to go back inside and sit down, then brought him a drink of warm tea, poured from a kettle steeping on a small stove. Once settled, the older man nodded.

"Well said, my son. Indeed. Though there is no longer any threat. The English let us do as we wish, with no news of any more incursions. The colonial militia having lost their appetite for coming west. Again."

Aaron nodded, watching Eliza as he replied. "You are safe in *that* regard, with the threat—somewhat reduced, though not yet *eliminated*."

"We shall not speak of such things. Enough to have you home. With your wife. A celebration to plan. And a *feast!*" Lukas beamed, as Noah came through the door. "Our intrepid provider of God's four-footed bounty enters. Look, Noah, and see who's returned to us. Home, from the wilderness."

Noah came over and hugged Lukas, careful not to press too hard. "I already met him, Father. In the woods. With a doe in hand."

"Then tonight we shall dine on fresh venison. And marrow squash. With berries, on biscuits!"

Later that evening, once the people of the community made their goodbyes, filtering back to their own homes, Eliza stood beside Aaron. They were outside the door to the small house she shared with Noah, who'd come and gathered up his things, making his bed in the church.

Aaron waited to see where he stood, regarding his place in Eliza's heart. She took his hand, leading him inside, letting go as she busied herself stirring the coals of a fire to life, adding a split of wood. Aaron finally broke the silence. "I can easily find a place in the woods to lie down in."

Eliza looked over, slowly undoing her hair, leaving it hanging in a dark wave across her shoulders. "I imagine so. With it being your bed these past few—*months*. Since you left me. Your wife. All alone."

"Hardly alone, surrounded by your family and the others."

"But *not* with my husband. Which you were *then*. Your vow made in front of Anna, and those who were witness *to* it."

Aaron sighed, aware of the fervent energy of Eliza's faith was as strong, if not stronger, than before. Her eyes were bright with the light of her steadfast belief. Difficult for him to find the woman he'd married, hidden behind the glow. Or the young woman who helped Anna nurse him back to health. He lowered his eyes, his voice soft. "And *now*? Am I to return as if nothing has changed between us?"

Eliza walked over and reached up, opening the topmost button of the cloth shirt he was wearing, pulled from belongings left behind by one of the larger men, lost in the massacre. "I have not forsaken *my* vows, husband."

He watched as she undid the rest of the buttons, revealing his wound, pressing her lips against the scar, and kissing it. The scent of her hair caused his heart to beat faster, his breath coming short as a swirl of emotions rose from within. The room spun as Eliza lifted her lips to his, parting them with the tip of her tongue.

Released to his need, Aaron gathered his wife in his arms, carrying her to a small bed in one corner of the cabin. He placed her there, then lay down, watching as she hung her clothing on the bedpost. Removing it layer by layer, until clad in a simple shift, with the curve of her breasts in his hands.

His mouth traced the line of her neck, then followed the curve of her shoulder, eliciting a soft gasp of pleasure as she arched her back, pulling him to her. As their bodies joined, the wind outside the cabin brought the faint howling of wolves, singing from a remote hilltop. Their sound soon echoed by Eliza, moaning in her husband's ear.

The next morning broke beneath a cloudless sky. Eliza prepared a breakfast of corn cakes, venison, and greens. And a pot of tea brewed with a mixture of herbs steeped in spring water. Palatable enough to serve the purpose of washing down the cakes. Aaron downed it with a heartfelt sigh, missing the blend of leaves back at Meghan's house.

The previous night had provided moments of quiet conversation, each feeling their way back to where they'd left off. Eliza had been hesitant to ask questions, afraid of the answers. Aaron determined to keep details of recent activities to himself, though he had no regret over the killing of former soldiers in retribution for their involvement in the horrendous massacre.

It was enough they knew his hunt was over. That most of the men responsible would live out their remaining days, haunted by memories of what they had done. Suffering from an itch they could never scratch away. Left searching every shadow they passed through, wondering when an arrow would find them.

Eliza listened to what her husband shared without comment or reaction, causing Aaron to question her sincerity. Another bout of love-making helped to push the worry to one side, leaving him drained of everything but his love for her, flooding back.

"You will make your accounting to God, not me. Your soul is in *his* hands. As it has *always* been. I am satisfied with having you at home. In *our* home. Surrounded by *all* of our homes. Here. Where we will continue his work."

"Then you'll not entertain the idea of a place of our own? Near to here, but *apart* from the others?"

She'd looked at him with a wry smile. "I will not leave our people.

Or my father. They opened their hearts to you, accepting you in. Saving your *life*."

"I understand and will honor the debt. But can we nae repay it from a wee bit further away? Someplace where nature can rub up against the walls. With trees overhanging the roof. A place of privacy to raise our children in."

"Meaning for us to be away from prying eyes?" Eliza sat cross-legged, bare-chested, hands in her lap. "You are afraid. Not of dying. But of *my* death, brought back with you to our home. Brought to our people, *here*. Others searching for you. To hold you accountable for what you were running away from. From what you did, back *there*."

"I was not *running* away, only searching for A'neewa. For Anna. Delirious with fever from my wound, moving on instinct." Aaron shook his head. "We're safe, *here*. No harm falling to our family. Or our people."

Eliza stared at Aaron. "You claim to know God's will?"

Aaron frowned. "I would dictate a lack of interest in lands *this* far to the west. The east, occupying everyone's attention. Filled with vipers. Each one killed, resulting in a dozen more rising in its place." He paused, his shoulders falling. "I'm not the *fool* my father was. Paying with his life, attempting to bring a measure of balance into the world."

"Your father—dead? You know this to be true?"

"He's dead." Aaron looked away, the light from a candle reflected from the side of his face, his jaw clenched. "Successful in having burnt out *one* of their nests. Rumors of him caught in the flames. With nothing gained from the effort except a slight delay. Enough of one to pull me into the *next* inferno. Able to find my way out, ending up here."

"To *me*. As God willed it." Eliza took his hands and held them to her chest, the swell of her breasts warming them. "You can *see* that, Aaron. I *know* you can. That God led you here to *me*. To help do his work. Living and working *among* his people, not apart. Giving you a *second* chance to find peace. Immersing yourself in his love."

Aaron nodded, aware his life with Eliza and all the others would be his destiny. A land filled with native people under the control of the English for now. The commander at the fort, unaware he was the Wolf, a notorious killer of their soldiers, once. Of Colonial militiamen, now. His fate, to have slipped halfway between one group and the other. A member of an independent community of pious people, living off the sweat, tears, and blood of their labors. Standing in the light of God's love.

CHAPTER TEN
PHILADELPHIA INN
SPRING, 1783

The air was crisp, driven by an ocean of salt air sweeping through a haze of smoke from the city. The weather was achingly clear, revealing the sails of ships arriving and departing, spanning the wide river port like water lilies shivering on a windswept pond.

Sinclair spun in a small circle, the dress she was wearing swirling in a flowing pattern of emerald-green, spun through with gold threads. She stopped, smoothing the silk with her hands, looking at Pierre with pursed lips. "Impossible for me to accept this. You *know* that. *Knew* it, before having it made."

Pierre glanced at the fireplace in his suite. The hearth was cold, left unlit during a recent bout of fine weather. "Then I shall have it burned. With no one else to wear it. The sight of you trying it on is enough for me. A memory I shall cherish forever." He came over and placed his hand on hers. Moving it down to her waist, then lower, stopping when she turned away.

"I am not a woman of society, Pierre." Sinclair lowered her head. "No longer my life. Those days—behind me."

Pierre reached out and touched the side of her face, encouraging her to look at him. "No one wants you where you don't want to be. I'm willing to become a man of the country. *Your* country. Willing to join my efforts to yours. To purchase land attached to your own. Building an estate with a great manor and stables. A place to host—" Pierre caught himself, recognizing the error in his logic. "A *farm*. With thousands of acres, producing crops. Where people will work together to create a bright future for their families. Education provided for their children. With an opportunity for employment. Helping to expand on *your* charitable efforts."

Sinclair shook her head, a smile on her lips. "And that would suit you? Living close to the soil, with dirt under *your* fingernails?" She laughed, her voice tinged with huskiness, the onset of middle-age softening the edges. "I hardly think so, my sweet, misguided friend."

"A compromise, then. If you will. A *small* manor on a hill above a valley farm. One with *moderate* stables. With a ballroom, capable of the occasional soiree with a hundred—no, with *fifty* guests."

"*Scoundrel.*"

"My *queen.*"

"*Idiot.* Though dashing." Sinclair grinned. "A *dangerous* combination. Especially in the French."

"And you, my lady, are both *brilliant*—and *forgiving.*" Pierre brushed a stray curl from her ear, tucking it behind her slim neck. "A dangerous *fault*, in a woman so beautiful. Trusting a dashing idiot, such as myself."

Sinclair turned around, raising her arms, fingers pointed at the ceiling. "Help me out of this dress."

Pierre came over and released the clasps on its back. He kissed her shoulders and spine as he slipped it over her hips, kept slim from long rides on horseback through the fields and woods on the outer edges of the city. "And then I am to burn it?"

She turned around and circled his neck with her hands, gazing into his dark eyes. "Unless you're able to convince me to *keep* it, hoping I'll give in to your use of—*French* persuasion."

He smiled, sliding his hands down her thighs, taking her pantaloons with them, revealing her body. He carried her over to the bed, laying her on the edge. Then he kneeled, drinking in her essence, loving her, losing himself in her cries of pleasure as she grabbed him by the back of his head, her body writhing in a shuddering release.

When they finished their lovemaking, Sinclair leaned on one arm, her fingers toying with the curls of hair on Pierre's chest. She regarded him with a smile, though her mind was spinning a dozen different scenarios about why he was still there. In Philadelphia. Staying in an expensive room. In bed. With her.

"What are you looking for, my friend?" She tugged a tuft of hair, eliciting a slight flicker of reaction from the slim, handsome face of a man she was enjoying the company of, though could never fully love. "Our paths are *not* the same. Our interests, running in angled lines to one another."

"Not *all* our interests." Pierre opened his eyes, reaching out and cupping Sinclair's breast, stroking her nipple, watching her eyes.

She removed his hand. "I would know your thoughts. Plainly spoken. Or as plainly spoken as you're *able* to do. With your Francophile nature set aside."

Pierre sat up and stretched, a wide yawn cracking the edges of his mouth. "To speak as an Englishman. Direct. Without —*panache.*"

"With *truth* will do for now." Sinclair grinned. "Later, perhaps, more of the *former* would be nice." She squirmed her hips and legs around, sitting up, trying to ignore the slight sag of her breasts, knowing how she must look, despite reassurances from Pierre that she was perfect in every detail.

"I would know your intentions toward me. Finding it difficult to believe you would ever consider making Philadelphia your home. Not in the same way as *I* regard it to be. And my family." She paused. "Those that are left, choosing to live *here.*"

Pierre reached over, pulling her into a warm embrace, feeling her tears on his chest. He kissed the top of her head, inhaling deeply, knowing he would leave her in the morning. His passage booked. Having waited to let her know, not wanting the affair to end.

Sinclair looked up, her eyes red, cheeks glistening in the afternoon light. "I'm —leaving you, Pierre. Today." She smiled. "Leaving this *wonderful* dream. This glass globe, with the outside world held at bay. Delightful hours spent floating inside it, swirling around like flakes of snow." She sighed, taking his hand and kissing each knuckle. "Ready now to release you back into your world. While I remain here, returning to *mine*."

"I'll not be able to change your mind?" When Sinclair shook her head, Pierre leaned forward, finding her lips, his own slightly bruised from the attention paid to her earlier. He kissed her softly, squeezed her hand, then pulled away. "Then I will honor your decision. For now." He stood up, his lean body resplendent, his skin a light shade of tan, indicative of a Spanish bloodline, somewhere in the mix. "And will go open another bottle of wine." He paused. "Shall I bring back two glasses, or one?"

Sinclair held up a single finger, watching him move away with a sigh, knowing how much she would miss his loving attention to her every need.

Meghan leaned down and searched Allwyn's eyes. He forced them open as wide as possible, causing her to smile, her lips tight with concern. "The pupils *look* normal. With no sign of cloudiness." She sat up, holding out two fingers. "How many?"

"Two. Blurry. But only *two*." Allwyn gazed up at his wife, wishing to have her mood lifted. His continued headaches and filmy vision were a weight on both their shoulders. Patrick had noticed as well, his usual playfulness dampened of late, watching as his mother helped guide his father through a never-ending list of chores, insisting on doing his share of the work.

Meghan had hired two additional men from the same families as the others. Doing everything needed to expand the services provided to the local community and those lying further into the hills. With two more wagons added into the mix, making regular trips into and out of the city. The stable and storeroom enlarged, along with the house, with another child on the way.

Sinclair had sent a courier, letting them know she'd be staying on in the city of Philadelphia for a few days. Waiting there for the loading off of a shipment of valuable goods from the hold of the ship she'd arrived on. A wagon to be sent her way once a second note arrived.

The news had frustrated Meghan, eager to go into the city to hear news about Marion and her family, though hesitant to leave her husband's side, with occasional bouts of dizziness still bothering him.

"I'm not *incapable*, lass." Allwyn walked arm in arm beside his wife, the two of them heading toward the storeroom. It still appeared tilted to his eyes, requiring him to focus on walking a straight line. The injury to his head had healed on the outside, the pressure within reduced by the poultices Meghan applied. But his eyesight still troubled him, leaving him wondering how much longer it would be until he could regain his place as the unofficial head of the community.

"Of course not, husband. No one thinking that of ya'. I'm only leery of you doing something foolish, causing yourself a setback. One we *cannae* afford, not with the new crops going in." She squeezed her hand around his. "We've found a balance, with the new men handling things with no issues. We must place our faith in what's helped get us here. Our trust and love for each other."

Young Patrick, held in his mother's other arm, laid his head on her shoulder, then coughed, causing Meghan's eyes to narrow in concern.

Pierre strolled along the length of a narrow dock. It stretched like the finger of a hand, pointing straight ahead, the pilings filtering the near edge of the river, laced through with a mixed collection of grasses, lost ropes, and discarded trash. He peered down into dozens of small boats, moving between ships sitting at anchor, bearing passengers and their personal effects. Impatient travelers, unwilling to wait for the ships they'd arrived on to find a spot at the crowded docks.

Then he smiled, knowing that Sinclair, back on the shore in the harbormaster's office, would be firmly pressing the harried man for an update on her shipment. She'd sent him outside while she tended to her affairs, giving him the perfect opportunity to do the same. He came to a stop, standing by a section of stacked goods marked by odd symbols in red paint, identifying the place where a messenger from the cabal was to meet him.

A slight cough from one side caused Pierre to start. He hesitated a moment, then turned around. A wave of a hand invited him into a narrow space between several head-high crates. Once sheltered from view, he eyed a small man with an outstretched hand, a leather envelope clenched in his dirt-stained fingers.

Pierre handed him a small purse of silver coins, receiving a curt nod and the package in return. Once he was alone, he broke the wax seal and opened it, scanning through the report. Then he folded the papers, sighing, aware he'd need to put a new plan in place. An extremely capable and nameless man missing, soon after passing on a report that he was hot on the trail of Sinclair's son. A man remaining a thorn in the cabal's side. His removal made a priority, before growing into something far worse.

A loud squawk startled him as a large gull landed on the stacked goods, head tilted to one side, staring at him. Pierre smiled. "To be a bird, free to fly away, leaving the earth and all my problems far below." With a deep and cleansing breath, he slipped the pouch into the pocket of his tailored jacket, then headed back to the grounded end of the pier, where he'd bid a sorrowful and heartfelt goodbye to Lady Sinclair.

CHAPTER ELEVEN

HIGHLAND MANOR
LATE SPRING, 1783

M arion shoved Lorna away, causing her to fall onto her back, with two tiny fistfuls of weeds spilling from her chubby hands, scattered by a cool breeze. Her daughter laughed as she rolled to one side, struggled to her feet, then headed off to pull another two handfuls from the edge of the flower garden. She started back, a devilish smile on her face as her father encouraged her to toss them at her mother.

"There'll be a price to pay, *husband*, for such actions." Marion stood up, hands on her hips, a glare on her cheeks, red from the rub of a raw spring breeze. Declan grabbed their daughter as she passed by, lifting her into the air, placing her legs around his neck, her hands dropping the clumps of grass as she grabbed onto tufts of his thick hair, causing him to swallow a curse.

Marion laughed, feeling a stir within her lower abdomen, aware another bairn was in place with the father, clueless, as yet. "A reward earned. For courage in the face of—*greenery!*"

Angus came around the corner of a thick hedge, his face locked in a stoic expression, carried with him from morning to night. The only exception, when holding young Lorna was in his arms, giggling with delight as he made faces. He was in no mood for such frivolity now, a dark cloud before him as he came up.

"I've just now heard from below. Your Frenchman. Coming here alone. Without an escort." Angus turned and spat on the ground, then cleared his throat. "I'll take two men and go to meet—"

Marion shook her head. "No. *I'll* go. Prepare my mare." When Angus turned to comply, she raised her voice, a gust of wind sweeping through the thick, highland grass, ringing the hedges. "*Alone*, Angus. The ride down to and through the Pinch will help clear my restless mood."

He hesitated, then nodded in agreement, Marion watching as he walked away, knowing he'd follow along behind, taking up a cold perch at the high lookout. His face wreathed in a stubborn scowl, anxiously counting the minutes until she came back into sight.

Pierre pulled on the reins, stopping his mount, a wide smile on his face as he watched Marion guide her horse through a shallow run of water, remnants of a recent storm racing down from the highland mountains.

"I'm honored to be greeted by the beautiful matriarch of clan Scott."

"An unexpected and *foolhardy* visit from a man who should *know* better than to *test* my trust. Dark eyes abound on dangerous ground between Glasgow and here, with the potential of harm to travelers from away. Especially those sporting such—*resplendent* attire."

Pierre doffed a plumed cap, his wide shoulders bedecked in a black cape with a silver pin holding it in place. "I left small purses in the hands of those I met before. When escorted here by my good friend Angus. People *he* trusted, who remembered me for my *previous* generosity." He raised himself in the saddle, legs straightening in the stirrups, easing the ache in his lower back. "Speaking of my erstwhile traveling companion, he must be close by. No doubt with musket in hand, my chest in his sights."

Marion came up, the two horses exchanging touches of their noses, shaking their heads, then lowering them to graze on tufts of grass growing beside the well-traveled path. "He is in a *seethe* of anger, high above. Armed with nothing more deadly than a *glare*."

"I've felt it, before. And lived to tell the tale." Pierre leaned over and took Marion's hand. He raised it, kissing the back, her pale, flawless skin warmed by his soft lips. "Well met, Lady Marion. A genuine pleasure to see you again." When she didn't respond, he sighed. "I apologize for my unexpected intrusion into your lands. I carry a message from your mother. Regarding news of your sister's husband." He paused. "And your brother."

"From my *mother?*" Marion pulled back. "When? And where?"

"From her own hand. Lady Sinclair's." Pierre hesitated. "Fortunate enough to spend time with her while making a crossing to the colony of Pennsylvania. Returning here at her bidding. To deliver a letter updating you on recent events." He pulled it from beneath the cape, holding it out. "Honored in being asked to do so."

Marion sniffed, the chilly air making her nose run. She ignored the letter, turning to look on high, measuring the sky. "We'll just arrive by fall of night, in leaving now." With a tug on the reins, she turned her horse and started back.

Pierre slipped the thin packet away, then nudged his mount with his heels, urging her to follow along behind. He fixed his eyes on Marion's thin waist, admiring the fluid movement of her hips, allowing himself a moment of consideration of how the daughter might compare to the mother. Then he dismissed the possibility. His thoughts refocused on the reason for his self-assigned mission.

Declan poured another helping of Aqua Vitea into Pierre's glass. It was the product of a recent attempt to rekindle the work of his wife's great-grandfather. Charred barrels used to smooth the liquid, helping to mature it. Angus had led the effort, with knowledge gained of such things from one of a multitude of books he'd gathered, then placed in the manor library. He'd drawn off a dozen bottles, the rest stored away in the cellar beneath the manor.

Pierre closed his eyes, comparing the notes of flavor to a rare bottle of wine. "This is a—*pleasant* surprise. Strong. A bit spirited on the tongue, though with a smooth gait." He kept his eyes closed, the image of his host's wife lingering in his mind's eye. Then he took another drink, able to down it without losing his breath.

Declan nodded. "I have stayed as close as possible to the original blend, with Angus suggesting a few key alterations to the process. By rights, the credit goes to him."

Pierre reached for the bottle, looking for a label, the brown glass unadorned. He looked at Declan, his eyebrows raised. The younger man smiled. "It's unmarked for a reason. Not allowed for distribution outside clan lands. The English looking with a sour eye on such things as that."

"A foolish attitude. The world would be a far better place if men of ambition were to filter their greed through the occasional glass, surrounded by those with a more—common view of the lay of the land." He poured another finger's width of liquid into his glass, then raised it. "Not that I consider you, or our young professor of spirits, to be *common*. In thought, *or* deed."

Declan nodded, then leaned forward, touching his glass, still a quarter-full, to that of his guest. "I believe we're seen for who we *truly* are, whether sitting at a highland table, or lowlander's hearth."

Marion, standing in the doorway, having come from putting Lorna to bed, smiled as she walked over and took the glass from her husband's hand, downing it with a toss of her thin wrist, knowing Declan was not a drinker, the spirits causing him sickness when over-imbibed. She gave Pierre an appraising gaze, holding it until he raised his eyebrows in response. She crossed her arms over her chest. "I find it interesting, with you making the journey here alone. Without an escort, like the *last* time."

"Meaning it is my *close* friend, Angus, the one with the question."

"The question, regardless of its source, stands." Marion handed the empty glass to Declan, then crossed her arms.

Pierre shrugged, taking a moment to stare into the fireplace, watching the flames. "I had heard of the—*unfortunate* event. News of it provided from sources of information in the port of Glasgow." He swiveled his head, taking in Declan's uneasy demeanor. "I fear I was a

Judas goat. Used by a *selective* group of powerful men I've had an occasional association with. They offered their services to facilitate the transfer of money and arms to the colonials' cause."

Pierre looked down at his glass, reflecting the light of the flames. "My hands, tinged with the stain of it. Albeit not red—" He sighed. "With the blood of innocent animals—as were your own, from the story told me."

Declan leaned forward, placing his hand on Pierre's forearm. "It has been a dangerous game we've played. One with significant risk to us all." He glanced up at Marion, who held a look of neutrality on her face, her eyes fixed on Pierre. "A message sent us. Warned to stay clear, which we have. Our part in this—now finished, with the war all but over. According to the news brought to us by couriers, from below."

Pierre nodded. "True. With darker days to follow." He stood up and came over, stopping in front of Marion. "I spent considerable time in discussion with your mother while on our passage to the colonies. Lady Sinclair filled me in on events *here*. Presenting me with your opinion as to my role in what transpired. Your doubts warranted. My position, without justification."

He paused, looking straight into Marion's light-colored eyes. "Associates of mine searched for the men involved, looking to exact a heavy punishment upon them. The men responsible—gone missing. Themselves, or their bodies, not yet found."

He stepped back, waiting to see Marion's reaction, detecting no change in her stiff posture, though her eyes softened slightly about the edges. "Men, dressed in dark clothing, confronted me. To discern for themselves the depth of my involvement. Saved, when several of the members of the group interceded on my behalf. My life spared."

Declan stood up, his voice firm. "We danced with the Devil, in trying to do what we believed to be right. Lucky to have suffered no serious harm, beyond a handful of animals to bury, with no further trouble for our efforts, made." He gave his wife a quick nod, then left the room.

Marion sniffed as she went to the window and leaned against the frame. When she spoke, her voice was soft. "I would hear what you know. *All* that you know, as to the latest news of my family."

Pierre hid a smile of satisfaction, keeping it from his lips. He came over, standing across from the woman who looked as if a younger version of her mother. "Your brother is alive. Your sister saw him again when he rescued then returned her husband to her and young Patrick. The lad, Allwyn, left with an injury to his head. Of some concern to your mother, on hearing of it."

"Aaron—is *with* them?"

"No." Pierre leaned forward. "I've learned a few details of his background. That he is a marked man, by both English and Colonial groups. With his head placed in one of two nooses if he's caught. His aggressive talents *stinging* those on both sides." He hesitated. "I can share more, though fear it might disturb your feelings towards him."

Marion gave Pierre a sad look, her eyes glazed with unshed tears. "I've learned what he's seen. Been involved in. Of what he experienced. From his *own* words written in journals. Including images drawn by his—" She turned away, looking through the glass, the sky a silver streak of clouds beneath a full moon, racing by. "By his hand. Along with the number of deaths he's dealt to the enemy. *Our* enemy. Mine—" She locked eyes with his. "And *yours*."

"Then I shall leave off with this." Pierre stepped back. "I am in love with your mother." He paused, receiving a quiet look. Then he cleared his throat. "Your father, who was once my enemy, had become a good friend. Then lost to us all. His death, along with several others, related to me by someone I place *great* trust in. Your mother, having sensed it herself."

Tears trailed down his high cheekbones as a genuine feeling of loss painted a look of sadness on his narrow face. "I shared what little I could. What I'd been able to find out. Your mother—she allowed me to share her grief. The look of pain in her-"

"You've *lain* with her." Marion watched as Pierre lowered his eyes, hands clenched at his sides. She didn't wait for a reply, moving away from the window, and heading toward the door leading to the bedroom shared with her husband.

Pierre's voice, strained with emotion, stopped her. "I *did*. And offered her everything I have, in return. Including my *name*. Freely given if she'd chosen to accept it. Rejected. Bid by her to come here. To provide her daughter answers to any and every question asked."

He closed the distance. "Which I have openly offered you. And offer once again, in begging your forgiveness for my inability to have refused my desire—no, my *need* to be with her. My infatuation with your mother began from the moment of our *first* meeting. Shamed by those feelings, then. Your father a—a *good* friend, and far better man than I. And then, upon seeing her again, I could no longer resist sharing those feelings."

Marion paused halfway through the doorway, with one hand on the frame, her head lowered, back to him. Her reply, when it came, was dark in tone. "Together. On a *ship*. Making a crossing to the colonies. One of the dozen or more departing from Glasgow that very week. After you showed up at the *same* establishment where *she* was staying."

She turned around. "Angus has eyes everywhere, keeping a close watch over the members of our clan." Marion was silent for a moment, then gave Pierre a wide smile. "Such a *wondrous* stroke of luck for you *both*." Then she spun around and strode away, the sound of her shoes echoing off the walls of the narrow hallway.

Once settled in bed, with Declan's arm curled around her shoulders, Marion rested her cheek on his chest, listening to the slow, steady beating of his heart. He reached up with his free hand, brushing back a few strands of her fine black hair, then gently kissed her forehead. "Are ya' satisfied, my love, as to his telling of the truth of things?"

Marion pictured her great uncle Shaun's face, remembering the lessons taught her about the telling of truths. To strangers met, and kin alike. "Yes." The lie rolled off her tongue. "I am."

"Then we agree. With no more said on the matter of his honesty."

Marion nodded, an honest reply finding its way to her full lips. "Aye, husband. No more *said*. I promise." Then she began composing a letter in her head. One she'd carefully encode, confirming to her mother that her own concerns about Pierre, discussed in a previous message sent her way, were valid.

The wind picked up, causing the windowpanes to rattle. Marion lifted her head, gazing at Declan. "We're to have a child. By the spring. A boy, I think. A son." She felt him turn toward her. "Calum. With Aaron, his middle name. A longbow placed in his hand, soon as he's able to hold one."

Declan nodded, his hand on the side of her face. Cupping it as his lips found her earlobe. "I love ya', lassie. More than words can ever tell it, true." Then they clung to one another as a storm enveloped the manor, tumbling down from the rounded shoulders of the mountain, on high.

Angus watched as the Frenchman rode away from the end of the Pinch. He pursed his lips, returning the other man's half-wave, then nodded, his first task completed. Lady Marion having bid him escort their guest through to its further end, after taking him aside, handing him a satchel, whispering additional orders into his ear before kissing him on his bearded cheek, wishing him safe travels.

He waited until Pierre disappeared, then retraced his path, heading uphill until he reached the end of an old clan trail, known to a handful of his most trusted men. With a shrug of his hips, he coaxed the large mare to follow the steep, winding climb, promising her a feast of oats when they reached the other end. She responded with a shake of her head, moving ahead with short, steady strides.

Angus settled back, his thoughts centered on what Marion had told him. Her feelings aligned with his own. Both seeing eye to eye, despite their disparity in height. A message to Lady Sinclair in hand. A purse of coins at his waist, enough to buy passage to a place he was looking forward to seeing. To a reunion with Lady Sinclair, Meghan, and Allwyn. And a young laddie he'd yet to meet.

As for Pierre and plans made in his direction, he'd deliver the letter, then wait to see what transpired. Patient, as always, with a job in hand, waiting to provide whatever service Lady Sinclair might ask of him.

CHAPTER TWELVE
CAPTIVE'S TOWN
AUTUMN, 1783

Noah shook his head, giving each of the young native men facing him a hard look. "There's nothing good coming from what you're asking. With nothing gained worth the risk. With no *reason* for it."

Their leader, the oldest son of the chief of the Wyandot tribe, glared at him. "You've lived too long in the shadows of the fort, bowing to the men *in* it. Making *friends* with them. Gone over to their God. Letting the English tell you where *your* land is. And where it *isn't*." The one speaking, named Two-Spirit, was larger in body and stronger in voice than the others. He hit his open hand with a fist, his eyes narrowed in anger.

"Denied right to our rightful claim of ancestral ground. Where we've walked for as long as any can remember. Game trails followed. The water, *ours* to move on as *we* wish. The English said to be giving it away to those who would come here, stealing our way of life. *Butcher*ing our people, taking our *hair*."

The tip of his finger came close to Noah's chest. "The same ones who *butchered* your adopted people. All of you, *blinded* by the white-skinned liars who turned your eyes away from your own heritage.

Your hearts and minds ripped away from the Great Mother's embrace."

The older boy shook his head, stepping back. "We will make them hear *our* voices. Answer to *our* ancestors, calling out for us to protect our way of life. All we ask from you is to help us find a way into the English fort."

Noah shook his head. "You will *die. All* of you. The soldiers, cutting you down before you can climb over the walls." He looked at the sullen-faced group. "Too few of you. Too *angry*. Too inexperienced in dealing out death." Crossing his arms, Noah looked around. "Where are the elders of your tribe? Why are *they* not here?"

"*We* will act in *their* place." Two-Spirit straightened up, head held high. "They will join us once we show them the English are *not* our friends."

Noah gave the leader of the group a sad look. "You will die. For nothing." Then he walked away. Once he cleared the edge of the woods, he swore under his breath. He'd left his longbow behind, the sudden appearance of the young men catching him off guard. When he returned to the small opening to retrieve it, a young woman was there, with his bow and quiver in her hands.

"My brother, the one who spoke—is wrong. I have heard our father counsel him to be patient. Telling him his anger has twisted his thoughts. The English have protected our lands from incursion. But he will not listen. His youth, making him deaf to the words of the elders."

She hesitated, holding out his weapons, her face wearing a shy smile. "I am Tindee Utehke. It means Two-Women, in the white language."

Noah walked up and took them. "I am Noah. My given name." He spoke to her in his birth language, having used it while speaking to her brother, struggling to interpret some of what Two-Spirit had said. He stumbled now. "I am Lenape. I mean—I *was* Lenape."

"I know of you. The Shadow Hunter, with the strange bow. As long as a tree." She smiled, the tip of her teeth white against her doe-brown skin. "A *short* tree, now that I have held it."

A moment of silence followed, deafening in the hush of the thick woods. When she turned to go, Noah called out to her. "You are worried. For your brother. And for the rest of your people."

Two-Women slowly turned around, her face angled down, slim hands clasped before her. "I saw a vision. Of my brother hanging from the limb of a tree. With the wind stirring his unbound hair. His eyes staring down at me." She raised her arms, crossing them on her chest. "Feeling cold, though the sun was shining on me."

Noah felt a pull, wanting to go to her. He stayed rooted in place. "I will talk with him. Alone. No one else to come."

She nodded. "I will tell him. There will be no one else." When she turned to walk away, Noah called out.

"*You* could come, to remind him of what he stands to lose, in pursuing this pointless gesture. One doomed to fail."

Two-Women paused, her back to him. "You will need to find a *better* way of showing him a path leading away from violence. He is— stubborn. Determined to walk a crooked path."

Noah watched her until she disappeared into the woods, able once more to take a full breath as the ache in his chest eased. Then he whispered. "I can be stubborn, *too*. But am learning how to bend." With a last glance in her direction, he sighed, then started home.

Aaron listened as Noah related details of the impromptu meeting. He held his opinion while the young man finished and asked him what he should do.

"It's *your* decision to make. Whether you try to guide him from this foolish idea or leave him to his fate. You're unlikely to succeed. Those looking to make their mark in the world *difficult* to reach. A curse that comes with young men wanting to earn a name."

"Like you. Walking in your father's shadow. The Wolf, surpassing the Fox." Noah sucked in his breath, seeing a flare of anger in his mentor's eyes, dissolving away as Aaron shrugged, then nodded.

"I hadn't thought of it like that. Not until this very moment." He eyed Noah. "You have wisdom. Far beyond your years. The sign of a good leader. Your first opportunity in front of you, trying to convince this angry boy to follow your advice."

Noah made several visits over the next few weeks to Two-Women's village, meeting with her brother and explaining the difficulties in trying to attack the fort. Two-Spirit showed little interest in what he shared concerning the strength and capability of the English forces.

The native boy's stance remained unchanged, his words filled with anger, frustrated at Noah's lack of willingness to help. Challenging him with taunts of cowardice, testing the young Moravian's belief in non-violence. The elderly chieftain had intervened, causing the young would-be warrior to walk away, muttering under his breath.

Two-Women, near in age to Noah, had been eager to visit Captive's Town in return, speaking with Eliza about her belief in God. The language barrier prevented a straightforward exchange of information, with Noah caught in the middle, his head left spinning by the rapid flow of conversation.

Two-Women rewarded his tireless efforts during their long walks between villages, a full day of travel each way, holding his hand as they moved through the countryside, speaking on a diverse range of subjects.

The seeds of their conversations soon grew into discussions about religion, covering the concepts of God, church, and the sanctity of marriage, with each of their cultures holding opposing views. Two-Women confused about the need for a minister to bless the union of man to woman, with the God person looking over their shoulders.

"He is to be there with us as we —*join?*"

"Yes. Along with *all* the people of the community."

"We are to —*lie* with each other? While they *watch* us?"

Noah blushed, stopping in the middle of the trail. "*No!* Not *that* kind of joining." He looked away, unable to face her. "The binding of our *hands* together, with vows spoken before God. The others, my people, standing as witnesses, praying we will follow God's law, as a couple. Honoring him with our faith."

"And if we do not, he will get *angry*. And make us die." Two-Women looked at him, her dark eyes narrowed in an expression of reluctant acceptance. Noah took her hands in his.

"God is—he's *not* like that. Not as the others—not as *we* know him to be."

"He allowed *your* people to die. The ones who were evil—to live." Two-Women shook her head, her twin braids dangling down the front of her shoulders, threaded through with twists of blue beads, a gift from Eliza, gleaming in the mid-day light. "The Great Mother allows us to decide how to bring balance into the world. Our people expected to fight back when threatened. Our women and children stand *alongside* the men. Some of them dying, yes. But many of them *live*. Allowing the *tribe* to survive."

"Yes. But—" Noah shut his mouth, unable to repeat the words he'd grown up listening to, knowing in his heart he hadn't fully accepted them. That what he'd seen had damaged his faith, along with the distant look in Aaron's eyes, when leaving him behind.

Two-Women touched his face. "I will do the marriage if someday you *ask* it of me. I will *say* the words. Try to obey you and your God. But I will *still* walk the path, listening to the Great Mother."

Noah shook his head, trying to piece together a response that would meet both their spiritual needs. Then Two-Women leaned in, pressing her lips to his, her hands on his waist, eyes open as she pulled him in against her. Noah released his troubled thoughts as a rush of warmth spread throughout his body, joined by the rapid beating of his heart.

⸎⸎⸎

A large contingent of natives joined the Moravian parishioners for two days of thanksgiving, having traveled to attend a splendid feast held in Captive's Town. The two groups had agreed to come together, convinced by the combined efforts of Noah and Two-Women, hoping to ease the tensions caused by her brother and his band of young warriors.

The elders had agreed to make the journey, stirred by the gifts

delivered by Noah, along with a promise from the leader of the Mora-
vians to help them with their claim for independence. Talks between
the Iroquois nation, the English, and the Colonial government were
ongoing, with a treaty hanging in the balance, waiting for a final round
of negotiations between all sides.

Two-Spirit and his followers accompanied the Wyandot tribe but
refused to eat with the others, staying at the edge of the forest, sullen-
faced, looking at the fort with dark eyes. The commander of the
English force, invited to attend the meal, along with his officers and
men, pulled Lukas and his son aside, demanding to know the reason
for the younger men's lack of participation in the festivities.

Lukas had turned to Noah, allowing him to answer. "They are
unhappy because Two-Women chose me over one of their own.
Displeased, but willing to support the elder's decision. Though
unwilling to break bread with *my* family."

The commander pursed his lips, giving the matter a moment of
consideration, about to offer further comment when Eliza stepped in.
She asked him to lead her in a dance, music from a handful of soldiers
with instruments wafting through the heated air of the large common
building, used as their church.

Food, music, singing, and dancing proved enough of a distraction
to avoid further discussion, with Noah able to slip away and visit Two-
Spirit and his followers. He tried once again to convince the angry
young man to let go of his need to make a name for himself at the
expense of his and his followers' lives.

"You know the fort is too strong for you to make your way over the
walls or to break through the gates."

Two-Spirit leaned in, his eyes reflecting the light from a half-full
moon. "Not if you're willing to *open* them, then helping to provide a
distraction."

Noah shook his head. "Leaving you rushing inside, with men
pouring out of their barracks, muskets in hand, their bayonets lowered.
With you facing them with—*what?* Tomahawks and war clubs? A
handful of old weapons, most of them unreliable. Leaving all of you
caught, then hung by your necks."

"We will *have* guns. Taken from their hands, killing them before they know we are inside if you *help* us. Help *me* send a message that they will *not* set us aside as people of *no* value. Sent to the furthest edges of our lands to live as animals. Without pride." Two-Spirit straightened up. "Without honor."

"You will *all* die. The tribe hollowed out, collapsing from within, with the English exacting their revenge on your people. They will wipe away your stories, leaving nothing behind but ashes and the tears of the women. Those who survive, *cursing* your name."

Two-Spirit turned away, then spun around, a war club in his hand, eyes blazing with the light of a false dawn. Noah didn't flinch, standing his ground, hand to his back, a knife near to his fingers, though he knew he would not need to use it.

Hesitation bloomed across Two-Spirit's face, turning into a sneer. He lowered his hand and stepped back. "You are as much an enemy to *me* as them. Drinking their lies. Eating their promises. Left with an empty belly, until their sword falls on *your* neck." He turned away, leaving with the others, disappearing into the woods.

When Noah started back to join the celebration of thanks for a bountiful harvest, Aaron slipped into place beside him, stepping from the shadows of a large tree, bow in his hand, strung, a sign he'd been ready to defend his younger brother if necessary.

"He'll bear watching. His fever grows within him. Seen it happen before with men, especially the young ones. Blinded to reason by their ambition."

Noah faced him. "And that duty falls on *me?*"

Aaron nodded. "It does. Unless you're ready to cut ties with your girl and her people." When Noah shook his head in response, Aaron reached out and squeezed his shoulder. "There's no good in denying it or trying to find a way out from under. You're *no* different from anyone else, including me. Left facing a choice that offers nothing but pain, either way. Yours. Hers. Standing together or forced apart. A cross you have to bear from having an open heart to the world. Which you do."

Noah looked down, his hands open, fingers curled as if holding onto Two-Women. When he looked back up, he watched Aaron's eyes as he asked the question. "Who was she—the one *you* lost?"

Aaron shrugged. "As fair a flower as your sister. Wanting to make her my wife. Cut from the same bank of clay, with as big a heart, and as incredible a mind." He sighed, wondering where Skye was. Unwilling to picture her married and bearing another man's children.

"And you had to let *go* of her?" When Aaron nodded, Noah softened his stance. "Would you change it if you could?"

"No. She was well clear of what happened next, with me coming here to help steer a friend clear of the war. The one just finished up. Another on the horizon, with your people's lives and traditions, pinched between what's coming their way."

Aaron fended off the next question, giving Noah a hard look. "And no, I wasn't able to forestall his destiny, any more than *you'll* be able to with her brother. You'll just have to try your best when the moment arrives, trusting your own set of instincts on what to do, and when."

Noah let a look of frustration cross his wide-cheeked face. His body thickened by the work and hard miles spent combing the wilderness for game and hours spent working in the fields. With a nod of his head, he turned around, heading back to the feast. "Then I'll need to be getting back, so I can let *her* know."

Two-Women stood beneath the limbs of a sheltering tree, eyes lowered. "Are you sure?"

Noah took her hands in his. "Yes. It's for the best. For my people, and yours." He hesitated, then squeezed her fingers. She shook her head, her braids swinging as she did so, glistening in the light from a lantern, the two of them standing outside the gathering place, people moving in and out through a large door.

"In front of your people *and* mine?"

"*Our* people. When the time is right. United by the vows we'll speak. With words of our *own*. One's honoring *both* traditions. Of God, and the Great Mother."

Two-Women gave Noah a shy smile. "Together. You and I." She leaned her head against his chest. "I would enjoy that. *Very* much." Noah reached up and cupped her cheek, pulling her in, aware there would be blood on the ground before long. Swearing a vow to himself that none of it would be hers, knowing he'd do everything possible to protect her and her people.

Aaron watched from the doorway of the church, the air cool against his temple. The scent from the spread of food and the crowd of bodies gathered inside fed an urge to disappear into the woods for a few days, bow in hand, helping to clear his mood.

Eliza found him there, taking his arm, coaxing him to hold her, with her arm curled around his waist. She noted the young couple standing a few paces away, aware a change had occurred in the budding relationship.

She smiled, happy for her brother. Happy for all their people. Satisfied that the life they would share might help draw the natives closer to the light of God. A school built, with classes open to all, continuing work Anna had begun so many years ago. With the torch passed along to the next generation.

With a warm smile, encouraged by the laughter of the mingled communities, she wondered when she should let her husband know she was expecting. Concerned with how he might react, his mood of late troubled. Sleep disturbed by sudden lurches, waking with a start, then going outside. Found lying in woods near the edge of the pasture, an oiled cloth sheltering him against the morning dew.

It will be different now, she promised herself, with their child bringing him closer to her. Back to where they'd been before. A call from her father pulled her head around. The elderly man held a glass of wine in his hand, beckoning her to join him in making a toast.

Aaron felt her pull away and released his grasp, returning to a study of the woods as the two young lovers slipped past him, coming back inside. His thoughts filled with the memory of a tavern in Glasgow. Of a good friend, lost much too soon. And an incredible woman he'd loved and then let go of.

CHAPTER THIRTEEN
CROSSROAD STORE
MID-WINTER, 1784

Sinclair wrapped Patrick in a thick shawl, then tucked him in between his mother and father, the three of them heading to the port of Philadelphia. Leaving on a ship bound for Glasgow, then by carriage into the highlands, so that two young cousins could finally meet.

"I wish you were coming with us." Meghan gave her mother a searching look, her hands pulling a blanket in place, the weather gray, with the promise of snow.

"I'm where I need to be. Here, with the first school going up. Supplies on their way, with no place to put them. Yet." Sinclair placed her hand on her daughter's lap, sensing there was something Meghan was hiding. She smiled, allowing her daughter to keep her secrets, knowing she'd reveal them to her in time. "Take loving care of my grandchildren. *All* of them."

A flash of reaction colored the freckled skin of Meghan's face, filling it in with a soft blush. Then Allwyn shook the reins, moving the small carriage ahead, a young boy of ten years in back, his head sticking out of a thick blanket. Securely bundled up between the luggage, it would be his job to bring the carriage back once the family was at the port.

Once her tears cleared, Sinclair walked over to the store, expanded in size for the second time. The same with the storehouse and the barn. Along with an additional thousand acres of riverside land surveyed and purchased. Half of it cleared of trees, with stumps pulled and countless rocks removed, forming stone walls. Fields plowed. Ready for spring planting. Hundreds of trees felled and hauled to the mill, producing lumber intended for the construction of new homes, soon occupied by people, arriving each season. And the raising of a church, hoping to find a minister willing to leave the city of Philadelphia to lead their flock.

For now, Sinclair would settle for a trip into the city, alone. She'd received a message from Angus, letting her know he was there, tucked away at an out-of-the-way inn. Another message arrived soon after, brought by a courier with news from Pierre that he was in Philadelphia as well. Busy with meetings the next few days, then free to spend the rest of his time with her, if she were willing.

Sinclair brushed her hands down the sides of her heavy woolen skirt, imagining them to be Pierre's, a warmth spreading from her abdomen to her loins. A sigh of longing slipped from her throat, then she scolded herself before heading inside the store.

It was still early. The December weather, turned cold and gray, leaving the thick panes of glass in the windows struggling to hold in the heat from a masonry stove, kindled by one of the young men tending to such things. It emitted a blanket of heat, doing its best to offset the chill air. Sinclair went over and held out her hands, sighing as she felt the heat embrace them.

"A *braw* day."

The thin-toned voice from behind drove a shard of ice through Sinclair's heart. She strengthened her will, refusing to show any untoward reaction, then turned her head to the side, watching as a man separated himself from an alcove in the back end of the store. He came toward her, his hands open, hanging at his side.

"I mean no harm to ya'. Only wanting to talk."

"Which conveys no sense of comfort, as someone with foul intent might say the same." As Sinclair spun around, slipped her hand though the slit in her skirt, fingers on the hilt of the knife strapped to her upper thigh. A set of fingers formed of steel, moving as quickly as a viper's strike, grasped her wrist, stale breath warming the side of her neck as the man pulled her in, holding her close.

"You'll have no need of such as that." He paused, a smile lifting the corners of his thin lips. "Which is *also* what a person with foul intent might say." He released her lower arm and stepped back, his arms crossed on his chest. "If one *had* foul intentions toward the other. Which I do *not*."

He glanced through the window, seeing a shadow pass by. "Better for us all, if left undisturbed." Sinclair moved toward the door, the man's eyes on her as she opened it a crack and called out, a youthful voice responding.

"Go to the house, Benjamin. Rouse the coals in the stove, putting a kettle on to boil. Keep watch until it does, then add the tea, already in the diffuser. Let it steep, before bringing it here."

The man nodded as she closed the door. "Nicely done." He pointed to a chair, a frown tightening his thin lips, when Sinclair hesitated before sitting down. He followed her over, standing beside her. "Won't be but a moment or two, then away I'll be, leaving you to your business."

He held out his hands, the palms scarred, two of the outside fingers missing from his left hand. He noticed her stare. "Result of a small keg of gunpowder packed amongst sacks of lead balls. With a *short* fuse." He hesitated. "A painful lesson learned."

"Your purpose? The air—holding an *unpleasant* odor."

The man, dressed in gray clothing with simple boots and no adornments, smiled, his eyes remaining as cold as a midnight frost. "A friend of a friend bids you a fond hello. His message one of fair warning. Given me, to give to you."

Sinclair slowly closed, then opened her eyes, conveying no outward sign of her emotions as she racked her brain for who it might be, having sent this vile creature her way. Pierre flashed into her thoughts before dissolving in an immediate denial. She compressed her lips, waiting for the man to come to his point.

"Your daughter. The one in the highlands. She'll need to be careful, as well. Having placed her trust—where it ought not to be.

Liable to turn and bite her hand like a *mad* dog if she reaches out *again*."

"You will *not* touch my daughter—with no *cause* for it. Removed, as she is from politics. Outside of what might affect the interests of clan Scott."

"Gold coins paid. For the purchase of arms to the colonies. Twice."

"Impossible. There's not enough—"

"Paid. With monies moved from highland to port."

Sinclair narrowed her eyes, sudden understanding widening them. The thought of Marion having done such a thing filled her with a sense of dread. "She's not to be—"

"Touched. Yes. *Heard* you. The first time. And she *won't* be. Her hand already spanked, with some lovely animals left paying the price." Sinclair stayed silent, Marion having filled her in on the incursion, leaving her and her family stranded on high.

"Your daughter. The *other* one. Visited by a—*brother* of mine. Come here to let her know of his interest in locating your son." The man paused, taking a deep breath, and letting it out in a long sigh. "Himself, gone *missing*. Without a trace. A regular and *concerning* occurrence of late."

"I've got people enough of my *own* to keep track of. With no interest in the whereabouts of *yours*."

He nodded. "Be wary in your dismissal of our concerns, with numbers *easily* reduced on *both* sides of the ocean between." Her intake of breath brought a flicker of a smile to his lips. "I believe we have reached an accord, with questions needing to be asked, seeking information from people close to you, known to have been in the western reaches of late."

Before Sinclair could respond, the man placed another cold shard of ice in her heart. "Which will need to wait on *their* return. The one's just left. Not that we can't reach them. Anywhere. Anytime."

He bowed his head, leaving without a sound, closing the door behind him. Sinclair stayed seated, her face pale with fear, her hands trembling as she twisted them in her lap.

Angus carefully measured Sinclair's unsettled mood, then nodded a greeting as she stepped through the door of a tiny room, perched at the very top of a small building. The air was stuffy, with only one small window, kept closed against the unusually cold, late Autumn weather.

Her voice was taut, eyes narrowed. "I am late. By half a day. My apologies."

Angus shrugged, coming over and taking Sinclair's hand, his skin warm, the look in his eyes comforting. "You've got worries. Written all over ya' face, my lady."

"Hardly a lady any longer. As far from being one as is possible, living over here." She sat on the edge of a small bed, the mattress torn, straw poking through, digging into the back of her legs. "You had the funds to choose a more *suitable* establishment. One with — more room."

Angus shrugged. "And a *better* class of clientele." He'd been sitting outside his door, watching from an elevated perch on the second floor as several whores greeted Sinclair with arched eyebrows when she'd arrived, her head covered by a shawl, entering with a stiff posture through the front door of the seedy inn. A concern, if recognized, though no one in her social circle or of high status would spend their days on the seedier side of the city, running alongside the expansive docks.

"It suits my purpose. Staying low. Out of the way." Angus paused, his thick lips pursed. "I should have thought of the potential of your exposure. Only focused on my own." He gave Sinclair a rueful smile. "A mistake, my Lady. One I *shall* not repeat, I assure you."

Sinclair smiled, noting the fluency of the smaller man's speech. An improvement, no doubt prompted by the book on a small table. Common Sense, by Thomas Paine. "You've not missed *much*, my friend." She clasped her hands in her lap, head high, steeling herself for his reason to have come so far to meet with her. "No doubt you have news of my daughter and her family."

Angus nodded, going over to a small dresser, and tilting it to the side with one hand. He slipped a thin, leather-bound packet out from beneath it, then walked over to Sinclair, pulling it back as she reached for it. "The information contained within — *may* cause you a measure of personal discomfort. Regarding a man you've become close to, of late."

Sinclair stiffened, the words and tone of the young man's speech unsettling, as well as his opinion concerning whom she associated with. "The packet."

Angus handed it to her, then went to the door and leaned against the frame, watching with hooded eyes as she slipped the papers out. He saw her eyes widen as she reached the second page, her hands trembling. She looked at him, her voice thin.

"This—is *true?* Marion, *certain* of her facts, with no possibility of a mistake?"

Angus nodded. "As certain as were my own feelings regarding the man. From our *first* meeting. Nothing changed since then. My thoughts kept to myself. Hers—" He pointed with his chin, staring at the papers. "Her *own*. Based on time spent with him."

Angus hesitated, clenching his lips. "Declan, without doubts as to our Frenchman's honor. Our laird, much too trusting. His *only* flaw." He paused. "Lady Marion—asked for and got my advice, before deciding to send me here with the message. Delivered to you, by *my* hand."

Sinclair closed her eyes, the unnamed visitor and this latest news leaving her with a sour stomach. Threats, from every quarter, bearing down. Her instinct's shouting to head back home. To hie to the hills, with her family safely tucked under her wing. Less one. She drew in, then released a long breath before rising to her feet, a determined look on her face. "*Pack* your things, my friend. We're off to an *improved* class of accommodations."

Sinclair knew what she needed to do, a second note from Pierre in hand. Waiting for her when she'd checked in at the inn she'd stayed at before. Letting her know he'd finished with his meetings and was back at the port, aboard a transport ship, waiting on the offloading of a large shipment of goods. She'd reply with a message of her own, informing him to call on her tomorrow morning. At the same inn, and in the same room. Then she watched as Angus leaned over and slid a leather pack from beneath the bed. He brushed the surface with his fingers, dislodging any vermin collected during his brief stay.

Pierre hummed to himself, moving with confident strides between stacked crates filled with materials of all kinds. A series of letters and numbers burned into their sides, detailing their weight and contents. Information stevedores used to keep track of where in the holds of ships to place them, helping maintain center balance, with ballast stones used to fill in the space between.

He grinned, knowing it had been a roll of the dice, separating his lot in life from that of a gang of workmen passing by. His lofty position in life ensured, born into a family with money, prestige, and ties to those in power. Which assured him of absolutely nothing, with each member of the cabal judged on their own merits, or lack thereof. A terrible end for anyone failing to complete tasks assigned to them, no matter their rank of nobility, or position of privilege.

Pierre made his way along the pier, his mood elevated by a note delivered to him while still aboard. A response from Sinclair, the perfumed message flavoring the air of his cabin, letting him know he'd soon be in her arms, using her body, while enjoying her incredible mind.

He moved aside, letting several workmen pass, wishing he could wave a wand and remove a dozen years or more from Sinclair's age, making her a viable choice for a permanent position in his life. Then he smiled, allowing the image of Marion to slip through his thoughts, entertaining, once again, the possibility of both women sharing his bed at the same time.

A fantasy, he told himself, and nothing more. One he'd recently entertained, hiring two women of similar ages and builds, wearing wigs purchased at significant cost. The charade had left him displeased, with the harlots tossed out while he drowned his sorrows with a bottle of fine Scottish whiskey.

Pierre smiled as he entered the foyer of the same inn where he and Sinclair had whiled away several wonderful days. He took the steps leading to the second floor two at a time, surprised by how much he was looking forward to holding her in his arms once more.

Angus held out a small packet of medicinal herbs, watching Sinclair closely, wondering if she'd take them. Wondering, as he waited, if she'd use them. Their purpose explained to her, along with the reason he'd brought them with him.

Sinclair reached out and took the waxed paper, her hand trembling as she faced her second moment of trial by fire. The first time, the horror-filled day at Gran Ma's Mill. Failing to perform then, the gun left half-cocked. No room for such an error now. The decision looming in the air between her and the cold-eyed young man staring back.

Her fingers closed on the waxed paper, the flap sealed with a smear of red wax. "How?"

"Mixed with tea. Or wine. Warm enough to dissolve it. Stirring it in, then allowing it to sit. Swirled for a few moments before serving."

"How—long?" Sinclair's eyes brimmed with tears. "Before?"

Angus shrugged. "Depends on the size of the person. And the amount used." He stepped forward, closing his fingers around the packet. "I'll prepare it for you. Wine is the better choice, considering the reason the two of you are to meet." He blushed, releasing her hand.

Sinclair pulled the packet away. "*I'll* do it. My opportunity, as Harold always said—to help bring balance to the scales."

Angus nodded. "A fitting expression, this man—wearing *two* faces. Part of *his* true nature, unlike yours or any of your kin. Caught up in doing dark things. With no choice given to him. *Most* of the time." He watched as Sinclair nodded, her eyes softening, the packet dangling in her fingers, her hand dropping to her side. Then he hardened his tone. "But *smart* enough, and thus *fully* aware of what he's done. Of the people placed in harm's way. With the threat of violence against you and yours. People who welcomed him into their homes. Their trust in him, abused."

"My family—means *everything* to me. As it has ever been and will *always* be." Sinclair clenched her hand, crinkling the packet as she walked over to a small table, a bottle of red wine sitting there, cork removed in anticipation of Pierre's visit.

She poured the wine into a large decanter to breathe, then placed two color-twist glasses alongside it. One in red tones, the other blue. Sinclair hesitated, looking over, holding the packet over the opening.

When Angus nodded, she poured it in, using a spoon to stir the mixture, before pouring the wine back into the bottle. "It's done."

"Not yet." Angus handed her another packet. "You'll need to use this. It negates the effect of the other, though it will cause some measure of cramping. And you'll be sick to your stomach later on." He slipped a third packet from one of his pockets. "*This* will help with that. But not to be used until after the symptoms first begin."

Sinclair widened her eyes. "How are you so—*knowledgeable* about such things?"

Angus shrugged. "Books. Trips made through swamps, fields, and woods. Long walks taken alongside wise women, tucked away in remote glens and shadowed hollows. Careful to keep their heads down to avoid accusations of practicing witchcraft."

"Something I've always considered myself to be. One of them." Sinclair noted Angus's look of confusion. "A *wise* woman." She shook her head, looking at the bottle of wine. "Played for a fool. An *old* fool, thinking someone like him could find me—"

"Enough." Angus hardened his tone once again. "You're *Lady* Sinclair Haversham-*Knutt*. Responsible for gifting opportunities to those most in *need* of them. Mother to a clan of *incredible* people, extremely capable, no matter their role. No matter *where* they are in the world."

He stood up and came over, placing his hand on her forearm. "I'll find a place of observation, then return once the *bastard* arrives, staying near the door. Waiting for you to let me in once it's finished." Angus took her hand and squeezed it gently before letting go. Then he headed to the door, closing it softly behind him as he left.

⁑ ⁑ ⁑

"I've missed *you*, as well." Sinclair poured two glasses of wine, handing one to Pierre, touching hers to it with a smile. "To our *mutual* interests."

Pierre bottomed his glass, then reached for her, his eyes revealing his need. Sinclair took a sip of her drink as his lips traced a heated line of kisses down her neck, causing a shiver of reaction, dampened by the thought of what would happen once the poison found its way to his duplicitous heart.

He pulled back, a look of concern on his face. "What is it, sweet lady? Has there been news from your family, causing you concern?"

"No. Nothing heard *lately*. Though I miss having them near to hand. Alone as I've been these past weeks, with my son still not returned to me. Leaving me—out of sorts. Wondering why I'm here, and not back In Scotland. Or England." Sinclair gave Pierre a quiet look. "Or France."

Pierre angled his head, lips pursed, as he reached to pour another glass of wine. He offered to refill hers, Sinclair refusing with a shake of her head, her hair in ringlets trailing over her shoulders. Worn the way he liked it, hanging down, shimmering in the light from two lanterns, hanging on the walls.

"If only it could be so, my lady." He paused. "Over *here*, the far better choice. As offered to you before. A place in the countryside, with an expanse of land purchased for the raising of horses. The planting of crops. Enough to provide for *anything* you could ever want."

"Better if the monies required for such were to go into housing and places of businesses for those needing it most. With investment in their skills, returning both interest and principal, in due time. Allowing—"

Pierre cut her off, his eyes revealing his need for her. "Yes. Of *course*. The model you've created will be a *splendid* legacy, to be sure." He swallowed the rest of his wine, then took Sinclair's hand, squeezing it as he looked over at the bed. "Speaking of a *splendid* exchange of mutual interests—"

Sinclair pushed him down, a soft smile on her lips. She gazed at him, feeling a stirring in her abdomen, the antidote to the poison making an appearance. "A lady needs a moment to—prepare herself for such a *cunning* tongue."

Pierre watched as she stepped into another room. The door gently closed, with the sound of water being poured into a basin exciting him. Five years younger, he decided, telling himself that would be enough to cause him to reconsider his earlier assessment of a long-term relationship.

He lay back on the bed, arms crossed beneath his head, a feeling of lethargy pulling him down into the cozy mattress. A slight rumble in his stomach caused him a moment of discomfort. He yawned, choosing to ignore it, then stared up at the ceiling, listening to the sound of the wind rattling the windowpanes, until the light slowly faded from his eyes.

Sinclair called out to Pierre, with dead silence the only response. She returned to the bedroom, finding him lying there, his chest stilled, his beautiful eyes open. She looked down at him, surprised at her lack of tears, then went over and opened the door, letting Angus in.

"How will we —"

Angus shook his head, holding up one hand. "Dress yourself, Lady Sinclair. Then head back to your home. A carriage is out front, with the driver waiting." He walked over to the bed and slapped Pierre on the face, without a reaction noted. "I've got things well in hand, here."

"People—his associates, they will search for him. Track his movements. Arriving here, asking questions."

"The man at the counter below, checking in guests." Angus stared up at Sinclair. "Is one of *mine*." His eyes searched hers. "*Go*. Now. That I can do what's needed *here*."

CHAPTER FOURTEEN
CAPTIVE'S TOWN
SPRING, 1785

Eliza held her father's arm as she guided him from the church, back to a small cabin where he spent most of his time alone. She could feel the frailty of his body, his steps a slow shuffle as the soles of his shoes scuffed the ground. Kept clear of twigs, pinecones, and other detritus by several children assigned the daily task, to help him avoid falls.

"Your sermon—is it ready for me to review?"

Her father tapped the back of her hand, shaking his head, his hair white, having thinned over the winter. His skin was pale, with small spots revealing the onset of age. Old, before his time, Eliza thought as she kept to a halting pace. Knowing the trauma suffered had caused his decline, despite his rock-solid faith in God.

"All but done, daughter. The *bones* of it laid down, with the rest of the words left lying where I can find them." He looked at her, a soft smile on his lips. "No worries. Three days yet until Sunday service."

She caught her breath, knowing it was Saturday. A glimmer of tears filled her eyes, realizing the day was swiftly approaching when the man she loved second only to God would be with him. "I can look at it if you like. Helping you to *complete* it."

He squeezed her hand in answer, without making a reply, the two of them having reached his home. She opened the door and followed him inside, ignoring the scent of his soiled nightclothes, lying on the floor, stained with urine.

Eliza filled Aaron in on her concerns regarding her father's deteriorating state. Aaron looked at her, taking a moment to soften his response.

"Your father is close to making his—journey." Aaron crossed his arms, staring at the floor of the small home shared with his wife and Noah. Another issue on the horizon for him to deal with once the babe in Eliza's womb was born, with the news of the impending birth causing mixed feelings. A moment of happiness, closely followed by concern over his wife's frail body and the uncertain future of their child, if born a boy. Fearful the lad would one day follow in his foot-steps, as well as those of his father and grandfather.

"Saw it happen with friends of my great uncle, Shaun. Going low with him to visit them. Listening to the sharing of old stories. The same ones heard the last time we were there. Him nodding, encouraging their re-telling with a smile on his lips. And a sad expression in his eyes."

Aaron looked up. "Another misery in my life added to a pack, over-stuffed with them. Missing out on seeing my great uncle off. My sister Meghan, in our brief time together, told me of his passing. With me not there." He hesitated. "Not around for *any* of it. The birth of my niece and nephew. Missing out on seeing my mother, having gone back to Scotland."

"While you were finding then *saving* your friend. Your brother by marriage, returning him to *his* family. One that is *still* there, waiting for your return." Eliza came over and grasped his forearm, pulling him around and leaning in against him. She placed his hand on her swollen abdomen, the fabric of her shift stretched tight, the birth of their child a few months away. "And another family *here*, with time enough for you to make your way there, and back again."

Aaron hesitated, then pulled away, causing Eliza to turn around, a surprised look on her face. He shook his head, his lips compressed in a line of exasperation. "You've *no* idea of the world outside these walls, wife. *None.* Despite all that you've suffered through. With your eyes forced open, able to see the depravity that exists in people. The willingness of some to inflict it on others. The inability to escape it, when aimed your way."

He paused, gathering his emotions as he saw the hurt in her eyes. "I mean no disrespect. And don't wish to upset you, especially now." Aaron stepped forward, placing his hands on either side of her round belly. "It's only that I've seen the world *beyond* this place. Beyond the words written in the Bible carried with you everywhere you go. The beliefs you share with your—with *our* people. Counseling them, guiding them, as your father has always guided you."

Noah came through the door. He stopped, registering the look on his sister's face, then turned around, leaving without a word. The two of them remained silent, the moment stretching until Eliza sat down, giving Aaron a slow nod. He took a deep breath, letting it out slowly, then joined her at a small table, centered by a clay pot holding sprigs of mint, helping to flavor the air.

Aaron took one, folding it between his fingers, his thumb rubbing the waxy leaves. He gave it to Eliza as a gesture of goodwill. She held it to her nose and inhaled, her eyes guarded, aware her husband had more to share. "You're an intelligent, sensitive, and caring woman, with much to offer and little needed in return. Your faith *sustains* you. For valid reasons, having helped you to survive what—"

He looked down. "No need to remind you of it." With a sigh, he stood up, moving to the window, looking through a pane of thick glass, acquired at great expense from the English by Lukas and the community, as a wedding present to the couple.

"I've read *hundreds* of books. Treatises on subjects covering mathematics, history, science, and war. All of them imparting seeds of wisdom, sown in the soil of my soul. For me to work out for myself. To harvest opinions, ideas, and thoughts from those growing within me, sprouting with vigor. Letting go of those failing to take root. Casting them aside."

Aaron shrugged, his voice dropping to a faint rumble of regret. "And then, once armed with *all* that knowledge, and unlimited opportunity to use it to the greater good—I ended up with the blood of men on my hands." He held them up, staring at the myriad scars covering their battered surface. "Leaving scars on my body. On my soul."

He leaned back against the window frame. "As *you* well know, having helped heal me. Holding me while I poured out an endless list of my sins upon your shoulder. A'neewa—your mother, with her arms surrounding us both. And, despite all you've done to bring me closer to God as *you* know him to be, I'm still as far away as ever. Unable to bridge the gap created years ago in a highland draw. Two men left staring up at the sky with sightless eyes. Slain by *my* hand."

"You were—" Eliza gave him a searching look. "You *said* you were protecting your family."

"Aye. I was." Aaron nodded. "*Then.*" He paused, looking down at the floor. "All the ones *since*—no. Killing them was an act of revenge. Or done for survival, at first. Changed to a cold-hearted strategy, helping drain the enemy of vital resources. Of supplies. Of the blood and lives of their soldiers."

"It was war, Aaron. No different from those written about in the Bible. Believers, resisting evildoers in the name of the Lord. Brought to the *same* end, as he delivered to them, through you." Eliza stood up and came over, taking one of Aaron's hands in hers. She straightened his clenched fingers, slipping hers in between them.

"God led you here. Not some random breeze, or unmapped path. *God.* With a plan for you then. A plan for you *now.* Here. With me. With our child."

Aaron looked at her, seeing the face of a genuine believer, as if an angel, surrounded by light. He pulled his hand away. "You're wrong. Eliza. God has no plan. The massacre—not of *his* doing. What's coming, in these next few years and beyond—not a part of *his* plan."

He tightened his expression and leaned in, his lips inches from her own, noting the shocked look in her light-colored eyes. "The world of modern man is coming. Bringing misery in every form imaginable. Evil intentions, mixed with good. Hard things, and soft. With offers of genuine friendship and lies. Told with false smiles by men carrying tools in one hand, weapons in the other, willing to do whatever it takes to get what they want. Whether welcomed as friends or made enemies. Intent on eradicating native populations in their wilderness homes."

Aaron leaned back. "*Everyone* daring to stand in their way. Those here or living beyond the edge of the fields. All made victims of a society willing to quote the *same* sermons as your father. Laying their hands on the *same* book, with a fervent belief in what they say. What they believe to be true." He stepped back and moved toward the door, his mood as dark as the moonless night to come. "Willing to set it aside, going out and tearing pieces of this land away from the grasp of others. Claiming it for themselves, whether it's traded for, bought, or stolen."

"Wait, husband." Eliza reached for him, then hesitated, her hand poised in the air. "*Please?*" Aaron stopped, refusing to turn around, knowing if he did, his will would soften. His resolve would weaken. Aware his destiny was still before him. Unchanged, despite the love she had for him. And his, for her.

Eliza softened her voice. "I believe in God because I know *no* other way. Willing to stay open to you, accepting your lack of belief, hoping one day you'll have an unclouded vision of him, letting him enter your life. *Our* life." She touched his shoulder, pulling back as she felt the dark energy within him. Tears overflowed her eyes, spilling down her cheeks. "I will be here. Our *child* will be here when you're able to accept the light of God's love for you."

Eliza rested her forehead on the back of his shoulder. "You should go. Go to your family, being away from them for far too long. Let them help heal your wounded spirit. Then, when you're able to, return and bind yourself to me again."

Allwyn glanced up, seeing a tall, broad-shouldered man slipping out from the shade of a large oak. He squinted, his vision not yet fully returned, still hazy about the edges. Then his face brightened, recognizing who it was. He opened his mouth to call out, then stopped, looking around to see if any of the other men were nearby.

Aaron nodded a greeting, motioning to him, pointing to the woods. Allwyn complied, leaving the axe head buried in a block of wood, grabbing a satchel, and hurrying over. "You are a sight, for—" Allwyn reached out, taking Aaron's hand in his. "For *blurred* eyes!" He released his brother's hand, embracing him, feeling as if he were hugging a hardwood tree. The other man's body was thick, and muscular, though still lean in build.

"My sister and your son?"

"Healthy. Growing. Both of them. Meghan, with child again."

"Your sight—still bothering you?" Aaron's eyes held a look of concern.

Allwyn shrugged. "A bit. Not enough to keep me from my work."

"Or from *lying* with my sister."

Both men smiled, staring for a moment, adjusting to seeing each other again, not having known if they ever would. A shout from the opposite end of the field brought their eyes around. A tall woman was walking their way with a basket in hand.

Allwyn twisted his head, gauging Aaron's reaction. "I'll go let your mother know you're here. Gently. To prevent a stir." He moved away, crossing to Sinclair, taking the basket from her hands, setting it on the ground, then pulling her in, his head against hers, whispering in her ear. After a moment, Sinclair's knees buckled, Allwyn supporting her as she lowered her head, her shoulders shaking. Then she recovered, her head held high, walking with determined steps, coming to greet her long-lost son.

Aaron held his mother, her hands formed into fists, pounding him on his back, head burrowed into his neck, unable to speak. Minutes passed while she released every one of countless hours of worries on his behalf, compressed into the time it took her to pull away and look up at him, seeing a stranger's eyes in a lined face.

"You've changed."

"*You* haven't. You're still the image of the woman my father met in a doorway, placed in one of his journals, long ago."

"He's dead. Your father." Sinclair hesitated, taking a deep breath, and letting it out slowly. "But you must already have *known* that. Or sensed it."

"Both. Heard it from Allwyn's lips, before. When I brought him home."

Sinclair's lips trembled, tears flowing as she shook her head, staring at him. "*Pinch* me. Or *slap* me, that I might know this is not another dream."

Aaron leaned down and kissed her tears away, then pulled her in for another long embrace. The sound of Meghan calling to Allwyn let him know another woman would soon be there, sharing the same embrace.

⚜⚜⚜

"You're married. To a woman living so—far away." Sinclair peered at her son, having trouble making the emotional readjustment to him having a life outside her own. As if she'd placed his portrait over a mantel in her mind, remaining the same boy last seen heading off to university. Left there, unchanged, until he would return home again.

An oil lantern in a small cabin, newly built on the outer edge of the spreading community, emitted just enough light to see. Aaron was extremely cautious, based on the reality of the world he lived in. His mother was fully aware of the dangerous game played by hard-eyed men, considering her son to be a prime piece. Eager to remove him from the board.

"I've lost *so* much." Sinclair shook her head, her tears dried up, eyes still haunted by memories. "Your father. Your—*youth*. With you living beyond my reach, with half my family over there." She waved an arm in the general direction of Scotland, letting it drop to a small table in the tiny, two-room structure.

Aaron shrugged, his hands clasped between his knees. "It's why I hesitated in coming here. Not wanting to aggravate you. Sent this way by an understanding wife who insisted I bind the tie between us." He paused. "With a child on the way. Not due until after I'm safely home again. Named Jackson if a boy. Gela, if a daughter. It's from the Lenape language. Meaning happiness."

"She's—your wife—is a *native* woman?"

"Nae. She's German. Her father is a minister. Her mother, of the same ancestry, passed shortly after her birth. My wife, Eliza, named for her."

"A beautiful name." Sinclair leaned back, some of her tension released as she pictured another grandchild. There were tears in her eyes as she reflected on the name of Harold's brother. "And a wonderful name for a son." She nodded. "I will need to prepare gifts. For them both."

Aaron nodded in agreement. "I'm certain she'll be pleased when I bring them—"

"Not *you*, but *I*." Sinclair gave him a look of maternal defiance. "I'm not *daft*, son. Still with a mind capable of subterfuge, knowing the danger to you lying in every nook. In every cranny." She paused, licking her lips. "And I'm not without the capability of striking a blow myself. I've managed the elimination, with another man's help, of an agent of discord and destruction. Belonging to the same group your father fought against. The *same* group you've come to the attention of."

"You—can't *possibly* mean that."

"I *do*. With the help of a man gifted with incredible vision, not unlike your own. Helping me attend to what we *needed* to do. Protecting our clan, guarding against dangerous men lurking in the shadows." She paused. "As the shepherd guards the flock."

"Against people like *me*. Wolves, lurking in the shadows." Aaron narrowed his eyes in concern. "Sharp-toothed and willing to bide their time before striking."

"*My* worry, Aaron. Not *yours*. With a flock of your *own* to tend to if I'm not mistaken."

Aaron leaned back, his head angled down as he considered everything his mother had revealed. Then he looked up. "I'll *not* be able to dissuade you?" When Sinclair shook her head, he sighed. "It will be the *two* of us, moving at night along animal paths. Careful to avoid contact with others."

Sinclair considered the offer, then nodded. "Yes. With you. Soon.

Tomorrow, or the next day." Aaron angled his head, giving his mother an open look of appraisal, no different from the one given Chatte when she'd made her approach at a small, out-of-the-way tavern. A leather bag stuffed with the ears of redcoat soldiers in hand.

"With *me* in the lead. You, to follow my *every* command. Without hesitation *or* questions asked of me. Agreed?" He stuck out his hand, waiting until his mother took it, her grip as firm as his.

"Agreed."

The woods spoke to Aaron, whispering their secrets. Images formed from marks in the soil. Found in the scattered pattern of leaves. Felt, in the pressure of eyes, watching for the slightest movement. He tilted his head to one side, his eyes closed, reaching out with his senses.

Lessons learned as a young boy, shown him by his father, teaching him to use more than his ears and nose. To make use of all his instincts. Knowing where to step before making your move. Driven home again as an adult, with mistakes measured in blood and shattered bones. Death, the prize awarded for coming in second. Handed to the losers, tipping the needle of the scale to one side. Or the other.

Sinclair waited, kneeling in the shadows beneath low-hanging branches. Her hands were on her knees, feet cloaked in soft leather. Her hair formed into a thick braid, wrapped in a thin leather covering, then laced in place.

She watched her son transform, becoming something outside of himself. A being of the wilderness, more feral than human, with civilization left far behind, lying miles away beyond foothills and mountains.

The two of them had skirted countless marshes, with a handful of rivers, carefully crossed as they moved from dusk through to dawn, passing through places where other men stood watch from overlook posts. Aaron, familiar with every step of the twisted path they were following, was a gifted woodsman, no longer seen by his mother as the boy she'd helped to raise.

Sinclair shivered, not from the temperature of the air, or fear. She clenched her hands, her fingernails digging into her palms, aware of how foolish she'd been, assuming they would have moved the same way as when Harold had led the trek into the wilderness to visit her father's burial site. Permission sought to pass through native territories granted by tribes holding sway in the area. With no risk of danger, then.

The steady encroachment by colonists into native lands had changed everything, building pressure in a sealed pot. Leaving the local inhabitant's emotions overheated, watching interlopers hunt and trap without limits. Taking what they found, staying as long as they wished. Moving freely among ancestral sites. Hard men, seeking to escape pressure from the east, wanting to stake a claim to fertile lands lying to the west.

A slight motion from Aaron caught Sinclair's eye, letting her know to come to him. His hand held parallel to the ground, signaling her to stay low. She complied as quietly as she could, stopping once she gained his side, his hand out, pulling her in, lips pressed against her ear.

"There. Twenty paces ahead."

Sinclair narrowed her eyes, trying to spot what he'd seen, the thick woods a maze of unfamiliar shapes and colors to her untrained eye. Her son pointed, his voice relaxed. "A fawn. Newborn. The mother, off browsing."

Sinclair followed the line of his finger, finally able to see the small white spots on a red coat of hair. The recently born animal lying prone, its head down, long ears twisting, listening for its mother's call. "I see it. So tiny." Her lips were almost touching Aaron's ear, tickled by a curl of his dark hair. One she desperately wanted to slip back behind his ear, barely able to resist the urge.

"Do you see the *coyote?*"

She stiffened, looking, trying to define the shape in her mind. Aaron shifted the line of his finger, a horizontal line appearing several yards from the small fawn. "There."

"Can you shoot it with an arrow?"

Aaron turned his head, looking at her. "Why would I do *that?*"

"To *save* it."

He shook his head, his eyes dark in the subdued late afternoon light. "Nature will see to that, or not. Both to live or die by other hands than mine." He muttered something beneath his breath, Sinclair hearing the word God used. She closed her lips, trying to send out a message for the mother to return and chase the predator away with sharp hooves.

The coyote moved on, missing the scentless fawn, focused on the scent of the mother, her body a gray shadow a dozen paces away, feeding back toward the spot where she'd left her young one.

Aaron stood up, moving back, his hand on his mother's shoulder, easing her away. Once clear of the animals, he cut a wide circle, leaving the beasts to their destinies while focused on their own. Aware they'd need another night to reach, then clear the pass. The same one where he'd met up with Allwyn, clearing it for him and his party of traders.

Once through to the other side, four days would see them to where his expectant wife and members of the community would be. A clamp kept on his heart, his emotions secured safely away. Moving ahead as silently as water in a deep-run river, slipping past its bank.

Later, once dawn was near to hand, Aaron started a small, all but smokeless fire, using it to heat a meal of dried meat, left to soak in a small tin, along with a handful of oats, mixed with corn meal. Filling, though bland. Each of them swallowed the mixture in silence as birds called out, letting them know the woods held no threat from man.

Aaron smiled, his teeth white in the early morning gloom. Sinclair looked at him, then reached up to check her hair. "What?"

"You." He shook his head. "Lady Sinclair Haversham-Knutt, crouched in a huddle of drab clothing, eating with your fingers from a tin. Acting as if it's normal. As if you've been living like this for years."

"I could say the same. About *you*."

Aaron nodded, bowing his head, picking up a canteen, and handing it to her. "We're both a far piece from the clear air of a highland glen. Miles traveled across unsettled seas. Then inland, through lands involved in a deadly dispute over who'll end up in control of them." He paused, taking it back and drinking, using the rest to put out the fire.

He used the sole of his moccasin to cover the wet ashes with a thick cover of leaves, Smoke's voice whispering in his memories that an empty canteen is a silent canteen. His mother noted his unfocused gaze, her eyebrows raised. Aaron shrugged. "Only a passing thought. Of no real importance."

Aaron reached out and gathered their things, keeping them near to hand, then nodded at his mother, each taking turns sleeping while the other kept a silent watch. His mother settled back, curled between the upturned roots of a fallen tree, using her pack to cushion her head.

"How long until we can move without caution?"

"Now. If no one's about with ill will intended those passing through, acting as if they have a right to trespass in another man's house. Uninvited."

"Wouldn't they know *you?* Know your people?"

"My *people*, yes. Most likely. But *not* me." Aaron leaned back, searching his mother's face. "You *still* have little understanding of the threat hanging over my head. Hunted by men who —" He stopped, his voice caught in his throat.

"Those who killed your father?"

He nodded. "And grandfather. Great uncle Thomas. And my aunt. On orders given, or in compliance with people once named friends. Charles, for one. Nathan, another. And George." He saw his mother's eyes flicker at the mention of the last name. "All of them torn between their love for him and the pull of their ambitions."

Sinclair looked away, her eyes shadowed. "And yet another. Someone even closer to your father. Having saved his life. More than once."

Aaron narrowed his eyes. "Uncle Shaun?"

"*No!*" Sinclair looked at her son, lowering her voice. "Why would you *think* that?"

"I don't. Not really." Aaron paused. "But there *were* secrets kept by him. Held from father. Things Marion shared with me shortly before I left for university. Of dark deeds, done. The stories gleaned from long talks with him. Not the details, of course. But something in his eyes, she said. Shadows, where none had been before."

Sinclair shook her head. "Impossible — for anyone to *think* that of him."

Aaron leaned in. "I've learned from experience that *nothing* is impossible when people want the reins of power in *their* hands. Whether they be foe, friend—or family." He waited for his mother to respond, seeing a flicker of a repressed emotion cross her face. "What is it?"

She sighed, reaching out, touching his pack, twisting at a rawhide tie, pulling it tight. "I—can't believe I *killed* him."

"Father?" Aaron leaned forward. "How? In letting something slip? Providing his enemies—"

"*No.* A man named Pierre." Sinclair lowered her gaze, shaking her head. "Your father's death was something he did to *himself*, trying to strike back again, based on tales shared with me of the scene of his death. Along with the deaths of several others. With two bodies—one of them his—in tatters. Scattered around a large hole in the ground." She paused, rubbing the toe of her moccasin into the earth. "Another senseless act, changing nothing."

"I'd heard some of it from Allwyn." Aaron shifted, leaning back, waiting for his mother to continue, pressing her when she remained silent. "And what of *yours*?"

"Mine?" Sinclair paused, then nodded. "It was—a more *personal* act, with no purpose other than to remove a man long overdue for his comeuppance. His life spared if he hadn't threatened our family. His callous heart—earning him his death."

"Pierre—Coulombe? The soldier from Father's journals?" Aaron waited, seeing his mother nod, then leaned back, staring straight ahead, measuring the light growing in the early morning sky. "A man who might have changed *all* our destinies long ago. With the pulling of a trigger."

Sinclair nodded. "Your sister, Marion, having planted the seed, reaching out to—"

Aaron held up one hand, silencing her, shaking his head. "Say no more. What's unknown can't be told." He hesitated. "A saying used by men I once served with."

"Along with a woman."

Aaron lowered his eyes, then looked up. "You've read *my* journals." Then he looked away, his shoulders slumped. "I *killed* her. To prevent her capture." He closed his eyes. "Then put her body in a well. Keeping it away from those who were hunting us. Keeping it from being—defiled." He paused, then exhaled, his voice a whisper when he spoke. "Then I ran away."

Sinclair leaned forward, her eyes fixed on his. "Why?"

Aaron stared back. "To lead them *away*. Try to escape."

"Why—did you *kill* her?" Sinclair's voice was as soft as the whir of wings from a small wren passing by.

Her son's face softened as he stared at her. "It was a suicide agreement. Made between us. One I sensed she'd break." Another sigh sounded, followed by a shrug of her son's wide shoulders. "Which she *did*. Wanting to keep fighting. Thinking she'd be able to talk her way out of it. Blame me for the things she'd done. Not that anything she said would have changed the result. The death I gave her—the *easier* one. At least it was for *her*."

"Why?"

"Why did I—*care* for her?"

Sinclair shook her head. "Why did you *love* her?"

"I—don't know."

"Because you were both surrounded by death and misery. Each day, another challenge. Trying to find your way through it, then rising and doing the same thing again. Over and over, with no future assured beyond the next battle. Two people fighting to stay alive. Taking advantage of what you both *needed*, and each had to give. Sharing your bodies. Your love. And your pain."

Sinclair saw a flush cross Aaron's sun-bronzed cheeks, and reached out, touching the back of his hand. "A bond formed between soldiers. Along with a deeper level of intimacy. With shared experiences, horrible as they were. As your father found it to be for him." She paused, allowing her words to settle in. "Your mutual survival left you with a feeling of exhilaration. Fortunate to have someone to share your emotions with. Leaving you alive. To begin again. Which you've been able to do, with Eliza."

Sinclair waited again, reading her son's mood. "Could she, this other woman—could Chatte have done the same if losing *you?*"

Aaron shook his head, a gleam in his eyes. "No."

"Then we shall not speak of it again. The past, for us both, is the past. With its sorrows and pleasures, *ours* to hold on to." She leaned back, a smile on her lips. "As for today, I need you to take me to meet your wife. For I'm soon to be a grandmother, again. With another child added into the bosom of our family."

CHAPTER FIFTEEN

NATIVE VILLAGE
LATE SPRING, 1785

N oah made his way from Two-Women's family lodge, angling into the woods to void his bladder. He found a suitable tree, closing his eyes as he released his stream, held far too long while listening, without interruption, to another long, wandering story from her grandfather. The old man was full of accumulated wisdom with valuable lessons taught. Most of them scattered along dozens of winding trails.

"You'll never put *that* into my sister."

Noah opened his eyes, his hand going to his belt, a skinning knife in his hand as he turned around. The brother of Two-Women stood there, sneering at him. "Which weapon were you planning to *use*, half-white?"

"You're quiet enough when it *suits* you." Noah closed his pants, replacing the knife in the sheath at his side. "Making up for it other times, with the incessant screeching of a jay."

"You will *never* lie with my sister. Only a warrior of *our* tribe will bed her. Not some half-white *coward*."

Noah turned to go. A hand on his shoulder spun him around. The other man, taller by a hand, lashed out. Noah ducked the blow, his fingers finding Two-Spirit's throat. His other arm wrapped around the angry man's chest, trapping him in place. "If I *squeeze* —you *die.*"

Noah released the would-be warrior, shoving him away. Glad none of his followers were there to witness the altercation, with no loss of face suffered by the prideful man.

Two-Spirit rubbed his throat, his voice a hiss of anger. "I will see you *dead!*"

"Plan on a *long* life, then." Noah walked away, his hands trembling from the threat of physical confrontation, outside that of facing down an occasional bear, taken by an arrow. When Two-Women found him, he was standing by a small river, staring into the water, his head down, eyes still. She came up and took his hand.

"I know you are worried about my brother. His behavior is worse with each moon. Sickened by hate, with little cause. Or none that I can see."

"He's no different from those he proposes to —"

"To —what?"

Noah shook his head. "Foolish words. His *and* mine."

Two-Women pulled him around. "I *know* what he plans. And that he is *afraid*. His threats, empty words. Meant to bind the others to his side. Taking power from them, as if he is a respected leader and not a man made up of shadows."

"More dangerous, then —if forced by false pride to act. Fearful of his cowardice, leading him to take rash actions." Noah squeezed her hand. "I've *seen* what men, afraid to show their true feelings —*seen* what their leaders led them to do."

"You speak of what happened to your people. At the hands of the colonial soldiers."

"Yes. *Most* of them, though not all. Some with the courage to face their leader and try to stop —" Noah released her hand and turned away. Two-Women reached out, touching him on his shoulder.

"I will talk to my father."

Noah shook his head. "Nothing he says will matter. Only make your brother angry. Defiant. The son —rising against the father."

"Then *I* will speak to him."

"Bringing his anger toward me to a full boil."

Two-Women shook her head, her two braids swinging to the sides. "What then, am I to *do?*"

"Nothing." Noah sighed. "Your brother will find his path, as all men do. The Great Mother, or God, will leave it to him to decide his direction. It will be Two-Spirit's destiny, not yours, or mine."

The community was a beehive of activity when Noah returned, Two-Women at his side, carrying packs of trade goods on their backs. Noah watched as a stream of people made their way toward the largest building, their faces lit with smiles of excitement, helping to ease his concern.

Two-Women paused, her eyes narrowed, one hand finding his, holding tight. "What is happening?"

Noah smiled. "No worries. Only a calling together, without a tolling of the bell." He widened his eyes. "There must be *news.*" He hesitated. "Of *Aaron's* return!" He started forward, pulling Two-Women with him, shedding their packs at the small home where he was now living, before running to the sound of people's laughter.

Aaron, surrounded by the members of the community, held Eliza, her arm around his waist. His mother's hand clung to his as they stared at the young child in his wife's arms, its head covered with a thin blanket against the cool air. Unable to understand how it could be, with the birth not due to happen for several more weeks.

The infant stared back. Dark complexioned, with tears in its deep brown eyes. Upset by the excitement in the air, tiny arms pulled tight against its chest. Aaron looked at Eliza, his mouth half-open, confused by what he was seeing. Her face beamed back at him with pride.

"He is *our* son. Jackson. Arriving soon after you left."

Aaron was about to ask her how that could be when he heard his name shouted over the light-hearted voices of the gathered members of the community. He turned to one side, recognizing Noah's voice, deeper in tone, sounding more like a man full grown.

The excited crowd parted, allowing the young man to approach, Two-Women at his side. "You've returned. As I *knew* you would." Noah reached out with his free hand, the other held tight by the beautiful young native woman, standing slightly back. "Bringing a *guest!*"

Aaron nodded, releasing himself from Eliza's grasp and taking Noah's hand. "I have. This is my mother. Sinclair. Eager to visit. To meet my family." Then he spotted Lukas, who was waving a hand, standing in the large opening of the church, one hand braced against the frame. The older man looked frail, his body shaking, roused from his small cabin by the quiver of energy spreading throughout the grounds.

Aaron rushed over and gathered him in. Eliza was at his side, having handed the infant to his mother. They supported the elderly man, helping him inside and sitting him in a chair brought over by one of the older men.

Lukas, his face pale from exertion, waved a hand, telling them he was fine. Eliza kneeled beside him, her fingers on his pulse, a sad smile on her face. Sinclair watched, holding the child, who was smiling up at her, uncertain what to do, wondering if she should go check on the man's condition.

Noah's hand found hers, his face wreathed in a wide smile. "*Welcome!* You must be footsore and trail weary. The journey here from the colonies is not for the faint of heart."

Sinclair smiled, lips tight with concern for Eliza's father. "I've never stood accused, by those who know me, of having a *faint* heart. Though there were moments in our journey through the wilderness that tested its limits."

Noah nodded. "It can be an unforgiving place, or a paradise, depending on who you are with." He turned, looking at Two-Women who stood back, her face lowered, uncertain of her place. "The one who walks it with you." Noah reached out and pulled her in against his side, his arm circling her waist. "This is Two-Women, my—*close* friend." He shrugged. "More than that. To me."

Sinclair "I'm happy to meet you, Two-Women. Aaron has told me about you." She smiled at Noah. "Told me how proud he is of the man you've become. About you and your sister, both. And your father."

They all turned their attention to the knot of people standing in a circle around their spiritual leader, everyone with worried expressions, several holding hands. Aaron eased away, coming over, his face pinched in concern.

"Your wife's father?" Sinclair leaned forward, kissing the top of the infant's head, drinking in his scent, her heart swelling with love. "How is he?"

Aaron shook his head. "I—I don't know." He glanced at Eliza, still kneeling beside her father, head on his thin chest. "Lukas is a pious man. The focus of her—of my wife's attention, of late."

"I understand, having gone through the same myself. With *my* adopted father, who took me in as his own." Sinclair handed the child to Aaron, then went over and kneeled beside Eliza, taking her hand, and whispering in her ear.

Aaron watched as the two women exchanged words. Saw his mother reach up, touching the aged man's neck, looking into his eyes, their voices lost in the swirl of low-toned murmurs, filling the air. Lukas nodded, a smile creasing his thin lips, their color pale.

Eliza stood up, smoothing the sides of her plain dress with her hands as she came over. "He will be gone by morning. Your mother, sensing it the same as I. An inauspicious way to begin our relationship. Celebrating a new grandson, while witnessing the passing of my father." She reached out for the infant, taking him from Aaron, then passing him to Two-Women. Then she hugged her husband, surrounding him with her arms, pulling him in against a stomach, no longer swollen.

Aaron stared over her shoulder, a lost expression on his face. Eliza let go of him, then took back the infant, returning to her father. He turned to Noah. "Tell me what happened here."

Noah glanced at Two-Women, then looked at Aaron. "My sister. She should be the one—"

"What happened to *my* child?"

"Eliza lost him soon after you left. A boy. My sister burning up with a fever, standing on the threshold of death's door. Cured by medicine provided by a wise woman. One from the Wyandot village."

Two-Women stepped forward. "Noah saved her *life*. Running to our village, then back with medicines. Returning in time to heal her. To heal your wife."

Aaron stared, then turned and looked at Eliza, seeing the child cradled in her thin arms, a smile on her face. As if the death of their child and the impending end of her father's life were of no matter. Her eyes shone as she held her head high, leading the people of the community in a psalm.

⚘⚘⚘

Aaron shook his head, watching as Eliza placed the young boy into the cradle he'd built for their child. He stood by the door, a shocked look on his face, waiting until his wife turned around.

"Our son. *Dead*. Why didn't you tell me?"

"Dead?" Eliza came over with a confused look on her face. "He's *not* dead. Our Jackson is a fine, *healthy* boy."

"He's—" Aaron paused, then pointed. "That's *not* our son." He reached out, taking Eliza's face in his hands, forcing her to look. "His *eyes*, woman. *Brown*, not blue." He released her, going over and staring at the child. "His skin—brown."

"He's Jackie. *Our* child. Our beautiful little boy."

Aaron stared at her, aware something had changed, leaving Eliza in denial of the world he lived in. "Eliza. Our son—Jackson—was born too *early* to survive. With you left with a fever. Almost dying."

"No. *God* saved him. Saved us *both*. Breathing his love into his body, then into mine." Eliza smiled, looking at Aaron. "We've *both* been reborn, Aaron. Our Jackson, our blessed son—a *miracle* from God."

⚘⚘⚘

The sky was a haze of golden light, attended by drifting tendrils of fog. Moisture, left over from an early morning rain, reaching for the sun glowing through the trees. Wispy curtains of gray drifted over newly planted fields.

Aaron stared at them, imagining them as lost souls, seeking to be reborn. Released into the warming air, rising to touch the face of the sun. He sighed, listening to the sounds of people moving about. Clusters of mournful followers, on their way to the church. Their leader lying on a raised platform, arms crossed, eyes closed. His journey had reached its end, his voice stilled by the infirmity of a traumatized mind, collapsing beneath the weight of advanced age.

The English commander and several officers were in attendance, showing their respect for a man worthy of their trust. Admiring him for his faith and resolute leadership of his people. A handful of soldiers stood in a solemn line outside the door, heads bowed, showing respect, remaining silent as the parishioners slowly passed by.

Eliza stood with the native child in her arms, her husband a few steps away, standing just outside an arc of wildflowers, placed around her father. Noah and Sinclair stood on the other side, their hands clasped, eyes lowered, waiting for her to speak.

Eliza turned and handed the child to Two-Women, then moved into place behind the pulpit. Once there, she took a moment, sweeping her eyes across the group gathered in the church to pay their respects. Too few, she thought, allowing herself to recall the faces of those lost to God's will. The small hall was barely half-full. Most of those in attendance were old and weak, unable to have made the trek to Gnadenhutten. Mixed in with a scattering of young children sitting amongst them, the newer members of the small community.

"I welcome all, in celebration of the life of my father. Your minister. Our friend. Gone to God with an open heart and mind, embracing his faith, as he embraced us all." Her voice was firm, though tinged with a soft reflection of pain. Aaron listened, sensing his mother coming to stand beside him, the warmth of her hand joining with his, offering her support.

"It was truly a blessing, my being raised by him. Raised by *all* of you. One family. With many fathers and mothers. Sisters, and brothers." She hesitated, looking down at her father, before continuing. "My father—*our* father—did not leave us without guidance. His words live on. Still here, within each of our hearts. Found whenever trials or tribulations await us. With a host of loved ones ready to share the burden, however great, or small. None of us made to walk alone."

Her eyes found Aaron. "No need for *anyone* to stand apart. Our arms are open to *all*. A lesson made clear to those who knew my father. Shown to us by the words, actions, and love he gave us, every day."

Eliza's voice grew stronger in tone, causing Noah to look up. He could feel something stirring within him. A spiral of warmth rose from his chest to his head as he heard the words of his father reflected in his sister's voice. Telling him to be resolute. True to his faith, throughout God's test of it. He squeezed Two-Women's hand, getting one in return, knowing his path was to help bring her and her people to the light. To help guide her brother, Two-Spirits, away from his anger. From his fear.

He looked over at Aaron and the tall woman standing at his side, adding his mentor to the list, sensing his disquiet from the tragic loss of his son. One he would help him come to terms with. In time.

Sinclair let Eliza's words wash over her, the message unable to pierce her thoughts as to the meaning of God's will. Or his plan for his followers. She didn't question his existence, but after what she'd been through, witnessed, and survived that day in the Pinch and highland draw, she'd learned how frail life could be when facing death at the hands of men, lacking faith.

Aaron gazed at Eliza, admiring her ability to speak openly and honestly. Frightened by her blindness to reality, causing her to have lost some part of her mind. He felt his mother lean in against him, her hand slipping into his, her voice in his ear.

"She is an *amazing* person. Her energy—so *pure.*"

Aaron frowned. "Isolated. Her *entire* life. With a *horrible*, unimaginable event, challenging her faith. Leaving her face-to-face with the world *we* know. Though her view of it is *severely* limited."

Sinclair leaned back, surprised by her son's stiff-toned whisper in response. "She must have read books. On literature and history. Her use of language is superb."

Aaron turned, giving his mother a quiet look. "None of those exist *here*. Only the Bibles her father brought. Forming a *closed* society with one focus. To spread the word of God."

They returned to silent poses, listening while Eliza spoke to the people, carrying on her father's work. Aaron, questioning his wife's sanity. Concerned by her zealous faith, balanced against his own beliefs, conditioned by a more worldly view. Scrubbed clean of the illusion of man's love for his fellow man. Erased by the screams of men dying, calling out to their mothers, not to God.

Sinclair stood alongside her son, aware of his feelings, wondering whether he would accept a child, not of his issue, as his own. Or if his wife's inability to deal with what had happened would force him to choose another path. One leading him back into an endless war.

Sinclair found Aaron sitting alone, his eyes fixed on a group of people gathering wood. She slid in beside him, the stone he was on cool against the back of her legs. Her hand found his, holding on for a long moment before letting go. Several minutes passed, the sound of voices at work slipping through the breeze-stirred air.

Aaron sighed, his eyes shadowed as he looked at his mother. "I'm not able to do this. To stay here." Sinclair nodded, holding her thoughts, biding her time. "I mean—it might be possible if she would admit that our child died, as often happens with families." He paused, regarding his relatives. "With *some* families."

He sighed once more, tossing a small stick he held in one hand away. "But her ability to reason is *gone*. The light she claims to see— nothing more than a shard of a broken mirror. Held up to the truth, reflecting a false image of what happened to her."

"She's a woman *lost*, Aaron. Her faith was *all* she had after the death of your child. All she had to hold *on* to. Her mother, dying. With another mother lost to *indescribable* violence. Then a babe, gone. With you not here to help guide her through her pain. The misery was too great a burden to have carried. Alone."

"I can understand *why*. To know the—loss suffered." Aaron looked away, his voice soft. "He was *my* son, too."

"Yes. *Your* son. And *her* child to carry from conception on. Feeling it moving within her. Bonding with it. Imagining how it would look. The color of its eyes and the texture of its skin. The face, imagined, with shades of herself and you in each feature."

Aaron dropped his head, chin against the top of his chest. "She won't return the native child. Refuses to give him back to his mother.

Claiming him as ours. Saying he's been reborn. God's will. The young woman, the child's mother, left with heartsick eyes. Torn between her faith and the claim of her womb. Eliza, *angry*—in my suggestion of it."

"She *will* find her way to an end of her grief. Will see her way through it, as all mothers do. In time. With *your* help."

Aaron shook his head. "And what of you?" He looked at Sinclair. "What of *your* community, needing your presence back there? How long are you willing to be away while I remain here?" Aaron took her hand. "There is *no* one else to take you back. No one else is capable *of* it."

Sinclair took a deep breath, holding it for a moment, then releasing it. "I will speak to her. Help her find her way back. As a woman, and as a mother." Aaron nodded, then stood up, helping his mother to her feet. She looked up at him, sensing a change in his demeanor. His face set in a firm expression. "And you? What will *you* do?"

Aaron nodded, his eyes on a group of older women, one of them dressed in skins, hair worn in a single braid, woven through with white beads. "I'm going to find my son."

The native woman stepped to one side, her hand pointing at the ground beneath a towering oak. Her eyes, lined with deep wrinkles, sought his. "Here is where I placed him. Between the roots. Covering him with a stone." She looked over at Noah, standing alongside Two-Women. "They dug the hole."

Aaron looked up, staring through the thick limbs above his head. The ends of the branches danced in a soft breeze, the air clear, the weather warming. Then he turned around, looking down into the valley where the fort and town were located. The view was expansive, stretching to the western horizon. "It is a *perfect* place for him to be." Tears flowed down his cheeks. "More perfect than you can know."

He took her hands, holding them up to his lips, kissing them. "I will never forget your kindness. For helping to heal my wife. For bringing my son *here*."

"The Great Mother guided me. As she does with all who are open to her voice." She collected Aaron's tears, then bent over and touched the stone, placing them on the resting place of his son. "I will go. So that you can speak to him. Alone."

She reached out, Noah taking her hand, helping her back along the narrow path leading down the steep rise. Two-Women stood on her other side, the older woman's head bowed, shoulders trembling as she moved away. Once the shadows of the thick wood swallowed them up, Aaron sat down, his legs angled toward the stone.

He leaned over, tracing the surface, a large piece of limestone. Weathered gray, with a layer of leaves and soil filling in around the edges. Time moves on, he thought, erasing the work of men. Then he opened a pack left sitting on the ground, removing a hammer and chisel.

He set himself to placing his son's name in the limestone, one letter at a time. Using a canteen to wash the powdered rock dust away, leaving Jackson's name revealed in white. Along with a single date, marking his birth and death.

"Be at rest, my son. Never to know the touch of my hand. The sound of my voice. Never to learn the ways of the world, as I've experienced them and would have taught you about. The same lessons I learned from my father. And his father, before him. A family curse, broken on the shoal of your innocence."

Aaron gathered the tools, then stood up. He took a drink from the canteen, pouring the rest onto the roots of the sheltering tree. Then, without a backward glance, he left his son's marker behind and headed downhill, joining the others.

"He *is* the *resurrection*. Returning to me *three* days after they said he'd died." Eliza swung on Aaron, hands on her hips, a determined look in her eyes. "*Our* child, Aaron. Brought back as a sign of God's love for *all* his people. Converted natives, and those from *other* lands. Surely you can *see* that." She came over and grasped her husband's shirt, gazing up at him with beautiful eyes. Her mouth parted. Breath sweetened with mint.

"No." Aaron removed her hands, denying himself the love he felt for the woman standing there. "I cannot."

"You *will*. Given time to do so." Eliza stepped away, her mood unchanged. She moved across the floor of their home, going to check on a child who belonged to another mother.

Aaron left standing by the door, shook his head, refusing to refer to the boy by his uncle's name. Known to him from his father's journals, with images of Jackson. One of a young man, wooden sword in hand, striking a pose. Another of him lying in bed with a thin face, eyes wide, reaching out, wanting to go to the sound of bugles. "You are not—in your *right* mind. About what happened to you. To our son. Dead and buried."

Eliza turned around, holding the babe in her arms, eyes narrowed. "How so?" Then she smiled. "Were you *here*, witness to what the other women saw? The miracle God provided. A *healthy* babe, placed in my arms." She looked down, looking at the child's face, tears streaming down her cheeks. "A miracle, indeed. His life returned to me. My *son* returned to me. *Our* son, Aaron, whether you accept him into your heart. Or not."

Aaron turned around and walked away, the woods calling to him. His bow, calling to him. His past, calling out to him. He ended up on the ridge, kneeling beside the limestone marker. His head bowed, listening for God's voice. Wanting to believe. Wanting his son to have lived. For his wife, not to have lost her reason. Wishing everything had been different. Wishing so many things hadn't happened.

Sinclair found him there, following the narrow path with Noah showing her the way. Leaving her to make the climb to where she found her son. On his knees. Joining him there.

Aaron whispered. "I—*can't*." He touched the stone, the surface cold. "I'm not able to find it in my heart to accept the child as my own. I wish I could, but I *can't*."

"I know."

"Do you?" He looked at his mother. "You feel the *same?*"

"No. But I *understand*. Your wife's unable to provide you with what's needed so the two of you can move on together. To bring herself to accept the loss. Together, man and wife. Open to trying again." She paused, touching Aaron on his shoulder. "The child—belongs with his mother. And *you* belong with your wife."

Aaron shook his head. "There is falseness behind her faith. Moving her beyond the word of God, as written. Believing she is—"

"Speaking *for* him. Or rather, believing *God* is speaking through her." Sinclair sighed, reaching out, touching the stone, tracing the letters her son had inscribed. "I spoke with her. She listened. Then told me something that chilled me to my bones."

"About the resurrection."

Sinclair nodded. "Yes. And when she finished, I asked about the mother of the child. If God planned to trade one mother's suffering for another's. The elderly native woman who tended to your wife, telling me how they'd taken the babe from its natural mother. Placing it in Eliza's arms when her fevered mind heard it crying. Eliza, screaming at the women gathered around her to see it. To hold it. Given her, hoping to soothe her sorrow. Shocked when she claimed it was Jackson, reborn. Refusing to let go."

"And her *answer* to that?"

"Your wife told me the child was *hers*. That God has told her to cast the other woman out. To declare her guilty of apostasy."

"She—is *beyond* my reach."

Sinclair nodded. "I'm afraid so. For *now*. Unless the others band together, forcing her back to the path, helping her damaged mind, her body—and *spirit* to heal."

"And you believe my place is to remain *here*? To help her through it?"

"Could you? Stay here, helping to raise someone else's child? With the young mother lurking in the shadows, grieving, her babe torn from her arms?"

Aaron shook his head. "I—could not."

Sinclair rolled to one side, easing the ache in her knees. "You will take me back to the settlement, letting the journey show you your path. Whether it leads you back here, or across the sea, home to the highlands once more." With a press of her hand on his knee, she rose, standing over him, her fingers caressing the top of his head. "You can release yourself from a hand-fasted vow—if your union wasn't consecrated before God."

Aaron looked up and shook his head. "Her father—emotionally unable to do so when we returned. Then I left. Going off to do the Devil's own work."

"Then you can dissolve it. Here, and now." Sinclair stared at the horizon, remembering the morning she'd kneeled before her father's marker, so many years ago. "No better place, and no better time than now."

Aaron sighed, pressing his hand on his son's stone. "How?"

"Say how you *truly* feel. Tell it to the wind. That you are no longer bound by love. That you no longer carry it in your heart."

She listened as her son repeated the words. Watched as he leaned down and kissed the marker. Waited as he held up his hand, letting her help him to his feet, tears in her eyes as the two of them walked away.

CHAPTER SIXTEEN

HIGHLAND MANOR
LATE SPRING, 1785

Patrick, his small face pinched in a scowl, came on the run, chased by Lorna. His legs were a blurred churn of pale skin beneath clan Scott tartan, carrying him into his mother's skirts, clinging to her leg. Meghan gathered him in, chiding him for not wanting to play with his cousin.

"She's *mean* to me. *Pushing* me down. Calling me a *flatlander*. Saying I'm *Irish*." He stuck out his lower lip, his aunt Marion coming over and easing him from his mother's grasp. She leaned in, whispering something in his ear, bringing a smile to his small face. He looked up at her, his head angled slightly. "*Can I?*"

Marion nodded, then sat him down, watching as he ran over and shoved his cousin in the back, knocking her to the ground. Lorna came up in a boil, spinning to confront him, knocked down again. Lying there in a daze as Patrick held out his hand, offering to help her up.

"You *pushed* me!"

"I know. I like *this* game." Patrick smiled, ready to shove his slightly older relative again, stopping when he saw his aunt raise one hand, shaking her head.

Lorna gave her cousin a considered look. "Well, I *don't*." She frowned, then turned and looked at a flock of sheep wandering near a stone wall, marking the end of a pasture just beyond the flower garden. "Let's go chase *them!*" The two children raced away, with Lorna slightly in the lead.

Meghan stared at her twin, younger by moments, with the two of them formed in the same womb. "I would not have thought that to go so well. Without ending in bloodshed."

Marion shrugged, hands on her hips, a second child filling out the fabric of her shirt, a linen top. One of her grandmother's, embroidered with an ivy-green pattern. "She has *my* blood and, thanks to the good Lord above—more than enough of her dear fathers in the mix. Helping to keep her *emotional* tendencies well in hand." She paused, sucking in her lower lip, biting down, as she saw Patrick take a tumble, his cousin laughing with delight, picking a handful of grass, tossing it in his face. "Not *always*, mind you, but enough to keep me from sending her to the city, to live under Aunt Milly's roof."

"How is *she* doing? Must be well along in age by now." Meghan saw Patrick lining up on one of the sheep, with Marion closing fast. A quick step to one side nudged her off her stride, her legs flashing as she went down in a swirl of tall grass, skirts in a twist, legs flailing.

"Her days of running the house in Bath are over. Limited to spending most of her time in the kitchen for the greater part of the day. Holding court, glass in hand, telling endless stories to whoever is there. *If* anyone is there. Her mind often caught betwixt and between, with her memories hazed by age."

"And *drink*." Meghan cupped her hands to her face to call out to Patrick, carrying a large armful of grass in his arms, ready to dump it on Lorna. The young girl lying on her back, crying in anger and the pain from a bruised shin.

Marion gave her sister a touch on the shoulder. "Leave the two of them to work it out, as *we* used to do." Then she paused, sighing loudly. "I've *missed* you, sister. Our connection *is still* there, no matter the distance between."

Meghan nodded, taking Marion's hand and placing it over her heart. "The same for *me* and for Aaron, who sends his love and congratulations. For your marriage and the birth of your daughter."

Marion narrowed her eyes, studying Meghan's. "You have tales of our wayward brother to tell. A mix of light and dark. I can see them on your face."

"I have read his journals, added to those belonging to father, in the chest at the wee croft house."

Both women held their thoughts as a wave of emotions washed over them. Marion, given the news of her father's disappearance and rumored death by her mother during her visit. Told there had been no attempt made to recover his remains, buried in a common grave with the other men killed. The risk of exposing her family to the attention of men with hooded eyes and stony hearts, too great a risk.

Marion lowered her eyes, staring at the garden path. "Our father — damaged by his war. As had been our grandfather/ And now, our brother added to the list." She gave Meghan a sideways look. "Do you fear for young Patrick, with the generational curse hanging in the air?"

"I do. For it seems no measure of peace will last long enough to allow him to skip the *next* senseless bloodletting. Brought on by pressure building in the colonies as we speak. With this latest war all but signed, ready to stuff away in history books. The next one looming. Inland. The tribes living there soon to feel the sharp tip of the bayonet."

"Is there no possibility of an agreement between reasonable men, on all sides, to seek a peaceful resolution?"

Meghan gave her sister an incredulous look. "Based on everything our mother shared about what happened *here*, what *you* went through, and handled with such — such *shrewd* actions taken? You *can't* believe it of us." She shook her head, her copper-colored hair glowing in the sunlight. "We're to be a *new* country. One locked in place, with our backs to the sea. With an entire wilderness to move into."

Marion stepped back, surprised by her sister's frustration, who looked at her, hands on her hips. Meghan snorted in derision. "You have a *directed* mind, in being able to see what needs doing, then *doing* it. You always have. But as to your understanding of how *others* perceive their place in the world to be, you lack the *external* vision our brother and I share in common."

Marion lowered her eyes, her hands clasped as she allowed the words to soak in. Then she sighed, listening to the shrieks of laughter from the young cousins in the field, chasing the flock of disturbed sheep. Red-faced, playing a game of dodge, divert, divide, and conquer. Cornering the agitated animals, using underhanded tactics inherent in the traits of the family that formed them.

"Then we must pray." Marion pointed at the two children, walking hand in hand, herding a knot of nervous sheep, squeezing them into one corner of the field. "For *them*."

Angus dismounted from his mount, a broad-chested mare with a deep brown coat and black mane. The beast waited patiently as he slipped from the saddle, hanging onto the stirrup, finding the ground with his toes. He'd just turned eighteen years of age, his full growth reached, standing a full hand shorter than the youngest of the men working in the stables, paddocks, and fields surrounding the manor.

The height difference didn't bother him, as the members of clan Scott were eager to defer to his suggestions, based on dark stories circulating throughout their lands, high and low. Croft farm families, whose homes he visited when making his way between manor and Glasgow, refusing to believe the more salacious tales. The short-legged man claimed as one of their own, their children and dogs drawn into his lap, or standing at his side, eager to share his easy-going banter and gentle embrace.

It was enough for him, being the firm hand needed to deal with threats to his people. Doing all he could to direct the actions of laird Declan, and Lady Marion, each of them capable enough of making hard-edged decisions when dealing with surface issues. Though neither one was aware of the store of secret information held in his large hands, detailing subversive elements, capable of doing them harm.

Shaun, the former laird of the clan, had bid him recover a small chest sealed with metal bands and two large padlocks, secreted in a corner of the barn. Wooden boxes, filled with odd tools, and gear, and an assortment of rusty chains piled on top. A finger raised to the old man's lips with a devilish glint in his eyes as he leaned down, his voice a raspy whisper. "Held in trust—*your* trust. Until you feel the time is right to open it."

A key provided, hanging from a silver chain, handed him. Angus, young as he'd been, aware his laird was not fully in his proper mind. With serious slippages noted. Morning finding him late to rise. Evening catching him sleeping in his chair in the manor salon, with Angus helping him to his bed.

The time of revelation had arrived immediately after the attack on the manor, with innocent beasts made to die from a pointed message sent. One Angus had answered in return. The chest pulled from beneath dust-covered crates. Opened in the light of a lantern during a midnight hour. The papers within gone through, refolded, then placed away. He'd spent the rest of the night in silent consideration, weighing a dozen options on what to do in response to the attack. With a decision arrived at, producing a grim smile on his youthful lips.

Now, as he led his mount into the barn, Angus took a moment to admire how easily the large doors slid open, then closed. The metal rollers he'd designed had worked as intended, with a dozen crofts wanting the same. Additional sets ordered, then distributed to any who asked for them, further securing people's trust in him as their de facto leader.

Two youthful voices erupted, shouting his name, rushing from the shadows, their bodies clad in tattered strips of dull-colored cloth. Adorned in old ghillie suits, outgrown by Lady Meghan and her brother, Aaron. The children stopped when Angus raised his hand, a dark look on his face as the mare jerked its head in alarm. He soothed her, his voice low and reassuring as he removed her saddle and bridle, then eased her into a stall. When finished with the watering, feeding, and grooming of his trail-weary mount, Angus turned around, facing the children.

He spread his arms, a grin on his face, urging them on. They came in a rush, gathered up in his brawny arms, giggling as he lifted them from the floorboards and spun them in a circle, tossing them onto a mound of fresh hay. His eyes gleamed with a mix of pleasure and pain as he listened to their unfettered screams of delight, hearing the heartbreaking echoes of horses dying in the night.

⅏ ⅏ ⅏

"You'll need to *come* our way, visiting Pennsylvania to see the excellent work mother's been doing there." Meghan, with Patrick and Lorna, tucked between her and Marion, reached out, taking Declan's hand.

Angus, aboard his mare, held the bridle of one of the two geldings hitched to the carriage, the animals quivering, eager to strike out. He heard his name, and turned his head, seeing Meghan and the two children beaming smiles his way.

"And *you* must come too, Angus." Meghan nodded. "It would do you good, crossing over, seeing the world from *our* side."

"I will consider it, Lady Meghan." Angus stuck out his tongue, eliciting grins from the two children. Then he released the bridle, leading the carriage away. Once they reached the lowlands, he pulled up, waiting for Lady Marion to coax the spirited pair of matched geldings to a reluctant, head-tossed halt. "I'll leave you now, ladies, with the road ahead cleared of any potential for trouble." He smiled at Meghan, her son cradled at her side. "Bidding you and your son, a safe journey with fair weather for your crossing."

Angus nodded, receiving her soft-voiced reply, then swung aside, waiting for them to pass. Once they'd cleared the turn, he headed off along a narrow path twisted through a draw, leading to a small, rock-faced gorge. A group of clan Scott men waiting on him there. Messages sent and received in return, naming the day, with the time of his arrival left pending.

The sound of two muskets brought to half-cock sounded. One from ahead, the other from behind, bringing him to a stop. Angus grinned. "You're getting better at concealment, though I spotted ya' coming over the brook. Your heads raised, like young stags in heat, scenting the air for a mate."

Two young men, identical in build and looks, rose from their hiding place, adorned in dark cloaks. They dropped their eyes, their lips tightened into thin lines of chagrin, waiting for admonishment. Left disappointed.

"The day is *well* along. I suspect the hours waiting on my approach have *strained* your patience. Old men, like me, being less susceptible to the making of sudden movements."

One of them responded. "You're *nae* old, Angus." The other finished the sentence for him, a wide smile on his face. "Just *overly* experienced. With an *all-seeing* eye."

The lads came up, waiting as the man standing in as the leader of the clan dismounted. Everyone in the valleys, glens, and draws fully aware of who held the power. The little man, with enormous hands and a mind, to match. Along with the will to see dark days through.

"We're all here. The entire kit *and* caboodle. Assembled, just as you asked."

Angus nodded, handing the reins to the first boy, who reached out, taking them in hand. "Is our *friend* ready to talk?"

"The money offered and counted. Seemed happy enough with the food you had sent down. And the bottle."

With a nod of his head, Angus moved along the narrow path with a measured pace. As he neared a squat shouldered hovel, he wondered if he would accept what the man waiting inside the small hut would tell him. If he'd allow him to ride away or end up placing him beneath the sod. He paused, took in a deep breath, then let it out, watching with hooded eyes as it drifted away, the air cold enough to color it gray.

When he entered the building, a thin man, his lower leg twisted from an accident or a hard entry into the world, looked up. "I'm *not* to blame for the value of the information, given ya' people. They asked. I answered." He crossed his arms, then nodded sharply, staring at Angus. "Exactly as *I* heard it told and have shared with *you*. No blame to fall on me if you're—"

Angus held up one finger, bringing the seated man to a stop. "The purse." The man hesitated, then reached toward his pocket. Angus stopped him with a shake of his head. "Nae. Not from you." One of a handful of men squeezed inside the building handed a second purse to the frightened informer. A man found huddled in the corner of a tavern on the outskirts of Glasgow, identified based on information in the chest at the manor. One of several dozen descriptions of nameless men, provided by a man wearing blood-splattered white clothing. Left babbling in fear, terror, then misery, his grandiose plans cut to shreds.

"I'll need *another* name. And *description*. Now." Angus kept his voice even, his tone relaxed, knowing he was at a crossroads. That the man's answer would be vital to his plans to infiltrate the lowest rung of a secretive group. One Shaun had become involved with, with no one else in the clan aware of their former laird's role.

Not a single person told of Duncan's fate, Shaun's former protector, who'd disappeared under a cloud of suspicion. Along with another. A young man tasked with taking down the words of a broken man under sharp-edged questioning. Discovered a few months later with a broken neck, having suffered a drunken fall from a skittish horse. The true story of what happened told to Angus by Shaun in a mumbling voice, drifting between whiskey-blurred memories of a deteriorating mind.

The crippled man stared, then half-opened his mouth before clamping it shut, his breath hissing through a gap in his stained teeth. "Kill me *here* and *now*. I'm dead—soon as it's said."

Angus waved his hand, clearing the room, the sound of boots moving away, with the small door left open, allowing the crippled man to peek through, verifying no one stood in earshot other than the one facing him.

"Your *word*! Sworn before *God*."

"I'm not much of a believer—in all that."

The man swallowed, his fear staining the air. "*Your* word, given. Sworn on the honor of clan Scott." The man held out his hand, fingers bent by accident or disease, his body shaking beneath a tattered cloak.

Angus took it, a momentary spasm of recalled emotion running through him, hearing the nasal, spittle-flecked voice of his first father in his mind's ear. "*Cripple!* The *Devil's* own spawn. A *waste* of life. No more to me than a rat. *Less!* A rat in the pot is worth twice as much to me as *you!*"

Angus tightened his expression. He leaned in, meaning every word offered to the other. "You have my word. No one but *me* to hear what's said. No one told. My word on it, as protector of clan Scott."

Once the man provided the information asked of him, Angus called out. Two men came back inside and collected the cripple, taking him outside and setting him on a small horse. Angus gave him a short wave as he rode away, then headed toward his own mount. One of a handful of men trusted to see things done followed him, waiting as he gathered up the reins of his large mare.

Angus turned around. "See that it's done *quickly*, with as little pain as possible. Then take him high. Somewhere with a clear view into the valley. On the *east* side, so the sun will find him there each morning." He hesitated. "Gather the purses. Take the smaller one to the third croft down, the next valley over. Handing it to a family with a crippled son. The larger one, delivered to the Catholic church in Glasgow."

The two men crossed themselves, then headed to their mounts. Angus placed his hand on the stirrup strap, his eyes closed, remembering the moment his father had died. The flux had stolen his strength, leaving him on his back, gasping for air. Helpless, his eyes widened in fear as death approached. His young son, called a deformed waste of life, standing over him with a wide smile on his broad face.

Then he pulled himself into the saddle and headed along a path toward Glasgow. A grim smile stretched across his weather-worn lips. A name in hand. A man to meet.

CHAPTER SEVENTEEN
WESTERN WILDERNESS
SUMMER, 1785

Aaron kneeled, longbow in hand, with an arrow nocked. He lifted his head, his nostrils sifting the air for stray scents of tobacco, sweat, and the odor of unwashed flesh. Finding none, he sighed, having verified what his instincts had already told him. The energy surrounding him was native to the local environment. Going about its business without interference from man.

He closed his eyes and focused on slowing his breathing. A lethal decision to make as two deer moved along the near edge of a narrow clearing, heads down, searching the ground for shoots of sweet grass. One of them, unaware of its imminent fate.

The weather had cleared with no further sign of rain, leaving behind a peaceful scene encouraging a relaxed mood. Aaron ignored the deer as they approached, his attention fixed on locating a shadow on the other side of the opening. One in the shape of a man he'd spied earlier that day from an overlook spot tucked into the ridgeline behind him. Aware someone was tracking him. An experienced woodsman, though lacking critical knowledge of his quarry's capabilities. The table turned, with a painful lesson taught.

A whisper from behind froze Aaron's next breath. The words not registering at first as adrenaline coursed through his veins, preparing his body for sudden violence. His eyes widened as he caught up to what he'd heard and slowly turned around, the movement spotted by the two deer, their tails raised in white flags of alarm as they bounced away.

Smoke, with a gap-toothed smile on his scarred face, reached out, using a dead branch to poke his friend in the ribs. "I said you're *dead*. Again." Then he laughed, covering the sound with one hand, his eyes glistening with pleasure. "Didn't recognize ya' at first, thinking I'd have ta' *kill* ya'. Until I saw the bow in your hand." He turned his head to one side, spit, then wiped his fingers across his lips.

Aaron smiled. "I should have *recognized* it was you. Spotted you earlier. From above." He pointed with his chin, looking up at the rock-faced ridge. Then he frowned. "You *let* me see you, then swung around, reversing the trap. Catching me out from behind."

"Yup. Just like I taught ya'. The lesson—*wasted*."

Both men stared at one another for a long minute, coming to terms with each one still alive and not planted in the ground. Aaron was the first to break the awkward silence. "Glad to see ya'." He paused, the question in his eyes.

Smoke shook his head. "No one else made it out. Not that I *know* of." He lifted one edge of his shirt, revealing a large scar on the side of his abdomen. "Caught a stray ball. Passed through the meat, with minor damage done. I lit a backfire, hiding my tracks, then slipped away, staying ahead of the flames." He paused. "Like someone *else* that I served with. A long while ago."

"At the Big Burn, as you named it when telling me the story."

Smoke nodded. "Got to admit it *pains* me some, hearing that name. Like I'm back there again, looking at your Da. With yourself a close match to him in looks. And *capability*." The older man pursed his lips. "Though he made a serious misstep that day. Ended up paying a *high* price. Along with most of his men."

Aaron nodded, then looked down, using the tip of a moccasin-clad toe to scuff the leaves. "Mine was worse. Resulting in the loss of —everyone."

"Not so. *You're* still here. And *me*." The older man reached out, offering his hand. Aaron took it, a sad smile on his lips.

"Good to see you, my friend."

The next day found them tucked into a hollow, two trails leading out the back of it, already scouted. Both men prepared to leave in a hurry if discovered. A force of habit, honed by years of caution, with each man aware of the risks of moving through lands claimed by people on both sides of an uneasy truce. Everyone waiting on the signing of a treaty by the major players on each side of the board. The result of months of negotiations, with copies released to the public for distribution throughout colonial towns and settlements. The English left to deal with explaining the agreement to native villages lying further west.

"A fair mess ahead." Smoke grinned, his teeth white against the nut-brown color of his tanned skin. "With thousands to pay the blood price on *both* sides. On *all* sides, one way or t'other." He leaned in, adding a small pine knot to the coals of a small fire. Kept as smoke-free as possible as it glowed between stacked rocks, heating strips of fresh venison, sizzling above the flames.

The scent of it tweaked the nostrils of the two men, their stomachs rumbling at the thought of a hot meal. The air was still, a thin column of spiraling embers rising straight up, carrying the odor of charred meat, preventing it from spreading into the surrounding walls of tumbled rocks and thick woods.

Aaron stirred a cup of tea with the business end of his knife as he considered Smoke's words, the last of his leaves used for the brew. "I suspect so. With false promises as thick as horse shite, covering the ground."

Smoke coughed, shaking his head. "Nothing's changed. Not for us. Same rules *still* apply."

Aaron nodded. "Blood, the next thing to cover the ground. Heading from there—" He pointed to the east, then swung his arm. "To there." Then he leaned back, testing the tea, his thick-skinned hand not bothered by the heat of the metal cup in his palm. "I won't ask where you're headed."

"Planning to meet up with a few friends." The older man gave Aaron a grin. "One of them who knew your Da, back in the day." He paused, his voice drifting away. "Too damn *many* days ago." Then he shook his head. "But I'll admit there were *good* ones, too. Squeezed in between God and the Devil himself."

"You knew who he was. My father." Aaron leaned it. "When he showed up during *our* war. I could tell he thought he knew you, too. Just couldn't place you."

"He never *saw* me again. Not after I got *this*." Smoke reached up, touching the scars on his neck and face, using his damaged hand. The tips of his fingers chewed off at the ends by a cannister round. One the battle-hardened man said had landed too *damn* close.

Aaron nodded without comment, aware the veteran had served with his father, until the fight where his friend and mentor, Robert Scott, had caught an arrow in the back and died. Left buried on a ridge, just over a week's walk away.

Smoke stared at him, his eyes narrowed in thought. "Your father, he told you of it — of what he did."

"It was in his journals. All of it. No need for secrecy back then. Not like the fight *we* were in."

A flash of light came through the sky, painting a green line in the evening sky. There and gone, leaving both of them looking up. Neither spoke, the fire burning down, the meat ready. They ate without words, their mood subdued as the night folded in around them. The woods filled with the sound of birds calling out. Tucked safely away in their treetop roosts.

The next day arrived wet. A light mist, with the promise to thicken up before noon. Aaron followed Smoke, a silent agreement reached to tag along, with a decision made whether he would join the veteran and his friends once they reached the outer edge of civilization.

Aaron, having delivered his mother safely back to her Pennsylvania valley home, kept his head down, trusting the wily woodsman to lead the way. Wondering, as the two of them moved along animal trails and untracked passes, whether he could trust the men his friend was leading him to. Left asking himself if it even mattered anymore. He was a man without a home, having come east, leaving Eliza clinging to another woman's child. Leaving Noah and the other members of the community behind.

The parting from Eliza and the community had been difficult. His mother waiting at Jackson's grave. Aaron standing in the church. Eliza poised behind the pulpit, staring down at him with an eerie look in her light-colored eyes, listening as he explained his decision to leave.

"The lad—he's *not* ours. Not *yours* or mine."

Eliza looked at Aaron, her head moving from side to side. "He's *our* child, Aaron. Returned to us by God. To replace the one lost. A *gift* from heaven. One that we—that you—*cannot* refuse."

"He's the child of a woman whose husband died. Taken by you from her after *our* son died, lost in a premature birth." Aaron hardened his stance. "If that is a measure of *God's* love, allowing the massacre of people grown closer to him than any I've ever known, along with the theft of a child from its mother—then I *renounce* him. *Your* version of him, warped by—"

He caught his anger too late, seeing Eliza's eyes blazing with righteous intensity. Her features were a mask of anger. Voice high-pitched, trembling with emotion. "*You*, who came to us in *need*, healed by a *miracle* from the very God you would renounce—"

"It was *not* God, bringing me here. Nor the one who *healed* me. It was a *native* woman, offering me life when death was in a close hover. A death I would have *welcomed*. Then."

"You speak *blasphemy!* With no regard for the love of God. Of God, or *me*."

Aaron turned away, unable to find the young woman he'd sworn a vow to, then held in his arms for two days and nights with plans made to travel back to his family. Given an opportunity to experience a world outside her cloistered upbringing. Raised under the cloying influence of her father, a man dedicated to building a new world deep in the wilderness.

"I'm leaving. Leaving you. Leaving the community."

"*Go*. And *don't* return to our home until you're ready to kneel and accept God into your heart again."

He'd left that day, Noah catching up to him, eyes wide in shock at what his sister had shared with him. "You *can't* leave. We need—*I* need you."

"I've not *been* here in full. Not since—"

"She said—my sister—told me you've let go of your faith." Noah reached out, touching Aaron on the shoulder. "It happens. To all. Even to Lukas. But he *regained* it, stronger than before. Eliza, too. It *will* happen to you. I know it."

Aaron smiled, a sad look on his face. "Too late for me. Having brought nothing but darkness to her life. Your sister's life, and mine. Not here, when needed most. A punishment from God, if you will, landing on everyone. The weight of the cross carried on my shoulders, my *own* to bear."

He spun around, leaving without looking back. Without seeing Noah, his hand half raised, his voice a whisper, telling him he'd see him again. Someday.

CHAPTER EIGHTEEN
CAPTIVE'S TOWN
SPRING, 1785

Noah watched as a column of soldiers marched into the English fort, led by several officers. The commander came over, shaking his hand.

"We appreciate your efforts with the Wyandot. You, and your father before you. A stabilizing influence. I commend you for everything you've done. Helping feed your people. Gathering of wild meat for their tables, as well as my own. The venison loins you delivered me, of *excellent* quality."

Noah nodded, liking the man despite his nose-down attitude toward the community. Seeing them as wards of the English Empire and not as members of a thriving group of people of faith. And his lack of awareness of the behavior of the soldiers under his command. Men with wandering eyes, making crude, suggestive comments whenever he entered the fort with his sister or Two-Women at his side.

"Thank you, sir. I have tried to do my best, as God requires of us *all*."

The commander nodded, then sniffed. "Yes. Of course. By God's will and our *own* hands. Held accountable to orders, performing the roles we're assigned. Especially out here, on the far edge of civilization." The tall man sniffed, then headed through the gate, off to the routine of filling out the hours, days, weeks, and months left before his replacement would arrive.

The English government had remained intent on maintaining a military presence in the Ohio region, with everyone waiting for the results of treaty negotiations, taking place thousands of miles away between colonies and the crown. Including negotiations brokered between government agents and the heads of the combined tribes of the Iroquois nation, making decisions that would affect all tribes throughout the greater Ohio Basin. Everyone with a voice, though some were louder than others. Those of the leaders of the Wyandot people and tribes further to the west barely heard. Along with those of the people of Captive's Town, whose concern for their future was only a whisper in the wind.

The woods were in full voice, laden with evening noises. The sharp yip of a coyote in a pale imitation of the howl of a wolf in the distance. Calls from doves, in their evening roosts, competed with the less frequent but penetrating hoot of owls. Crickets, hard at work, adding their high-pitched notes into the mix. The sounds stirred by a stiff breeze, building into a storm that would arrive before dawn.

Noah held Two-Women's hand as they passed by the walls of the fort, on their way to his sister's small house, where his native friend stayed when visiting the community. Two uniformed soldiers, standing watch, called out, their comments tightening Noah's thick shoulders and neck, his fingers clenching, causing Two-Women to wince.

She leaned her head against his shoulder. "They are only the *sounds* of the night. No different from the noise made by coyotes." Noah relaxed his grip, bothered by the lack of courtesy shown. The men, recent arrivals, had little knowledge of the people they were there to watch over.

The two of them continued their walk, hand in hand, with Eliza looking up from her writing as they knocked on her door, bidding them to enter the house. "Welcome, my brother, and his good friend, Two-

Women." She graced them with a warm smile, then returned to working on the sermon for her next service, two days hence.

Noah hugged Two-Women, taking a moment to look into her dark eyes, every detail of her perfect face captured anew. "I will find you. In the morning. Take you to your parents' lodge. Hoping to find a fat doe as a gift to them. Allowing their daughter to walk with me."

She smiled at him, her voice low. "I might find a gift for *you* along the trail. A *special* gift. From me."

Noah cut his eyes to one side, watching his sister's face. The two of them had been speaking English, with no sign of Eliza having overheard. He nodded, his eyes bright with the love he felt. Then he left, heading to his small house where he collected his bow and sheath of arrows, intending to sit watch over a staked chicken, its frantic movements and complaints intended to draw four-footed predators in, reducing any additional losses in the small coops scattered between the houses of the settlement.

Noah sighed, missing Aaron. His mentor had headed off two months earlier, returning his mother to the colony of Pennsylvania. He looked up, knowing a night spent under the stars with an arrow poised, waiting for dawn, would help soothe his mood. His thoughts troubled, wondering when Aaron would return. The trip there, and back, filled with risk, with Noah aware his mentor was a wanted man. Sought by men on both sides of the struggle between colonies and their king.

As he neared the fort, carrying an oil-skin cloak under one arm against the storm to come, Noah noted the guards were not at their usual post. A court-martial offense, if discovered by an officer. He shrugged, letting go of any concern on their behalf, still feeling the sting of their coarse remarks.

A shout from inside the tall wooden structure brought him to a stop. A loud voice with English accent called out, followed by the muffled sound of a blow. Noah stepped inside, seeing a door swinging open, light from within revealing the huddled form of a soldier on the ground, a man in buckskin standing over him, war club raised.

Noah dropped the hen and his bow, running over, colliding with the native, and knocking him to the ground. He wrestled the club away, hearing a rising chorus of voices streaming through the air as soldiers with bayonet-tipped muskets in hand came on the run.

The English officer in command of the fort straightened up, perfectly attired, every inch of his uniform tailored to his tall, haughty frame. He peered at Noah, his pale eyes framing a long, thin, aquiline nose. The man's voice, over-flowing with outrage, was tight with restraint as he spoke.

"An *assault*. In his *Majesty's* fort. By a handful of *miscreants!* Assisted in their efforts by a man I believed *trustworthy!*"

Noah, his hands tied behind him, feet spread to keep him in place, tried to focus. His head throbbed, with a large knot on his forehead from the blow of a musket stock, leaving his vision blurry. A line of ten young men in similar poses stood with him. One of them, Two-Spirit, wearing an angry glare, underlain by a shadow of fear.

"The *penalty* for such action is *death! No* exceptions. With sentence carried out on the *morrow!*"

Two of the soldiers took Noah by his elbows, leading him away, while the others remained behind, held in place by irons clamped around their ankles. After they escorted him into the commander's office, Noah tried to come to terms with what had taken place in the hours since leaving Two-Women. It seemed a dream. A bad dream, without the ability to force himself awake.

"Release his hands." The commander entered the room, tossing his jacket on the back of a chair behind his desk. His voice was soft, his fingers rubbing his forehead. "I know you had nothing at all to do with this—*wretched* affair. Boys playing at being warriors. Overstepping their boundaries, deserving of my having sentenced *them*. But it need not include yourself. If I'm provided compelling evidence of your innocence."

A nod of the officer's head left Noah sitting down, his hearing muffled. His vision clouded at the edges. He struggled to remain upright, his thoughts heavy with fatigue.

"Have you *nothing* to say? Tell me you had *no* part to play in this affront to our stewardship. My officers and men posted here to protect *your* people. To protect the rights of natives, already converted, and those in outlying villages."

Noah tried to speak, his throat dry, producing a series of coughs that wracked him with pain, as if shards of glass, piercing his temple. Another nod from the commander produced a glass of warm, watered wine, held to his cracked lips, helping to slake his thirst.

"I knew—knew of the plan. Not the details. Or timing. But aware it was a possibility."

The officer pursed his lips, looking at the wall past Noah's injured head, taking a deep breath, releasing it slowly. "Not the answer I'd hoped for, leaving me in a quandary on what comes next."

His second in command, one of a handful of men stationed at the fort since the beginning, spoke up. "He has a wound, sir. To his head. Perhaps causing some confusion. If I might have a word with him. In private. Sir."

The commander sniffed, then yawned. He stood up and left the room without comment, bringing the two soldiers with him. Once the door closed, the older officer pulled a second chair over and sat down. He leaned forward, studying Noah's eyes, seeing the haze in his expression. "You knew. And tried to stop this—nonsense. Your nature to *do* so. Your reputation is impeccable."

He refilled the glass, handing it to the young man, and encouraging him to drink. "You've always told the truth of things. No reason to doubt you now. Whatever you say, accepted as a defense, with no one wanting to upset the locals. Enough of a headache having to deal with the potential for trouble with the Wyandot. Your efforts are vital in helping allay their anger. Allowing you to serve a *greater* purpose. Do you not *see* that, Noah? That you can help to minimize this—minor event. Before it becomes something greater."

"I knew. And failed to stop it."

"Do you know who their leader is? The others refuse to name him."

"I know. And will *not* name him."

"Then *all* will pay for *his* decision. His friends. His people. You."

Noah nodded, knowing he would not speak, even if it meant his life. His faith in God sustained him as if had his mother. And his sister, despite the challenges faced. "I will *not* name him."

The older man nodded, his respect for the young man immense. "I accept your decision, difficult as it is to do so. And will let the commander know. You'll remain here, untethered, to await *his* decision in return."

The cell was small, without room to lie down. Straw, scattered over the soil, was damp, reeking of rat urine. The air, thickened by the scent of fear, was musty with mold spores.

Noah leaned against a wooden wall, his head pounding. The voices of the other boys were a buzzing whine of complaint, with accusations tossed back and forth. The would-be warriors were afraid and angry. Their heads hung in shame, with no one to blame but themselves for having come along.

Their leader remained silent, his thoughts centered on how to pin the blame elsewhere. "He is responsible." Two-Spirit pointed, his hands bound before him, his finger aimed at Noah. "We will tell the English when they come to speak with us, that their *half-white* pet betrayed them. Leading us here with false tales of the soldiers having despoiled my sister."

Noah stared, a blank look in his eyes. The others stopped talking, their eyes on Two-Spirit's face. One, larger than the others, got to his knees. "*You* are the one to blame. Your words are *lies*. Your spirit is *weak*."

"And *you* will die. Along with the rest. They will let *me* go, to protect themselves against my father's revenge." Two-Spirit smirked, confident of his eventual release.

"The Great Mother—" Noah forced the words from his mouth. "She will take away your spirit. Your lies—will lead you down a shadowed path. Unable to find your way back to her."

The other young men exchanged glances, seeing the pained look on the Moravian's face. Their leader shook his head, about to respond as the cell door opened, pulling their heads around. The English commander stood framed in the doorway, looking down at them with an imperious stare.

"Your leader *named*. *Now!*" He gave Noah a nod, implying he should translate, making the meaning of his words clear. Noah complied, his voice steady, now that his headache had eased. When he finished, no one said a word. The commander nodded, then turned to leave. The larger native spoke up. "*He* is the one. There." His bound hands pointed at Two-Spirit.

The officer looked at Noah as he translated, his eyebrows raised. "Tell him to answer me himself. To *admit* he is their leader." When Noah remained silent, he narrowed his eyes, his voice tight. "*Ask* him." He paused. "Now."

Noah looked at Two-Spirit. "Will you let all these men die? Turning your back on them?"

The other man sneered. "I name them *cowards* and *fools*. Their lack of resolve is why my plan *failed*."

Noah started speaking as soon as Two-Spirit spoke. "He denies it. Refusing to name the one who leads. Said he would rather die. Along with the rest." Noah looked up. "Including me."

"Then so it shall be." The officer left without a backward glance. The heavy door pulled shut, its latch sliding into place. Once the sound of boots faded away, Two-Spirit glared at Noah.

"What did you tell him? What did he say?"

"That you will die. With us. Together."

Two-Spirit glowered. "I *hate* you!"

Noah nodded. "Which is why we are here. Your anger *blinds* you to the truth. That you were born with two sides. Light and dark. Strong —and afraid."

The largest man nodded. "It is our path to die as brothers." He gave Noah a searching look. "*You* are innocent. And will not join us. You will tell the tall English man to let you go. That you can help to prevent blame from falling on our people's heads."

"I will stand *with* you. As guilty in their eyes, knowing of your plans and not warning them." Noah looked down. "If I'd told them, they would have prevented the attempt. My mistake. One we all will pay for."

The man nodded, accepting the truth, the discussion at an end. Two-Spirit continued to moan in fear, with harsh curses aimed at Noah. The others sat back with stoic expressions on their youthful faces, awaiting death.

"Surely you cannot believe my brother is capable of such an action. He is an *exemplary* citizen of our community, with no malice in him." Eliza faced the commander, her Bible in hand. News brought to her by his second in command, asking her to intercede, begging for clemency. One he was ready to grant on her brother's behalf, but not the others. Unless they would relent and name their leader.

"I quite agree, Miss—" He paused, giving her a confused look. "I cannot seem to recall your married name. My apologies for having forgotten it."

"I have never provided it, sir. I choose to go by Eliza, according to my faith's custom."

"Then—Eliza, my agreement stands. Wanting nothing more than to put this behind us. Needing only one name. Releasing the others to their homes. Or lodges. A task you can help me with. Or your native friend, standing behind you with a worried look on her face."

"It is in God's hands. Each one involved will have to find their way to the truth. Then share it with you."

"Including Noah. Your brother."

Two-Women gasped, hearing Noah's name, still struggling to catch up to the undulating flow of English words. She stepped forward. "He is *mine*."

The commander looked at Two-Women, then nodded. "I am the leader, here." He swung his hand, taking in the fort. "Need the name of the leader of men there." He pointed to the far wall, where the cell was located, tucked among a collection of storage buildings.

Eliza opened her mouth, prepared to explain that the native woman understood and spoke English. Interrupted as Two-Women shouted out, telling Noah to name her brother. The officer looked at Eliza, waiting for her to translate. She returned a frown, unable to do so, the Wyandot language unknown to her.

The commander shrugged. "I *am* sorry, but there's nothing I can do unless your brother loosens his commitment to the others and tells me *who* I am to hang." He paused, his eyes pleading with her to help him solve the problem. "I *must* act. To prevent another occurrence. We need to maintain order here. Until we have signed treaties in place."

Eliza put her hands on her hips, her eyes lit up with frustration. "Paper, with meaningless words. Not a single settler held accountable when they arrive from out of the east, trampling down the woods. Taking furs that do not belong to them. The only ones punished—these *foolish* boys. Thinking they could change anything."

"It's the way of the world. The one we both awoke to, my dear Eliza. And no one, short of God himself, can change the ways of man. Ensuring the good. Eliminating the bad."

The officer, second in command of the fort, leaned forward, looking at Noah, his eyes filled with concern. "This was *not* your idea. With no blame assigned to you for having tried, then failing to prevent it. A noble position, though *misguided*. Your death will only produce grief for your sister. Your people. For your friend." He paused. "I *implore* you to reconsider."

Two-Women reached out, taking Noah's hand, a concerned look on her face as she stared into his eyes, speaking in her language. "My brother, *he* is the one to pay for his blindness. Not you. Or the others. Only *him*."

Noah shook his head, a smile on his lips as he looked over at his sister, giving Eliza a long, considered look, his voice soft. "That day in Gnadenhutten, when Aaron carried you away with your hands pounding his back, your voice—a wail of anguish. Did you wish to join the others? To go to your death *with* them?"

Eliza hesitated, seeing Two-Women turn and look at her, a questioning look in her doe-brown eyes. "I—*yes*. I did. Caught up in the moment." She saw her brother's expression of victory. "My faith, rising to an elevated level of love for God, having spent hours of prayer to him, knowing my fate. *All* of us, knowing our fates."

She reached out and took Noah's hands. "But Aaron *saved* me. Part of *God's* will. Taking me with him. Saving you. Taking us away as Anna asked of him. To help our father continue his work. For the *greater good.*"

"And, if given the chance to have saved them, by trading your life for theirs—tell me, sister, what would you have done?"

Eliza nodded, having arrived with her brother at the moment of God's test of his faith. She turned to go, Two-Women crying out, aware of what had happened. Two soldiers stepped forward, easing her away from Noah, half-carrying her out of the room.

⚶ ⚶ ⚶

The native infiltrators, lined up along the back wall of the cell, faced three soldiers with leveled muskets, bayonets attached, flanking their commander. He stood braced, hands on his hips, giving each one a long stare. Then he shook his head and pointed at Noah, bidding him forward.

"I've decided that *one* of you will wear the noose. On the other's behalf. Yourself, excluded."

"Yet I am the one *most* guilty of the crime. One made against the King."

The commander frowned. "Failure to have stopped them is *not* a crime."

"Failure to report the attempt beforehand—*is*."

The tall officer spun about, facing the opening, his face reddening in exasperation. He slowly turned back around, opening his mouth to have Noah removed, allowing him to proceed with his plan to put the problem behind him.

Noah kept his voice level, his words clear in the foul air. "You risk hostilities if choosing one at random. The Wyandot people known for their pride. Especially their chief. A blemish on your record should an uprising occur under your watch. Especially at such a *critical* time, with the treaty all but agreed to and signed."

He paused, allowing himself to return to a state of harmony, then shrugged. "Whereas I, a member of a people known for their peaceful posture and unshakable faith, will gladly sing my soul to heaven. My story added to the others. To those of all the martyrs of Gnadenhutten."

The second officer came into the room. He stepped forward and conferred with his superior, their words exchanged in whispers. When he stepped back, the commander nodded. "I will accept your offer. You will hang by the neck until dead. Tomorrow morning. May God watch over and comfort you this night." With a nod of his head, he turned away, leaving without another word.

The second officer gave Noah a long look, then did the same. The soldiers locked the door, the group of prisoners looking at Noah, waiting for him to let them know what had just happened. He related the news, causing them to scowl at Two-Spirit, their angry muttering filling the cramped space.

As Noah explained the reason for his actions, the door opened and the soldiers came back in, placing irons around his legs and wrists, half-dragging him from the cell. Voices of protest from the others rang out, muffled by the thud of the heavy wooden door.

🌲🌲🌲

The day dawned clear of clouds, with the sky speckled by a large flock of crows winging by. Their cries brought a smile to Noah's face. His mood was light, feeling refreshed, having slept soundly, uninterrupted by any visitors other than the second officer who'd handed him a Bible. Refused by Noah, telling him he had everything he needed, pointing to his heart.

The commander waited, two soldiers standing at attention at his side. He gave them a nod, watching as the men removed the restraints from the condemned man's wrists and ankles. Noah frowned. A confused look on his face as he stood in the center of the yard with no one else around.

The commander came forward and reached out, taking him by the elbow, guiding him around the barracks, then stopping, facing the back wall of the fort. Noah stared, his mouth open in shock, staring up at Two-Spirit, the boy's body suspended from a twisted length of rope.

His hands bound behind him, face drained of color, the tip of his tongue extending from between his teeth.

Noah looked over at the commander. "*Why?*"

"His punishment—deserved. Named and found guilty. Deliverance belongs to the faithful. Which *you* are."

"The ramifications, once his father—"

"I had a visitor yesterday, not long after I had you placed in shackles and taken away. An elderly native. Leader of his people. Willing to trade one life for the other. His son's, for yours."

"How—how could he have known?"

"My second officer, and a young native woman on horseback. The two of them made the trip to the Wyandot village and back. Bringing their leader with them, who spoke on *your* behalf. Gave me his word there would be no trouble between us." He paused. "Did you not wonder why she didn't visit you last night? Two-Women. Able to find a solution to this—*regrettable* situation."

Noah twisted his head, taking in the sight of the young man who'd lost his way. He lowered his voice and his eyes. "May the Great Mother guide him on his path. May God hold him in his loving embrace."

The commander nodded his head. "Amen." Then he took Noah by his arm, gently leading him back to and through the front gate.

CHAPTER NINETEEN
CROSSROAD COMMUNITY
FALL, 1785

S inclair wiped her hand across her forehead, sweat clinging to her skin. Patrick glanced up, straining to hold up one end of a small, heavy desk, He reached back with his foot for the first step of the new schoolhouse, smiling, his lips tight with effort.

"I've got it, Gran Ma. I'm ready."

Sinclair nodded, feeling the weight of the wooden desk shift into her hands as the boy lifted his end. They cleared the steps, taking the desk inside and putting it down with tired gasps. Sinclair took a moment, needing to catch her breath, looking around the room, light from three large windows highlighting the interior.

She'd hired men to deliver the desks, enough to hold the children of the rapidly expanding community. With every child encouraged to attend, learning in a structured environment, one more conducive to advanced studies. The delivery men who delivered the furniture had shrugged when asked to help bring the furniture inside, leaving it in the yard, laughing among themselves as their horse drew the large wagons away.

All the members of the valley settlement had contributed their time, tears, and sweat helping to build the school. The materials needed provided by a grant from a fund set up by Sinclair. Along with funds to construct a church, additional housing, and several large storehouses. Several wells added to a mix of half a hundred home-based businesses run by women, producing a steady flow of goods. Purchased by citizens of Philadelphia, with the city expanding at a rapid pace. Monies, flowing to and through community coffers, reinvested in a mill and smithy, along with a huge extension to the large communal gardens.

"I'm ready, Gran Ma." Patrick came over, taking her hand. Sinclair tugged him into a hug, then leaned down, kissing the top of his head, his scent dragging memories of her son to the surface.

"We'll do *two* more, then find others willing to assist. Part of becoming educated is learning when to ask for help."

Allwyn glanced up at a crescent moon as he closed the large door of the barn. The new rollers sent to him by Angus helped to ease the task, with a dozen orders from local farmers already placed, waiting for the new smithy to get them made. He took a deep breath, smelling wood smoke hanging in the air, mixed with the scent of offal. One of few disadvantages, he thought to himself, as the door slid shut, with too many people living and working in too small an area. Leading to issues of adequate waste disposal, along with a host of other health-related concerns.

As the unofficial leader of the community, the position given him by default with no one else willing to run for the job, Allwyn spent far less time with his hands in the soil or holding the reins of a team than he cared for. Constant calls for his attention elsewhere to intercede in disputes between neighbors, or find a solution to communal issues, had soured his stomach. And his attitude. The distant hills called to him, tempting him with dreams of building, then living on a remote farmstead.

A deep voice sounded out, followed by a figure stepping from the shadows, arms to the side, hands empty. "My brother. You walk as if carrying the weight of the entire world on your shoulders."

Allwyn shook his head, then stepped forward, taking Aaron in his arms. His friend's body was thin, rangy in build, with all its assorted parts still attached. "It's from the weight of *this* place, alone." He paused. "This place, and the outlying group of new homes filling in the valley. East to west. North through south."

"And your family?" Aaron softened his tone. "*My* family?"

Allwyn smiled, dusk hiding the gleam in his eyes. "In *fine* fettle. Those of us who are here, with *another* wee one on the way. Those still in Scotland are the same. Last we heard." He clapped his brother by marriage on his shoulder. "Come into the house and greet them yourself."

Aaron pulled away. "Better if you send my mother to the barn. Alone."

Allwyn tilted his head. "I ken from your tone there's dark news to hand." He gave Aaron a searching stare, then turned to go, stopping when his friend's deep voice caught him up. "You're the rock, Allwyn. The one all this rests on. Laying the foundation of something that will outlive you. Will outlive us all. You should be proud, my brother."

Allwyn hesitated, then moved on. He headed toward the front door of the newly expanded house, watching the shadows of his family within, crossing in front of the windows.

❦ ❦ ❦

Sinclair stared at her son, her joy at seeing him alive and hale, leaving her at a loss for words. Aaron walked out of a stable, the horse he'd been grooming stretching out its head, whickering a request for more attention. He stroked its neck, missing the daily contact with the long-legged animals from childhood, on. Not a practicable choice for moving about the trails of the western reaches. The wiser choice, shank's mare for getting from one place to another. With less risk of drawing undue attention.

Sinclair gathered her son in her arms, tears in her eyes, the moment of reconnection stronger now than ever before. She pulled back, looking up at him, wondering where he'd been, and the things he'd done or had done to him. Both of them were silent, recalling their journey made to the west and back again. Then the sound of feet coming on the run pulled their eyes to the large door, watching as it rolled open, with Meghan stepping through, fire in her eyes.

"*Aaron!*" She started toward her brother, seeing his hand raised, finger to his lips. She continued over, reaching for the hug Aaron offered her. Sinclair forced to step aside, a tight-lipped smile on her lip that failed to reach her eyes.

"Allwyn *didn't* want to tell me. Tried to keep it *from* me. Left having to work it out of him, knowing he was hiding something. With our mother—" Meghan swung her head, giving Sinclair a pinched look. "Not choosing to share news of your arrival. With *me.*" She separated herself from Aaron's arms, hands on her hips, her abdomen swelling with a bairn on the way, two months off. "What is it?"

Sinclair opened her mouth to respond, stopping when Aaron raised his hand. "It's *my* tale to tell." He reached out, cupping his sister's cheeks, gazing into her wide-set, sky-blue eyes. The light from a turned-down lantern painted a gleam of copper in her red hair. Her freckled cheeks dusted a light tan from working outside. "So beautiful a woman you are, sister. Mother to a fine son, with another child soon to arrive. Wife, to a man of strength and integrity. And every bit as *willful, prideful,* and *incredible* a woman as is our mother. As are *both* of my sisters, with families of your own."

"You're leaving. Again." Meghan's eyes filled, then overflowed, tears falling down her cheeks, stopped by her brother's wide palms. "Am I *never* going to have ya' back in my life?"

"I don't know." Aaron shrugged. "My path leads me to where I'm destined to go."

"*Fook* all to you. And your *path!*" She shoved him away, then looked at Sinclair. "Am I *wrong,* Mother? That I'll ever be able to—" She ran to Sinclair, burying her head on her shoulder, unable to speak.

Sinclair gazed at Aaron, seeing the look of desolation on his face. She gathered in her daughter, her son's arm outstretched, left hanging in the air as Sinclair slowly guided Meghan to a pile of crates. She sat down alongside her, both women with broken hearts, staring at the man they loved with sorrowful expressions.

Aaron came over, kneeling before them, reaching for their hands, Meghan refusing the gesture, keeping hers pressed tight to her swollen abdomen. "I've no *choice* in it. Impossible to stay here. Or go back to where I've been." He leaned in, finding Meghan's eyes, holding them with a solemn look.

"My war—not yet over. Embroiled in the same struggle our father was involved with. *Still* going on with myself having a role to play. Vital to securing a future for what you're building here. Laid down by thousands of people like *you*. You and Allwyn. Creating a bright future on blood-soaked ground. Bringing meaning to the sacrifice of other people's lives. All of you—men, women, and children—helping to bring about a *new* beginning."

Meghan looked up. "Then *stay*. *Join* us. Help us do so. The people here trusted to keep your secrets. To hide you from whatever's following in your wake."

Aaron shook his head. "You've no idea what's out there beyond the fields. Over the hills. Forces aligned against the common good with every side of the board in play. By the same group of vainglorious men. Their sole intent is to *sow* discord, while people like you are busy sowing seeds. Raising families. Attending church. Sending your children to school."

He stood up, placing his hand on Meghan's shoulder. "I am the *hardened* edge of the blade. Of both the tool and the weapon. Myself, and many others like me, helping this country to survive, doing whatever's needed to *strike* back. Protecting those most deserving of a chance to make it their own."

Aaron stepped back. "And the only *sin* I've *yet* to commit, and one I shall avoid at *all* costs—is that of *complacency*. Believing myself out from under the death sentence of those I'm fighting against. Eager to see me and men *like* me removed from the game. With the constant risk of them bringing their evil *here*. To my *family*."

Sinclair turned toward her daughter. "He's right. Your brother. He's right in what he says. I've seen it *firsthand*. Your sister, too. The roots of it, the evil described, run deep. Requiring caution. Their removal—*carefully* done, lest it leaves pieces of root behind. Allowed to spread underground if left unchecked."

Meghan stood up, giving both of them an uncertain look before focusing on her mother. "You—*too?*" When Sinclair nodded, she stepped back, holding her hands up. "I *cannae* understand it. The *reason* for it. Unable to find the *sense* in it. In *any* of what you've told me." She paused, shaking her head. "Or *haven't* told me, in wanting to protect me from some *unnamed* threat. To myself. To my family. To everything we're—" She stared at her mother. "From everything *you're* doing, creating opportunities for all."

Meghan lowered her head, looking at the floor, the silence deafening. She took in a deep breath, then slowly released it between her full lips. When she looked up, her eyes were open. Her face wreathed in a soft smile. "I do so love ya', brother-o-mine. More than I have words enow to express it fully."

She came over and rose to her toes, kissing his cheek, her fingers running through his hair. "Go—head to the sound of the bugle's call, finding your salvation there. I'll pray for ya' *every* night. Loving ya' 'til the day I pass. Missing ya', until seeing ya' again." Then she turned around and walked away without looking back. Sliding open, then closing the large barn door, leaving mother and son staring at each other. Aaron sighed, his shoulders sagging, head lowered, as Sinclair stood up and touched his cheek.

"Go."

Aaron shook his head. "I'd stay if I could. You *know* that."

"Aye. I do. Your sister, too. With no doubt of our love for you, ever and always."

"I'll see you again." Aaron looked at her. "I'll see *all* my family again. Somewhere. Somehow. When I'm able to get clear of this."

"I know." Sinclair smiled. "I *believe* it. I *do*."

The door slid open and closed once more, leaving Aaron standing in the barn, the lantern flickering, the horse offering a soft whinny, seeking his attention. He walked over and stroked its neck, recalling the twisted journey he'd made since leaving Skye and Scotland behind. Leaving Chatte, and then Eliza behind.

He reached out and lowered the wick of the lantern until it died. Then went outside, stopping to give the farmhouse a long, searching look. Then he walked away, disappearing into the shadows of a nearby wood.

⅏ ⅏ ⅏

A thick-built man greeted Aaron as he approached a humped mound of growth, centering a small opening in a thick grove of fir trees. The short, thick-chested man held out his hand, a grin on his face. "Good to meet you're still in *one* piece." He straightened up, wincing, his hand on his lower back, rubbing at an old ache. Result of a musket ball that had partially numbed his spine after passing through a fellow soldier's body. Tearing through skin and muscle, leaving the vertebrae severely bruised.

"Image of your father, you are. Not like *my* sons, blessed with their mother's fair looks." He hesitated, then sighed. "A great patriot, your Da. Always there, speaking for the rights of the common man. Native people included."

"I assume with you speaking so openly, it means we're beyond the need for secrecy." Aaron looked around, taking in the surrounding woods. "Just the two of us?" He repressed a shiver of apprehension. Cautious, despite Smoke having told him where and when to meet. The veteran had shaken his head when asked why he wasn't coming along. "My part to play is in finding *capable* men. Guiding them to a place where others will measure them, seeing if they pass muster."

The sturdy-framed man nodded. "Aye. With myself to meet with ya' first, then guide ya' to the others." He shrugged. "Gives us a chance to speak of things the others need not know of. Nor ever will." He spat into his palm, then held it out. Aaron stared at it for a moment before taking it in his, sealing the offer of friendship.

"I have a jug—" The man angled his head, looking at two horses, their heads down, cropping at grass, leads tied off to limbs of an ancient elm tree. "In a bag tied to my saddle. Along with information to share, letting you get an idea of what we're offering you, and asking for in return." He stepped back, hand at his waist. "If'n ya' still of a mind to join forces. A paper in waiting at the end of our ride for your mark in red *ink*—not blood. Unlike those *pox*-ridden *bastards* on the other side of things."

Aaron nodded, following the man as he made his way across the uneven ground, noting his slight limp. The meeting with the old veteran marked the end of his former life. A new one, soon to begin. Once they were on their mounts, they worked through a series of narrow paths, coming out to a wet, muddy track through a large marsh threaded through with small islands of alder trees where the man pulled up.

"People. They're always going on about rights. Those of *every* man, as if there's only *one* type of people. Not allowing for the darkness lying beneath the surface of some men. Lurking like a catfish, ready to suck in whatever opportunity comes its way. Its whiskered maw unable to resist the temptation."

The older man laughed, a flask of potent liquor having loosened his mood. And tongue. "Like *Adam* himself, talked by Eve into a bite of the fruit. Leading all of us to a place left halfway between heaven and hell. With room enow for the Devil himself to come along, nudging people away from the righteous path."

Aaron glanced over. "A minister—your *original* vocation?"

The man twisted in his saddle, wincing as he took another pull from the thick-walled bottle before handing it over to Aaron. He wiped his lips. "*Nae.* A farmer. Standing in the mud. Watching shit from a mule falling out of its ass. Not worth a damn in helping to boost the soil." He sighed. "Then allowed opportunity to become a *captain.* Of a *fine* ship. Handed a bag of *gold* coins. More than enough to purchase a new life for me and my two sons."

"My father. The one providing the funds for your first purchase."

"He *told* ya'?"

"It was in his journals. Not the names of those involved, but the plan. One enabling him to get back to us. To his family, in the highlands."

"You have the right of it. A *fine* ship, matching her name. The 'Nee-wa." He smiled. "Unlike *any* of the ships in ports up and down the eastern seaboard." He squinted, the moon a half-sliver hanging in the sky. "He never told me the reason behind it. For the name given me to use."

"That of a native woman. One who saved his life then saved mine. Dying, a few years back. Killed by a Pennsylvanian militia. Responsible for the slaughter of nearly one hundred men, women, and children. A handful of them babes. Their hair taken, bodies burned, along with the rest." Aaron paused. He looked down, the reins in his hands tugged by the horse as it dropped its head, searching for grass alongside the muddy rut. "Myself, a witness to it. Asked to help get her children free. Which I did. Then spent a half-year hunting them down. Killing some of them that were involved. Starting with those leading the rest. Until I realized their lives weren't worth the effort. The ones I let go of left looking over their shoulders, wondering when justice would arrive."

"Heard something about that. About the killings. About the deaths of men. Arrows used. A tale told of some who took their own lives, haunted by their cowardly actions. Most of the stories heard in taverns hereabouts mentioned there was a measure of *justification* for the slaughter. Savages killing families in outlying areas. With their hair removed. *First.*"

"They aimed their wrath at the *wrong* target. Murdering a group of peaceful people. Natives, long converted to God. Carrying no weapons. No hate in their hearts. No involvement in what took place around them."

"Easy pickings, then. The hair bringing coins to those as done it." The man nodded, his mood dour, the effect of the drink worn off. "You did right by them. And might soon have an opportunity *again*. With the tools and men needed to see things through."

With the conversation at an end, both riders moved on. Silent as they reached a collection of lights in a small town, with the smoke from dozens of chimneys mixed with the ever-present scent of waste, human and animal, flavoring the early morning air.

$$\text{♼♼♼}$$

Angus looked up as the door to his room at a small inn swung open. A man he knew must be Lady Sinclair's son stood framed in the doorway, his head almost touching the top, with wide shoulders that filled the opening. He stayed in his seat, resisting the temptation to rise and greet him as a member of the family, knowing all there was to know of the boy who'd ridden down from a Scottish mountain, never to return.

He saw a small flicker in Aaron's eyes, gone between one heartbeat and the next. "Welcome to you. The prodigal son—returning to the fray."

Aaron closed the door with an elbow, taking a moment to study the oddly shaped man sitting behind a small desk. Thick-set, with a square jaw and wide-set eyes, his broad face edged with thin lines. He centered his thoughts and took a single step forward, his instincts telling him he was looking at a serious man.

"It seems you have the *advantage*." Aaron kept his voice low, soft-edged, poised like a wolf, facing a bear on a recent kill. "In knowing more of *me* than I know of *you*."

"I *am* a stranger, though well known to your family. Made part of clan Scott, over there." Angus tilted his head toward the eastern wall of his room. "Where your great uncle Shaun claimed it to be in the clan's best interest to take me in. Trusting me with the keys to—" He stopped, finding it difficult to let out a secret long held in trust, even to the grandnephew of Shaun, doted on since childhood.

"He gave me a chest. One filled with documents. A handful stained with blood. With descriptions of dangerous men, without names. Other papers with the names of men. *Known* men. Most with fancy titles. A collection of financial reports put together by *another's* hand. One with exacting penmanship. The information gathered *extremely* detailed."

Angus reached up and scratched his head. His reddish-brown hair, normally kept short, curling as it grew out. He straightened up, yawning, then gave Aaron a nod. "I read as much as I could find out about *each* one. Discovering they're in firm control of events on *both* sides of this—continual war. The one just ended, and the next, soon to arrive." He paused, raising his eyebrows as he shook his head. "Followed by another. And then—well, you get the gist of it."

"The descriptions of *nameless* men. Did they include the one who killed my father? And my grandfather before him—along with an aunt and uncle? Did they include those who came high, wanting to kill my entire family?"

Angus hardened his expression. "Yes."

"You, along with the man who brought me here, are working

against them. Against the efforts of those who paid them. Are *still* paying them. Men, responsible for my family's deaths."

"Yes. The one's *still* alive." Angus nodded, leaning forward, his hands on the desk. "A dozen or more gone missing. Those who headed into the highlands. With others having disappeared in the war. Information I've been able to gather pointing to *you* as the primary cause, with your subversive group doing considerable damage. Under *your* leadership."

Aaron stepped back and leaned against the door. He crossed his arms, eyes fixed on the other man's, who returned his gaze without blinking.

"Your name?"

"Angus."

"Are we *related?*"

"No."

"How then do you come to be—*here?*"

"In the right place. At the right time." Angus grinned. "The laird of your clan took me on high. A place offered me there. Measured by my wits and will. Your sister, Lady Marion—trusting me to protect her family."

"Yet you are not *there*, doing *that*."

Angus lowered his eyes, his thick lips pursed. When he finally looked up, his eyes revealed a softer edge. "I have been to this side of the ongoing effort *twice*. Once on the direct ask of Lady Marion. To deliver a message to your mother, Lady Sinclair. With the two of us, your mother and me—dealing with a threat."

Aaron waited, watching as the stocky young man stood up, stretched, then went over to a small window and stared into a darkening sky, his eyes fixed on the eastern horizon. Then he turned around, arms crossed. "I hesitate to continue. Not wanting to mar the image of your mother—as you *know* her to be."

"My mother is a woman, nae, a *person* in full. As was my Da. With shades of gray *in* them both. And occasionally—*between* them." Aaron stepped away from the door, finding a seat on the edge of the one bed, studying the strange man. "You're torn between your vow, given her. And the one you're looking for from me."

Angus nodded. "A narrow bridge. One not *easily* crossed." He extended his hand. "To a first step, made." Aaron leaned forward and took it, giving as firm a grip as received. Then he watched while the other man went over to the small desk and sat down, his eyes lowered. "We—your mother, and I—killed a man deserving of it. Poisoned him, then left him in—her bed. Made to look as if his heart had given out." He blushed, then looked away.

Aaron tightened his lips. "With others left assuming my mother to have been the likely *cause* of it?" Aaron shrugged when Angus refused to answer. "She would have had the right to a—*friendship*. My father tossed away his claim to her as a wife. Coming here, years ago. Returning to us, a man believed dead. In hiding. Aided in his attempt to rebalance the scales by the man who brought me here to *you*." Aaron shrugged. "The circle, drawn anew. With yourself wanting to enlist me in *your* group."

"Not to be *mine*." Angus nodded. "But *yours*. Information and monies provided, helping set you on the path." He glanced at the desk, a satchel lying on its top. "Enough in there to make a decent start. More in gather as we speak. Back in Glasgow."

Aaron pulled back, remaining silent, wondering if he still had the stomach, or will, for what the other man was asking from him. He sighed, feeling each of the years he'd spent trying to survive unspeakable violence. "How many men can you provide? Men with *experience*."

Angus shrugged. "Only one. So far." He walked over and opened the door. Aaron watched as it swung open, revealing a gangly man, his leathery face covered with scars from a fire, a full set of good teeth framing a wide smile. "Good to see ya', *Wolf*."

Aaron stood up and went over, placing his hand on the man's shoulder. "And you as well. *Smoke*."

CHAPTER TWENTY

HIGHLAND MANOR

WINTER, 1785

Declan stood in the shadows of a dock outside Glasgow, waiting for the harbor master to secure the ship carrying Angus, now returned from his second voyage to the colonies. Notified by a young boy on a windblown horse a day earlier that it had finally arrived. Marion insisting her husband head low and gather him in.

He watched as stevedores finished attaching the gangway, the first one down it a familiar shape. Squat in body with bowed legs, trudging with a confident stride between stacked crates, kegs, and heaped sacks of foodstuffs, a somber look on his weather-beaten face.

Declan lifted his hand to wave, then quickly lowered it, remembering the advice given him by the height-challenged member of his family. Eyes everywhere at all times. Watching. Reporting. Tracking the movements of anyone with a name or reputation, drawing the attention of men in dark clothing.

Their reunion came later, at an out-of-the-way house where Declan had left his horse and the mare belonging to Angus, the two animals placed in a small stable owned by an elderly couple. When they arrived to collect their mounts, the couple invited them inside with smiles of welcome and endless hugs for Angus.

After another round of long, embracing hugs, they departed, a bag of food tucked into each of their pockets. Once clear of the rolling lowland hills, Angus pulled up, waiting for Declan to come alongside. They were at the lower end of the Pinch, called the Squeeze, with barely a trickle of water coming through.

Angus gave Declan a questioning look, his eyebrows raised. The other man leaned back, tugging the reins, stopping his mount. The large-bodied stallion snorted, impatient to get back to its highland stable.

"One of *Marion's* ideas. A dam. In process of construction. Built to control the valley run-off during storms. Along with a mill, providing those lower down the valley with a site for grinding wheat. Saving them silver spent at mills outside the city, further below. The coins used for the purchase of other things."

"Seems more like an idea of *yours*." Angus's eyes narrowed, pinned to Declan's. "Focused on *others'* needs, outside those of the immediate family."

Declan looked away. "My *suggestion* of it. Yes. Her the one willing to *fund* it."

Angus let his next comment go unsaid. The nominal laird of the clan was kind-hearted, finding it difficult to do the things needed to further the interests and security of his people. Needing a well-tempered hand kept on his reins, guiding him through what promised to be troubled times. Irish Protestants, a majority of them Presbyterians, arriving each week by ship, disembarking through the Glasgow port. The city had swollen in numbers, with dozens of linen mills under construction. Built on riverbanks with flow and head enough to power the looms.

"You have a *keen* mind, laird Declan. Looking after your clan's financial needs. This valley is a decent place for mills or every kind." Angus noted the look Declan gave him, knowing his arrow had hit close to home. With a click of the tongue to his lovely mare, he started home, both their mounts picking up the pace, eager to get back to a familiar stable and stall.

⚉⚉⚉

Marion called out to Lorna, hearing her in the kitchen, the sound of a spoon in a mixing bowl filtering into the salon. She had her nose buried in reports, delivered every few days by young boys on horseback, using secret clan trails. Leaving for Glasgow at night, arriving at the manor two days later, slipping sealed messages through a slot in the manor door.

She resisted an urge to go look out the window, having expected Declan several hours ago, with Angus in hand. She frowned, considering it more likely to be Angus having Declan in hand, her husband a gentle soul, always willing to follow. Finding it difficult to lead.

Marion sighed, then felt a rumble in her stomach, the scent of scones from the kitchen stirring her appetite. With a tap of fingers on her swollen abdomen, a bairn within, soon to be born, she smiled. A boy, she told herself. A son. One she would raise to rule the highland reaches. Bow in hand. Looking to the mountains. Staying firmly in place, protecting clan Scott. Unlike his uncle, who supported the colonial cause, with a large bite taken of his highlander's soul.

The sound of hooves in the yard pulled her to the front door. She swung it open, one hand cradling her belly as she stepped down the wide, granite steps. Declan gave her a rueful grin as he dismounted, coming on the run.

"We stopped to check on progress at the dam. Angus with several ideas on how to maximize the flow once it's finished. A worthwhile investment of our time."

Marion nodded, extricating herself from her husband's arms, going to Angus, and greeting him warmly. "My family?"

"Your mother tells me they are of good health and *extremely* busy. With the settlement becoming a town. Allwyn, doing what he can to prevent the inhabitants from placing the title of mayor 'round his neck."

Angus heard a high-pitched squeal of delight, arriving a moment before Lorna landed in his arms. The reins to his mount let go of as he picked her up, swinging her in a full circle. "You've gone and *grown!* Despite my asking ya' to wait a *wee* bit longer. Holding off until I returned."

Lorna gave him a peck on his cheek, then reached up, rubbing it.

"And *you* have a *prickly* beard. One, I will shave, soon as you've had some of my scones, just now out of the oven." She took him by his hand, pulling him toward the back door, Angus glancing at Declan, who nodded, gathering the reins of his mare, handing them to Marion, with the two of them walking side by side toward the barn.

"He seems none the worse for his journey made." Marion squeezed Declan's hand. "Was his trip without issue?"

"As much as he told me of it, yes. Though I sense he's held some things back. Perhaps waiting to share them with you."

Marion nodded, with the stables reached. She stood back as Declan swung open the gates of two stalls, allowing the horses to enter. He gave the mare a small helping of oats, rewarding her for the work, then used a curry brush, working it along her neck and shoulders. His mount whinnied in protest, with Marion delivering him a feedbag, soothing the stallion's mood. She took a brush, following her husband's lead.

She raised her voice, piles of hay dampening the sound. "I sense there is more to his recent journey than he'll ever be willing or able to share. With you *or* me. Having to do with what Shaun left him, locked in a small chest, secreted away in his room in the manor."

"A chest? Left him by your great uncle?" Declan stopped grooming the mare, her nose swinging around, nudging his elbow. "What does it hold?"

Marion sniffed. "I've never asked. With no key offered *me* to open it with. Whatever it contains, or once contained, unknown." She sneezed, wiping her nose with the back of her forearm, another in build. "At least, to *me*." She sneezed again. "Angus—the one trusted with possession of it."

Declan handed his wife a handkerchief, neatly folded, pulled from a shirt pocket. He considered what she'd revealed, waiting until she finally sneezed a third time, wiping her nose, handing back the thin cloth.

"Would he share it with you? The information, if asked?"

Marion stared at him, then shook her head. "I—don't wish to find out. Enough on my plate, here, with the running of the manor. The grounds. And now the new mill, below. My days of stepping outside the boundaries of clan lands are over."

Declan shook his head, done with currying the mare. He came over, taking the brush from his wife's hand, intent on giving the stallion equal time. "Trusting whatever *he* decides to do. Angus. Trusting *him* to protect us from any harm ever coming our way. Again."

Marion gave him a puzzled look. "Don't *you?* The lad's proven more than capable of doing the work. The *hard-edged* work, coming with the responsibility of seeing to things, no matter the weight to one's conscience."

Declan frowned. "You diminish my role, wife, with your choice of words." He shortened the strokes of the brush, using more force than required, the stallion swinging its head, forcing him to step back. "Your feelings made *clear*. That I'm *weak*. Too soft—"

Marion closed the distance, removing the stiff-bristled brush from her husband's hand, and tossing it aside. She placed his palm on her belly. "Not *weak*, husband. *Compassionate*. And *caring*." She reached up and caressed the side of his face, draining away his anger. "And a far *better* parent to our girl. And will be to our *son*, moving just beneath your fingers. His mood growing mild beneath your gentle touch."

Marion moved closer, forcing her body against his until she felt his arms surround her. His nose pressed to her head, taking in a long draught of air, letting it out slowly. "I depend on you, husband mine. To help curb my baser tendencies. To temper my ire. Redirecting my mood when I'm angry."

She pulled away, far enough to look into his eyes. "Loving me—is your *greatest* gift. To me. Our children. Our people. All of us looking to you when in need. When in fear. Knowing you'll turn over heaven and earth to see to what's needed. The dam and mill, *your* idea. Our clan, fortunate indeed, having you as its laird."

"A *kind* man." Declan leaned in, touching his nose to hers, handing her the linen, another drip forming on its narrow end. "But not leader *of* it, in times of trouble."

"Nae. You're not." Marion used the square, dabbing her nose and the corners of her light-gray eyes. "But you *are* the man I love. And one Angus respects. As too, all the others. The three of us are enough,

together, to carry on the work of my great-uncle. To carry on the work
of my mother, seeing to the needs of our people, low or high. Looking
as far into the future as possible, preparing them for the changes lying
in wait. The world is an ever-changing place. With us doing our best to
stay balanced in it, from one day to the next."

Decan pressed his lips to hers, stopping the flow of her words. His
love for her, grown stronger each day. Aware she was right, that it
would take all their energy and as much luck as they could conjure up,
to guide them and their children, and everyone else through what
promised to be a turbulent sea change, hoping to reach a safe harbor.

Angus placed his dish in a large soapstone sink, using a ladle of water
to rinse it, with a scrub of lye soap before giving it another rinse. He
stacked it with the other plates, aware Marion was watching him.
Waiting to ask the first of dozens of questions. Many of them he would
be free to answer. Some of them met with a shake of his head, eliciting
a frown from her in return.

"Your messages brought, from my mother and sister both, a relief.
As I'm certain were mine, delivered to them by you."

Angus didn't bother to nod, waiting for the next question to fall
from Marion's lips. He could see they were trembling, her eyes locked
on his. He nodded. "Your brother is hale. I met him. Though he has
aged since leaving these hills."

"He is well—in *spirit?*" Marion had read the journals, with Angus
forced to explain to her the realities of men at war. Bending her mind
around the horror described. Forcing her to land on loving the man
her brother had once been, and not the one he'd had to become.
Accepting, if not understanding, the actions taken by him. By the
woman who'd shared his life.

"He—is."

"My mother sent word he'd married, with a son dying. Born too
early. Living in a community in the wilderness far beyond the Pennsylvania colony. A farmer and hunter, both. His wife, a woman of God.
With ties to converted natives, sharing the same belief."

"He is. Or rather, he *was*."

Marion opened her mouth to ask why, then stopped, Angus shaking his head, one hand raised. She leaned back, arms crossed above her abdomen, the babe stirring, sensing her unease as she stared at the man she trusted beyond all others, including Declan. He finally sighed, relenting just enough to satisfy her need to know.

"He's following a path he *needs* to walk. Leading him from one form of wilderness, into another. Desiring to keep his family—all that matters to him, to keep them safe until he can return to them."

"Like our father, before him. A second generation caught in the same snare." Marion looked down at her belly, feeling a foot moving within. "I fear for my own. In wondering if he too—"

Angus leaned forward, taking her hand in his. "I'll not allow that to happen. Not while I'm alive to see to it. Making certain that he remains *here*. Where he belongs." He stood up, leaving her to the heat of the kitchen, the stove mulling away as the coals died down.

Once she was alone, Marion went over to a large window, cracked open against the chill air. She closed it, latched it, then turned around and leaned against it, tears in her eyes. Her voice was soft, words left to float through the stew-scented air. "As my mother wished her son to do. Remaining here, a bonny lass in hand, with children soon at his heels. Running the hills. Bow in hand, leading all of us on *grand* adventures in highland hills, and the mountains beyond."

CHAPTER TWENTY-ONE
OHIO WILDERNESS
SPRING, 1786

Three men in weather-stained gray cloaks crept toward the light of a small campfire, focused on two men sitting with lowered heads, staring at a spit of meat roasting over a bed of glowing coals. The night air carried the rich scent of seared venison, causing the men's stomachs to rumble. Fresh food was difficult to come by due to lack of woodlore, leaving them living off dried meat and hardtack stashed in their packs.

Their journey into the wilderness of the western hills had proven to be a challenge to their limited skill set, left having to cross rivers in full flow, with the trails washed away. All of them bone weary, with strained expressions on their faces from their trek through rugged terrain.

The leader raised one hand, freezing the others in place as one of the two men stood up, staring into the night, hand on the butt of a pistol in his belt. After a long moment, he spat, then sat back down. A muffled comment from the other man caused him to laugh, then shake his head.

The mission assigned to the cloaked men by their leader had ordered them to seek a man their employers were eager to find. To take, then torture him for information. Eliminating him, his body made to disappear, with a checkmark placed beside his name. One he was born to, not the name given him by the group of insurgents he'd led during the war.

News of his whereabouts, provided by one of their spies, placed in an outermost settlement, had instigated the release of the team to his general location. And now they'd found him, along with a cohort, known to them as well. A whispered plan made to bring both men to account. The leader and his two men eased forward, slowly closing the gap.

Aaron leaned back, his eyes reflecting the light of the oversized fire. He looked up at the sky, thin clouds filtering the light of a half-full moon. "The crickets have gone silent. Our dark-cloaked friends disturbing their singing, no doubt."

Smoke shoved a thin stick into the coals, raising a swirl of embers, watching as they spiraled into the air. He grunted, then turned his head and spit. "The invitation given them, *bright* enough, with us doing all we can to make ourselves available, short of tying ourselves up, left sitting in the middle of the *damn* trail." He reached out and took the spit, setting it to one side, the meat cooked through. "Think they'll be time to eat before they make their move?"

Aaron listened as several men from his group of experienced outdoorsmen slid into position, prepared to spring a counter-ambush. The trap baited. The quarry in furtive approach. The next move left to the three foot-sore men to make. Far outside their normal environment, dangerously exposed.

� � �

Smoke poked one of the two infiltrators they'd captured in the shoulder with the tip of a long-bladed knife. The man's skin sizzled, a line of heat blisters growing in the firelight from the fire, brought back to life with a handful of dry wood. Added by Aaron after the removal of the metal spit, with the seared pieces of deer meat eagerly consumed by the members of his group.

The lanky, second in command pulled the steel blade away, reheating it in the coals. "A shame, the one leading you to your doom getting away. Leaving you and your friend behind to take on the full weight of our frustration. A real pity. Him the one we wished to have a —*pointed* conversation with."

The man refused to respond, his eyes fixed, staring straight ahead, hands tied behind his back. A low moan came from another man, lying on the ground beside him, his head bloodied, the result of a blow from one of Aaron's followers, preventing an attempt by the man to fire a pistol aimed in their leader's direction.

Aaron nodded to Smoke, the older man bringing the point of the heated blade out of the coals, touching it to the ear of the man lying on the ground. An agonized scream, deep-seated, rose to an unearthly shriek, penetrating the cloak of night. The man's shoulders arced back, his legs stiffened, heels drumming the ground in agony. The other man turned his head away, sickened by the odor of smoke coming from the tortured man's head. His ear burned halfway through, hair scorched, a cloud of smoke slowly drifting away.

"A tale told us if deemed *true*—will end his torment. Both of you promised a clean end. Your choice." Smoke placed the knife back in the coals. Several of the youngest men of their group, new to the game, stepped away, the sound of them retching in the shadows bringing a smile to the veteran's fire-scarred face.

"We *know* the group you belong to. Boys from the sewers and rat holes of cities throughout England, France, and the rest of the so-called *civilized* countries. Made part of a family, of sorts. Becoming men, trained to mark the faces of those moving from port to port. City to city. Following them between places of worship, politics, and financial houses. Tracking people of note, wherever they go. From pillar to post. Whorehouse—to the manor. Attending secretive meetings, held behind closed doors. No one escaping the eyes of men like you, lurking in every shadow."

The unmarked, nameless man, his teeth clamped tight, glared at the man kneeling next to the flames, reaching for the knife. His eyes tracked the movement of the glowing tip as it neared his face, hovering near his eye. He broke down as the heat blistered the skin on his upper cheek, aware his eye would be the target of the serious-faced man.

"I'll — I'll give you what you ask." He licked his lips. "A clean death — promised me."

Smoke nodded. "Agreed. And yes. You'll give me *everything* you know."

⍦⍦⍦

"They didn't suspect we allowed the one leading them here to get away." Smoke shook his head, giving Aaron a look of satisfaction. "As you predicted. Our best tracker on his heels, following the bee back to the hive."

"The one who *sent* him will be suspicious. His man's life, forfeit. With ourselves left with a finger on *one* strand of a small web." Aaron shrugged, then stretched. He'd watched Smoke give both men a quick death, their bodies buried with rocks rolled over the holes. "What they won't realize is we've little interest in gathering information from the spider in the middle of *this* spider nest."

He gave Smoke a dangerous smile, then raised his voice. "We're to dig out what we can from the man in charge, then burn it out. Eradicating it from under the foundation of *our* home. One we've sacrificed for. Bled and died for. Allowing others to build a decent future here."

The group of men dressed in drab clothing nodded their heads. They were eager to follow the marked trail left by the native, tracking the fleeing man. To learn the next phase of their leader's plan. One that would cause powerful men in countries around the world to sit up and take notice.

⍦⍦⍦

A small man with thin-rimmed glasses stared at one who looked as if Satan had sent him straight from hell. The leader of the group of men sent to locate his adversary stood in front of his desk, hands to his sides, his skin covered in deep scratches. His face scraped and badly bruised. Clothing rent, with bloody abrasions showing through the ragged openings.

"*My* mistake. In sending someone, not *of* the wilderness. Leading others, without the skills needed to complete the task." The small man leaned forward, small hands resting on the surface of the desk, his eyes appearing overly large behind thick lenses. "Not *your* burden to bear, my friend."

"It was *me*, sir, making the mistake. Wanting to—prove myself." The wretched figure of a man lowered his eyes, along with his voice. "I ask that you not blame yourself, sir. The fault is mine."

"Commendable attitude. Hallmark of a good leader. Willing to admit, then *learn* from the error of his ways." The thin man smiled, then reached up and removed his glasses. He fogged them with his breath, then wiped them clean with a small square of linen, pulled from a pocket of his jacket.

He set his glasses back in place above a thin, angular nose. "We are mere mortals. Men with feet of clay, and such. Mistakes—a part of the dangerous game we play." He paused, then pointed at a chair, sitting against the outside wall of his office, at an angle to the desk. Placed in front of a window, opened to the early morning air. The sound of doves in nearby trees called out as they greeted the sun.

Once the battered man complied, he nodded. "I have heard the gist of your story told. Of your travels there, and back. Of your verification that the man we are searching for, have *been* searching for, is still alive. Still *exists*. Real, and not some ghost from the shadows, releasing arrows with phenomenal skill. And speed."

A long pause followed. "I'm *most* encouraged by the news of this information. Balanced against the loss of your two men. Encouraged enough to consider making an *exception* to the rules. Allowing you to start anew, albeit from the bottom rung. From there, *another* ascension begun, based on your past success." Then he sighed. "But rules *are* rules, as they say. With *all* of us required to abide by them."

A strangled sound, followed by the drumming of heels on the wooden floor, vibrated the still air. Felt in the soles of the small man's feet beneath his desk. He stared at his fingers, focused on a fingernail with a slight discoloration of ink staining the skin beneath it. He placed it in his mouth, wetting it, then pulled the linen from his pocket once more, using it to wipe the stain away.

With a satisfied smile, he glanced over, watching as the body of the man who'd failed him was being pulled through the window. A garrote around his neck, eyes bulging, with a protruding tongue. Turned a light shade of blue, the color barely visible in the slant of rose-red light streaming into the small room.

A few minutes passed, the door swinging open as a large man with a thick beard and hooded eyes stepped through. He stood there, blocking the light as he removed thin leather gloves from a pair of immense hands. When he spoke, his words were the rumble of distant thunder.

"What do you want me to do with him? Left as a warning to the others — or disappeared?"

"Better if he's *never* seen again. As a *man*."

"Turned into pig shit, it is." The mountain-sized man spun about, quick on his feet, moving through the door, closing it without looking back. Once he was gone, the thin man pulled out a piece of parchment and began composing a message in code. Aware that the man he most wanted to see removed from the board had taken the bait, at the cost of three men's lives, sacrificed to bring him and his deadly group from out of their wilderness lair.

Aaron watched the movements of unnamed men in the small town below his hilltop perch. Made conspicuous by their lack of verbal contact with the local inhabitants. Coming from and going into a large warehouse with an attached office, sitting on the outermost edge of the town. A hive, with the drones in steady flight at all hours. Not one deviating to a small tavern and inn or make use of a stable or store. Living a sterile existence, meant to draw the eye and attention of someone like himself. A bright target, designed for him to focus his attention on. An obvious trap. One he would be more than happy to step directly into.

"Don't like it. *Any* of it." A hack and spit from Smoke drew a thin smile to Aaron's face. The veteran lay alongside him, his head turned to the side, giving him a questioning look. "We've tracked them *back* to their leader. He's all but begging for us to go down there and remove him and the others from the face of the earth."

"And — ?"

"And *what?*" Smoke's reply was a hiss of frustration.

"Okay. Then I'll rephrase the question." Aaron looked over. "*Why?*"

Smoke twisted his mouth, then cursed beneath his breath. "I don't *like* it when you make me try to reason things out. It hurts my *brain*."

"Proof — barely — that you *have* one."

Smoke narrowed his eyes, staring at the building, watching as a man entered, his shoulders near as wide as the door. "Fair enough." Then a grin tucked up the corners of his mouth. "A Judas goat." He sighed. "Inviting us in with a reverse trap laid. Wanting to snare us. To *end* us."

"*Me*. Not *us*. I'm the one they're after." Aaron nodded. "And it's me they'll soon have in hand. When I'm ready."

Smoke gave his younger friend a confused look. "*Why?*"

"To strike a greater blow. Helping us make a bold statement that this land is *not* theirs. We're the ones who *fought* for it. Bled for it. Hoping to build something a shade better than most of what civilization's spread around the globe. Since men started putting square corners on things."

Smoke cursed again. "*Fook* ya' education. Your words wasted on me. Along with *most* of the men with us." He rolled onto one side, removing his knife, keeping the blade at his side, angled away from the sun, crawling its way above the near horizon. "*This* is the measure of what most people understand." He held out the knife. "Whether it's the sharp or dull side pressed to their throats. Bringing death or life, depending on the *fookin'* whim of whoever's running the place. No matter what name's given him."

"Or *her*." Aaron watched as Smoke worked the idea through his rigid mindset with a clenched jaw.

"More *fookin* nonsense, no slight intended."

Aaron grinned. "None taken." Then he returned to his study of the scene below, watching the men moving back and forth. Actors, in their assigned roles, with one hidden from view. A dangerous player in the larger game, waiting for his opponent's next move.

CHAPTER TWENTY-TWO
CROSSROAD SETTLEMENT
SPRING, 1786

The settlement had grown over the past few months, edging up against the foothills lining the sides of the valley, filled with the sound of saws, hammers, and animals. Horses, large shouldered with straining legs harnessed to ropes threaded through pulleys, helped raise wood-beamed walls into place. Roadways, filled with rip-rap pulled from granite quarries, ran in veins of white-gray lines, carrying wagons loaded with lumber from mills located upstream on a decent run of water.

A communal effort, building on the foundation of monies loaned, then reinvested. Returning benefits to hundreds of people, earned with aching backs and hands. Citizens of a new world, with bright smiles on their weary faces.

Allwyn looked up, holding a hammer in one hand and a hardwood peg in the other. He inserted the tip into a drilled hole at one end of a hemlock beam, a crosspiece forming the frame of a new warehouse. Intended as storage for barrels of supplies, along with a hundred or more items vital to the needs of people, throughout the winter to come.

A stir of activity from below pulled his attention away, a crowd of people gathering together, shouts of joy flavoring the air. Allwyn bent to the task at hand, setting the first peg along with another, leaving the sawing off of the pointed ends on the back side for later. He climbed down, untying a rope from around his chest. Worn each time he climbed into the frameworks, honoring a promise sworn to his wife.

Sinclair, surrounded by children with outstretched arms, smiled, moving with difficulty through the throng of people welcoming her home. She'd been away in Scotland, drawn by news of another grandchild born. Going there to stake a grandmother's claim to the laddie, born with dark eyes and fair hair. A handsome mix of both parents' features, with more than a fair share of his uncle's.

Allwyn shouted, waving a hand, catching Sinclair's attention. "You're a *pleasant* surprise, with your ship not scheduled to arrive for three days, hence." He closed the distance. "Meghan is away, teaching settlement children in the hills. Not due back until the morrow." He paused, seeing the question in Sinclair's eyes. "The wee bairn, Lochlan, with a wet nurse. Back at the house. A fine boy, with strong lungs and clear eyes."

Sinclair let out a long sigh. "It seems I'm destined to be caught in between births of late." She disentangled herself from the crowd of well-wishers, making her way to Allwyn, and giving him a heartfelt embrace. "The wind was in our favor. Reaching the coast of New Scotia three days ahead of our schedule. With the southern run, as fair." She kissed him on his sun-bronzed cheek. "My other grandson — is *he* here?"

Before Allwyn could answer, a youthful voice called out, closely followed by a gangly body attached to a set of long legs and arms. Patrick ran up and enveloped his grandmother in a hug that threatened to squeeze the air from her lungs.

Sinclair kissed her grandson on the top of his head, now reaching a level with her chin. "You've grown so *tall*. Sprouting up *much* too fast, Patty. Too fast by *half*."

The boy released her, then stepped back. "My cousin, Lorna? Has she grown as much as me?" He hesitated. "As much as *I*."

Sinclair smiled. "You can see for yourself. She's back at the farm, out with the horses in the stables. Said she'd wait for you there. With a gift in hand."

Allwyn opened his mouth, about to ask Patrick to take the team of draft horses back with him, the animals in need of water and feed. The young boy raced away before he could form the words. He shook his head, going over and untying the work-worn beasts, leading them back to where Sinclair stood.

Allwyn gazed at her, noting signs of age, revealed in the color of her hair, with silver threads threaded among the dark. Her eyes, with small wrinkles at the corners. Still as beautiful to his eyes as ever, her stance proud, cleft chin outthrust. He delivered a kiss on the back of her hand.

"You're truly a vision, my lady. Welcomed back home, deservedly so, by those who've benefited from all you've provided them."

"Sweet words, Allwyn. But money left stacked in a chest or bundled in a purse is of *little* value. It's what's done with it that matters most. And—" Sinclair swung her head, taking in the expansive works of the community stretching from the hills to the edge of a small river. "You have made the most of *each* coin."

"*We* have. My lady. Your daughter, the engineer of your own ambitions. With myself, along with the labors of many others, only tools placed in her capable hands." He began the walk back to the farmhouse, using the new roadway, a layer of packed gravel topping the fractured granite stones beneath.

Once they arrived at the crossroads, the sight of two children on horseback greeted them. Patrick, with a new longbow strung and placed about his shoulder, a sheath of arrows in hand, using them to urge his mount on. Lorna, lying with her head stretched out alongside the neck of a slim mare, coaxing it to a greater effort as they approached a fence lining the far end of the field.

One the mare cleared with a leap of hooves, the sound of Lorna's laughter trailing behind. With the race over, Patrick pulled up, knowing better than to break the rules, with his mother forbidding the leaping of fences. Until he could convince her to relent for having fallen from the saddle, bruising his ribs, causing her several nights of nervous pacing until the raps of his ragged breathing eased.

"She's a *magnificent* rider." Allwyn glanced at Sinclair, having left it to her, as to remonstrations made concerning Lorna's actions. Pleased to see his niece was capable. Certain of herself. Confident in her abilities, and those of the mare.

"I taught her. But only the fundamentals. The rest—well, she has a way with animals. As you can see."

The mare made another leap, easily clearing the top rail, landing with a smooth transition to a gallop, its mane, and tail flowing in the wind, along with the bright sun-kissed hair of its rider. Lorna made a wide turn, coming to a sliding stop in front of her uncle and grandmother, her face beaming with pride.

She dismounted with a leap, reins in her hand. *"Uncle!* So good to *see* you." Patrick came over, taking the reins so Lorna could hug his father. He led the horses away, stopping when his cousin called out, asking him to wait. She kissed Allwyn on his cheek, then ran to Patrick, the two of them heading toward the barn. The horses exchanged gentle touches of their noses as they followed along behind.

※ ※ ※

Meghan dropped the pack on the counter of the kitchen, her lower back aching, eyes heavy with fatigue. She'd given lessons to the outlying settlement, the students infused with excitement. Eager to work out the magic of letters, turning them into words, used to paint pictures in their minds.

The call to assist in a difficult birth had interrupted her last class, leaving her spending the entire afternoon trying, and finally succeeding, in getting the stubborn babe turned around. Everything had worked out, leaving her satisfied, though late for the long ride home. Two men and a young boy had escorted her there. Giving her their thanks, then turning about, heading back into the hills despite her invitation that they stay the night.

Meghan poured a glass of water and brought it to her lips, then stopped, staring at a familiar pack. Her eyes widened, realizing her mother had arrived. A call of joy rang out, bringing the others in a rush down the narrow stairs, having waited up there to surprise her. After things settled down with an exchange of hugs, tears, and stories told of things on both sides of the big briny, Sinclair took her daughter in hand, stepping outside the house into the light of a crescent moon.

"Has there been any news?"

Meghan knew what her mother was seeking. "None. Not even rumors."

Sinclair squeezed her hand, a sigh slipping free from lips parted in a sad smile. "He's alive. I *know* it. Feeling it in *here*." Her fingers brushed the line of her abdomen, thicker in girth as age made its claim. "Can still feel the tug of the cord tied to him."

Meghan was silent, holding her thoughts close. A dream had come to her a week earlier. Of her brother in dark clothing. With a defiant smile on his face. Blood on his hands. Death, whether his or another's, stalking the edges of her dreams since then. "You'll—see him again."

Sinclair turned, giving her daughter an open-eyed look. "You see it true? Another *vision*?"

"No. Not a *true* vision. But I ken he will find you again. I know it. In here." Meghan touched a finger to her breast, then nodded, a serious look firming the line of her full lips. The moment now at hand, with the two of them alone. "We need to discuss—*things*. Of interest to us both."

"You're not with child again, are you? So *close* together?"

"Nae. I'm not. Though the women I work with are always in my ear, determined to see me so." She paused. "I'm curious as to the reason for your return, so—soon. Had thought you intended to stay the summer on high." Meghan measured her mother's face carefully. Hesitant to pry, aware there were secrets between them, still and ever. "Though your return *is* a pleasant surprise to our family. As well as those of the entire valley community."

"I came in *pressing* need to help someone to deliver a message." Sinclair lowered her eyes. "Escorted here, as part of an effort to deflect attention from me. By a young highlander." She looked up, seeing her daughter's interest written on her face. "A young boy with a *good* mind. Trusted to do whatever was needed of him, without question. Finding me here, with his errand finished."

"My sister—the one behind it?" Meghan waited until her mother nodded, then shrugged. "Had *thought* there was something in the wind.

Word brought me you were in residence at the same manor we visited on our *first* trip here. Or rather, there—in the outskirts of the city."

"Word? Brought you?" Sinclair stared at her daughter, who returned a quiet look, her lips pressed into a thin line. She sighed, shaking her head. "You're of the *same* blood your father was. Able to see beyond the horizon, ever watchful." Then she shrugged, eyes narrowed in thought. "Your messenger—is a worker in the household, no doubt. Their secrets purchased."

"Willingly *exchanged*." Meghan's eyes beamed with a look of pride. "A home provided to her *here*, with support for a desire to improve her lot in life. Leading to the need for more homes as lads continue to arrive, hats in hand, looking for work. Introduced into the mix, a traveling minister performing the marriages, with children following close behind."

"Wise. *Beyond* your years." Sinclair nodded. "Beyond what I'm prepared to accept, with both daughters having surpassed their mother. Time slipping away, leaving me behind. Same as it was with your dear departed grandmother."

"Nae, Mother. You're *still* Lady Sinclair. Founder of everything we've accomplished. Here, and in *every* major city in England. And Scotland. *Thousands* have benefited from your vision. Nothing I've done, or might yet do, in compare." Meghan nodded. "And I'm *good* with that. Truly. Enough that I'm known as a daughter to ya'. As a sister to my sister, much closer to you in what she's done in carrying your vision into the next generation. And those beyond."

Sinclair took Meghan's hand, holding it to her breast. "I would have the two of you together again if it were possible to draw the hills o'er there to *here*."

"Marion—*requires* the distance. Hard as it is on you. And *I'm* wed to the land we've tilled. *Here* is where we belong. With our children born, then raised *here*." She paused, thinking about her brother, and how much he was missing from his family's lives. "Where my husband and I will one day die, adding our dust to that of all the rest. Natives and colonists, both."

"But not *this* day, or the *next*." Sinclair took her daughter into a warm embrace, drinking in the scent of her hair. "Not for as long as I have left. The good lord protecting me from *that* misery. Every parent's nightmare."

Meghan nodded, her eyes widening at the thought of losing her children. Or her mother. Tears in her eyes as she thought of losing Allwyn. Or Marion. Or any of those she loved. Especially Aaron. Out there, somewhere. Caught between the end of one war and the next.

A young man waited in the shadows of trees behind a line of privies. The night was dark, beneath thick clouds. His eyes, adjusted to the darkness, tracked a steady flow of men coming and going to relieve themselves. Their business quickly accomplished, then a razor-straight return to a nearby tavern. Lanterns inside the bustling interior painted the ground with a yellow wash of light as they went inside, fading to black as the large door swung closed behind.

A hand on his shoulder robbed him of several years of his young life, leaving his stomach wedged in his throat. He swallowed, forcing it back into place, then turned around. Hoping for a greeting. In fear of a blade.

"You the lad, sent by my friend on high."

He nodded, daring to breathe once more, about to form a reply. Stopped by a finger pressed to his lips, followed by a hand on his back, moving him away. They slipped into the middle of a grove of fir trees, the needled ground and drooping branches absorbing the sound of their voices.

"Him. The one sent me to you. Said to give you this." The messenger held out a leather satchel, with a twist of leather in a thick knot securing it. Tied in an intricate pattern around a metal stud protruding from the inner surface.

Aaron worked the knots loose, each one tied in a unique sequence of loops. Difficult to recreate, with a single strand of hair, plucked from his sister Marion's head to seal the flap, the ends held in place by a thin smear of wax. He felt a surge of love flow through him, then suppressed the emotion with a shrug of his shoulders. He felt the boy's eyes on him.

"Yes?"

"I'm sorry. I mean, for staring. In my knowing who you are." The young man stammered. "Was told by him, the one sent me, not to do that."

"It's not an issue for *me*. As long as it remains a *secret* between us." Aaron opened the flap, the scent of mountain heather wafting from inside. He smiled, knowing his sister was sending a message of her own. One he would dearly love to reply to in person. Knowing, from a vision years ago, that if he were ever again to touch Scottish soil, it would be from inside a wooden box.

"I'm to leave?" The boy swallowed, his voice tight with fear.

"Yes. That being the *wiser* choice."

"Any message in return?"

"No."

The young man nodded, then turned to go, stopping as a large shape materialized from out of the shadows. His heart leaped into his throat, hands clenched at his side, not daring to breathe again until the shape slipped past. A whispered conversation ensued, ending quickly.

"You're to come with us. *Now*." The first man took him by the upper arm and guided him uphill, moving without hesitation, as if it were daylight. "You've been followed."

The messenger, sent by Angus, shivered despite the cloak of balmy air, having done all he could to remain out of sight. Moving at dusk through to dawn, staying close to the edge of the woods. Maintaining secrecy, following the order given to him by the man who was second to the laird. A short man, with a clan-wide reputation as someone you should never cross or disappoint. "I'm *sorry*. I tried my best not to—"

"You did a *bonny* job. Exactly as *expected* of you. No worries." Aaron ducked into a small shelter, holding the oiled flap open, inviting the lad inside. Once they settled in, he offered his hand. "Thank you. For bringing the messages. The information is vital to our efforts."

"Will I be—can I go *back?* Someone is there, waiting for me to return."

"No doubt a lady of note. One with raven hair."

The boy hesitated. "The one mentioned *is* a lady. But with hair more the color of silver than black."

Aaron nodded, a thin smile on his lips. "Best to keep that observation between the two of us." He paused, another pang of loneliness finding him, allowed to linger for a moment before letting go, knowing how easy it would be to give in to its call to go to her. "She is in —*good* health?"

"Aye. Right as rain on heather. She said to give you this—if I were to see ya'." The young man held out a letter, blank on the outside, with a hint of floral scent. One he'd held to his nose several times a day as he'd made his way to the point of its delivery. Lying in the woods during the day, waiting for dusk, imagining such a letter given to him by a feisty young lass. One with gold and red hair, back at the highland manor.

Aaron took it from him and placed it in his pocket, saving it for another time. Silence fell in around the two of them until the sound of men moving about outside the shelter drew their attention.

Smoke stuck his head inside. He gave the messenger a curt nod, then grinned at Aaron, his voice as thin as the shadows on the fabric walls. "We're clear. They sent out a patrol. Off following the false trail laid out. Just as you said they would." Then he gave the boy a hard look.

Aaron held out his hand, taking the boys and shaking it, then letting go and motioning toward the opening. The youthful messenger rolled to his knees, his head bowed as he passed beneath the flap held open by the other man. A hand on his shoulder, from a wide-bodied man waiting outside, guiding him away. Smoke waited until they moved away, then joined Aaron inside the shelter. "He seems *solid* enough, for one so young."

Aaron nodded, lighting a small candle with a flash of sparks from a flint. "Got here in one piece. Delivered the papers. Our Scottish friend, the one sending him our way—*knowing* his people. Trusting them to do what's asked of 'em."

Smoke was quiet, though Aaron could read the thoughts behind his silence. He sighed, then leaned forward, giving the old veteran a searching look. The other man shrugged, his eyes reflecting the light of the candle. "How much *longer* are we to be here? Close to the hornet's nest, without a lit torch in hand, burning it out of existence?"

"It's one of *many* others. A dozen or more, scattered throughout the colonies." Aaron straightened up, running a hand through his hair, scratching at an itch. The thin, moss-stuffed bedding he'd been sleeping on needed a dose of bright sunlight, followed by a scrub of lye soap. Or tossed in a fire, left behind when they decamped. "The one I'm after is aware we're out here. Somewhere. Knowing *we* know it's a trap he's set on the ground, down below. Each of us poised on opposite sides of the board, waiting for the other to make the next move."

Smoke shook his head. "*That's* your answer?"

"No. Only an explanation." Aaron hesitated. "The answer is one you will *not* like."

Smoke stared, his eyes fixed on his leader's. "It's not another lesson taught me, having to do with them little pieces? With one of them small pieces offered as a sacrifice?"

Aaron shook his head. "No."

Smoke lowered his head, a frown on his lips. "It's *yourself*, then. The *King*."

"Nae. Not the king." Aaron paused. "The *Queen*."

Smoke cursed, the sound absorbed by the oiled cloth of the shelter. He clenched his jaw, giving Aaron a hard stare. "And I'll not be able to convince you otherwise?" Aaron shook his head, eliciting another curse from Smoke. "Why not deal with these men *here*? *Now*. We've got the numbers. More than enough to do it, causing a real setback for *their* side."

"A cup of water removed, against a rising tide."

"*Fook all!* Your words *twisted*. Not *clever* at all. Not to *my* ear."

"We've got to give them *something*. A large enough bite to satisfy their appetite. The meal I'm offering intended to engorge their bellies, making them sleepy-eyed. Careless. Thinking they've struck a blow. Unaware of what's coming next."

"With you maimed. Or dead."

Aaron shrugged. "Perhaps. Though I believe the results will fall well short of *that*." He paused, pursing his lips. "A period of forced negotiation, at most, with an offer made. A false feint, meant to turn my flank. Though the one in charge—is too smart to think I'd fall for such as that. I expect he'll play it straight instead, offering me a way out, hoping I'll turn. That I'll end up leading his people to *our* leaders."

"And *then* what—when you refuse to give them up? You left tortured, minus a few choice pieces?" Smoke looked away, unable to face the prospect of losing his friend. "If'n ya' no longer capable or willing to lead us, then *leave*. Go back to Scotland. Or the town your family's building over here. *We'll* carry on the fight. Not as *you* would. But doing our best to strike blows when and where we can, as we can. Until we're placed face up in the dirt."

Aaron shook his head. "We need to do this *now*. And *I* need to be the one doing it. In coordination with events that are soon to happen on the *other* side of the line." Aaron held up the package of information delivered by the messenger, sent by Angus. "It needs to be *me*, the one used as bait. Knowing enough secrets to avoid the *worst* of it. Keeping things in play until you come along with the others, setting everything right with the world again."

Smoke sighed, his eyes gleaming as he stared at Aaron. "Then ya' need to tell it to me, true. *All* of it. Every *part* and *parcel* of your plan. Convince me it's a *braw* one, laddie. That I can let you go with a clean conscience, knowing there's no other way to get *to* it and *through* it. With you still breathing, when all's said and done."

The small man, his name unknown to the others, having signed his true identity away in red when invited to join the game, looked up. A looming figure filled the door of his room at the inn where he was staying. He frowned, a sheaf of papers in his small hands, glasses perched on the end of his nose.

"Yes?"

"We found him." The man stood as if a tree, rooted in place. Unmoving. Making the room seem smaller by his massive presence.

"Where?"

"Above. The boy followed. Left untouched, as you ordered. Let to get on about his business."

"The false patrols?"

"Sent out where you told me to send 'em to. Where you pointed to, on the map."

The thin man considered for a moment, running through every variation of the plan he'd put in place over the past few weeks. Creating an exquisite symphony of strategic movements and counter-movements. Seeking the least hint of a sour note, aware of how easily the man he was after could turn the table, leaving him empty-handed, facing the dire consequences of failure.

With a satisfied nod, he dismissed the large man with a wave of one finger. Then he picked up a message he'd prepared for the cabal. His hands trembling as he held it, trying to resist counting the coins about to fall into his lap. Along with a title of nobility, purchased on his behalf. A reward for having finally found the one they'd been hunting for years. A deadly ghost, like his father before him. One he'd soon bring to heel.

A small bird hit the window, leaving a knot of feathers stuck to the thick glass. He went over and opened it, staring down at the puddled shape of a small wren. Unmoving, with a broken neck. He pursed his lips, wondering if it was an omen. Then he smiled, closed the window, and returned to his desk. Confident his quarry was about to step into an ingenious trap, with his foot on the pan, causing the jaws to snap shut.

"It's a *shit* plan." The large, heavily bearded man stared at his employer, his dark eyes glowing, deep voice thick with anger. "I'll have *no* part of it." He turned away, stopping when he heard the thump of a leather bag on the floor behind him. He turned around, looking down.

The unnamed man gave him a quiet look as he removed his glasses, cleaning them with a small cloth. "Understood. Your reluctance to perform the role, as directed." Then he nodded at the bag. "An additional payment—for your *continued* service."

The mountain of a man shook his head. "Not much good, silver in hand to a man with a *slit* throat."

"*Gold*. Not silver." The small man sniffed, replacing his glasses. "And you'll suffer nothing worse than a headache."

The large man tried to look away, failing. The scent of wealth, far beyond his expectation, held him rooted in place. He nodded, then bent over and collected the money, leaving without another word.

The small man smiled, allowing himself the rare pleasure of a sip from a pewter flask. His plan was working to perfection, with a slight risk assigned to the man he'd paid to do his part. The moment close to hand when everything would come together. Then he returned to his scheming, focusing his attention on a myriad of potential outcomes. Anticipating his wily opponent's next move.

Aaron stood outside the shelter, staring into the woods, feeling a familiar itch crawl along his spine. One impossible to scratch away. It reached his shoulders, then spread down his arms, into his hands, causing them to clench. He took several deep breaths, forcing himself to relax. The moment at hand when he and his men would begin the first move in what might prove to be his last effort at striking a telling blow.

Smoke came up from behind and leaned in, his voice low. "We're ready." Aaron nodded, then stepped aside to allow his men to head to the settlement and take up their assigned positions. His second in command whistled, a signal to three men passing by their leader to stop and toss a thick blanket over his head. Using leather straps around his shoulders, arms, and legs, preventing him from freeing himself.

The men ignored Aaron's muffled shouts of anger as they carried his thrashing body to the trunk of a hardwood tree. They sat him down between its large roots, helping hold him upright. Two of the younger men kneeled to either side, the fire-scarred veteran having given them strict orders not to release his friend until the others returned.

Smoke nodded to the rest of the hard-eyed group of veterans, the original plan still in play. Albeit with a change of who it would be, entering the lion's den. The risk falling to him. Aware of a sea of pain might lie in store. One he'd gladly wade into, allowing his long-time partner to live.

The large man stood outside the small office building, keeping watch. His senses were in a heightened state of awareness as he pried apart the night, trying to discern movement in the trees across a narrow road. He swallowed his impatience, his role to draw the first move. Told it would not be an arrow or blade, but a blow to the head used to disable him. Not fatal. A necessary inducement, intended to bring their wary quarry fully into the reverse trap. He frowned, trying to spit, his mouth gone dry, then focused on slowing his breathing, feeling the adrenaline subside as he contemplated how he would spend his money.

"A fine evening. Don't you think?" A prod of something hard against his spine caught him off guard, his reaction one of genuine surprise, followed by inky darkness as a blow to the side of his head felled him. Smoke looked down, measuring the man's size with a shake of his head. Then he turned to the four men selected to join him, willing to risk all to accomplish what their young leader had planned. Volunteering to trade their lives, against his own. "Gather him up. Bring him in behind me." Then he turned around and walked over to the door of a small building. He hesitated a moment, then opened it.

The small man, sitting behind his desk, looked up, his eyes going wide, frozen in his seat, as he watched a group of strangers pour through the opening. The first man walked over and stopped across from him, with four others close behind, holding the thick arms and legs of the man left outside on watch. They dropped him in one corner of the room, two of them standing over him with pistols aimed. The other two fanning out on either side of the desk.

"Can I *help* you?" The seated man reached up, sliding his glasses back in place, squinting in the light from two small lanterns hanging on the walls of the small room. Smoke leaned down, his hands on the top of the desk.

"We have words to exchange, you and I. Enough to determine what's coming *next*."

"Sounds—somewhat *ominous*." The man leaned back. "Are you certain you have the right place? The right *person?*"

Smoke smiled as he toed a chair, sliding it into place and sitting down. He crossed his hands behind his neck, giving the other man a long, penetrating look. "You're the one described to me. In every detail." He shrugged, turning to look at the man lying in the corner. "Your man left alive. For now. Not made to pay with his life for associating with people like you."

The small man nodded, slowly. "A fortunate break for him. With myself left trembling in fear. And *confusion*."

"You've been hunting me. You and your group. Sending men into the wilds, where we buried them." Smoke paused. "I've come here to find out what your offer is. Willing to hear you out before deciding what happens next."

"The lives of your men, spared. With a negotiation between us, to determine *your* future." The small man leaned forward, hands clasped together, resting on the desk. "A position of influence and wealth offered you, balanced against a—*hard* end if you refuse." As he waited for a response, he reached up and removed his glasses, holding them with one hand, pulling out a linen cloth, and polishing them.

Smoke glanced over at the large man, lying still as death. He smiled as he swung his head around, pinning the man seated across from him with a firm look. "I'll offer *you* the *same* opportunity. Tell me everything *I* want to know or suffer the pains of the Devil himself. With me holding information about your group in here." He pointed at the side of his head. "Enough to pin your words to your forehead, if'n ya' try to tell me any lies."

The diminutive man replaced his glasses, then pointed at the window, left open to the air. Several men with muskets leveled moved into view, the barrels poking through. Then the door swung open, with several more men stepping inside, pistols in their hands, fully cocked. "Your weapons. Placed on the floor."

One of Smoke's men lifted his pistol, stopped by a small motion of the veteran's hand. "*Easy*, gentlemen." He gave the grinning man across from him a look. "What guarantee offered, *if* we are to comply?"

"The fact you and your men are *still* alive should suffice." The man raised his hand, motioning toward the door. "Your men are free to leave. It's *you* I want."

Smoke nodded. "Go, lads. No need for everyone to pay for *my* decision. Poorly made."

The room quickly emptied. The large man on the floor left behind, shaking his head, moaning as he regained his wits. Smoke listened for sounds of a struggle outside, his eyebrows raised when a murmur of voices bounced back and forth, followed by footsteps, heading off in opposite directions.

"It would seem you're an—honorable man. Of a *sort*."

The small man smiled. "And yourself? Is *your* word good?"

Smoke sighed, then leaned back. "Depends on the situation. And who it is I'm dealing with."

"You spoke of having information. Does it include knowledge of *me?* Are you aware of *who* I am, and why I'm here in this god-forsaken wilderness?"

"You're a *cog*. In the works. Helping to spin the wheel, churning out profits made off the flesh, blood, and bones of men on every side. Good men—and bad."

"And what about you? Known to have been involved with the torture of soldiers in red coats?" The small man pursed his lips, brushing them with the tip of one finger as he considered his adversary. Older than his reported age. His face lined. Eyes, the correct color, with a build close to the description given by a handful of men who had some knowledge of the man known as the Wolf. "Are you not also a mix of the good, along with the bad?"

Smoke smiled, eyes tight with anger. "As are *most* men, having to deal with the chaos promoted by those *you're* associated with."

A moan sounded, along with a rustle of cloth on wood, the large man sitting up, rubbing his head, his fingers coming away wet with blood.

"True. As it has *always* been." The small man opened the drawer of the desk and picked up a small bell, ringing it. Several men came back through the door. "One of you see to him." He nodded toward the large man with glazed eyes, still staring at his fingers. "The rest of you will escort our guest to where we might continue our conversation in a more *suitable* environ."

The men looked at one another, confused. The small man sighed, rubbing his temples in frustration. "Take him to the warehouse. *Now!*"

"They seemed prepared to have a meeting of—minds." A short man, second to Smoke, had led the rest of the men back to their campsite. He gave Aaron a curt nod. "Which is what he—what Smoke said it would be. With us ordered here once it took place." The man shrugged, his face pinched in confusion. "They had the drop on us. Then let us go, with our weapons left behind. Just like Smoke said, in telling us of your plan."

Aaron, released from the blanket, stood up, the press of men standing back, with nervous expressions. He gave them a slow nod. "*His* idea to remove me from it. From *my* plan. One I shared with him, then shared with you."

The leader of the men nodded, several of the older veterans lowering their eyes, refusing to meet Aaron's gaze, aware of what Smoke had done to preserve the life of his friend. The younger men, with less experience, left milling about with confused expressions.

Aaron shook his head. "Our misguided friend has subverted my plan. With no blame assigned to anyone *but* him. His actions, taken against my wishes, intended to protect me." He fixed each of the co-conspirators with a hard look. "A *mistake* on his part. One he'll end up paying dearly for. Unable to provide answers to what's asked of him. Unable to prove he's *me* and not an imposter."

Aaron reached out to one of the younger men, left behind to guard him. The man handed him his weapons with a shame-faced expression on his face. Once rearmed, Aaron looked at the others. "We'll return to the settlement and punish those holding him. Retrieve our friend. Bring him back." He moved off, the others falling in behind, his voice a faint whisper in the evening breeze, too low for the others to hear. "Then bury what's *left* of him."

☡☡☡

The pain was a thick wet blanket, wrapped around Smoke's body in a tight compress, squeezing the air from his lungs. Unable to draw in a full breath as waves of agony emptied them. Words, unbidden, falling from bloody lips in broken sentences. Saying anything, everything, trying to stop the pain. Beyond the ability of flesh and bone to bear up to. Darkness, falling, bringing a merciful end to the torment.

"He's passed out. *Again.*" The small man stepped back, a heated blade in his hand. He removed his glasses, the lenses fogged on the inside, the outer surface covered by speckles of blood. One of his men handed him a clean square of cloth, which he used to wipe them clean. "Bring water. Drawn from the spring. *Go!*"

Two of the men spun away, racing to a small doorway at one end of the building. Several of the younger men watched them go. Following them with their eyes, wishing for a release into the night air, the scent of shit, urine, and blood overpowering. The rest of the men, hardened by years of exposure to violence delivered by the edge of honed blades, remained stoic-faced, their fingers touching purses tied to their belts.

Smoke hung from the end of a thick rope, his wrists bound to it with thin strips of leather. His toes were barely touching the dirt floor, leaving thin lines drawn on its surface where he'd tried to escape the damage done to him. Unconscious for the moment, a reprieve granted him by a mind driven beyond its limitations.

The small man came over, lifting one of his victim's eyebrows, revealing a blue eye. He pressed a finger against the man's neck, monitoring his pulse. Weak and uneven, the blood-soaked cloth of the man's tattered shirt barely moving, his breathing labored. Enough strength left, he told himself, to begin the next phase. One that would leave the man whittled into pieces. Beyond the ability of his body to repair. Death preferred over life as a cripple. The black void waiting to bring an end to his pain. Eventually. But not yet.

He sighed, having realized early on his victim was not the one he'd been searching for. His carefully designed plan lay in ruins, starting with the sacrifice of the three men he'd sent to bait the trap. Two of them, missing. One returning. Proof his quarry knew someone was on his trail. Resulting in a false representative hanging from the rope, protecting the one he'd planned to have met with. Trying to convince him to alter his path. Or die.

A door to the building swung open. Two men entered with buckets in their hands. The small man stepped back, making room for them to come over and soak down the comatose man. His narrow jaw dropped as he watched them pull a brace of pistols out. The buckets let fall to the ground as a flow of men in dark clothing rushed into the warehouse.

A flurry of shots rang out, echoed by the shrieks of pain from men spinning to the ground. Others stumbled back, their arms raised as war clubs struck their heads and shoulders, used by the intruders to significant effect, bringing a quick end to hostilities. The small man's men dead or dying. Their assailants left bruised, with several bleeding, but still alive, staring at him with murderous looks.

Aaron came over, knife in hand, his club tossed aside as he cut Smoke down. He lowered him to the floor, placing him atop a cloak spread out by a burly man kneeling beside him. They ignored the small man who was still holding his paring knife, its blade stained with blood. Focused on Smoke, studying his wounds, wondering what they could do to ease his pain.

Aaron cradled his friend's head. "Water." One of the younger men grabbed a bucket and ran outside, bringing it back half-filled. Aaron used it to wash the blood from his friend's face, a flicker of an eyelid giving him hope, lifting of its own accord.

Smoke's lips parted, the skin peeled, his front teeth missing. "Told —him—enough." A wet gurgle of bloody phlegm pulsed from the man's damaged mouth. Aaron wiped it away with a finger, tears in his eyes, blurring his vision. "To—make him—you. Think—" Then his eyes rolled back, showing white.

Aaron leaned down and listened to the sigh of his friend's final breath as his resolute heart came to a stop. Men gathered around, one of them taking the knife from the small man's hand, forcing him down to the blood-splattered ground. The others placed their hands on Aaron's shoulder, then stepped aside. Going to check on friends with wounds of their own.

Aaron stared at Smoke's cloaked body, arms and legs strapped, lashed to the back of a small horse. He touched the material, bidding goodbye to a warrior who'd sacrificed his life for his own. Another debt added to the burden he carried. Each life lost, another memory to haunt his dreams.

He turned about, reentering the building, eying a pile of bodies stacked in one corner. Tossed there, their eyes still open, staring into the cobwebbed beams, as if wondering how they'd come to such an inglorious end. The largest man, several musket balls needed to knock him from his tree-trunk legs, lay to one side. As dead as the others, but with one last duty to perform.

Then Aaron turned his attention to the small man sitting on the ground. His eyes looked small, his glasses removed. The frames bent, with the lenses crushed. He went over and stood over him. "You thought him to be *me*. At first. Prepared to discuss terms." The man swallowed, his fear ripe, staining the air, his pants dark with urine.

Aaron leaned down. "Gathered from him what little he could give you, hoping it would be enough to keep you in your *club*. Knowing you'd lost out on the gravitas of having brought the Wolf to heel. A fine feather in your cap—if you'd been successful."

"End me." The frightened man trembled in fear. "Winning this hand, poorly played. Others to follow in my place. Plaguing you unto your last day."

"You'll die. As all men do. A bloodless death, yours. But not by *my* hand." Aaron took the man by his upper arm and pulled him to his feet. He guided him outside, leading him back inside his small office. Once inside, he released him, then pulled the door closed behind them. He motioned toward the desk, watching as the small man went over and slid into his chair.

Aaron went over to the window and secured it, then dragged a chair over, sitting down across from his adversary who was staring back, his eyes pinched with confusion. "Do you have another pair?" The man hesitated, then nodded. He slid his desk drawer open and reached inside, bypassing a small pistol, left half-cocked in case of an emergency. He pulled a small cloth bag out and opened it, slipping another pair of spectacles in place. Then he slumped back in his chair, waiting for judgment.

Aaron smiled. "Why so *glum*, friend? I promised you that *no* harm will come to you by my hand or those of my partners." He paused, then lifted one hand, gently stroking the sides of his chin. "Though *your* partners in the cabal might hold a *different* point of view. I understand them to be a *prickly* bunch. Especially toward those responsible for causing disruptions to their worldly plans."

The thin man cleared his throat. "My failure *will* disappoint them." He sighed. "Your plan was *masterful*. Using your associate like that. Willing to sacrifice a major piece, in winning the game."

Aaron kept his eyes hooded, hiding his feelings. "The decision was his. Not mine."

"An admirable, though *foolish*, gesture. Having failed to convince me of his false identity, lacking *key* knowledge. Revealing himself to be a *false* wolf. If you will." The man leaned forward, his confidence returning, the drawer left open, the handle of the pistol near to hand. "We are at the precipice of an opportunity. Imperative that we clarify *each* of our group's intentions. Our positions are not as much in opposition as you might think."

He sat back, one hand on top of his desk, his expression relaxed as he returned Aaron's steady gaze. "If we work *together*, we can help to smooth the way forward. There are substantial financial difficulties ahead for the new government, still in its infancy. Nations soon to come knocking at its door, bills in hand for monies lent. Funds needed to help pay the high price for what many would mistakenly name *freedom*." He snorted. "As if that word holds *any* meaning in the world as we know it to be. As it has always been. One *all* men are born into."

"And eventually *die* in. A guarantee, for all." Aaron paused. "One day."

"But *not* today." The man smiled. "Having given me your word. Which allows me to provide you with information you would not otherwise discover. Enough *leeway* in my assigned mission to judge what to reveal. And to *whom*."

"I'm listening."

"My name, before having signed the membership book in red, was Pritchard. Raymond Pritchard. Of minor note, outside my family's group of businesses. My education—"

Aaron sighed, his voice stiffening. "*Time*. Of the essence. Decisions to make before first light."

"Yes. Of course. Whether away to your wilderness lair, or in company with myself, a far more comfortable path to follow. Leaving all this—" Raymond waved one hand, his fingers grasping the handle of the pistol, slipping it into his lap. "To those without higher ambitions. Content to wrest pieces of it away from the grasp of savages. Pretending, once they've done so, it will belong to them."

Aaron gave him a quiet look. "Will it not?"

Raymond smiled. "You know the answer to that as well as I. Nothing belongs to *anyone*. Not their homes. Their lands. Their holdings. All of it is merely an *illusion*. People, like us, with control over the value assigned. The masses allowed to *claim* ownership, though we both know that *everything* is ever in play. At *all* times."

He closed his hand around the butt of the pistol, finger on the hammer, ready to draw it to full cock. "Those able to see the board from above standing to gain the most. Men with foresight, wisdom, and the will to see things through, will always reap the greater reward. Climbing on the back of huddled masses of people. Ignorant of the games played by those with their fingers placed on the strings of power. Men perched on the shoulders of royalty, whispering in their ears, suggesting every move they make."

Aaron leaned forward. "Harder to accomplish with an open-minded, *democratic* social order. Led by men who've bled to build it, left disillusioned by the alternative. Willing to lose everything with little gained in return, if successful. Placing their trust in, as you would name them, the huddled masses. What others name the *common man*, willing to stand the line when called upon to do so. Each with equal say in how things will play out."

Raymond stared, uneasy, his finger on the trigger, the barrel aimed. "You *jest*, of course. Knowing better than to believe such nonsense."

Aaron's face hardened into a look of greed. "*Fook* all to the commoner. And to those thinking themselves better than the rest." He

stared, his eyes cold as ice. "You'll give me what I want. *Now*. Everything you know, put down on the papers in your drawer. With your
tiny pistol left *inside* it. My sworn promise to you—*kept*. When you've
finished, we'll talk about the path ahead. The one we're both destined
to walk." Then he stood up and went over to the window, cracking it
open, measuring the height of the moon.

Raymond nodded, his hands trembling in excitement. *"Agreed."* He
replaced the pistol and removed a sheaf of parchments, along with a
vial of ink and a quill. He began writing out the names, places, and
descriptions of men huddled in their manors throughout the colonies.
Along with those skulking about every inn and tavern throughout the
colonies.

Aaron listened to the scratching of the pen, holding back a sea of
emotions, biding his time until he could dole out justice on his friend's
behalf.

Raymond twisted his body, trying to break free of the taller man's iron
grip on his upper arm, leaving his flesh pinched, but unbroken. Not a
single drop of blood shed, though his pants were urine stained again.
Sweat beading his forehead, with fearful tears blooming in the corners
of his eyes, his glasses held in his free hand.

Aaron half-dragged him across the lane, ending up at the privies.
The largest of them tipped to one side, exposing a deep hole. Ripe with
the leavings of his men, their bodies burning in the warehouse, set
afire.

"No!" Raymond squirmed, trying to break free. His voice climbed
through a scale of extreme distress, ending in a shriek as Aaron
dropped him into the odorous hole, leaving him standing chest deep,
staring up, his face gone pale.

A group of men brought the body of his largest man over, having
pulled it from the barn before igniting a pile of oil-soaked wood and
hay. They looked at Aaron, who gave them a nod, watching without
expression as they dropped it in on top of the small man, who cried out

in terror, his knees buckling as he struggled to hold up the man's dead weight.

As Raymond strained to keep his head above the noxious liquid, he moaned in fear, his tormented cries turning into grunts of effort as he fought to keep the body, its thick girth filling the space, from slipping further down into the hole.

The men put the privy back in place, then moved away, leaving Aaron standing there, listening as the small man blubbered, choked, then gagged. He remained rooted in place until the sound of his last gasp, followed by four hundred and twenty seconds of dead silence.

Aaron turned away, joining the others, placing one hand on his friend's body as a small mare carried the old veteran with a fire-scarred face away, heading back into the hills above.

CHAPTER TWENTY-THREE

CAPTIVE'S TOWN
SUMMER, 1786

E liza watched as Noah came out of the woods with two large turkeys on his shoulder. Two-Women walked beside him, carrying his bow and quiver. The two of them were engaged in conversation, talking with each other as young people in love often did. The sight brought a cloud to her face, recalling Aaron at her side, engaged in lengthy discussions on events and cultures far beyond her isolated knowledge of such things. His serious tone painted a smile on her lips, with her responses limited to an occasional nod of her head.

Eliza looked at the spire of the new church, pointing like a finger at God. Far smaller than the one on the church built in Gnadenhutten, but enough to draw the people's eyes to their savior. She smiled, cradling her son, who was cooing in her arms as she sang a psalm, walking toward her home.

Noah saw his sister and waved, then looked over at Two-Women and nodded. "The *suggestion* of it is sound enough. But the thought of having to fight off dozens of hen turkeys for their eggs leads me in the *opposite* direction." He grinned, heading toward an offal pile behind the stables, where they would pluck, then clean the large birds.

Once there, Two-Women kneeled beside him, a hen in hand,

removing the feathers with a practiced hand. Noah reached for his knife to open the body cavity for her, but she beat him to it. A knife of her own slipped out from beneath her skirt.

Noah stared at the blade, then sighed. "I miss her. Anna. In seeing you do that." He gave Two-Women a soft look. "You have many of her features. Her eyes, lips. And—" He stopped himself, his face darkening in a blush.

"These?" Two-Women lifted her hands, cupping her breasts, having come into full growth now she was of age. She giggled, the sound of it like spring water falling over stones in a brook. "You're caught between two worlds. Here. And *there*." She pointed to the west with her chin, eyes focused on slipping the tip of her blade into the abdomen of the plump bird. "One place or the other, always wanting to make its claim on you."

Noah yanked at the feathers on the other bird, several getting loose, floating in the warm air, one landing on his forehead. Two-Women leaned over and blew it away, her breath cooling his sweat-beaded skin. He leaned back, looking at her, his dark eyes focused on the side of her face. "The same for you, with a decision to make before Sunday service. My sister is eager to convert you. To rename you, bringing you fully into the church. Not only in body, but *soul*." When there was no answer, Noah bent to the work of cleaning the other bird, readying it for hanging in the communal smokehouse.

The two of them remained silent, focused on preparing the turkeys for the smokehouse. Once finished, they made their way to the windowless structure, its ceiling stained black with residue from herb-scented smoke. Noah went inside and tied the birds in place, then stoked a fire left burning night and day. He closed the door and latched it, making sure it stayed sealed.

Two-Women had waited for him, her head down as they started toward the house shared with his sister. Noah reached out, finding her hand, taking it in his, holding on until she relaxed. He knew she was struggling to accept the version of the Christian faith as told to her by Eliza. One she'd altered from what their father had preached. His sister convinced God had chosen her to speak through. Chosen by him as the arbiter of his plans for the community. Making every decision, large or small. Calling out the good or bad of each person's behavior.

"I—am not ready. Have not decided. Not yet." Two-Women's voice was soft. Noah stopped and pulled her around, then leaned in, his hands on her waist. "As to the name she's chosen for you?" He paused. "Or to acceptance of our *faith?*"

Two-Women looked up, her eyes filling. "I don't want to disappoint you. Not after everything you've given me. Given my people. Your willingness to exchange your life for that of my brothers. Helping to keep the peace. Protecting *all* of us."

"There's *no* possibility of that happening. Your decision, whatever it is, won't disappoint *me*." Noah paused, a small grin crossing his lips. "*Eliza*, yes. A fight on your hands trying to get *her* to step back." He saw Two-Women's face tighten, her lips pulled down at the corners. "With me ready to step in on *your* behalf, helping to divert her —*passionate* insistence on it being done this week."

"She will be *angry* at me."

Noah leaned in, kissing her, his eyes open, looking deep into hers. "*Us*, my lady of buckskin and wood-smoke." He paused. "And turkey feathers—tangled in your braids."

Two-Women reached up, pulling them over her shoulders. No feathers showing. With a wide smile on her perfect lips, she reached out and shoved him away. "Teller of *tales*!" Then she took his hand and pulled him into the woods, seeking a moment of privacy in a thick grove of pines.

⸹⸹⸹

The second officer watched Noah, copying his every move. He was now the temporary commander of the English fort while a new officer was in route to replace the former commander, his body shipped north in a barrel of brine, dying from a lingering sickness.

He walked a few paces behind Noah, carrying a loaded musket, left half-cocked. They were on the trail of an enormous bear, the beast insistent on killing cattle belonging to the King. Two of them killed, then partially eaten over the past few weeks. The large boar recently spotted over a third kill, earlier in the day. Driven off by soldiers with badly aimed muskets, leaving tracks difficult to follow in the leaf-littered woods.

The English officer, second in command, and a close friend of the Moravian hunter, cursed under his breath, having lost the trail again. Noah provided a verbal nudge, guiding him back to the line of tracks. They finally swapped positions, the officer deferring to the native man's experienced eye as the tracks led them deep into a dense growth of trees.

"We'll pause there, just ahead. To assess the lay of the land." Noah's voice, barely a whisper, caused the officer to close the distance between them. He stopped alongside the young man, the end of the musket held out to one side, the hammer at half-cock. Noah kneeled down, placing his finger on the edge of a track. The claw marks extended well beyond the press of its wide pad. He straightened up and strung his bow, slipping an arrow in place, his eyes probing the undergrowth.

"Are we getting *close?*" A nervous tone in the officer's voice revealed his tension, though he was a decorated veteran of war. Seeing action in the eastern theater until wounded in battle. Then sent west, after recovering his health. Noah nodded, not wanting to speak, his instincts singing, encouraging him to seek the nearest tree or boulder large enough to climb. Spotting one, he edged away from the large boar's trail, glancing back, making certain the officer was close to his heels, with the end of his musket kept pointed away.

The next few steps were a mix of tension and release as a turkey ran across the path, launching itself into the air with a rattle of wings. Their hearts leaped into their throats, each of them pointing their weapons at the bird before lowering them again, with chagrined looks on their sweaty faces. They gave each other a tight-lipped grin, then Noah's eyes widened as he stepped to one side, releasing an arrow. Another on the string before the officer could turn around. Quickly released, chasing the first into the chest of the oncoming bear, its mouth popping in anger, a roar from its throat vibrating the air.

The thud of the musket caused the beast to stumble as it closed the distance. Another arrow, brought to full draw, driven into the heart of the bear a moment before it reached the two hunters, where it finally collapsed, its lungs filling with blood. With a large hole torn in its cheek, the thumb-sized lead ball buried somewhere deep in its neck, helping to stiffen its hind legs.

Both men fell back several steps, the mouth of the bear gnawing at the air, claws tearing at the ground, unable to move ahead. Its dark eyes focused on Noah as it shuddered, then stopped moving. Dead before the officer could reload his musket with trembling hands, barely able to ram another round down the barrel.

Noah slipped his knife back into its sheath, prepared to have used it in defense of himself and his hunting partner. He gave the officer a wide-eyed look, gasping with relief at having survived the charge. "The answer—to your question—is *yes*. We're *close*." He looked at the officer's hands, trembling as a surge of adrenaline began burning off. "*Too* close."

The two men shared a moment of mutual appreciation for the other's quick reflexes, with neither man having turned to run. Then Noah tested the bear for signs of life, gently poking the tip of an arrow into the flesh around its eye, with no response.

"I will admit to a level of fear—beyond *any* felt before." The officer wiped a line of sweat from his brow with a forearm, his hands bloody from helping Noah dress out the bear. "My exposure to imminent death made against colonial militias, standing in line. A moment of pause as the lead balls sang past. The whimpering of shells, falling from the sky. Over before you could blink. Then leveling of weapons, returning the same. Focused on reloading, then firing again. Unaware of the next wave of shot or shell, until given the order to charge. One side or the other, pulling away. Leaving their wounded and dead behind."

Noah glanced over, almost done with the odorous chore. He dragged his hands through the leaf-littered soil, using them to clean the gore from his fingers. "Seems like a—*foolish* way to go about it. Exposed like that. Out in the open, as if standing in a field in the middle of a thunderstorm, waiting for the lightning to strike."

The officer nodded, using a sliver of wood to clean the blood from beneath his fingernails, his skin as white as snow, having stripped down to his underclothes to help the young bowman dress out the bear. "The way *I* see, too. *Now*. In having witnessed how your people—the natives. How they use every bit of cover. Staying close to the ground. Avoiding senseless injuries, or death." He used water from his canteen to clean himself, then put his uniform back on.

Noah handed him his officer's coat and wig, the officer having placed them over the end of his musket, leaning against a tree. Then he quickly fashioned a drag, the two of them rolling the body of the large boar into place, securing it with long twists of pine roots. Once finished, they bent their backs to the effort of pulling it back to the fort.

Noah had offered to wait at the kill site until the officer could retrace their steps, bringing back soldiers to help. The older man had considered for a moment, then shook his head, knowing he'd never find his way out of the tangled woods. "We hunted, then slew it *together*. Seems only appropriate we haul it back ourselves." Noah had nodded, pleased by the decision.

They hauled the heavy load until dusk, arriving at the top of a small rise with a sweeping view of a large valley. They reached a silent agreement to stay in place with a small fire built. Enough to keep them warm. Fresh bear meat on greenwood spits, a reward for their efforts.

The officer sighed, his appetite satisfied, bone weary but light in spirit. "It impressed me, your reaction to the beast's charge. With your arrows released—so quickly. Amazing to witness." He paused, recalling his moment of frozen panic. "My effort delayed. Due to surprise."

"It was me with a first sight of it. My arrows—not enough to stop it. The shot you fired breaking its neck before it could reach us."

"Appreciated. Your comment." The officer hesitated, then reached out, using a grease-stained wooden stick to stir the coals. "I meant to ask you, after the unfortunate event at the fort—" He paused, eyeing Noah, wondering if he should revisit the death of the young native man. When there was no untoward reaction, he tossed the stick into the coals.

"You were prepared to give your life to save the others. With yourself, innocent of the crime. More so, for having tried to stop their leader long before that night, based on what your lady friend told me." He shook his head. "I could *not* have done the same. Have thought about it since. The answer, always the same. Leaving me with a question."

Noah stared out at the western horizon. "You want to know *why*."

The officer nodded. "I do."

Noah swung his hand, pointing at a ridge in the distance, crowned with oaks. A half-moon revealed one towering above the others. "The answer lies out there. The sacrifice of one man's life for another's. In the name of a cause greater than his own survival." He gave the officer a long, quiet look. "The story of it told me by a man who knew what happened there. Taking me to the very spot where I watched him kneel and touch a stone. Saying his words. Telling me his father and mother had done the same thing. A long time ago."

The officer pulled up his legs and crossed his arms around his knees. He listened to the crackling of wood as it burnt down into coals, glowing in the firepit, background to the younger man's soft voice.

"The one buried there was a sergeant major. Of the English army. Had sacrificed his life to get his officer, my friend's father, to get him clear of an ambush. Left with a mortal wound. Dying right there, where the tallest tree stands. Buried between its roots, with the help of a French officer and a handful of natives. An enemy officer, returning a favor owed. My friend's father released, allowed to make his way back to English lines."

"A *remarkable* story. Such—*nobility*. On *all* sides." The English officer paused, considering the meaning behind the story. "You were prepared to sacrifice yourself. To keep the Wyandot people from rising in protest, leading to conflict. To protect the people of your—of Two-Women's tribe."

Noah shrugged. "It seemed the only way out from having failed to have warned the commander. To have failed to share the potential for threat—with *you*."

Both men settled back, their arms crossed beneath their heads, the day's efforts having taxed their reserves of energy. The English officer looked up at the sky, identifying points of light. Using them to draw constellations familiar to his eye. Different images formed by Noah, matching those known to his people.

He closed his eyes, picturing Two-Women's face, warmed by his love for her. Slowly drifting off to sleep with a smile on his lips.

CHAPTER TWENTY-FOUR

HIGHLAND MANOR
FALL, 1786

Angus stood at the far end of the manor path, watching a rider approach. The weather was gray, with a low overcast, painting the fields in a light haze of moisture. The end of a dreary day at hand. With more rain in the offing. The young horseman dismounted, then handed a satchel to Angus, who offered him a small purse in return. Rejected with a wave of the lad's hand, laughing as he led his mount toward the stables, having completed a task he'd gladly have done in bare feet, over rough-faced crags.

Angus shook his head, amazed at the quality of young men, eager to make the climb when called high. Willing to bend their backs to the demanding work. Drawn by rumors of decent food, fulfilling work, and the respect of the clan's laird and lady, both. He nodded, deciding to gift the young stallion to the boy, along with its saddle and tack. Adding him to the steady stream of riders making the journey to Glasgow and other cities throughout Scotland. Returning every few days, weather permitting, with sealed leather satchels in hand, tied up with uniquely knotted strings.

Angus stared at the latest packet, held in his thick fingers, wondering if the news would be good or bad. He shrugged, knowing it could wait until after dinner, his stomach grumbling, not having eaten since morning. Lorna had taken him by the hand, asking him to accompany her to the croft house to lay flowers on her family's markers. More of them placed there, each generation turned.

He'd been happy to go, hoping to have his stone placed in the glen one day. Alongside those marking the bones of Lady Marion's great uncle Shaun and her great grandfather. Their headstones lined the far end of a long narrow glen, where a handful of large, red-coated shaggy bulls liked to feed, plastering the ground with their shite.

Angus grinned, having heard the story told many times, wishing to have met the old man in self-isolation at the wee croft house, known for his irascible manner and cunning mind. Along with the double-edged blade of visions, come true. His own were of a different type. Flashes of light, preceding images of short duration, with the depth of the message defined by the color and intensity. He shrugged, head down as he neared the back door leading into the kitchen, supposing all people to experience similar things from time to time.

Marion looked up, the door letting in a cool draught of air, stirring the heat from the stove, cooling her forehead. Her hands were white to the wrists, with the bread she was kneading ready to form into loaves. A roast in the oven would soon be ready to pull out, with a rack of bread slid in, completing the making of the bones of a meal to feed her family and field-hands kept busy working away on the manor grounds. Steamed vegetables simmered in a pot, the trimming to their dinners, along with tankards of ale or spring water for those deemed too young.

Her son, Calum, eight months old, stirred as the currents of cool air swept over his face. His eyes, blue like his father's, opened on hearing a familiar voice, bringing a smile to his face. Marion grinned as Angus swooped in, plucking the babe from his cradle, holding him close as he slid out a chair, sitting down, already engaging the wee laddie in conversation. She finished up with the bread, then rinsed her hands, wiping them with a towel as she listened to Angus, his voice as soft as summer rain.

"To the mountains, on high. Where the tops touch the sky. Where the stags call in search of a mate. Someday you'll go, and once there you'll know all the answers to questions, in wait."

"That's new, and it suits him." Marion made a cup of tea, using honey to sweeten it, setting it down in front of the man she considered an uncle, even if he was nearer to her age. She knew no one would ever see him as a true laird, though he carried himself with an air of maturity and self-satisfaction.

His hands held the reins of power, acting on behalf of her husband, with everyone aware of whom to look to when problems arose. Angus prepared to respond with insightful, and sometimes forceful, responses as he oversaw the interests of each member of his adopted clan.

"Every child, once they arrive, given one of their own. My gift to them. For allowing me to love them." Angus smiled down at Calum, the wide-cheeked babe giving him one in return.

Declan came into the room, a worried look on his face. "You have the reports? The ones with the delivery date of the materials for the second mill?"

Angus shook his head. "Nae. Only a satchel from Glasgow with the latest news from the colonies." He glanced at the leather case, tied with a knot, intricately fashioned, knowing there would be a strand of dark-gray hair fastened with a dab of wax on the inside of the flap. Broken, if anyone tried to tamper with the satchel.

All messages produced were based on a cipher of his design. One created by the use of financial figures and legal disclosures, with the underlying story buried between hundreds of numbers and mind-numbing lists of transactions. Plucked by experienced eyes, gathered together, revealing recent events regarding Aaron and his group of dark-garbed men.

Declan cursed, frustrated by the constant delays in bringing another mill into production. Then he glanced over, seeing Calum awake, his son's small arms reaching out. Angus held the babe up, his father taking him into his arms, carrying him over to Marion, and kissing her on her forehead. He looked back at Angus. "Sorry—for being so short. It's from worry in getting the other millworks completed before winter."

Marion leaned up and kissed Declan's cheek, knowing her husband had fastened onto the project with both hands, desperate to have some-thing of his own to be responsible for. Willing to leave Angus to represent the clan's interests, under his paper-thin title as laird. Understanding his limited role in the clan's various businesses, firmly under his wife's control.

Angus waved a hand in dismissal. "A laird's worry for his people's welfare is nothing to apologize for. It's one of many reasons they love you so."

"I *agree*, husband." Marion reached out, pulling Declan in against her, kissing him, feeling Calum's head pressing against her breast, his fingers grasping at her dress, scenting the milk beneath. "Take the roast out shortly, with the bread put in. Use the large timer, setting it over onto its side." She pulled away, bringing her son with her, heading to the salon to nurse him. As she approached it, the sound of her daughter playing a Scottish song on the piano let her know Lorna had finished with her reading.

Once they were alone, Angus watched Declan. His stare forced the other to look away, then sigh, turning back around, an exasperated look on his thin, high-cheeked face. "I am *less* their laird than you. The clan *knows* it. *I* know it." He paused. "*She* knows it, too."

"Aye. You're right. You, holding the title. Me, with the reins in hand. In control of when, where, and how *firmly* to pull them. The clan led where *I'm* to guide it to." Angus paused. "But as for my *loving* them —no. That's not me. Beyond my interest or ability to do so."

He stood up and came over, taking Declan's hand. "It's to *you* they look for that. For love, when in need of reassurance. Knowing a note sent to ya' will bring you to them on the run. Listening to their tale of woe, tears in your eyes. Feeling their pain, their fear, as if it were your own. You—the one they'd die for in return. Not me. Nor Marion, sweet lady though she is. Only *you*." With a nod of his head, he gathered Calum in and walked away with a song on his lips.

Declan was silent, the wind rising as rain swept across the fields, slapping against the glass of the large kitchen window. He nodded, then went over and opened the oven door. He pulled out the roast, releasing a wave of richly seasoned air.

⁂

The report from Sinclair was a mix of positive results, and sad. There was news of the successful eradication of a viper's nest, made up of a group of men in direct opposition to those Aaron was leading. The action had resulted in the loss of a close friend who'd made the ultimate sacrifice, supporting their cause.

Angus offered a prayer for the veteran's soul, followed by a heartfelt sigh, then continued reading through the transcribed notes sent by Sinclair, adding the information gained to what he'd gathered from his side of the board. The game was always in play, with groups like his, Aarons, and dozens of others doing what they could to minimize the efforts of vainglorious men who believed themselves above the rule of law. Subverting the best intentions of governments while ignoring the will of God.

A cry from outside pulled him to the door of the small room he called home, located beside a large storage room on a downhill slope, tucked beneath the manor's thick wooden floors. He watched as Lorna rushed to help her brother Calum, who'd taken a tumble. The young boy just learning to walk.

Calum sat on the grass, his face red with angry tears, pushing his sister's hands away, looking around for his mother. Angus stepped forward, then stopped, seeing Lorna drop to her knees, watching as she hugged her brother, kissing his fingers. He smiled, hearing her singing him his song.

Angus closed the door, returning to his review of the reports, the view of the two siblings a tug to his heartstrings. The sight of them together reminded him of the small waifs living in the lower valley reaches. Coming on the run, their voices filled with excitement whenever he passed through, looking for coppers or sweets tucked into their hands. Gathering around him like ducklings on the small mill pond, circling their mothers.

He began crafting a series of messages to send out. Calling for a meeting at an out-of-the-way croft to propose new missions, carefully planned out and then performed by men determined to strike at the foundations of those in positions of power and privilege. Their targets were two-faced politicians and immoral heads of industry. All of those who felt the world belonged to them alone.

⅄⅄⅄

A tall man, who'd just raised his voice in anger, imposing his opinion into the conversation between Angus and the other men gathered together, stood with hands on hips, waiting to hear the much shorter man's response. The other members of the group leaned in, ready to defend their leader if called on to do so.

Angus waved a hand, bidding the thick-bodied man forward. "You raise a valid point. One I've *previously* addressed, behind closed doors. The purpose of our meeting *here*, and *today*—with everyone invited to attend, meant to assign what needs doing. And by whom."

"Leaving us men, standing on the outmost edge of the circle, without a say in the matter." The man leaned forward, towering over Angus. "Seems unfair, considering we're supposed to be fighting for the rights of *all*."

Angus nodded. "If you would, a moment in private. Just the two of us." He spun about, returning to a small room where the heads of each strand in the web he'd constructed had just come out of. He stopped, standing to one side, allowing the large man to squeeze past, closing the door with a muffled thud.

"Please. Sit. Partake of some wine if you're thirsty. It's a decent enough blend."

The sullen-faced man sat down, unsettled by the lack of reaction to his challenge to the smaller man's assumed authority. "You've taken the *role*. But not the *title*." He paused, gauging the reaction of a man with a reputation for cleverness and violence. "Why?"

Angus returned the scrutiny, his thick lips pursed. "Because I'm the one knowing *what* to do. And *when*." He joined the man at the table, his hands clasped before him. "And of *whom* to place my trust in."

"Meaning you have doubts. About *me*." He glared at Angus, then leaned back. "About my *bona-fides*. Suspecting me. The reason you brought me in here. To question my commitment, despite my having made my vow to the cause. My word, given ya', same as *them* out there." The man jerked his head toward the door. "Many amongst us would see someone *else* in your position. Our *real* laird. Not some messenger boy sent in his place."

"Pigs." Angus let the word slip from between his lips. The other man narrowed his eyes.

"Pigs?"

"Aye. A cunning animal. More so than a dog. Or even a horse." Angus lifted his arms, stretching them above his shoulders, yawning, his thick fingers pointing at the low ceiling. He lowered them. "As smart as *most* men, if allowed to prove their intelligence."

"I'm not here to speak of —"

"*Eating.*" Angus cut the man off. "Pigs. They eat *most* things. Same as us."

The man's face flushed red with confusion, turning to anger. He glared as Angus stood up and walked over to the door, leaving it open as he strode away. The man's eyes followed him, watching as he parted the others, stopping to whisper something in one of the older men's ears, before stepping out into the night air.

The big man leaned forward, about to stand, hesitating as the older man slipped in. He closed the door, then leaned down, murmuring into the large man's ear, causing his eyes to widen, his face going pale, voice trembling when he replied. "That's — *him?* The one who *done* that — to them?"

A nod in reply sat him back in his seat. The older man went out into the other room, leaving the door open. A moment later, the large man came out without stopping, his eyes down as he went outside and bent a knee, lowering his bulk, coming eye to eye with Angus.

"My apologies. For such *ignorant* words, rashly stated. I — I will take my leave, and never speak such words again." He rose to his feet, moving away. Stopped by the sound of the small man's deep voice.

"Stay. That we might speak openly. Sharing the truth of how each of us sees the world, in surround." Angus came over, his hand raised, waiting until the tall figure took it. Then he squeezed firmly enough to cause the other man to flinch.

"That you might come to an understanding of why *I'm* the guardian of clan Scott. With the backbone and *will* to see things *done* to any who would harm us. To reach deep into the darkness of an evil man's innermost fears. Pull them out. Hold them up to his eyes. Then drop them onto the blood-splattered ground, *grinding* them beneath my heel."

Angus released the man and walked away, going to his mount, releasing its lead, pulling himself up by the stirrup, and climbing into the saddle. His short legs thrust out to the sides, reins in his hand, riding away, his head held high.

CHAPTER TWENTY-FIVE
CAPTIVE'S TOWN
FALL, 1786

The English officer shrugged, having just notified a young man, considered a close friend of worrisome news. Noah, his eyes on the man who was second in command at the fort, nodded, then turned to go.

"I wish there were a promise of resolution, able to bring both sides —*all* sides—closer to a fair distribution of lands. Of the right of people to live their lives as *they* see fit, given equally to everyone involved."

Noah smiled, his head moving from one side to the other. "People. The word does not apply to those seen as *savages*. Uneducated in the ways and laws of those who are looking west, their leaders urging them to come here and spill lakes of blood. Ours, and theirs."

"The new commander and I committed to doing *all* possible to remedy any disagreements as they arise."

"Better for us if he carries a *large* stick. With the will to *wield* it." Noah walked away, having delivered the man a necklace formed of half of the claws of the bear killed several months earlier. Another strung around his neck. The two bonded as blood brothers in having taken the large boar's life. Their friendship strengthened during hours spent sleeping under the stars, then working together to drag the huge animal back to the fort.

The past growing season had been busy. Crops harvested, reaped, and replanted, now coming into a second growth with handfuls of soldiers from the fort lending a hand to bring it in. The community shared the food, with cattle offered in return. The meat hanging in the smokehouse, with the hides cured for use throughout the winter to come.

The Moravian community, having lost most of their married couples, young men, and single women, along with handfuls of children to the massacre over four years earlier, continued to struggle to gain in number. The native tribes had responded. Sending handfuls of their young people to join them so they could gain an education, helping to carry on the work started by Anna.

Noah bid his friend goodbye, then moved away from the fort. He headed toward a recently harvested field, smiling as he saw Two-Women kneeling along the far edge, young Jackson beside her. She was now his wife. Given the name Sarah after her conversion. The two of them having made their vows to one another in the small church, standing before God, Eliza, and the members of the community.

There had been a different ceremony performed at the Wyandot village by the chief, with the new couple surrounded by a sea of joyful faces. Noah smiled as he recalled the night spent with his bride in a small lodge, their union encouraged by the singing of his adopted tribe, urging the joining of man and wife with the sound of drums and rhythmic pounding of their feet on the ground.

Eliza, displeased when she learned of the latter celebration, had berated her brother, her voice strident with religious fervor. Noah withstood her anger, remaining silent, his head held high until his sister turned her wrath on Sarah.

"*You*, the cause of his *disobedience*. Turning him from *God's* path. Your faith is only *half-given!* Still clinging to your *native* beliefs!"

Noah had stepped in, taking his sister by her thin shoulders, cutting her off with a sharp tone. "You'll not speak to my *wife* in that way." He noted Sarah going over to soothe Jackson, the young native boy's nap interrupted by Eliza's shrill tone. "She is of *both* people. Her own and ours. Serving God's purpose. Leading members of her tribe *here* for conversion. By *you*."

Eliza turned her head, hearing Jackson cries, seeing Sarah holding him in her arms. She flung Noah's hands from her, going over and yanking the small boy away. "Don't *touch him!* He's *mine*, not yours. *My* son. Mine and my *husband's*. *Ours*. Belonging to God, not *you!*"

She spun around, facing Noah, her eyes wide, ignoring Jackson, now wailing, his hands clenched in fear. "And *you! Judas! Betraying* me, our dear *father*—and *God!*" She pointed toward the door. "Be *gone*. I *forbid* you to stay here. Leave. And take this *Jezebel* with you!"

The banishment had lasted all of a week. Noah, returning to gather the rest of his and Sarah's things, greeted by his sister with a warm embrace, asking about his wife, wondering why she wasn't with him. He'd shrugged, used to the frequent swings of his sister's fragile emotions.

Now, as he stood on the road between the community and the fort, Noah watched as Sarah stood up and started toward him, her arms filled with produce. Jackson, close behind, with an armful of marrow squash, forced to stop, trying to pick one up as it fell from his youthful grasp. Noah smiled, enjoying the sound of Sarah's laughter as she waited while the young boy struggled to regain his hard-won possession.

Then a shiver ran along his spine, causing him to look up as a gust of cool wind slipped through a grove of hardwood trees, stirring red and rust-brown leaves clinging to the limbs, as if afraid to let go.

The leader of the Wyandot people shook his head, a scowl on his lips, his dark eyes hooded as he spoke, his deep voice tinged with frustration. Noah translated, keeping his eyes fixed on the elderly man, showing him respect.

"These white men owe us tribute. The animals—taken from *our* lands. Hides removed. Bodies left to rot." There was a long pause as the leader looked away, his voice dropping to a whisper. "The Great Mother seeks balance. Opening her arms to those willing to follow her ways. As do we, my people and I." He eyed Noah, who stood at his side, waiting for him to finish speaking.

The commander of the soldiers in the fort nodded as he listened to Noah translate, his eyes reflecting a desire to move past the issue. Left unmoved by the native leader's words. "The King has ordered us to broker the terms of the treaty as *we* understand them. Not to the *letter* of the words, but their *intent*. Which is to maintain peace between *all* sides."

The native returned a stiff stance, his arms crossed, staring at the officer once Noah finished speaking. "You will not punish the ones who did this?"

"No. You must release them, so they can return to their people. Allowing them to take *half* the beaver pelts. And their horses. Returning *all* their belongings to them. Including their *clothes*."

Noah finished translating. He glanced at the white men. Three adults and a young boy, all of them holding their hands over their privates, their heads lowered in shame, waiting to learn their fate.

"The words of the Great Father across the sea have lost their way to *these* men. While we have *kept* our promises." The leader waved a hand toward the captives. "None of *them* harmed." He turned away, striding off, head held high, passing by the captives without stopping.

Noah watched as two soldiers went over and cut the bindings, tying the men's hands together. Slicing the short leather cords tied between their ankles, preventing their escape during their week of captivity while events unfolded around them.

"Will he advocate for violence?" The commander looked at Noah, who shook his head.

"The leader—has lost face with his people. Many of them will cry out for retribution. The young, and foolish. The elders will counsel them to be patient. To walk the path of peace. For *now*."

The English leader shook his head. "It is only the beginning. Incursions happening at an increased pace with people pouring through the hills, driven by promises in those *damnable* colonial broadsheets promising *free* land. Encouraging the cutting of forests for lumber. With dozens of mines dug for coal and iron ore. Wild game, killed by the hundreds. By the thousands. Land cleared. New homesteads springing up every day, along with countless acres of fields."

Noah nodded, his head lowered, staring down. "With *blood* spilled in those *same* woods and fields. Raids made against the mines. Gore staining the seats of heavily laden wagons, moving back toward Pennsylvania Colony." Noah sighed, then looked up at the English commander. "An offer—made in place of the *lack* of the men's deserved punishment might help soothe the frustrations felt this day. With face, saved. Which is as important to *my* people as it is to yours."

The commander nodded, then removed his hat, rubbing his forehead with a long, thin finger. He gave his second officer a nod. "See to it, Captain. Give the leader of the natives something of importance. Short of *military* use." Then he was gone, his long strides carrying him away.

"A difficult position to be in. Yours." The captain gave Noah a friendly nod. "Pulled between your people *here* and back *there*. Having to deal with the likes of *us*. And now, the colonists crowding in. With you standing with a foot in *multiple* camps."

"Life provides us opportunities. Most of them are easy. Some—difficult to look away from." Noah pursed his lips, eyeing the pale-faced men as they put on their clothes, their expressions tight with embarrassment as a line of British soldiers, who'd come along in escort of the officers, teased them. "Those men, the *harder* ones, will carry back tales of harsh treatment at the hands of *savages*." He gave the captain a soft look. "Like *me*." Then he turned away, heading toward a small lodge in the village. Shared with his wife during their frequent visits.

The officer watched as his close friend moved off, his voice a whisper in the air. "No savage you, my friend. Or your people. All of you made victims. The more so if, and when, we're ordered to leave you to fend for yourselves. Powerless to intervene. Our numbers—not enough to make a difference."

Sarah placed her head on Noah's shoulder, her arm draped over his chest, clinging to him. She felt his fingers on her head, running through the thick waves of her hair, worn down, the way she knew he liked it. Kept in a single braid during the day, no longer a maid. Falling over her shoulders as she slipped into their bed at night.

"Will there be another war?"

"Yes." Noah felt his wife stiffen. He lowered his hand, cupping her waist. "There will *always* be war. Here, or back in the colonies. Between the English and the French. The French and the Spanish. The Spanish and the English. In the colonies, again. Each generation asked to pay with blood price, fighting to keep a claim to land their parents fought and died for."

"A *dark* vision, husband. Not the energy needed now." Sarah lifted her head, a sly smile on her full lips. "I am ready. A handful of days since my flow ended. The moon—coming full. The Great Mother wants to send us a child. A son, I think. One of our *own*. Though Jackson is as much ours as your sister's."

Noah drew in a deep breath, then released it. "Is that *wise?* With the problems to come?"

"There will never be a *wise* time, husband. If everyone waited for that, *none* of us would be here." Sarah sat up, the movement of her breasts catching his eye. He reached out, cupping one in his palm. "Then we must do our part. And leave the Great Mother to decide."

Noah rolled over and gazed down at his wife, feeling her hand on him. He studied her face, losing himself in the love he saw in her dark eyes. Letting go of his doubts, he entered her, giving his worries about the future over to God.

CHAPTER TWENTY-SIX

CROSSROAD SETTLEMENT

SPRING, 1787

S inclair stepped into the barn, a worried look on her face, concerned about the health of a young mare. It was due to deliver in a matter of days. The swollen animal's behavior, normally docile, had turned tetchy of late. With a snap of teeth during grooming, exhibiting extreme displeasure.

She hung a lantern on a hook beside the birthing stall, then looked in on the mare. All seemed fine, though her sense of unease was still there, something unseen provoking her emotions. Unsettled, her dreams plucking her awake, leaving her staring through the bedroom window, trying to find answers to her instinct's whispered questions.

A soft noise from one corner of the shadowed barn drew her around, her face frozen in surprise as Aaron stepped into the light of the lantern. Age lay heavy on his face, his eyes etched with thin lines. His lips were stiff at the corners, though he still moved like the young man she remembered. With long, forceful strides, as if an alpha wolf moving in to claim its share of a kill.

"Hello, Mother."

Sinclair shook her head. A river of tears released, realizing the cause of her recent unrest. She opened her arms, her shoulders shaking with a mix of relief and pain as her son held her, having buried worries on his behalf away. Each packet of coded information, arriving in a hollow tree during midnight hours, forwarded to Angus, unopened. But not until she placed them under her nose, imagining they held the scent of her son on their stained-leather surface.

Overwhelmed on hearing his voice again, his words reassuring, Sinclair clung to him. Then she looked up, tears in her eyes, worried for her son, his body much too lean. "I've food. In the house. I'll go, and heat—"

"There's no time. I'm due back within the hour." Aaron slid away from his mother's tight embrace and stepped back, looking at her. She was still the mother he remembered her to be. Tall. Proud. Head held high, with a determined look in her light-colored eyes. He relented with a grin. "I'll eat whatever you're able to bring me, *unheated*. Without complaint."

Sinclair gave him a nod, then turned to go. Aaron reached out, handing her the lantern. He stood back as she opened a small door, closing it behind her. Then he went to check on the mare, having sensed his mother's concern.

When Sinclair returned with a basket of bread, the last of a roast, and half a jug of cider, Aaron met her with a tight expression, the lantern revealing lines of worry on his face. "She's in breach. The mare. A problem if you can't get the foal turned."

Sinclair looked over, hearing the heavy breathing of the mare. "I'll fetch Allwyn. And Meghan. And send Patty for a midwife, who'll be able to help." She handed the food to Aaron, then turned away. Her son reached out, taking her by the upper arm.

"There's time enough for that. *Hours* left before you'll be able to get it done." He smiled. "I'll eat, sharing what news I can. Listening while you fill me in on the family. The one here, and back in Scotland." Aaron sat down on a bale of hay and opened the basket, pulling out the food. "Will ya' join me, Lady Sinclair?"

Sinclair nodded. Her worry for the mare slid away, replacing with concern for her son, seeing the sag of his wide frame, as if he were carrying the weight of the entire world on his shoulders.

⁂

"And you've not been back—to see her or the child, since?" Sinclair watched as Aaron finished chewing, her eyes on his, knowing the answer before he spoke.

"No." Aaron shrugged. "Eliza's gone over to a place—someplace *outside* her mind. Shared with no one else. Where she's the *sole* arbiter of God's will, as she sees it to be."

"*Senses* it to be." Sinclair paused. "Correct?" Aaron looked over, holding two slices of bread wrapped around a large helping of the roast.

"*Sees*, mother. Claiming to have *visions*—sent to her by God. Words from his lips to her ear. Passed on to others. *Strange* things. Beyond reason. With no one allowed to question her. People left confused, wondering what will happen next."

"The babe? Is he—safe?"

"Noah and Two-Women had him safely in hand, last I heard." Aaron looked down, his voice dropping to a whisper. "His natural mother, a converted native—taking her own life, shortly after you left."

He sighed, a hard look on his face. "Eliza—wouldn't allow her burial in consecrated ground. Then she lost interest in the child, with Noah and Two-Women taking on the day-to-day care." He softened his gaze. "The two of them married. Two-Women having converted. Given the name Sarah, with a child of their own on the way. Based on the last word I got from him, with a message sent east with a native scout. One of several young men now working with us."

Sinclair clenched her hands, worried for them all, considering them part of her family, still. "The recent treaties, along with articles in distribution throughout the colony, have stirred people to turn their heads west. Promises on parchments made of land opened up to expansion. Encouragement made to go there and seek their fortunes."

She leaned forward. "Will they end up driving Sarah's people— Two-Women's people, from their land? As happened to those who used to live here?"

"They'll try. The attempt met with violence. Which will incite more of it in return. The English, bound by their alliances with native tribes, will do their part to prevent it. Failing in the end, with rivers of blood flowing up and down the valleys, between."

Aaron glanced at the remaining food, his appetite gone. "There are forces lining up, eager to create another conflict with thousands soon to die. Mountains of money spent on military supplies, in exchange for blood. With armies raised, intent on slaughtering natives defending lands *stolen* from them. Followed by hundreds of forts, providing security for tens of thousands of settlers staking claim to plots of farmland. Crops sold, enriching those responsible for the bloodshed to come. Supported in their efforts by articles in newspapers designed to incite young men to toss their lives away, fighting for liberties their fathers *already* fought and died for. Freedoms traded away, bit by bit, empowering men with control of the purse strings, allowed them to continue playing the game. One started by men drawing boundary lines on parchment."

Sinclair stared, swearing Harold was sitting there, hearing the echo of her late husband's words in her son's voice. Seeing the same look in his eyes, knowing he was beyond her reach, like his father before him. Her heart crept into her throat, knowing Patty was standing next in line. "You—Angus and the others. Can't you put a stop to it?"

Aaron looked at her, a sad expression on his face. "Stop it? No. *Resist* it, yes. Hoping this experiment in democracy might take root, deep enough to *survive* the fire to come. Sweeping over the ground already fought for. Bled for. Wasting the sacrifices made in wresting it away from those we were *part* of. Once. Our people. Our *tribe,* if you will, creating something *new.* Hoping enough pieces of it will survive, to be pulled from the ashes when all's said and done."

"Your words, *prophetic.* Others need to *hear* them."

"I am *not* my father." Aaron shook his head. "Can *never* be him. Forced to remain a lone wolf. Prowling in the darkness. My howling, if heard, will only lead to my death. To the deaths of men bound to me by their sworn oaths."

Sinclair leaned forward, a pleading tone in her words. "There *must* be *something* we can do. *You* can do, other than spilling blood in the shadows. To locate and then identify those involved. Threaten to expose them. Manipulating them into—"

Aaron shook his head. "The moment they're brought into the light, their lives are forfeit. Holding as little meaning to their group as if handfuls of extra pawns, removed from the outer edges of the board."

He paused, taking a deep breath, turning to look toward the door. "We can only *resist* their efforts. It's *all* we can do. All that I and my group can do *today*. And tomorrow. Hopefully, the *next* generation will have better luck if this experiment in self-governance, *by* the people, for *all* the people can survive infancy. Maturing into something worthy of the men who've given their all to make it so."

Aaron stood up. He came over and kneeled on the floor, taking his mother's hands in his. "Any birth, whether that of a child, foal, or a country to be—is a *messy* experience. With blood, tears, and tubs of sweat shed on all sides." He squeezed her hands, bringing them to his face. "It's up to *us*. To people like me and Angus—to reach into the deadly mix of men's greed and ambitions, trying to put things right. While people like you and Marion—and *others* with like minds and as clear a vision—to get the word out."

He sighed, kissing her hands, then letting go. "To find people willing to speak to the *truth*. To author articles placed on parchment. Distribute them to those who'll read them, then repeat what's written. Enough of them to alter the future, securing the efforts of men like me, willing to lead the way. Former soldiers. Citizens in cities. People with their hands in the soil. Dirt under their nails. Each with equal say in what happens next."

Aaron stopped, aware the time had come for him to leave. To continue the thankless task of standing against those eager for constant strife between disparate groups of people. Left counting mountains of coins earned engaging in trade with all sides.

Sinclair sighed, her eyes wide with every parent's concern. Proud of the man her son had become. The image of his father, a man she'd fallen in love with, then let go of. And lost. One still dreamed of. "A waste—with you locked in the dark. Your words are *vital* to bringing light to the vision you've painted. Wishing it could be *you* who's seen. Heard." She leaned forward and kissed his cheek, resting her forehead against his. "Know that I love you. Admire you. That I will carry you in my heart until its last beat."

Aaron blinked away his tears and stood up, walking away without looking back. The barn door closed behind him, the mare's soft neighing echoing Sinclair's hand-muffled sobs.

A man stepped out from beneath the branches of a large pine. He held two sets of reins in his hands, the horses quiet, trained to silence while saddled. He gave Aaron a long stare, then reached out, handing him control of his mount, a dark-colored mare, short-legged, with a sturdy build, ideal for the terrain they'd be moving through. Heading west. Using back trails or cutting new ones in wilderness tracts.

Their goal was to reach the tribes in the Ohio Basin, bringing promises of support. To help them resist the incursions to come. Men heading their way with sharp, thin-bladed skinning knives. Dreaming of deep streams and backwater ponds, filled with the glistening pelts of beavers and the scalps of any natives found. With bounties paid by governors in the east, using money collected from settlers eager to purchase a small piece of the vast territories, promised them.

Cabins built with fields cleared, planted, then harvested. Each successful attempt causing an increased flow of people eager to make their own move west. Intent on building a new country. One where every man was equal to the next. As long as he wore clothes, not deer-skin. And walked about without paint on his face or feathers in his hair.

Aaron mounted the mare, taking a moment to look down at the valley floor, measuring the size of the settlement spreading to both sides of a slow-moving stream. Then he shook his head, nudging the horse away, leaving one family behind, heading into the wilderness to check in on another. Thoughts of another, living on high in a land he'd left behind a lifetime ago, a constant itch in his soul. Wondering if he'd ever find his way back home to them.

CHAPTER TWENTY-SEVEN

WESTERN WILDERNESS
FALL, 1791

N oah eased into position, longbow in hand, left unstrung. He heard men moving around him, finding places to hide. A large opening ahead revealed hundreds of men in various colored uniforms, standing in circles, a dozen or more in each group. Part of a large colonial force formed of militiamen, gathered together to exact revenge for a one-sided victory by native tribes over General Harmar and his men the previous year.

Noah shrugged, ignoring the ache of a wound received during the former collision of men. A lead ball had struck him in the side, scoring muscles, without breaking bones. Fully healed, thanks to the administration of his wife's gentle hands, and poultices provided by the wise women of her tribe. The battle had ended with each side trading killing blows, with the heaviest losses suffered by those least familiar with fighting in the wilderness battleground.

The last few years had seen dozens of bloody clashes erupt, starting soon after the signing of a treaty in 1787, with leaders of the tribes living in the greater Ohio region forced to cede a large tract of land to settlers shoving their way into the interior. Resulting in a constant series of deadly raids by people living on both sides of reassigned borders with woods and fields left painted in blood from atrocities performed. Leading to retaliation, with the British poised in between, counseling peace while continuing to provide weapons, advice, and military support to the natives.

A warrior to Noah's side glanced over, watching as he strung his bow, preparing for what would happen next. The man shook his head, holding up a musket in his hand. Then he looked away, eyes focused on the nearest huddle of unsuspecting soldiers, waiting for the piper's call to assemble for morning muster.

Noah slipped three arrows from the sheath he carried, tied to a belt around his waist. Twenty-four shafts tipped with wide metal broadheads. Their edges darkened with a thin layer of resin, dipped in ashes, helping to dull the gleam of honed metal. Then he practiced the breathing technique taught to him by Aaron. Using it to calm his nerves, knowing it would help steady the draw and release of the bow in his hand. Each man targeted, reduced to a patch of clothing, or a button on a chest. No longer men with hearts, minds, hopes, and dreams. Only targets. Nothing more.

A vibrating call from a bugle rang out. The native youth holding it to his lips, sounding three long blasts, each one rising, then falling. The woods came to life as over a thousand warriors rushed out, their war cries reverberating across the encampment. The colonial soldiers watched, frozen in shock, precious moments wasted before rushing to collect their muskets, neatly stacked between their tents. Their hands, clumsy with fear, struggled to hold their weapons as they formed into a line, bringing them to their shoulders. Many left half-cocked, unable to fire as a wall of tawny-skinned men fell upon them.

Noah stayed to one edge of the maelstrom of violence, releasing his arrows at officers attempting to rally their men. Several of them stuck through with mortal wounds, slumping to the ground. Another one knocked to his knees, an arrow through his side, promising a lingering death. Others spun away, wounded in the shoulder, arm, or leg. Yelling to panicked soldiers to form the line. To rally to the sound of bugles.

Too late, Noah thought. Another shaft let slip, pinning an officer between his shoulder blades, the doomed man's legs stiffening as the broadhead severed his spine, dropping him to the trampled ground, his hands trying to pull him along. A native warrior caved in his wigged head with a blow from a war club. The false hair lifted into the air, then flung aside, his hand refilled with a bloody scalp.

The rest of the action descended into a melee of clubs and knives against bayonets, musket stocks, and pistol barrels. The colonial force left twisting away, eyeing the woods, seeking to escape with their lives. Native warriors, shrieking with excitement, chasing them down. Looks of hatred on their painted faces. The glow of a glorious victory in their eyes.

A handful of men, gathered in a solemn-faced group, sat with their heads down. Their officers' uniforms were bloody and torn, their boots removed, along with hats and wigs. The native warriors who'd captured them were smiling, parading back and forth, knowing their leaders would pay double for having taken the officers alive. All of them left undamaged, within reason, other than their egos at having suffered a second, one-sided disaster in the past year.

This defeat belonged to Major General St. Clair, his reputation stained by the devastating loss. Escaping with a handful of his men, retreating along their line of march, leaving behind over two hundred camp followers. Women and their children. Slain where they stood, having followed their men, serving as cooks, laundresses, and nurses to the militia force.

The wonton slaughter of those most innocent tore at Noah's soul the first time he was witness to it. Woefully unprepared for organized violence on such a large scale, shocked into nauseated silence, coming upon their blood-soaked bodies of innocents, not able to see them at first as people. His heart torn to shreds when a small hand appeared, trying to pull the child it belonged to free from a mound of mutilated bodies. A young boy, his shoulder deeply cleaved, dying in Noah's arms while crying out for his mother. For his brother. His father. His staring eyes closed with a rub of Noah's thumb, tears falling onto the boy's pale face, each one a measure of the insanity of it all.

Noah stayed clear of the back end of the encampment this time. Listening to the distant screams of women and children, draining away like water after a storm. Leaving an eerie silence behind, filled with the whine of insects in flight and calls of hundreds of ravens and crows. With buzzards appearing overhead, drawn to the thuds of muskets, eager to do their part to help put the sorry affair to bed.

"Your payment." An English officer came up, a thin leather purse in his hand. "Ten, the number of officers wounded or killed, by your hand." The man held it out, then gave it a shake, producing a muffled clink of coins. "Thirty pieces of silver. Earned." Noah stared at the officer, holding his unstrung bow at his side. The officer shrugged, then placed the purse in Noah's free hand. "More than enough to keep your family provisioned through the winter and beyond. With little chance of another incursion within the year. Not after *this* debacle." The uniformed man sighed, staring across the blood-soaked field. "Poor leadership, that. With no outposts set, or scouts sent out to keep watch. Leading so many to such a —*sorry* end."

"With *more* deaths to come." Noah pointed with his chin toward a group of prisoners. "*Entertainment* for the warriors. With no other purpose to it. Not now, with the survivors having fled. No one to carry back the tale of what will happen to *these* men. To help persuade the colonist militias to stop and wonder at the —*futility* of fighting us *here*. In *our* element."

The officer nodded. "I quite agree, being an officer myself." He paused, taking a moment to give Noah a long, considered stare. "If I might —you seem *unusually* aware, compared to most of your people. Stories told of your woodland skills. That your education is *far* superior to that of the others of your tribe." He gave Noah a considered look. "Known as a God-fearing man. One deadly with a bow. A *longbow*." The officer narrowed his eyes. "An *unusual* weapon. Especially *here*, on the edge of English influence."

"A gift. From a man passing through. His name, never given."

"Baseless rumors then. As I suspected." The officer removed his hat, scratching under one side of his wig. "Only tales, told by soldiers, about a man known to have carried such a weapon in the eastern theater of that *damnable* war. To *deadly* effect. Like yourself."

"I wouldn't know about any of that. Again —only a gift made in passing. Given me when a young boy, years ago." Noah held up his bow. "This one is mine. The arrows, too. And the heads, made on a forge, back at the *English* fort, where my community is located."

"Yes. Heard *that* story, too. Of you being a Moravian. A God-fearing group, abhorring violence of any kind. To the point of walking to their deaths, with songs on their lips."

Noah responded, his voice low. "Psalms, not songs. Led there by soldiers. Like these."

"I *quite* agree. The colonials known for—"

"*Soldiers*. Following the lead of their *officers*." Noah paused. "Murdering innocents, under the guidance of *men*. Not God." The Englishman stiffened, his features tightening. Noah took note, easing his tone. "Not that I'm implying that about *yourself*, or those *with* you. *Your* people were not to blame for the massacre that took place at Gnadenhutten." He looked to one side and spit on the ground, avoiding a puddle of dark blood. "Those guilty, only men. Little different from *any* group of people seeking vengeance."

"Ill-bred *rabble*." The officer spat out the words. "Not like those of us in the Royal army. Beyond *reproach*. Officers and enlistees both. *Discipline* the answer. A lack *of* it, the problem."

"With us—the natives—left in the middle. Squeezed between one group and the other. Trying to find a place to stand. On lands that have belonged to *us*—for *countless* generations."

The officer shrugged. "Your people must learn to change with the times." He pinioned Noah with a hard gaze, then relaxed, their exchange of hard truths at an end. "You carry a reputation as a leader, with your thoughts worthy of being *listened* to. Added to *ours*, helping to maintain a balance between your version of civilization and ours. Helping your people find their way to a peaceful arrangement, difficult as that may be to accept. Necessary, if you are to survive." With a curt nod of his head, the officer turned away, his head held high. He walked away with a haughty stride, the heels of his boots leaving deep impressions in the soil.

Noah slipped the purse into a leather bag hanging at his side, the money destined to purchase supplies for the community. He shook his head, knowing the native warriors would use the weapons, goods, and money looted from the colonial soldiers to support their struggle against further encroachment into their lands. To continue their fight for the right to survive.

The leader of the Wyandot people came up from behind, stopping alongside Noah, watching as the Englishman walked away. "He gave you money."

Noah knew it was not a question. He pulled out the purse and showed it to the man. "*Blood* money."

The older man, his face lined with heavy wrinkles, smiled, then slowly shook his head. "Is there *another* kind?"

Noah considered for a moment. "No. I suppose not." He sighed, staring at the native men as they moved through the battlefield collecting muskets, pistols, and ammunition. Stopping to search the dead for valuables. Many of them, with strings of fresh scalps dangling from their sides.

The screams of men sliced the night apart. The sounds echoed by waves of high-pitched native war cries in their wake. Several fires, built around the base of logs, their ends buried in the ground, teased the exposed flesh of colonial men tied to them. The flames were growing in intensity, fed by men with angry expressions, rushing in, waving war clubs in their victim's faces, dropping pine knots at their feet as they danced away.

The celebration of the one-sided victory would last throughout the night, with Noah staying clear of it, along with members of his group of native warriors. They sat on the ground beneath a canopy of trees, heads bowed, counting the blessings of the Great Mother for having protected them that day.

A few of the warriors, mumbling phrases learned at the Moravian church, glanced over at their leader, sensing his unease. Others slid their attention toward the men-centered pyres, torn between staying seated or joining the celebration.

Noah looked up. He gave them a nod, releasing them to the call of their heritage, aware they considered the deaths of those vanquished to be a transition from the waking world into the next. One each man must make, with the length of their journey measured by the looks of defiance shown to their enemies. Respect reflected on those with the will to meet their deaths without fear, becoming part of the great circle.

Noah watched as the young men raced toward the fires, aware the soldiers tied to the stakes stood outside such beliefs. Their shrieks of pain, delivered as swirls of flames spiraled around their bodies, were the only response they could offer to the leering faces and excited shouts of the natives.

Tears filled his eyes, knowing this night belonged to the men of the wilderness. Aware as well that a new day was approaching. One that would bring an end to the ways of his people due to lack of knowledge. Of how to make iron. Or powder. Or lead. He lowered his eyes, staring at the ground, unable to find the voice of God, or that of the Great Mother, in the screams of the tortured men.

The next day, Noah and his war party left the headwaters of the Wabash River, arriving at the Wyandot village several days later. Another day saw him home, his arms circling Sarah, with their infant daughter in her arms. Their son, Adam, now five, clung to his waist, with Jackson staying back, his dark eyes lowered. Noah reached out and pulled him into the family embrace, kissing the top of his head.

Sarah finally stepped away, holding out their angel-faced girl, named Brooke, looking as if a twin to her mother. "*Take* her. She's been restless these past two nights, able to sense you were coming back to us." Noah gathered his daughter in, aware his clothes still carried the scent of smoke and burning flesh. Sarah looked at him with understanding eyes, pulling the two boys away. Shushing their younger son as he erupted in a rush of questions asked.

Jackson, sensitive to the mood of his adopted parents, mentioned having spotted a fox skulking near the henhouses. Adam looked up, then began heading that way. Jackson, armed with a bow and quiver of his own, caught up with him, taking his younger brother's hand in his.

Noah watched his two sons walk away, his daughter nestled in against the angle of his neck. He felt the weight of the past few weeks slide from his shoulder as the youthful scent of the babe washed away the odor of death in his nose. Her soft breath on his skin, warming his soul. Her tiny hand, cupped in his, binding him to God's love, helping to heal his wounded spirit.

Sarah came over and pressed her head against Noah's chest, listening to the steady beat of his heart. Then she reached up, placing her hand over his, helping to cradle their child. Silent. Without the need to ask questions about his recent efforts to help protect her people. About their future. All her worries let go of with her man safely home again.

CHAPTER TWENTY-EIGHT
HIGHLAND MANOR
FALL, 1793

L orna eased her mount around a sharp bend in a rock-faced trail, having to pull her knees in as the sturdy, long-legged mare lowered its head, stepping carefully, as if aware of how close her rider's body was to the fractured granite face.

The trail was one of dozens of unmarked ways into and out of the high valley, treacherous to one's lower body if not protected. Lorna had on a thick pair of pants with leather patches from shin to mid-thigh. A gift from one of the younger riders making their rounds on rugged trails running between Glasgow and the manor. A collection of skilled riders kept busy delivering a steady stream of messages for Angus.

Once clear of the cut in the valley wall, Lorna gave a low whistle that raised the mare's ears, her pace picking up as she crested a ridge, revealing a thin ribbon of water threading through the center of the valley floor. A cascade of white water, slipping from pool to pool in a series of steep runs, formed a decent flow.

Further below, stone enclosures, erected alongside the curved faces of small weirs, supported large wooden wheels. The blades coaxed by the flow to turn heavy granite stones, grinding wheat kernels into flour. Other mills were spinning saw blades, turning logs into boards, beams, and other items needed to build housing, storage buildings, and churches for newly arrived Protestants, fleeing famine in Ireland.

The Irish had formed a swelling population of milliners and linen weavers, living outside the city limits of Glasgow. Catholic priests within the city left with frowns on their faces, mumbling amongst themselves, staring at the swollen bellies of women moving about the city streets. Nervously counting their rapidly increasing numbers.

Lorna leaned forward, a section of level ground encouraging the mare into a dash down a curved roadway, the horse with outstretched neck, ears pinned back as its hooves pounded along the hard-packed center of the rutted road.

A large hare, stirred from tall grass growing in a narrow field alongside the road, shot out between the front legs of the small mare, causing it to swerve to the side, stumbling, its shoulder lowered, causing its rider to slip from the saddle with a shriek of dismay.

Lorna landed with a tumble. She slid through a thick mat of highland moss and coarse grass, left lying flat on her back, the wind knocked from her lungs as she stared up at the sky, dazed and dizzy. A face shimmered into view, its masculine features dimmed by the haze of tears in Lorna's eyes. "Lie yourself there, lady. Dinna try to move."

She ignored his advice and sat up, struggling to catch her breath, in a panic when she couldn't. A firm hand struck her between the shoulder blades, hard enough to get her breathing again, her face flushed red, hands clenched in balls, twists of coarse grass caught between her fingers.

"There ya' are. Back ta' *this* side of the great divide." The voice grew clearer, along with the sharp-edged features of the face staring at her. "Are ya' legs and arms good? Can ya' move them—without causing ya' pain?"

Lorna tried, carefully testing each one, her breath still coming short. Then she noticed her pants had slid down to mid-thigh, a wash of embarrassment recoloring her fair-skinned cheeks as she tried to pull them up, while the young man looked away.

"I'll be off then, seeing ya' in fine fettle." He stood up and turned to leave, held in place by Lorna's call for him to wait. She rolled to one side and struggled to work the tight-fitting pants over her hips. Filling out, now she was of age. Then she got to her feet and gave her rescuer a smile of thanks.

"I'd know your name. Young sir." She judged the boy to be older than her by a measure of two years. "If'n ya' of a mind ta' share it wi' me."

The boy, a full foot taller, narrow in his shoulders with a shock of thick black hair, grinned. His teeth were white, framed by full lips. He stood with hands on his hips, a sling dangling from his belt. "That would depend on *who* it is—asking me *of* it."

"I'm Lorna. Of clan Scott."

"The *only* one?" He shook his head, angling it to one side as he waited for her to sort out his reply. Then he stepped closer, giving her a searching look. "You're wearing decent enow clothes. Your horse, standing just over there—" He pointed to one side. "A *fine* animal, with excellent saddle and tack." His face brightened. "Definitely not low born—nor do ya' have the wings on ya' back of a mountain fairy, come down from a secret highland glen."

"I'm of clan *Scott*. Daughter, to its *laird*. And Lady Marion, of Manor Scott."

The young man mimed the removal of a hat, sweeping his hand above the field grass as he bowed at the waist. "Honored, in making my acquaint of ya'. Lady Lorna. Of clan Scott." He straightened up. "*I'm* a penniless cur. Made to work for every meal, earned in hauling of materials to build the mills. Doing what's asked of me, helping where I can. Left to hunt hares in the grass to supplement my poor cupboard. Which I was doin' when *you* appeared, as if out of the face of the mountain."

"It was *you*, startled the rabbit. Causing my *spill!*"

"Or 'twas your *horse*—caused it to bolt, leaving me without meat for my *dinner*."

Lorna called out to the mare, who came trotting over, head down, as if guilty of having lost her rider. She stroked its neck, soothing its mood, considering the part she'd played in losing her seat in the saddle.

"It was an *accident*. *No* one's fault."

The boy stepped closer, hand outstretched. "Bayly."

Lorna shook it, his skin warm against hers. "Steward, it's meaning. Given you by your mother?"

"By a priest. Placing me with a family who'd lost their son. And myself, a young child in need of a place to live, blessed with a drip of water, poured on my head. Taking on the name they gave me."

"Your people — they are of clan Scott?"

"Nae. Of clan McLaughlin. From Argyll, near the end of Lock Fyne. Left clinging to the edge of a hovel somewhere down in Glasgow. With me sent off to fend as best I could. Which I've done when not having my meal scared off by one Mistress Lorna — of clan Scott. Daughter to its laird. A decent man and fine leader, from what I've seen." Bayly paused, looking toward the works below. "Himself, placing the coins in my hand for work I've done. Helping to set the geartrain in place. Me being wiry enow to worm into the workings, then out through the t'other side." He paused, seeing her yawn, covering it with one hand.

"Sorry." Lorna shook her head, still dazed by the fall. "My apologies made again for spoiling your hunt. I owe you a decent meal. Offered, above." She turned and looked into the foothills. "The mare's capable of taking two on her back if you're in agree to it. With a ride back down on the morrow."

Bayly took in a deep breath and held it while he sifted through his options before releasing it with a long sigh. "Aye. Seems the least I can do to help ya' right the *terrible* wrong done me."

He waited for Lorna to mount the mare, then took the hand offered him, using it to pull himself onto the horse's back, his legs pressed against hers. He slipped his hand around her waist with a smile on his face. Drinking in the scent of grass in her unbound hair.

※ ※ ※

Angus stepped out of the shadows of the large manor barn, arms crossed on his chest, studying Lorna's face as she returned from her journey down to the millworks near the far end of the Pinch. She was in the seat of a small wagon, with her young brother Calum pressed against her side, chattering away as always.

Angus swallowed a grin, having sent the young laddie along to keep his sister company while she delivered the young man she'd invited home, back to the worksite where Declan was staying. Wanting to keep a close eye on the project. He'd handed Lorna a satchel to deliver to her father, containing a set of drawings for him to review. One of them, with an innovative design for the mill under construction. A suggestion by the lad named Bayly when shown the papers the previous night.

Angus had guided him through each drawing, answering questions as the young man considered them carefully, offering a few respectful questions, and a suggestion that promised an increase in productivity at a lower cost of construction. A sealed note slipped into the packet, letting Declan know to keep the boy close to his side. Sent for several reasons, one of them having to do with the furtive looks exchanged between Bayley and Lorna during the meal at the manor.

"Did ya' have a fun time, Calum?" Angus greeted the boy, just turned six years of age, with a wide grin. Getting a nod and a wide smile in return.

"I *did!* Bayly—he told me stories of faeries hovering over the dark waters of the place he comes from. Of them feeding the dragons that live in the—in the—" Calum paused, gathering his thoughts, prone to letting them outrace his words. "The *loch*. With an *H* at the end. Not like a lock on a door." He paused, taking a breath, then continued. "Lorna, she never spoke a single word the whole way down and back again. Listening to everything we talked about. Bayly and me."

Angus noted Lorna's scowl. "I can only imagine, laddie. Now go on ahead inside while I help your sweet sister with the team and wagon." He waited until the boy cleared the yard, then helped Lorna down from the seat, getting a cat-eyed glare for his trouble. "The boy and the latest drawings—safely delivered?"

Lorna huffed as she went to the head of the team, leading them toward the barn. Angus moved ahead, sliding the heavy doors open, the metal wheels protesting a bit, a note made to himself to have them greased by one of the field hands on the morrow. Once the large animals were in their stalls, watered and curried, with the harnesses hung on wooden pegs, Lorna rounded on her uncle.

"You did that on *purpose*! Dinna' *trust* me to go off alone—"

"*Tone*, lassie. *Mind* your tone. The words—your right to offer me. Along with *respect* earned in caring for ya' since ya' was born."

Lorna opened her mouth to respond with a cutting remark, then glanced at the hands of the man who'd taught her how to walk, ride a horse, and stand up for herself. How to approach issues with eyes open to either side of the argument, made. And one with a firm hand that had provided her with rare, though memorable lessons on the merits of obeying authority figures. Taller or shorter than herself.

"You sent Calum with me. On purpose. To prevent the wagging of tongues, both here and below."

"Aye, lass. No distrust to you intended. Only meant to protect your place in the clan. Yourself, one day, to step into a role of leadership. Whichever one you decide suits you best, with *whomever* you choose to share it with."

Lorna nodded, her anger having flown away. "Do ya' *like* him, Uncle?" She blushed, looking away, unable to face the man she respected above all others, including her father. Sweet man, though he was.

"He's quick-minded. Which is as much an asset as it is a potential threat." Angus held up one hand, stopping her reply while it lay in the cradle. "Not a judgment on the lad's *character* or lack of known background. My own, equally suspect. Before my second set of parents took in me. Then invited on high by your great-great uncle. Former laird to the clan."

He paused, watching to see how his comment landed. "I sent a note to your father. Letting him know to keep the lad close to hand, with increased responsibilities—*and* pay. Enough to help him get set up. But *not* enough to marry, becoming a father to a brood of children."

Lorna twisted away, her face turning bright red, hands in balls of embarrassment. Angus stepped over, waiting to lay a hand on her shoulder until she regained her composure. "You're an *incredible* young woman, Lorna. As sly as the four-footed wee beastie you're named for. And, like a fox, you need to keep a watch out for the wolf, Mac Tire. Or the eagle, Iolaire."

She nodded, turning around, hands clasped in front of her, head lowered. When she looked up, a mist of tears filled her eyes. "My uncle Aaron. *He's* one of those. A *Mac Tire*." She paused. "I've heard him called that by the men visiting you here. Their voices kept low. Out of respect. Or *fear*."

Angus reached up and gently wiped away her tears. "*Respect*, Lorna. Shown your uncle for what he's done. What he's *had* to do. Protecting your family and countless others over there. His only wish when he left was to save a friend, then come back home. Back to the family. To the mountain, above."

Lorna leaned forward, resting her head on her uncle's chest. Not a relative by blood, all the closer to her for it. "Will I ever *see* him? *Meet* him? Is he *still* alive?" She sniffed, her mood gone over to the loss felt in wanting to see all her family. Patrick, Lochlan, Aunt Meghan, and Uncle Allwyn. "Would he even know who I am? Or only see me as a stranger?"

"Nae, lass. You've the look to ya' of someone he once loved—and let go of. A *fine* young lady, wanting to do the same work as your mother and grandmother."

Angus guided his niece out of the barn, then slid the large doors closed. As he walked toward the manor, he pursed his lips, the latest message from Aaron raising a concern. The war-weary veteran had mentioned a return to Scotland, using the same method as his father had before him. As they entered the kitchen, he let go of his worries, the scent of meat in the oven wrinkling his nose. Along with the odor of a wee bairn lying asleep in a cradle, in need of a change. Marion's third child, Isla. A healthy young lassie of two months with midnight hair, light-colored eyes, and a thin cleft in the middle of her narrow chin.

CHAPTER TWENTY-NINE

CROSSROAD SETTLEMENT
LATE FALL, 1794

Sinclair bounced a young girl on one knee, hiding a wince of discomfort, her hips sore from a trip to the city and home again on horseback, despite her sweet mare's smooth gait. She knew age was having its way with her joints, with medicinal herbs collected from the hills used to relieve the worse of the symptoms. Along with a small glass of wine before bed, providing a restful first half of each night's sleep. Broken along the edge of early morning by a mother's eternal worry for her children and grandchildren. Especially those not near to hand.

Meghan came into the store and stopped, watching her youngest child, named Eira after her grandmother, a healthy four-year-old girl with light brown hair and blue eyes, helping to improve her grandmother's mood. She was aware her mother was missing Marion and her growing brood. Knew it would soon trigger another voyage made there. One she planned to join, along with all three of her children.

Meghan pursed her lips, considering how Allwyn would respond when she let him know. Aware he would protest, unsettled by the thought of his family gone, though his duties as the leader of the community would provide enough of a distraction. As great as the constant calls for attention by Eira, long overdue for her nap.

"The tea is on. Fresh scones, too. The child needs her lie-down. And *you*, dear mother, in need of what I've added to the brew of leaves."

Sinclair handed her granddaughter to Meghan. "She's growing. Her weight now more than is good for me. Though I *love* our brief rides." Eira smiled at her mother, then raised one hand, trying to stifle a yawn. Failing to do so, resting her head on Meghan's shoulder, eyes closing.

"Come along." Meghan helped Sinclair to her feet, holding on for a moment while she found her balance. "I'll put ya' both to bed once you've had your tea. This little lady—sure to be asleep before we get to the kitchen."

Once Meghan returned from the bedroom upstairs, she sat down and took a sip of the tea her mother had poured for her. "It's good. The leaves left to steep. A mix of ginger and chamomile to help ease any aches or pains." Sinclair eyed her daughter over the rim of her glass.

"You've noticed."

Meghan shrugged. "Something we *all* suffer from. The work we do exacts a heavy toll."

"*Age*, daughter. No matter your attempt to gainsay it. I'm satisfied with the signs, having earned each wrinkle, gray hair, and ache." Sinclair grinned, holding the tea to her lips, inhaling the mixed aromas, before taking a sip. Then she closed her eyes and sighed. "Your grandmother—always with a tincture or poultice to hand." She opened her eyes, giving her daughter a steady look. "You learned your lessons at her knee. Fingers in the soil, pulling roots from the earth. She'd be proud of the woman you've become. Though there were more than a few *doubts* along the way."

Meghan nodded, her ear canted to the opening of the stairway, hearing a slight sound, her daughter mumbling in her sleep. "I was often on the *wild* side of things." She paused, sipping her tea while her mother remained silent. "*Most* times."

Sinclair acknowledged the comment with a nod, her eyes lowered. "Your brother, near to hand. Taking you to the mountain to soothe your mood. Guiding you to an occasional beastie when you were old enough. Brought to the ground by your arrow. Your blood—cooled by the hunt."

Meghan looked at her mother. "I'm going there with you. Back to the highlands the next time you travel home. The children, too, needing to get to know each other. Needing to know where they've sprung from."

Sinclair nodded. "Had the same thought, with passage booked on the next ship suitable. For us all."

"Allwyn will need to stay here. To see to the—"

"Him *too*. Enough men trained up to see to things, with plenty of women with eyes cocked, ready to step in with a suggestion or two if they can't seem to manage things for themselves."

Meghan nodded, a smile in her heart, eager to see her family back in the clear, cool air of the highlands, with visibility limited only by one's imagination. Able to see clear around the earth, as Aaron once said, the two of them at the top of the mountain, leaning against the rock cairn. With her brother's voice in her ear, telling her he could see the back of their heads from being so high. The rumble of his deep laughter as she twisted her head to look. A favorite memory still, hazing her eyes, wishing he were sitting beside her now.

"Aye. I agree. *All* of us, to make the journey there and back." Meghan hesitated, then asked a question she knew her mother might not be willing to answer. "Will I *never* see my brother again?"

Sinclair looked away, lips drawn in a tight line. "There's no gain to you in explaining the situation he finds himself in." She stood up, needing to use one hand on top of the table to catch her balance. "I've not *seen* him in—more than a while."

"But you have *news* of him." Meghan stared at her mother. "From dispatches delivered in the night. Left in a hollow oak on the far edge of the field." She stood up and joined her mother. "I've watched you leave in the mornings, just at dawn." The two of them stood framed in the kitchen window, Sinclair remaining silent, choosing to ignore the comment.

Meghan narrowed her eyes in concern as she watched Allwyn in the yard, working on showing his youngest son the proper jumping of a horse. Lochlan, who'd just turned nine, was astride a long-legged, dappled gray mare. Patrick, thirteen years old, sprouting in height and girth every day, alongside, sitting a large framed black stallion with a gray mane and tail.

"Let the jump come to the horse. She'll know when to rise." Allwyn touched his young son on his lower back. "Keep your shoulders square to the ground, head up, then lean back as she comes down onto her forelegs, with her hind legs landing next, helping absorb the shock."

"But what if she stumbles—or misjudges the leap?" Lochlan gave his father a strained look, his hands trembling, the mare growing anxious, feeding off the boy's fear. Patrick nudged his horse with his heels, the stallion sidestepping over to the mare so the two animals could exchange a greeting, their long noses touching.

"Come over here with me, brother, and I'll take you through it." Patrick slid back, making room in the saddle. "You'll see what I do, then have a go yourself."

Before Allwyn could stop his youngest son, the two were away. The stallion, given its choice of where to make its leap, bunched its hindquarters, the shouts of the two boys filling the air with a mix of deep laughter and a high-pitched squeal as the horse leaped over the nearest gate with ease. It landed in a cloud of dust, then turned an elongated circle with another leap made. Ending with excited shouts from both riders, their heads up, broad smiles stretching the corners of their mouths as the horse came on in a trot.

"He's *ready*. Aren't you, brother?" Lochlan nodded, dismounting with a leap, then climbed into the mare's saddle. Allwyn shrugged, knowing the lesson had moved beyond his control. He released the bridle and stood back, with Patrick coming up beside him. Both of them watched as the young boy and mare repeated the jump, albeit with less clearance over the topmost rail.

Allwyn hesitated, worried there'd be a boy with broken bones, or worse, rider and horse both. He leaned forward to wave them off from making another run when Patrick's hand found his upper arm. "Wait." His son gently squeezed, his fingers firm. "He'll be fine. I promise."

The moment of truth arrived, both animal and boy rising as one, sailing over the hurdle, landing without issue, and coming on in a gallop toward the center of the yard, pulling up in a shower of loose dirt.

"We *did* it! *Cloud* and me. Just like you and *Dancer!*" Lochlan gave his brother a look. "*Almost* as high."

"*Higher*, brother. Beating us by a hand."

Allwyn nodded, then looked away as particles of dirt found the corners of his eyes, his fingers dragging away tears of pride in the two boys he'd helped raise. With a clap of a hand on his oldest son's back, he went over and took the mare's bridle, giving Lochlan a firm nod of his head.

Sinclair, watching from the window, shook her head, amazed at how alike her two grandson's relationship was to the one Aaron and Meghan once shared. Her daughter, now a mother herself, standing alongside her. She turned, leaning against the frame, her arms crossed, looking at Meghan, seeing a woman in the prime of her life. Beautiful. Poised. Proud of her men. Matriarch to an incredible family. And worthy of the truth.

"Your brother is working with a group of men exposed to death at every turn. Dealing it out, when called on to do so. Doing what they can, in coordination with others back in Scotland, supporting the efforts of *good* men here to accomplish important work. Without interference from those with opposite intentions."

"Like our father, before him. Fighting in *his* war, which is why he *left* us. Left you. Coming *here*." Meghan got a nod in reply. "To prevent, if possible, the *next* conflict from happening." Another nod from her mother, who reached for a chair, and sat back down, reclaiming her cup of tea. Holding it between her hands. Meghan gazed at her. "Failing to do so, with my brother caught up in the mix. Leaving me concerned for the *next* generation. Another conflict looming over the horizon. With my oldest son—*your* grandson—pulled into the *same* horror. Like the three generations *before* him."

"Not if he's *home*. Back to the *highlands*. Not if you'd *agree* to make the move. To where he'll be *safe!* Where we'll *all* be safe. Protected. Kept from the senseless killings to come. With all of you returning there *with* me. Plenty of others here, willing to carry the torch."

Meghan stared at her mother. "You would have us run *away?*

From *everything* that we've accomplished. All we're doing. Tossing it aside like a pair of old clothes, no longer worth the mending of." She shook her head. "You'd have me—have *us*, my family, leave the land my children have been *born* in. My *blood*, *sweat*, and countless *tears* shed, along with those of their *own*, watering the very ground we're *standing* on."

Sinclair reached out, trying to take her daughter's hands. "*Please*, Meghan. *Listen* to me. You must see the folly of what's coming. This experiment in forming an independent country with men ceding power to the masses. An *admirable* enough concept, but a misguided attempt, doomed to fail." She shook her head. "There will *never* be another Athens. No *city-state*, this one. Hundreds of years of effort made to recreate it. Failing, every time. Made a target by men eager to pull it down. Stone by stone."

"It *still* lives, Mother. The possibility of it is *here*—" Meghan swept her hand in a half-circle. "Outside these walls. Beyond the ridgeline, soon to move deep into western lands. Spread along the entire coast-line, north to south. *Here*, where my father and brother bled for the opportunity before us. Where my brother *still* bleeds. Where—"

"I'll have *no* more of my family's blood *spilled!* Enough of it already *given!* Not a *single* drop more, for others' gain. My family—my children and *their* children—*will* be together again. Under *my* watch. Where—" Sinclair gasped for breath, her face going pale, hands clenched as she slumped in her chair, head striking the windowsill.

Meghan yelled for Allwyn as she reached to support her mother, holding her in place until her husband and two sons could reach the house.

Allwyn looked up, watching his wife's eyes as she entered the kitchen, looking for a sign as to her mother's condition. Patrick was outside, keeping Lochlan occupied, the two of them tending to the stock.

"She's—sleeping. Shaken by what happened, but her senses have recovered. Though I'm worried about her lack of strength. Her grip, weak, hands trembling." Meghan sighed, worry in her eyes. "A spell, no doubt brought on by distress. Her concerns for everyone's safety — more than she could handle. But she's a *firm* spine — and a *stiff* neck."

Allwyn came over and took his wife in his arms. "Like her daughter."

Meghan nodded, her head pressed against his chest. "She's stronger — *far* stronger than me." Her voice broke, hands rising to clutch at the fabric of his shirt, tugging at it. "She's had to carry a burden greater than any I've ever borne. For much longer. The weight of it — enough to break a strong mule's back."

"Can she not shed herself of her worries? Hand it on to others? To us? To me?"

"Aye, if pulled from her hands with a rope and tackle, with her feet anchored to the ground. Even then, she'd find a way out of letting go." Meghan looked up, her eyes filled with tears. "She wants us to go back. To move back home."

Allwyn rubbed her cheeks with the edge of his thumbs, drying her tears. "To the highlands?"

"Aye. To the manor home — in Scotland."

He released her, stepping back, eyes narrowed in confusion. "You're not in consideration of it, love. Right?"

"Nae. Not in the doin', but I am open to spending a half-year there. To see her made right again. See her back in balance."

"And why is *that?*" Allwyn saw his wife's eyes widen and hurried to explain. "Not in the *going*, but as to the sudden loss of her balance." He took Meghan's hands, holding them. "She's the toughest woman — nae, the most forceful *person* I've ever known. A rock." He lowered his voice. "What's caused the change? Is it news of your brother?"

Meghan shook her head. "It's about what he's been doin' all these years, since first arriving here. With more to his tale than she's been able to tell us."

"He's a *soldier*, wife. One without a war. Gone west to raise a family."

Meghan shook her head. "I sense he's never left off of the fighting, With the battle gone over to the shadows." She looked him in the eyes. "I could see it in his eyes, the last time he was here. A haunted look in the face of a hunted man." Tears filled her eyes once more. "My dear brother, wearing a mask with a false smile painted on it. Coming and leaving in the dark."

Allwyn held her while she cried, looking out the window, listening to the boys. His heart was in his throat, as he listened to the sound of sticks, used as swords, his son's engaged in a mock duel. For today.

"We'll go. As your mother *needs* us to do. And stay through the summer. Deciding then the next steps taken." He pulled back, raising her chin with a finger, staring into her eyes, tears on her cheeks. Then he leaned down and gently kissed them away.

CHAPTER THIRTY
BRISTOL
SPRING, 1794

Marion nodded, holding a financial report handed to her by a woman sitting on the other side of a small desk. She studied the figures, then gave the other woman, near to her age, a casual sweep of her eyes, taking in her clothes, hair, and demeanor. Poised. Calm. Wearing a dress with a small waistcoat. Both were of excellent quality, in black and gray tones. The fit, tailored to her build, the colors denoting she was a serious person, of high status.

"The numbers are—impressive." Marion hesitated, dropping her eyes to check the figures once more. "If *true*. Though the accounting house you chose is *above* reproach." She dropped the report, then leaned back, her hands flat on the surface of her desk. "As too are *your* credentials, Mrs. Harrison."

The other woman returned a tight smile, then looked away, watching a flock of blackbirds streaming by a small window of the nondescript office. Once they passed, she sighed, shaking her head. "No longer a Harrison, Lady Marion Haversham-Knutt. I've gone back to the use of my family name. Addison. Skye Addison."

Marion nodded. "Of course." She wasn't surprised by the news, having hired a firm to investigate the woman, verifying who she was and what she was about, before agreeing to the meeting. Her standard approach to anyone reaching out to her, offering their services, or seeking financial backing for efforts similar to the work started by her mother.

"Your father — I understand he was the rector at Marischal. Where my brother once attended."

"He *still* is, though expected to retire at the end of the term. His health — becoming an issue."

"Not *too* serious, I hope." Marion knew every detail of the man's condition. The man's doctor paid a visit from Angus, with monies exchanged.

"His leg, paining him more each year. An old wound suffered in the siege of Gibraltar. In service alongside your grandfather, if I have it right." Skye straightened up, aware the game was in play, with the opening moves providing a myriad of options for response. "Your father — *also* a veteran, as I recall. And a gifted speaker in Commons."

"He was. Though no longer with us. His death is a mystery, still."

"How terrible for you. A man of vision, clearly defined in the speeches made. A beacon of hope to the common man. A significant loss. For your family, and the British Empire, both." Skye hesitated, her voice soft. "Are they of good health — your family?"

"Three children of my own, scattered across more years than I am comfortable in the counting of. All hale. My husband, the same." She paused a moment, studying Skye's face, aware of her desire to learn of Aaron's fate. Fearful of hearing it told. "As too, my mother. Over in the colonies. My sister Meghan is there as well, forming a *new* clan. Three children in her capable hands."

Marion noted Skye's stiff posture, her hands clenched in her lap. "As to my brother —" She paused, noting the slight lift of the other woman's eyebrows. "He's well enough, last I heard. Having survived his — travails in the colonies." Marion, aware of Skye's past relationship with Aaron, had once hated her for having abandoned him, leading to his decision to head to Pennsylvania Colony. Learning the truth from her great uncle Shaun and letting go of her anger, understanding the pain of forced separation on both sides.

Skye nodded, then turned her head to the side, releasing the dread felt while waiting to learn the fate of the only man she'd ever loved in full. One forced to let go of her, honoring a promise made to her father. The story told her in a carriage bound from Marischal to London. Then another, when her father revealed she'd been promised to a man in an arranged marriage. Leaving her with a heart twice broken in less than a single day.

A brief engagement had followed, before her marriage to an older man. Decent enough, in his way, with a minor title of nobility and major expectations of a male heir. Her first child, a daughter delivered. A hard birth, with the child dying shortly thereafter. Found in her cradle, unresponsive. A second and third attempt had delivered two sons, perfectly formed, both having died in her womb, the cause unknown.

Her husband, devastated by the outcomes, reluctantly asked the courts to set their marriage aside, seeking dissolution on the grounds of infertility. Skye left with a sizeable dispensation as his measure of respect for her diligent efforts, harboring no ill will toward her. Or love. The emotion never having come to fruition during their eight years together.

Skye spent the next ten years of her life mirroring the efforts begun by Aaron in Glasgow. Moving back there and working in the outlying villages. Her focus aimed at helping to arrange financing for millworks, built on land alongside the river Clyde. The money earned, reinvested in the purchase of fields for communal gardens, and the provision of seed money for pocket industries, employing women and older children working in spinning and textile houses. Education provided them all. Taught by herself at first. Expanded to the other women, once proven capable of passing the lessons along.

Marion waited out the long silence, fully aware of the woman's tale of marital woes and subsequent activities. Meeting her gaze with a gentle smile when Skye looked back.

"He's there—*still?*"

"As far as I know. Not home again since—well, since the time *you* last saw him."

Skye lowered her eyes. "You know of our friendship, of course. As you should. Your brother telling—"

Marion cut her off. "*Nae.* Never a word of it heard from *his* lips.

With him leaving Glasgow behind, soon after you parted. With all of us, his mother, my sister, and I, never told of his plans. A decision he made soon after a conversation with your father, as told us by my great-uncle. With my brother lost to the chaos of that *dreadful* conflict, with a reconnection of sorts made with my sister and mother in Pennsylvania. Staying in contact ever since. As often as possible."

Skye stiffened her posture. "You have the advantage of me. Holding *all* the information about what transpired between us."

"Not *all*." Marion lowered her voice as she leaned forward, cupping her chin in her hands, elbows braced on the desk. "I know you came to love him. Beyond the kind that warms one's skin, quickening the beat of your heart, bringing an *ache* to the loins."

She smiled. "I've known the *lesser* kind, having suffered through it. Left paying the price, having to let him go. Finding the *other* kind. The heat of *true* love. One locked *deep* in my soul, to this very day. Unable to bear the thought of losing him, like I lost my father. And my second great-uncle. Along with my brother, for these many years. Each a blow, leaving me staggered."

Skye nodded her head. "I too left *staggered* by what happened. Delivered by my father, soon after, unto a man who was kind to me. Overlooking my—lowly status. Honoring me with his name, until set aside. Because of my—"

"I *know* what happened to you. My people were diligent in having established your credentials before I agreed to this meeting." Marion straightened up. "It's enough that we *both* know each has gained from our *painful* experiences. And gone through unbearable loss. As has my mother. A woman we've both pledged our efforts to, in helping others find their balance in an uneven world." She held out her right hand, waiting for Skye to take it. "To a collaboration. One promising to be of benefit for *all*."

CHAPTER THIRTY-ONE

LOCH FYNE
EARLY SPRING, 1794

The wind, coming hard out of the northeast, slung daggers of sleet, needling Angus's exposed cheeks. He stood huddled beneath an oiled cloak, staring at a small boat fighting its way through heavy swells. Its bow cut through a surge of green-gray waves, aiming for the ramshackle dock he was standing next to, the reins of two sturdy mountain horses held in his gloved hands.

Four men sat the sweeps, two to each side with a man at the rudder, head lowered against the icy spray, calling the stroke. He timed the last one, ordering the men to ship their oars as he turned into a narrow, water-foamed crack in a fractured headland. The boat slid into place alongside a water-soaked wooden structure. The man sitting in the bow, without a satchel or bag, leaping up, finding his balance, his legs swaying from having spent several weeks at sea.

The small boat retreated, with no words exchanged, leaving the way it came, heading back to a ship lying at anchor. A dark hull, with no sails, fit to the masts. And no lights showing on its deck.

"You've been long away, my friend." Angus smiled, regretting the movement, ice stinging his full lips. "And *coldly* welcomed back."

Aaron straightened up, his eyes on the one person outside his immediate family he knew he could trust. With his great uncle

Shaun's approval given to the short, stocky man, long ago. A solid reputation earned, many times over, as someone you could count on to see to the needs of each member of clan Scott. Whether born high or low.

Once he had his balance, Aaron reached for the reins, the two horses jerking their heads, snorting their displeasure, made to stand in the open. Angus handed him a small glass bottle, pressing it into his fingers.

"Agua Vitea. The last of your Grand Da's making. Saved for this very day. With your feet back home again on Scottish sod."

Aaron held the container up, the gray sky passing barely enough light to see through the thick glass. "I saw myself in a wooden box, the next time I touched Scottish soil." He stared out at the small boat, making its way toward the ship, then turned his back to the breeze, removing the stopper with his teeth. "Your message, sent by a man we shall not mention by name, suggesting a *different* point of disembarkation—" He looked around, taking in the desolate landscape. "The *wiser* choice."

"Knowledge of it provided me based on a young man's story of woe. Leading my eyes northward, before having sent the message your way."

Aaron offered the bottle to the much shorter man who took a small sip, holding it in his mouth until the tall, broad-shouldered warrior of note reclaimed it. Angus waited while Aaron took a healthy pull, swallowing it down with his eyes closed, then turned his head to one side, letting the whiskey drain from his mouth.

He watched as the stiff wind swept it away in a fan-shaped spray, staining the ground. Then he wrinkled his nose, the scent of it stirring bitter memories. "We've miles to go before the first stop. Best get moving. The horses, restless and liable to head off without us. Born clan Scott *stubborn*—and Scottish *strong*."

Night found them in a secluded croft, abandoned during the highland clearances. The owner of the vast estate, living back in England, leaving things in the hands of a bent-backed caretaker, minding the property. The man had remained silent, without a single word exchanged as he'd led them there. Leaving, without bothering to ask who or why the two of them were there, clutching a small purse that Angus tossed him.

Aaron yawned, a small fire in a slate stove heating the interior, the roof leaking, with a puddle forming in the center of the dirt floor. A satchel of hardtack and dried meat, their evening meal, with water carried in a small clay container from a nearby spring, used to wash it down.

"For all the times we've messaged, and the one time met—I've yet to hear *your* tale told, of why my great uncle called you on high."

"He knew my parents. My *second* set. The first, dying of a flux. The second, losing a boy to the same. With me gathered up by the church, then given to them. Taught my manners and how to read."

Angus paused, never having shared the rest before. With anyone. "He came through their door. Shaun—without knocking. Silent as a ghost, giving them each a hug. Sitting at their table, like he was there for a meal. My mother, the second one, handed him a parcel. My father, with a glass of whiskey in hand, a bottle pulled from a tall shelf."

Aaron took a bite of the tough meat, working it between his teeth while he studied Angus in the light from the stove, the small door left open, flames dancing in the firebox. After a few minutes, he gave the short man a look, his eyebrows raised.

"And—?"

"He looked over at me. Laird Shaun. Told me to stand. To come to him and shake his hand. Treated me like a blood member of clan Scott. Like a *man*." Angus paused, looking at the glass bottle, sitting on a small wooden slab used as a table. "Offered me a drink afterward. Gave me an odd look when I turned him down. I told him my Da, him that was my first, that he was a man possessed by the Devil when the drink was in him."

Aaron waited again, then finally sighed. "*And—?*"

"Your great uncle, he told me it was enough I'd shaken his hand. That he could tell my mettle, my spine, from the way I looked him in the eye while I did it. Told me I was welcome to come on high. Sent down a horse a few days later. A fine black stallion, with a new saddle, and stirrups sized to my short legs." Angus gave Aaron a sober look. "I *loved* that beastie. More than any since. Until bastards from down low come up and took him from me. Along with six others belonging to your family."

He reached out, taking the bottle in his hand and staring at it, leaving the stopper in place. Then he smiled, reliving a distant memory. "I tortured the one who put the blade to its throat. Fed him, inch by screaming inch, into the jaws of pigs. Right up to his knees. His pain — the shrieks of his misery — sounded just like those of the horses being slaughtered. Screaming in the night."

Aaron reached over and took the bottle. He pulled the stopper, drained the rest, then tossed it into the stove. A swirl of colors mixed with the yellow of the flames, slipping away through the chimney, coaxed by the wailing draw of the highland storm.

Angus tossed in a few pieces of peat, then closed the door and turned down the draft. He leaned back, hands in his lap, eyeing Aaron, who finally looked over.

"You're wanting to know the *why* of things. Why I've come home. Taking the risk of bringing danger to myself and my family."

Angus nodded. "And to those *still* in the fight. Your friends. Men, guided by you over the past eight years and more. With their leader over *here*." He paused. "With me."

Aaron looked away, studying the door, watching as it vibrated in the stiff wind flowing through the secluded valley from on high. "I'm *drained*. By the killing. The butchery. The — endless *insanity* of it all." He swung his eyes, staring at Angus. "Losing a friend —" He snapped his fingers. "Like *that*. In a senseless act, with him trying to protect me."

"I read the report. The information gathered of *immense* value. With several nests eradicated. One of them, near to where the interests of clan Scott lay. Gone now, because of your friend's sacrifice."

"An *unnecessary* one. Me, the one to have gone. Information provided, opening the door for a mutual exchange in return, leading to an offer of membership in their club." Aaron paused, lifted his hand, and wiped his eyes. "Information my friend *didn't* have. Leading to his death."

Angus shrugged. "Men make mistakes. Part of the cost of doing business."

"Business?" Aaron narrowed his eyes, lips drawn tight. "Is *that* how you see this? As a *business?*"

"Pigs."

Aaron shook his head, tired from the day's travel. Worn out from the weeks aboard ship. From additional weeks spent making his way to a secluded fishing village miles north of Boston. Weary beyond words, having parted from his new second in command under a cloud of anger. Charged with the betrayal of their cause. "*Pigs?*"

"A mainstay in the business of providing for people's meals. Pigs. Mutton. Cattle." Angus paused. "Along with stags. Of the *red* variety. Not to mention rabbits. Sagehens—"

"I *know* the list, Angus. The reason for its recitation, not clear."

"Then allow me to start anew." He paused. "*Butchers.*"

Aaron closed his eyes and cursed, his hands clenched. He shook his head, then got to his feet, intending to go out into the storm to cool his frustration, his memories heated by the words aimed at him over two months ago. The stocky man who'd stepped in when Smoke lost his life, stiff-legged in anger. His eyes lit with a mix of disappointment and fear.

"*Coward.* Running *away!* Leaving *us* to continue the fight. Leaving us to the *butchers!*"

"You're *clear. All* of you. Free to walk away, placing your shoulders to the wheel, along with the others, helping create something *positive.* Letting go of the *bloody* end of the stick. Using it to prod holes in the ground instead. Planting crops. Building homes. Families. Futures." The other man stood up and walked away from the circle of a small fire, leaving a trail of muttered curses.

Aaron stared at Angus. "Butcher?"

Angus gave him another nod. "*Butchers.* Plural. What they name people whose hands run red with blood. Doing the grueling work needed to keep people fed. Helping a community to thrive. Not work for the squeamish, or faint of heart." He paused again, giving Aaron a quick nod. "Butchers. Like *you.*"

"No longer, my friend." Aaron's voice was tight with repressed anger, Angus feeling a chill in the air, despite the heat from the stove. "I can *see* that." He yawned, stretching out his legs and wriggling his feet, watching the light from a small candle wash over their scuffed leather surface. "When a man's *done* with something, he should know when to set it aside. Same as it is with a carpenter, mason, laborer — or *butcher*."

"That word, uttered *again*, will be the cause for my leaving. Storm or no."

"No need for that. Your choice — a *commendable* one. With my full support. I assume it to have been the same with the men who followed you." Angus lowered his head, his chin on his chest, eyes fixed on Aaron's.

"They — came to understand. Accepted what I told them. Free to decide when to haul up stakes and go home."

"Which you've *done*. Arriving here. Your stakes pulled. No doubt tucked away in your sleeve, having arrived without a bag in your hand. When you stepped ashore. From a *wooden* box, in the shape of a boat."

"Why?" Aaron shook his head, looking away. "Why are you *chastising* me?"

"Because I have the interests of the *entire* clan to consider. Of you *and* your family. Of *every* member of *every* family, from low to high. And I need to know if you're *truly* out of the fight. *Never* to return. A *new* plan formed around your absence, if so. With no going back into the fray, my friend. Neither there *nor* here. *Ever* again." Angus hardened the tone of his voice. "I will need that agreed to. Tonight. *Now*."

Aaron gave him a fixed stare, his voice whisper-thin. "Or?"

Angus smiled. "One of us is going to get their *ass* booted. You, if'n ya' willing to kneel on the floor, that I might *reach* it."

Aaron nodded, letting go of his misplaced anger. Angry at himself for allowing his need to seek the high places again to have pulled him from the battleground. Other men made to carry on the struggle, including the short-legged giant of a man sitting across from him. He sat back down.

"If it comes to *blows*, I'll gladly bend the knee to you. *Both* of them."

∗∗∗

The wee croft house stood as a sentinel, framed at the end of a narrow valley floor. As Aaron passed by, he eyed the roof, covered in a thick layer of moss, noting it looked to be in decent shape. Repairs made years earlier with his father, the two of them sharing opinions about family, and the movement of stags in the hills. Of politics and war. Each question he'd dared to ask met with an answer. With occasional moments of silence as the veteran stared down, his hands working on the replacement of a cracked tile. His responses edged with emotion.

Aaron sighed as he followed Angus back toward the small shelter, the two of them having settled their horses into stalls further down the path. The foot-sore animals fed, watered, and groomed. He altered his stride, walking at a pace equal to that of the shorter man, feeling like a stranger to the place. As if his memories belonged to another man, from another time.

Once inside, he watched as Angus started a fire in the stove, the small room heating quickly, requiring him to crack open a window at the end of the wider of two beds, letting in a wash of dull, gray light. A thick-walled cast-iron kettle sat atop the stove, steam slipping from a spout blackened by hours of use on fires in highland meadows. Used during overnight hunts for red stags, the memory reaching out, tugging at Aaron's heart. The hiss of spring-sourced water coming to a roil around a linen pouch filled with tea leaves brought an image of his father's face to mind. A wide, crooked grin that framed white teeth. Eyes of blue, the color of his own, lined at the edges as he held his cup, hunched down in a swirl of Scottish gorse, tucked beneath the overhanging limbs of small trees, waiting on the tea.

The image resolved into the wilds of Pennsylvania. A similar kettle, heating under a canopy of pines. A moment of respite before the killing of men in red and white uniforms would begin again. Chatte with a smile on her perfect face as she tended the fire, confident of her hold over him.

"Hard, I imagine." Angus offered Aaron a cup of tea. "Being here. Near to ya' home. And still a thousand miles and more, away." He ignored the tears on Aaron's cheeks, falling into his thick beard. Black with gray strands. Too soon, Angus thought, as he sat down. Too soon to have so many signs of age, etched on the features of someone barely a decade senior in age.

"Thank you." Aaron sighed, holding the cup to his lips, testing the heat of the flavored liquid, glad there was no whiskey available. Too easy, he thought as he sipped and then swallowed. Too easy to fall into its numbing effects. Having witnessed far too many men, unable to force the flask away. Using it to help soften the memories of things they'd seen. And done.

"There are several casks of supplies near to hand, brought high by me alone, soon after your message arrived. Dried meat. Hard bread and cheese. Along with flour, salt, and a case of red wine. Enough to see ya' through 'til you've had time to settle in."

Aaron nodded. "Thinking of everything. As has been the case since first reaching out to me. Being able to *find* me across the ocean and land between. With you back here."

Angus shrugged. "The value of an *excellent* education. The books read throughout my life opened my eyes to a host of alternate viewpoints. Of countless options on either side of this endless game. Forced to play it without rules." He gave Aaron a measured look. "Assisted by information provided me by your great uncle. A trove of invaluable details about those opposed to our efforts. With a careful plan worked out, then employed. Carried out by people willing to deliver it to *your* side of the Atlantic."

"Risking men's lives for—*what?* Support of those behind the drafting of a proclamation of independence, with faint promises made of a seat at the table, should they succeed? Positions offered them should this experiment in self-rule work out?" Aaron shook his head. "A *thin* concept, placing your trust in the morality of men unable or *unwilling* to do the dark deeds required. Careful to avoid the stain of blood on *their* hands."

Angus returned a quiet stare. "My *trust*—placed in *our* people's honor." He hardened his tone. "*All* those used—loyal *sons* of Scotland. *All* of them—drawn from *our* clan."

Aaron felt a blush of shame wash over his cheeks. He looked down, staring into the cup held between his hands. The surface of the dark-bodied tea was a mirror. The eyes staring back belonged to a stranger. To a boy, now gone. Along with the bow. And the father. And the company of a sister, ever a shadow to him while growing up. Left behind, back in the colonies with her family. And Marion, a three-hour walk away, with a family of her own. The thought of meeting them was difficult to imagine. Greeting her with a shrug of his shoulders, a weak smile on his lips, as if the years between had been but a handful of days. Left facing the children as a stranger. With a deeply lined face and pain-dulled eyes.

Angus softened his tone. "You fought the fight that was in *front* of you. When first arriving there. Forced into war. The battles fought, left you alive against *great* odds. Toeing *both* sides of what's considered honorable behavior by those penning tales in books. Scribes, without direct knowledge of the burden to one's soul from the taking of other men's lives."

He leaned forward, matching Aaron's hunched posture. "What you, and those who followed you, accomplished, no matter the how of it — helped provide the foundation blocks for people like Meghan and her husband to use. Building on *your* efforts. Planting seeds in the ground you shed blood on. Given an opportunity to grow into something never seen before."

Aaron looked up. "You believe that to be true?"

Angus shrugged. "It's a bedtime story I tell myself *every* night. Helping me fall asleep, surrounded by the ghosts of those I've had a hand in the killing of while protecting my family. Sworn *to* the duty by the former laird. My solemn vow — made to him."

Aaron lifted the cup, draining it. "Easier on your soul, when eliminating a *direct* threat to those you love."

Angus looked over. "As *you* did years ago. Just down the valley."

"And the *rest* of them?" Aaron narrowed his gaze, searching the other man's eyes. "The bodies strewn in my wake, weighing down one side of the scale?"

"A *rough* game. With no clear winners or losers. No treaty to be offered in the shadow war *you* signed in red to join. With no quarter offered or expected in return. A *vicious* game played, with no way of telling if'n ya' on the right or wrong side of destiny's plan'." Angus grinned. "At least, that's what I tell *myself* when my feet hit the floor in the morning."

Aaron nodded, then yawned, lifting his arms, stretching them above his head, his fingers brushing against the low ceiling. "And the next step?"

Angus leaned back, his short, heavily muscled arms crossed on his thick chest. "You'll stay here 'til ya' ready to come down. Or until your sister—" He nodded toward the west. "Drags the story out of me, coming high, along with all the rest of them." He stood up and walked over, his hand on Aaron's shoulder. "*Your* call. For now."

"All?" Aaron stared, his mouth half-open, wondering if he'd heard right. "Meghan—and my mother? With her family?"

"The others are due to arrive within the week." Angus gave Aaron a wide smile. "So—when you're ready, it's down or up. I'll be back again, late on the morrow. You can let me know then." He paused, glancing out the window, seeing the sky was clearing, the night to come promising to be cold. "The mountain should be clear of snow if you decide to make the climb. I did it. Once. With your great uncle. Had to get behind and push him up the last rise. His hip gone sour, in pain every step."

"Thank you. For having done that." Aaron reached out, taking the other man's hand, holding on. "For that, and everything else you've done on behalf of the family. Of the clan."

Angus nodded, then turned around. He opened and closed the heavy door behind him, leaving without another word. A few minutes later, Aaron listened to the sound of hooves on flat stones. Fading away as Angus headed down to the manor below.

⚜ ⚜ ⚜

Meghan came on in a headlong rush, her eldest son, Patrick, beside her, both urging their borrowed mounts toward a line of bushes framing the end of a narrow field. They'd carefully scanned the ground while walking their horses the length of it, checking for rocks or other debris, which might injure the animals. Or themselves.

Patty held the lead by half-a-length, his body out of the saddle, angled forward, his black hair streaming in the sun-warmed air. His whoop of victory was short-lived, hearing his mother's scream of pain. He pulled back on the reins, turning his head to see the cause. Meghan flew past, with her scream turned into a shout of glee as she won the race.

"You *cheated! Unfair*, Mother!" Patrick pulled alongside her, Meghan with a wide grin, shaking her head.

"Not at all, son. You *had* it won, then *lost*. A valuable lesson learned." She reached over and squeezed his upper arm, feeling the muscles beneath his shirt. "One to remember, when a pretty lass catches ya' eye. Using her wiles. Turning you away from friends, or hunts in the hills."

"Never. My *bow* is all the friend *I* need. Hunting—in my *blood*." He nodded. "From two sources. Doubly blessed. Seeing the horns in the hall. Yours *and* Uncle Aaron's." He hesitated. "I plan to add a set there, once allowed to go high."

Sinclair stood at the manor door, using a small hammer to strike a gong, hanging to one side. The brass tone carried through the sweep of warm air rising from the lowlands, full of the scent of heather, easing into an early bloom. Marion was beside her, smiling, proud of her sister and her brood. Their early arrival had been a pleasant surprise upon her return from Bristol, London, and Bath, with a guest in hand.

"Father would be proud of the family she's raised. And with the work being done, in continuing your own." Marion waited until her mother hung the hammer beside the door, then took her hand, holding onto it. "And proud of *you*. Matriarch to clan Scott."

"Standing in the shoes of your grandmother. A wonderful mentor, and dear mother, welcoming me into this incredible family." Sinclair swept one arm, taking in the manor grounds, fields, and mountain beyond. "Now left in the care of yourself. And Declan."

"And Angus." Marion nodded toward the stables, where the short, stocky man was working with Meghan's youngest child, Eira. The child was safely in hand, placed aboard a small mare with a gentle disposition. One sent high with an appropriately sized saddle and tack. "He has such a gentle way with children and animals. All of them drawn to him—like bees to heather."

Sinclair nodded, aware of the other side of the man's unique capabilities. Standing in Shaun's shoes, doing the dark deeds required to protect the clan. Aware as well there was something Angus wanted to share with her when the moment was right. Her maternal senses whispered in her ear, her nerves drawn tight, knowing it would be news of her son. "A *good* man. Reminding me of another."

"My great uncle."

"Aye. In *some* ways. Though he seems more inclined toward your husband. Both of them with even temperament and a genteel mood."

Marion sighed. "Declan, with the *title*. Though lacking the will to do what needs doing." She shook her head. "No fault of his, with me loving him for the good and honorable *man* he is. With him caring so deeply for every member of the clan. Not one person turned away, come looking for help, or in need of work."

Sinclair nodded. Her bottom lip sucked in, watching as young Eira took the small mare over a low jump, her body rocking in the saddle, legs out to the sides, keeping her balance with a shout of joy. "The mill-works below—are a *wonder* of engineering. With sluiceways guiding water from mill to mill. A Scottish stream, indeed. Squeezing every drop of power from the snow in the mountains, on through to the valley floor, beyond."

"Angus—a large part of that, as well. Along with a new lad, having come into our Lorna's life. A boy by the name of Bayly." Sinclair twisted her head, giving Marion a lingering look.

"Is he a *worry* to you?"

Marion shrugged. "He's of a clan from the northern reaches. His family forced off their lands at the end of Loch Fyne, on the northwest coast. Ending up in Glasgow, where they cut the lad free to manage best as he could. Landed at the millworks, below the Pinch."

She nodded to her sister as she came up, her horse led away by her oldest son, heading to the barn. "I had my doubts, at first, with Angus putting them to rest, telling me he sees something of value in the lad. Declan, in agreement."

Meghan climbed the steps, removing a pair of riding gloves, her cheeks red from the ride with Patrick. She peeked over Sinclair's shoulder, looking inside the hall. "Where is our fair visitor, Lady Skye? Hope she's not still *leery* of me."

Marion shook her head. She'd invited Skye to accompany her to the manor. The other woman, reluctant at first to do so. Concerned with how the family might receive her. The issue soon resolved with Marion assuring her she'd spoken to her twin sister long ago, turning her wrath aside with the story, told true.

Sinclair responded. "Marion's guest is inside. With Lorna. The two of them going through closets, searching for riding clothes that will fit her." She pursed her lips. "Your sister bringing her high—without given *proper* opportunity to prepare."

Marion laughed, then returned her mother's dour expression with a grin. "There was a method to my *madness*. Wanting to see how she adapts to sudden changes in her environment. Finding out if she's worthy of a substantial investment, which I'm certain she *is*. Our brother having had his eye on her some years ago."

Meghan coughed, using her eyes to point over her sister's shoulder, Skye coming down the hallway, with Lorna alongside, a bright smile on the young girl's face.

"It took some *doing*, having to go through *several* closets. But we pieced an outfit together suitable for the ride." Lorna nudged Skye ahead, following her down the wide steps, coming out onto the walk. "Your skirt, mother. With *your* waistcoat, Grandmother. And *my* jacket, fitting her narrow shoulders perfectly." She paused, her tone softening. "And a pair of our great grandmother's riding boots."

Skye took Lorna's hand, squeezing it, then letting go. "I appreciate *everything* you've done. All of you. Welcoming me here to your home. Allowing me to meet your incredible children and everyone else. Truly, a wonderful family and an amazing place." She slid her eyes around the surrounding hills. "I can see why—" Then she hesitated, looking down in silence.

Marion reached out, placing her hand on her shoulder. "Why Aaron, our brother—why he loved it so much?"

"Loves it *still!*" Meghan came over and nodded at Skye, then headed down to where her youngest daughter and Angus were finishing their lesson.

"*Someone's* in a mood." Marion, seeing her mother's frown, held up her hands as she walked into the house, leaving the other two women alone. Several moments passed, with Skye about to offer a comment. Then she hesitated, closing her full lips.

Sinclair looked over at her. "My son, the last time I *saw* him—is no longer the man you knew him to be. The war changed him. Becoming —someone else. Someone both greater *and* lesser than the boy you knew. The one who grew up here. His time in the colonies exposed him to life and death decisions, far greater than *any* experienced here in the mountains."

She waited until Skye looked over with a shielded expression on her face. "He gained a genuine sense of his capabilities for violence. As any man does, involved in the *insanity* of killing. Losing pieces of his soul. Let slip through his fingers. Reduced to a shell of his former self. No longer the man you met and fell in love with. Forced by his destiny to let go of you."

Skye shook her head. "It was my *father's* doing. *All* of it. Sending me away, married off to a man above my station. A kind man, in his way. Needing children. An heir. My body, no longer my own."

"You were not—forced *into* it?"

"No." Skye sighed. "Only the *expectation* of an heir, every time. Himself in a constant hover throughout each month passed. His mood lightened when made aware of an impending birth." She gave Sinclair a look of abject sadness. "Disappointed each time, in my delivering death. A daughter, dying soon after delivery. Two sons left inert bundles of flesh and bone, dying in my womb. *My* legacy—*my* destiny was a failure to deliver him an heir."

"*Nae*, child." Sinclair took Skye's hand, pulling her into a side-armed embrace. "The deaths of your sons, when happening like that, point to the father as much as the mother. A problem, between seed and womb."

Skye narrowed her eyes, her head angled to one side. "Causing all my children to *die?*"

"As certain as poison, if happening under the *wrong* conditions."

"My two boys, dying in the womb—not *my* fault?"

Sinclair released her, stepping back, watching as Skye wiped her eyes. "Nae. You're innocent of that. The marriage, if sought for the provision of heirs—doomed from the start."

Skye lowered her eyes. "As was my other relationship. With *your* son."

"You've suffered much, through no fault of your own." Sinclair stopped, looking toward the mountains. "As too, my son. Suffering the death of his innocence at the end of a highland draw. With his morality left in tatters. Haunted by actions taken to support a *greater* cause. Protecting his family, *here*." Sinclair sighed. "Then trying to protect a friend, going with him to the colonies. Which led to his working with a deadly group of men helping to bring a new country into being."

A gruff-toned voice pulled them around, Angus standing a few paces away, his feet spread, having listened to them. "I need to go to the croft. Wanted to see if Lady Skye would care to ride along. To see the mountain, in full."

Sinclair gave Angus a questioning look. Sensing there was more to the invitation, she placed her trust in his judgment. "An *excellent* idea. With flowers gathered to place in the family plot." She smiled at Skye. "Would you be willing to take them there, my dear?"

"Of course." Skye nodded at Angus. "Seeing I'm already *dressed* for it."

Angus turned away, his voice tossed back over his wide shoulders. "I'll prepare our mounts while you two gather up the blooms."

Angus pulled up, nudging his sturdy mare to one side, allowing Skye's mount to pull even. He reached out and pointed to a narrow draw, a trail worn in the rocky soil. "It's just there, along the path. Not far." He slipped from the saddle, holding onto the stirrup, reaching for the ground with his toes.

"Is there a problem?" Skye watched as her guide led his horse to a patch of grass, its head lowered to feed while the short man lifted its front hoof.

"Nae. Just a slight limp. Needing a moment or two to check for a stone. It happens. The rocks here, sharp-edged." Angus looked up, then waved his free hand. "You go ahead, with your horse knowing the way. I'll catch you up, soon enow."

Skye looked at the three bouquets tied to his saddle horn. "The markers—should I wait there for you? To help place the flowers?"

"Nae. I'll see to it." Angus smiled, then reached out and tapped the mare on her hindquarters, urging her on, with Skye holding the reins in her gloved hands, looking back with a confused look on her face.

⸙⸙⸙

Aaron sat in the open doorway of the croft house, busy with the repair of a spade in need of a new handle. He looked up at the sound of hooves, then turned and checked the kettle on the stove. It was just coming to a boil, with a handful of tea leaves in a linen pouch ready to drop in. He'd been expecting Angus to show up. Two cups set out, along with a platter of bread, a bowl of preserves, and a small jar of honey.

His horse, grazing at the far end of the paddock field, came on a run to the railing. It thrust its head forward, calling out to the other animal, still out of sight. A soft whinny sounded in reply, unfamiliar in tone, causing Aaron's eyes to narrow, having expected Angus to arrive on the back of his large, broad-chested mare.

He set the spade to one side, then went over and dropped the tea leaves in, shoving the kettle to the front corner of the stove to let it steep. As he stepped back through the door, Aaron's mouth opened to call out, shocked to silence as he watched Skye approaching, her eyes angled to one side, gazing up at the mountain, it's top framed against an open sky.

When she swung her gaze back around, spotting the small house with a man standing in the shadows of a small doorway, Skye pulled back on the reins. "I'm sorry. For the intrusion. Angus, the one who brought me here."

Aaron looked down the trail, his voice low. "Don't see him. This Angus fellow." He stepped out into the sun, his face fully revealed as he came up and took the mare's bridle, watching as Skye's eyes slowly widened in recognition, his eyes still as blue as the first time she'd seen him, his face with a close-cropped beard.

"Aaron?" She stared at him, her face flushed with emotion, tears welling up in her eyes. "You—he—Angus *didn't* tell me. I mean, I *didn't* know."

Aaron reached up, taking her by her waist, swinging her down, holding onto her, searching her eyes, their hazel color as captivating as he remembered. Still as beautiful as he remembered. Then he leaned down, their lips touching, eyes open as they embraced.

When they finally pulled back, it was as if time had stopped. The years let slip away. Holding onto one another, under as bonny a bright blue sky. In a green glade far below in Glasgow, lying half a hundred miles away and what seemed to have been but a moment ago.

CHAPTER THIRTY-TWO
HIGHLAND MANOR
EARLY SPRING, 1794

Angus gave each of the three women a firm look, his face reflecting their expressions of disappointment. Sinclair stood in the middle, flanked on either side by her daughters, all of them with crossed arms. She stepped forward, her voice tight with frustration.

"You've been *hiding* something from us. Along with Marion's guest, gone missing. Leaving her alone in the hills. *Why?*"

"I can assure you, Lady Skye is *fine*. Escorted to the croft house, her saddlebags filled with food and drink, and suitable attire for the duration of her visit there."

"That's *no* answer."

"It's *all* you'll get, for now." Angus turned and looked at his horse, it's head down, searching the packed gravel for any sign of fodder. "I have a mount to look to, and a meal owed me. *Two* of them, by my count." He walked away, the horse following behind, both looking worn down from the ride up and back down again. Once Angus had slipped into the barn, the women gave each other sideways glances, then went inside the manor and started heating tea and a hot meal, along with a loaf of oven-warmed bread, with a pot of sweet honey set atop the table, hoping to sweeten the stocky man's dour mood.

⅏ ⅏ ⅏

With the meal finished, and the dishes washed and put away, Angus circled his fingers around a warm cup of tea, then nodded. "I have delivered your son —" He nodded at Sinclair. "And your brother —" He gave each of the two sisters a nod as well. "To the croft house. A day ago. Making my return here, finding the balance of the family gathered at the manor. Arriving early, along with an *unexpected* guest."

The three women exchanged looks, with Sinclair holding one hand to her lips, while Marion raised a single eyebrow. Meghan, standing with her hands on her hips, glared at Angus.

"You had *no* right to keep it from us. *News* of Aaron's return."

Sinclair reached out and took Meghan's hand, squeezing it. "My son — he is hale? In good health?"

"Aye. As much as *anyone* who's been through the same mill." Angus shrugged. "Time spent high, a salve to his soul if given time to let it heal his scars. Inside *and* out. Waiting for the mountain to call out to him, like it did *your* husband. And *his* grandfather, before him."

Marion came over, touching Angus on the shoulder. "You arranged his travel, getting him safely back home to us. Where he *needs* to be. Your efforts appreciated. And, as always, done in the *best* interest of us *all*." She looked at her sister, getting a reluctant nod of her head in return.

Sinclair had a solemn look on her face. "And your *decision* — to take Skye there?" She gave Angus a searching look. "How is *that* to play out in this *theater* of yours? With the two of them falling back in love? The years between — living their lives on opposite sides of the ocean, with their struggles and grief, to evaporate, like clouds in the sky? Leaving them to share memories of a distant relationship. Formed when they were barely old enough to know the meaning of *true* love."

Angus set his feet apart, his shoulders squared. "It will leave *two* wounded souls, having sacrificed body *and* soul on the altar of their devotion to a greater cause." He paused, then shook his head. "I'll happily leave the measure of their *love*, as *you* would name it, to *them* to decide as to its *maturity* and *depth*." He lowered his voice. "Not mine to judge. Nor any of you." Then he gave Meghan a quiet look. "I have *my* visions, of a different type from anyone else's. And they've served me well enough. Our former laird recognized that early on, entrusting me with tools needed to protect members of this family on *both* sides of the watery divide."

Angus stood up, his hands flat on the table. "If I've blundered *this* time, it will be the *first*." He paused, giving each woman a searching look. "I trust the most important thing I've learned from this family. Your *love* for one another, seeing you through *everything* that's taken place over the years. And it's *love* for each other that will help those two —" He lifted one hand, pointing toward the window, the top of the mountain visible in the last light of the day. "Will help them get through whatever happens *next*."

Smoke rose from the stone chimney of a small structure, squat in build, tucked into a nook at the end of a steep-walled draw. A thick-bodied horse, its saddle sitting astride a rail fence, wandered in a small circle on a patch of summer-kissed grass. It raised its head, making a whick-ering call to the mare Skye was on, getting one in return.

She'd awoken to the heated embrace from a slate stove, warming the air. A large window in the wall at the head of a bed left cracked open a bit, letting air in along with a thin slice of sunshine, washing one wall of the interior. A note, with a line drawn, let her know Aaron was just down the narrow valley, at a place named Gran Ma's Mill. The mare, left saddled, waiting in the paddock should she care to join him there.

A kettle of heated water, steam rising from its spout, was sitting on the front edge of the stove, along with the makings for tea. A small loaf of bread, with honey and a container of preserved fruit, sat in the center of a thick slab table. Skye had risen from her bed, a tired smile on her face, still in her clothes, with a tired smile on her lips. As she'd rubbed the sleep from her eyes, Skye hoped that everything she'd felt, seen, and remembered from the previous afternoon and night would turn out not to have been a dream. That she was really there, in the highlands, with a man she'd never stopped loving. A man who'd whispered in her ear during the night, telling her it had been the same for him.

And now, in the light of a new day, she approached the millworks with an empty belly and a basket of food strapped to the back of her mount's saddle. Trembling in a mix of anticipation and fear, aware the moment of revelation had arrived. Where she'd stand before him, fully revealed. Seen as the woman she was. Thirty and five years of age, with the birth of several children having left their marks on her body. No longer the image of the young woman she'd once been.

Skye dismounted the mare with a nervous sigh and tied off the lead. She started toward the mill building, her thoughts centered on Aaron, his rugged looks enhanced by his gray-salted, dark hair and piercing blue eyes. Still as tall, broad-shouldered, and handsome as she remembered him. And nude, standing in water up to mid-thigh, washing his body with a hand towel and lye soap. His broad back was to her, revealing scars on his arms and legs, his long dark hair unbound, hanging over his shoulders.

"There's water, heating in a tub inside the mill." His deep voice floated through the chilled air. "Along with another towel and bar of soft soap, carried in the saddlebag, brought here by your mare." Aaron turned around, facing Skye, offering her a shy smile. "Had planned to have my labors finished before you arrived. Been working on clearing the sluiceway of silt, hoping to encourage a greater flow to the works."

Skye averted her eyes, hugging the basket of food she'd brought with her against her chest. Then she turned around and reached for the saddlebag. She removed it, then ushered the mare into the enclosure through a small gate. As she moved toward the mill, she called over her shoulder. "I brought the breakfast you left me. I'll take it inside and wait for you there. While you—finish up."

"You're welcome to join me." Aaron grinned when she stopped, keeping her back to him. "The water's cold, providing for a deep cleansing of one's soul once you're at the far end of the pool. Standing up to your neck, with the Devil himself unable to find you here."

"I'll go inside, where you will find *me*. Warming my hands by the stove."

Skye entered the small building and let the saddlebag fall to the floor. Then she leaned back against the closed door, her eyes shut as she shook her head, unable to transition from who she was to the person she dearly wished to be. Too many years, with too many tears, shed. Too long spent living in the shadow of other people's expectations of her, setting aside her needs, again. Brought here by an invitation she'd dared not refuse. Shoved in front of two families, with children painfully familiar to her eye. Everywhere she looked, seeing pieces of the man taken from her by familial obedience. Her heart aching, seeing the joy expressed in the eyes of those who'd welcomed her with open arms. All of them left unaware of the hurt caused to her by their open, smiling faces.

And now, after a night with questions asked, some left unanswered, each of them withdrawing into moments of silence as memories threatened to overwhelm the delicate ties binding them to the past, Skye knew it was time for her to leave. To return to who she'd become. A middle-aged matron. Childless. Unwed. Spinster, the title assigned to her by fate.

The door moved, then stopped. Aaron called out, his voice low-toned. "I'd like to come inside. To share the warmth."

Skye stepped away, going to the far end of the small room, resting the basket on a wide-planked counter, busying herself in pulling out the food she'd brought, along with the kettle of tea, wrapped in a thick cloth to hold the heat. When she had nothing left to occupy her hands, she stiffened her resolve and turned around.

Aaron, his lower body wrapped in a towel, was rubbing his arms and shoulders dry with another. He watched her, his head angled to one side as he dried his hair. "You're at a place where leaving seems the wiser choice to make." He smiled. "A familiar look on your face. One I've seen in a mirror, or pool of dark water often enow. Of myself, poised between staying put, or heading to the mountain, looking for shelter from things I'd rather let go of than face up to. Memories of dark deeds done. To me. And *by* me."

Skye stared at him. Then she shook her head. "You can't understand what I'm feeling, despite your trying to name it. You don't know—"

"That you're seeing yourself as you think *I* do. As *others* do. The way you see *yourself*, measured against the girl you *once* were." Aaron paused. "I have a mother. And watched as she wrestled with the same thing. A strong woman. Intelligent. Capable. Left fending for herself and her family. Torn between being a wife and mother to her brood. Then, through no fault of her own, made to carry the burden alone. Doubting herself, with children trying their best to bear her up. To convince her to lean into their embrace, and not t'other way around."

Skye lowered her eyes, looking at her hands, her fingers clenched, tears threatening to spill down her cheeks. "I've had—*no* one else to lean on. To embrace me. Barely strong enough to cope, most times."

"Until *now*. If you choose it. My sister, in bringing you high, letting you know what's *here*. Your decision to accept it. Or not."

"Meaning *you*."

"Nae, lass. She wouldn't have known of my return when making the invitation to you. Unaware of my being here until yesterday, at the earliest. Angus, likely to have filled her and the others in by now."

Aaron came over and tossed the towel he carried over a wooden rod suspended above the stove. He took Skye's hands, his skin cold against hers. "It was a *family* she offered you. Not me. A place on high. Yours to come to when you need to set your mind straight. Seeing the world below as a place to work in. To *fight* in. Against those denying the right to others to live their lives as they want."

He smiled. "While up here, you're standing as near to God as you can get—the mountains bringing a clear view of yourself, unfettered by who or what the world sees you as. A chance to shrug off your sins, leaving your *true* self revealed." Aaron paused, swallowing, his eyes gleaming in the light through a small window. "The way *I* see you. Today. The same as the first time. My breath swept away, looking into your eyes again. Seeing an incredible future there. With *you*."

Skye let her tears fall. "I'm not sure I'd be able to recognize her. The girl I once was. If I can even recall what she looked like. Then."

Aaron reached out, taking Skye's chin in his fingers, angling her head back, and gazing into her perfect eyes. "*I* do. *Every* detail, as if it were today, the first kiss given to you, then." He closed his eyes, touching her lips with his, breathing in the scent of her hair, her skin.

They pressed their bodies together, for the first time since meeting at the croft house. Uncertain when first together how to make the journey back to when they'd been a couple. Balanced at the beginning of a new opportunity. One that would leave them fully revealed to each other, with their stories shared openly. Good and bad.

Skye pulled away. "I think—I think you should take me to the water. That I might wash away my sins. My sorrows." Aaron nodded, a warm smile on his face. He took Skye's hand, leading her outside. The sun had finally cleared the eastern ridgeline, warming the air. They stopped by the edge of the pool, where Aaron began removing Skye's clothes, one button at a time. Placing her outer clothing on a wooden rail, with her boots and stockings set aside.

Skye trembled, her eyes closed as Aaron undid the ties of her shift and slipped it over her shoulders. Then past her waist. Sliding it over her hips, then letting go, the thin fabric pooling about her bare feet. She stepped clear of them, one arm covering the stretch marks on her lower abdomen, the result of three pregnancies. The other draped across her chest, covering the swell of her full breasts. Hiding their slight droop, caused by the onset of middle age.

Aaron took her hands, pulling them away. He leaned down and gently kissed her stomach, then each side of her breasts. Skye with tears in her eyes as she watched him, seeing the look of love in his eyes when he straightened up. Holding onto her, his arm around her waist as they waded into the depths. Gathering her in his arms, standing up to their chests. Locked in a shivering embrace of lips and arms. Then Aaron lowered them beneath the surface. Staying there until Skye straightened up, rising into the sunlight. Her spirit, reborn.

Later that day, with afternoon turning over to early evening, the two reunited lovers made their way back to the croft house. They released the horses to the paddock, then went inside, leaving the door and large window open, letting in a soft breeze.

Skye began putting away the things brought back from the mill, hanging their towels to dry along one side of the stove. Aaron went over to the smaller bed and leaned down, sliding a wooden chest out from beneath it. He opened it, stared inside for a moment, then removed two journals containing details of the time he'd spent in the colonies, as well as what had transpired in the wilderness of the Ohio Basin.

He opened the first one and held it up to the spill of light, reading the words as if written by another's hand. The images were achingly familiar. Stirring memories of friends he'd made, then lost. Then he opened the other, coming to a drawing of a woman he'd loved, been hand-fasted to, then lost to a higher power.

A shadow shaded the parchment, the scent of lavender flavoring the air as Skye leaned over, touching Eliza's picture. "She's beautiful."

"She—was my wife." Aaron turned his head, looking up. "We were hand fasted. Together for two days, until—"

Skye sat down, her knees angled, touching his. Her hand touched his forearm, fingers in a gentle squeeze. "What happened? Did she die?"

"She lives. Still. The last I knew. In a small community, with the survivors of a people ravaged by hate. Or greed. Not much of a difference between the two. Her people murdered for—well, it didn't matter much to them, the reason for it."

Aaron closed the journal, staring at the cover, measuring the hours spent with a pen in hand, chronicling the lives of the people within. "I rescued her. Carried her away, her fists striking my shoulders, begging me to let her go to them. To her people. Natives converted to the religion she believed in. Killed by colonial militiamen. By people raised to follow the *same* God. Pledged to abide by the *same* rules."

"She—the woman pictured—does not *appear* to be an Indian."

Aaron shook his head. "*Native* is the word my father used to identify them. Having already been living there for thousands of years or more, with traditions of their own, followed. A rich heritage, inclusive of many of the same beliefs as our own."

"I meant no disrespect." Skye leaned away. Aaron slipped one arm around her waist, pulling her back in.

"Stay. Ask me anything." Then he paused, letting out a long sigh. "My wife and I, we never had our marriage consecrated. Our hand-fasting—set aside. By me. According to highlander tradition, citing irreconcilable differences. Caused by a tragedy of *another* kind."

He placed the journal in Skye's hands, watching as she opened it.

Prepared to face his past, openly. Honestly. Including her reading of the other journal. His first one. Filled with tales of horror that might end up driving away the woman sitting beside him.

A strong wind whipped the ends of Skye's hair, tickling the side of Aaron's face. The world lay outstretched before them, with England lying in the distance. Their climb to the top of the mountain had started in the clouds. Water running wild in silty rivulets alongside an angled trail. Their calves strained by their climb through the steeper sections, before easing enough to let them move, hand in hand, along a low-grade rise. Past bunched groves of gnarled pines, their eyes on the exposed bones of the mountain beneath their boots, feeling the slip of loose rocks beneath the soles. Ending up at the cairn of rocks, placed there by Aaron's great-grandfather, former laird of clan Scott.

"This is beyond *anything* I've ever experienced. Or imagined possible. It's as if I'm an eagle on the wing. Seeing into the *next* day." Skye snuggled into Aaron's firm-armed embrace, having listened to his stories of family and treks made to the top of the mountain. "Here, where you and your sister Meghan followed in your father's footsteps. Where he and his brother Jackson once stood, making the climb as children, like yourself." Skye paused, taking a moment to track the shadow of a small cloud passing by. "Hard to believe it possible. Standing all the way up here, on top of the world."

"A pilgrimage, made by each generation. Lured by stories told around the fire. Lured to it by the challenge. Getting here, discovering for themselves the reason for having made the climb. Finding something—*greater* than themselves."

Skye looked up, her cheeks bright red, eyes wide. Their hazel color, speckled with blue and gold tints by the arch of sunlit sky, overhead. "Which is?"

"You tell me."

She lowered her eyes, opening herself to where she was. Who she was with. To those waiting below in the manor house, further down.

Where her life was waiting to reclaim her. "To *escape*. To reflect—without doubt. Without fear. Worry. Or *regret*."

Aaron nodded. "And?"

Skye looked up, Aaron seeing himself reflected in her eyes. "To gather in what's been *missing*. Using the energy found here to heal a hole in my heart. To ease the pain. Stop the bleeding. Making me feel —*whole* again. Like a young woman. The one you met long ago. Down there." She pointed with her narrow chin to the west, toward Glasgow. "*That's* why I'm here. Today. With *you*." She buried her face in his clothing, taking his scent deep into her lungs, holding on, not wanting to let him go.

Aaron hugged her, his voice a whisper. "My father. He came here, after returning from *his* war. Damaged in body, spirit, and soul. Having lost the love of two incredible women, each with demons of their own to battle." He sighed. "One of them dying, unable to let go of her past. The other one, saving his life. Then saving mine."

He pulled away, reaching for Skye's hand, kissing it, then holding on. "She took me in. A'neewa, as my father knew her. Anna, the woman *I* met. Soon after I made an—*impossible* choice. Then forced to make *another*, later on. Not any easier. Losing her—Eliza—to a faith burning *deep* within her. Consuming her from the *inside* out. Her soul broken on the backs of near one hundred *deaths*. Of innocent men, women, and children."

Aaron closed his eyes. "Knowing that her adopted mother, Anna, had walked to God with an open heart. Singing as they killed her. Having led her people through their conversion, then to their deaths. All of them sacrificed on man's altar of greed. Of misplaced anger. Of —" He shook his head. "It doesn't matter, the cause. Or causes. Only the results. Eliza moved closer to God, while I pulled further away. Returning to find her drawn as a moth to the flame, her mind seared. My fingers thickened with calluses from the drawing of a bowstring. Arrows loosed. Men, slain."

Aaron stood up, pressing his hand on one of the stacked rocks they were leaning against. "Each of us lost to our own version of faith. Hers, a belief she spoke for God. Mine, that I was the means of his righteous wrath." He cursed, the wind coming on in a gust, sweeping the word away.

Skye rose to her feet and took Aaron's face between her hands. "You released yourself from the blindness of *your* false god. Able to see, clearly, your way back home again. To your family, where you belong." She nodded. "Back here, with me."

Aaron shrugged. "And what of Eliza, in my having abandoned her? And the dark path I walked? Is *that* not a concern for you? The thought it might happen again."

"No." Skye looked him straight in the eye, shivering before the press of cool air. "I have not lost *my* faith — in God, or *us*."

Aaron pulled her in, shielding her with his body. His deceased relatives gathered around them, many having met violent ends. A family tradition. One he was determined would end with him. With no son following in his footsteps, cursed to walk the same red path.

The End of Book Four

ABOUT THE AUTHOR

M. Daniel Smith is a writer of fiction, with interest in producing series covering various genres, including historical and speculative fiction.

His writing encompasses relationships between diverse groups of characters, real to life and gritty at times, helping connect the reader emotionally to people difficult to let go of.

Raised in a blue-collar environment, he spent hours in his mother's extensive library, reading the latest novels, exposed to every genre of literary works, from family sagas on through to sci-fi, military histories, and the like.

Retired, and able to write full time, Daniel fills his days putting down the words sent him by the characters who show up, compelling the telling of their stories, allowing readers an intimate look into their motives, desires, joys—and moments of pain. His own thoughts, beliefs, and experiences, garnered from a life lived full, liberally sprinkled throughout his writing.

You can reach Daniel at mdanielsmith@aol.com, or at PO Box 49, Phippsburg, ME 04562. His website is: www.bayledgespress.com.

Made in the USA
Middletown, DE
05 January 2023

17993027R00179